MIDDLE SCHOOL
MISADVENTURES

MIDDLE SCHOOL
MISADVENTURES
DANCE DISASTER

JASON PLATT

LB

LITTLE, BROWN AND COMPANY
NEW YORK   BOSTON

ABOUT THIS BOOK

The illustrations for this book were done in Corel Painter on the Wacom Cintiq companion and colored in Adobe Photoshop. This book was edited by Rachel Poloski and Esther Cajahuaringa and designed by Megan McLaughlin. The production was supervised by Kimberly Stella, and the production editor was Jake Regier. The text was set in MisterAndMeBook, and the display type is MisterAndMe.

Little, Brown and Company
Hachette Book Group
1290 Avenue of the Americas, New York, NY 10104
Visit us at LBYR.com

First Edition: April 2022

Little, Brown and Company is a division of Hachette Book Group, Inc.
The Little, Brown name and logo are trademarks of Hachette Book Group, Inc.

The publisher is not responsible for websites (or their content) that are not owned by the publisher.

Library of Congress Cataloging-in-Publication Data
Names: Platt, Jason, author, illustrator.
Title: Dance disaster / Jason Platt.
Description: First edition. | New York ; Boston : Little, Brown and Company, 2022. | Series: Middle school misadventures ; 3 | Audience: Ages 8–12. | Summary: "Newell's perfectly comfortable life is turned upside down when Mrs. Hendricks announces the upcoming school dance and he discovers his dad is dating his math teacher." —Provided by publisher.
Identifiers: LCCN 2021011925 | ISBN 9780759556621 (hardcover) | ISBN 9780759556638 (trade paperback) | ISBN 9780759556577 (ebook)
Subjects: LCSH: Graphic novels. | CYAC: Graphic novels. | Dance parties—Fiction. | Dating (Social customs)—Fiction. | Fathers and sons—Fiction. | Friendship—Fiction. | Middle schools—Fiction. | Schools—Fiction.
Classification: LCC PZ7.7.P55 Dan 2022 | DDC 741.5/973—dc23
LC record available at https://lccn.loc.gov/2021011925

ISBNs: 978-0-7595-5662-1 (hardcover), 978-0-7595-5663-8 (pbk.), 978-0-7595-5657-7 (ebook), 978-0-7595-5659-1 (ebook), 978-0-7595-5660-7 (ebook)

Printed in China

1010

Hardcover: 10 9 8 7 6 5 4 3 2 1
Paperback: 10 9 8 7 6 5 4 3 2 1

FOR MY FRIEND JOI

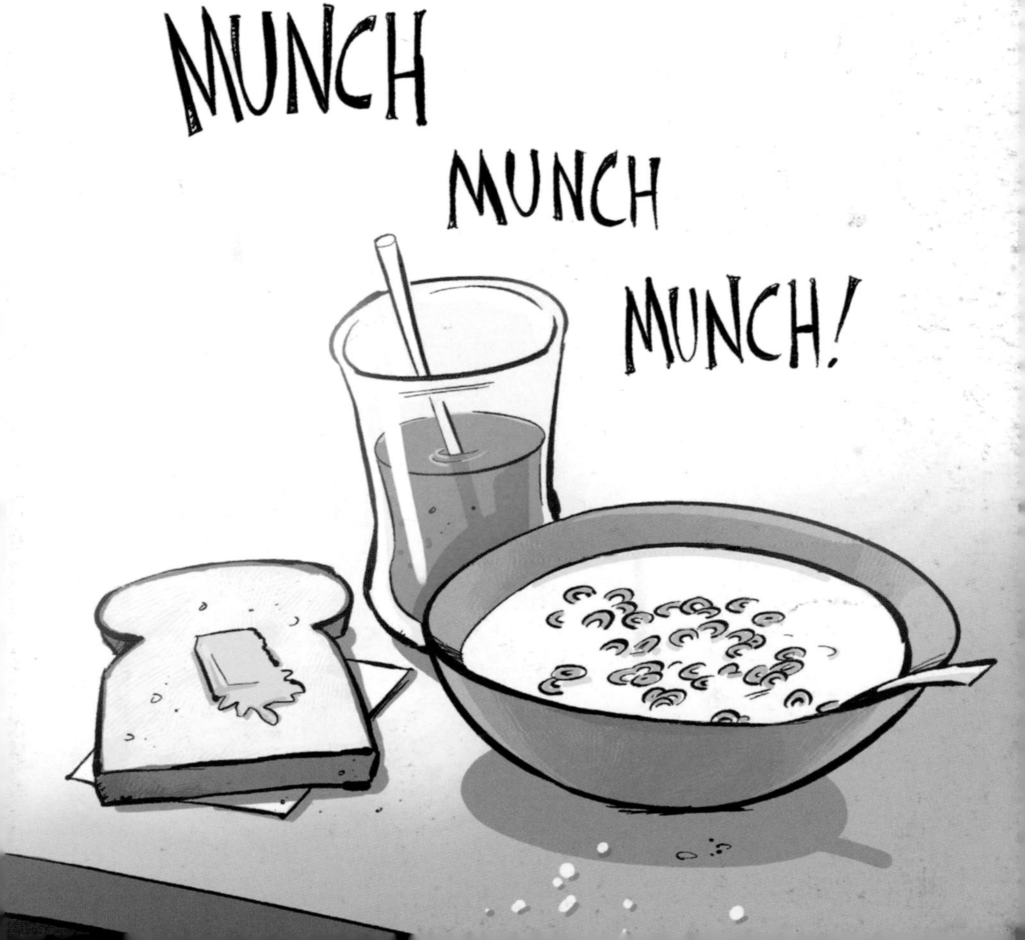
MUNCH
MUNCH
MUNCH!

CHAPTER ONE
I SWEAR THAT THIS IS A TRUE STORY

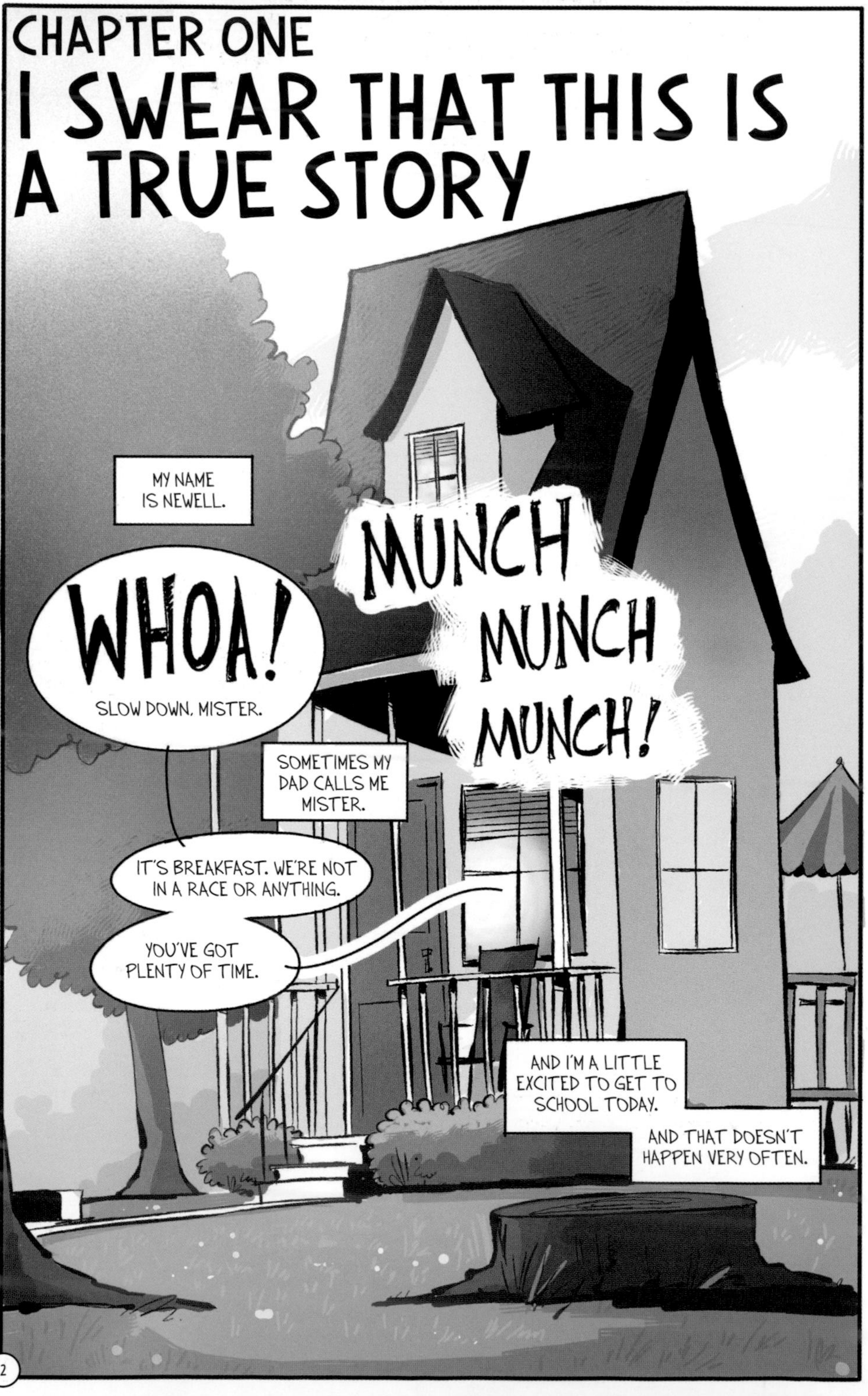
MY NAME IS NEWELL.
MUNCH MUNCH MUNCH!
WHOA! SLOW DOWN, MISTER.
SOMETIMES MY DAD CALLS ME MISTER.
IT'S BREAKFAST. WE'RE NOT IN A RACE OR ANYTHING.
YOU'VE GOT PLENTY OF TIME.
AND I'M A LITTLE EXCITED TO GET TO SCHOOL TODAY.
AND THAT DOESN'T HAPPEN VERY OFTEN.

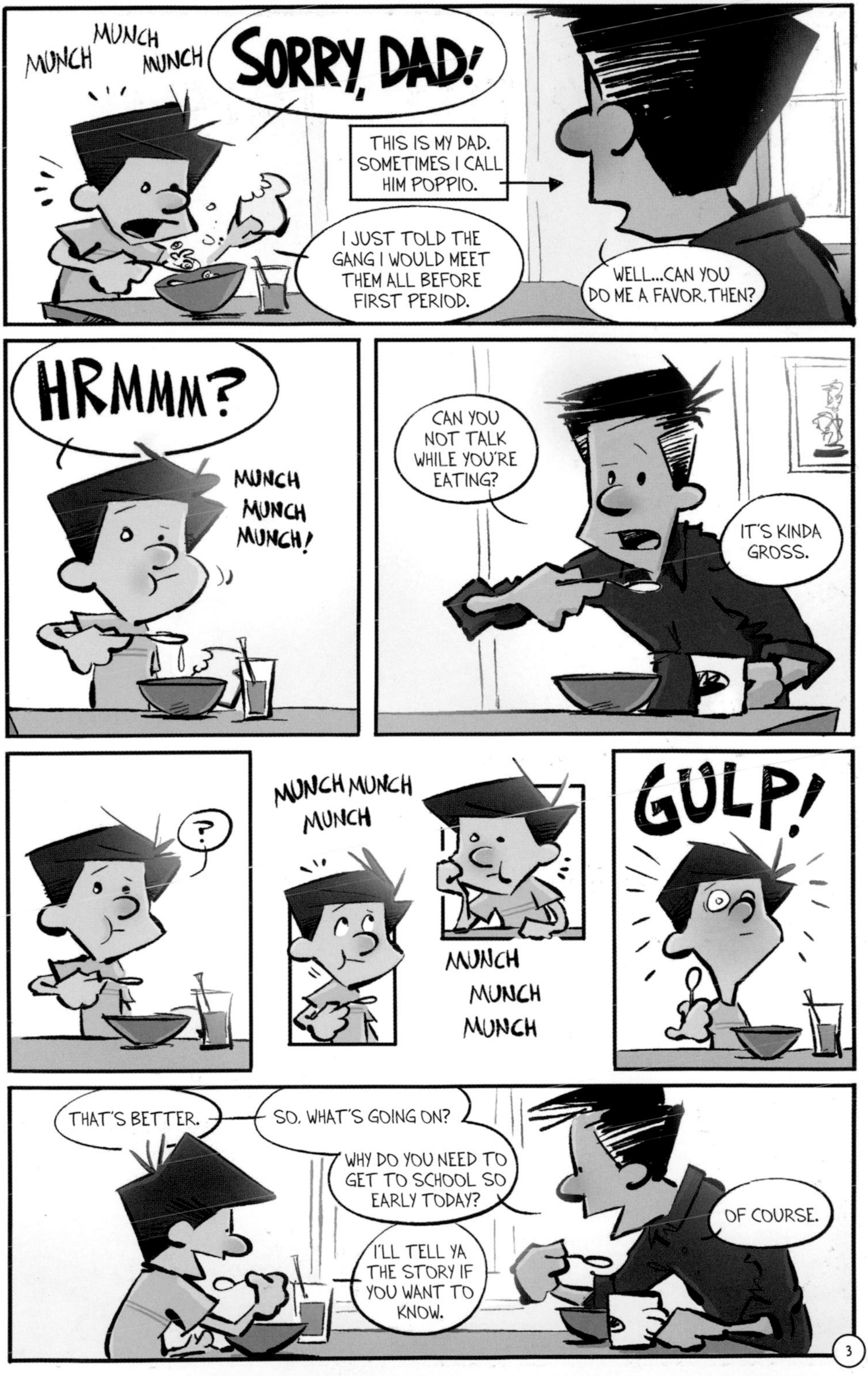
MUNCH MUNCH MUNCH
SORRY, DAD!
THIS IS MY DAD. SOMETIMES I CALL HIM POPPIO.
I JUST TOLD THE GANG I WOULD MEET THEM ALL BEFORE FIRST PERIOD.
WELL...CAN YOU DO ME A FAVOR, THEN?
HRMMM?
MUNCH MUNCH MUNCH!
CAN YOU NOT TALK WHILE YOU'RE EATING?
IT'S KINDA GROSS.
?
MUNCH MUNCH MUNCH
MUNCH MUNCH MUNCH
GULP!
THAT'S BETTER.
SO, WHAT'S GOING ON?
WHY DO YOU NEED TO GET TO SCHOOL SO EARLY TODAY?
I'LL TELL YA THE STORY IF YOU WANT TO KNOW.
OF COURSE.

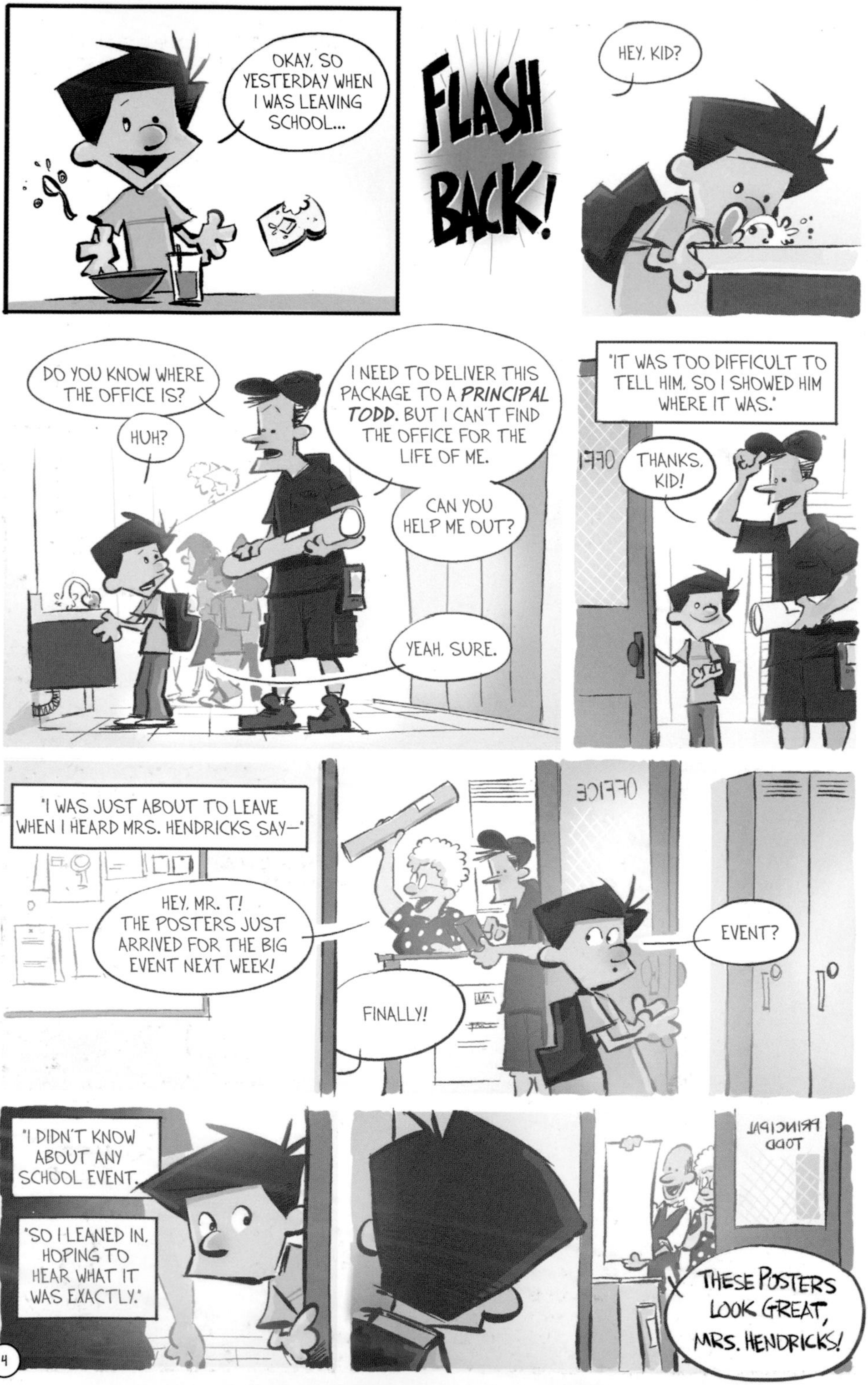

OKAY, SO YESTERDAY WHEN I WAS LEAVING SCHOOL...
FLASH BACK!
HEY, KID?
DO YOU KNOW WHERE THE OFFICE IS?
HUH?
I NEED TO DELIVER THIS PACKAGE TO A PRINCIPAL TODD. BUT I CAN'T FIND THE OFFICE FOR THE LIFE OF ME.
CAN YOU HELP ME OUT?
YEAH, SURE.
"IT WAS TOO DIFFICULT TO TELL HIM, SO I SHOWED HIM WHERE IT WAS."
THANKS, KID!
"I WAS JUST ABOUT TO LEAVE WHEN I HEARD MRS. HENDRICKS SAY—"
HEY, MR. T! THE POSTERS JUST ARRIVED FOR THE BIG EVENT NEXT WEEK!
FINALLY!
OFFICE
EVENT?
"I DIDN'T KNOW ABOUT ANY SCHOOL EVENT.
"SO I LEANED IN, HOPING TO HEAR WHAT IT WAS EXACTLY."
PRINCIPAL TODD
THESE POSTERS LOOK GREAT, MRS. HENDRICKS!

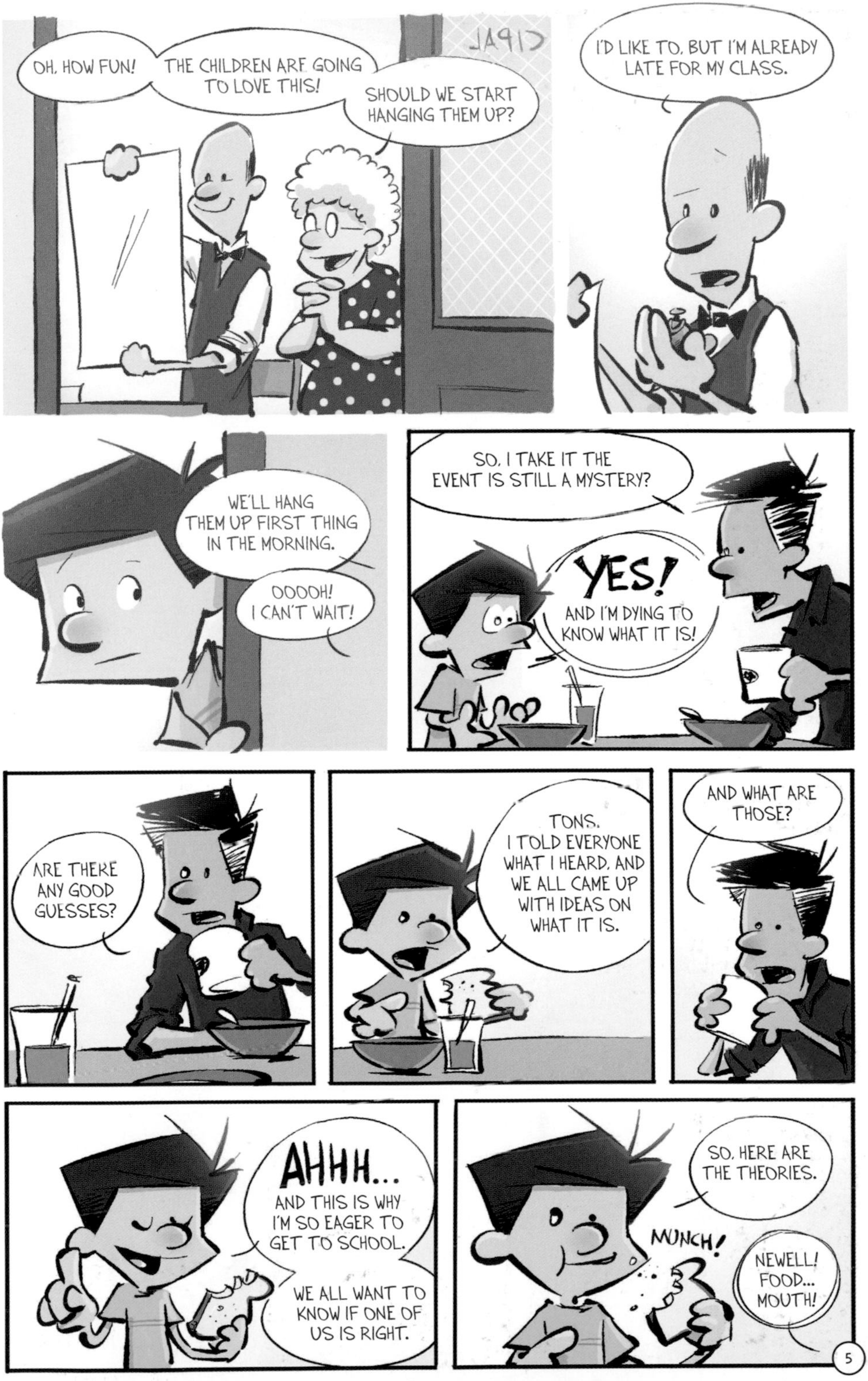

CIPAL
OH, HOW FUN!
THE CHILDREN ARE GOING TO LOVE THIS!
SHOULD WE START HANGING THEM UP?
I'D LIKE TO, BUT I'M ALREADY LATE FOR MY CLASS.
WE'LL HANG THEM UP FIRST THING IN THE MORNING.
OOOOH! I CAN'T WAIT!
SO, I TAKE IT THE EVENT IS STILL A MYSTERY?
YES!
AND I'M DYING TO KNOW WHAT IT IS!
ARE THERE ANY GOOD GUESSES?
TONS. I TOLD EVERYONE WHAT I HEARD, AND WE ALL CAME UP WITH IDEAS ON WHAT IT IS.
AND WHAT ARE THOSE?
AHHH...
AND THIS IS WHY I'M SO EAGER TO GET TO SCHOOL.
WE ALL WANT TO KNOW IF ONE OF US IS RIGHT.
SO, HERE ARE THE THEORIES.
MUNCH!
NEWELL! FOOD... MOUTH!

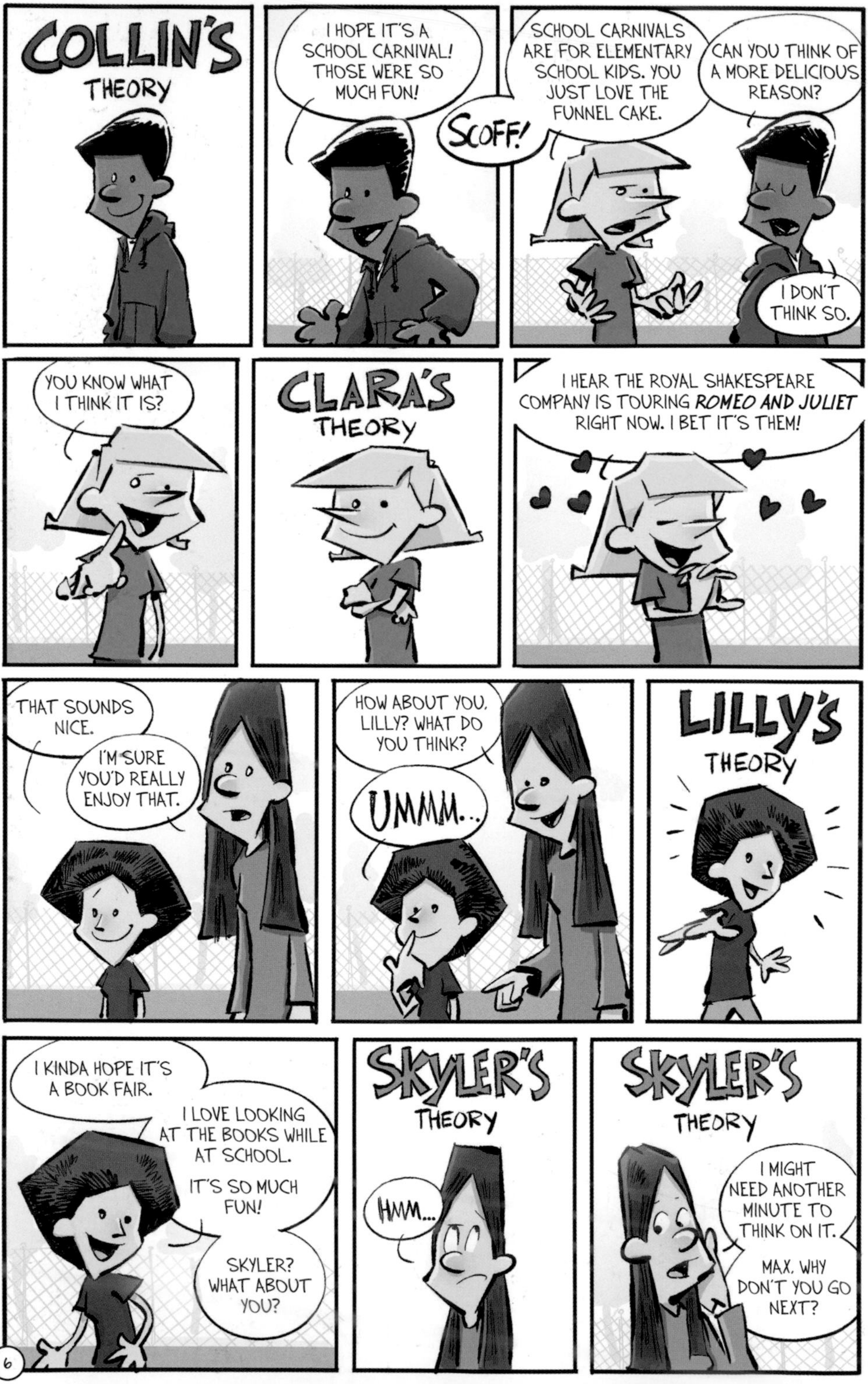
COLLIN'S THEORY
I HOPE IT'S A SCHOOL CARNIVAL! THOSE WERE SO MUCH FUN!
SCOFF!
SCHOOL CARNIVALS ARE FOR ELEMENTARY SCHOOL KIDS. YOU JUST LOVE THE FUNNEL CAKE.
CAN YOU THINK OF A MORE DELICIOUS REASON?
I DON'T THINK SO.
YOU KNOW WHAT I THINK IT IS?
CLARA'S THEORY
I HEAR THE ROYAL SHAKESPEARE COMPANY IS TOURING ROMEO AND JULIET RIGHT NOW. I BET IT'S THEM!
THAT SOUNDS NICE.
I'M SURE YOU'D REALLY ENJOY THAT.
HOW ABOUT YOU, LILLY? WHAT DO YOU THINK?
UMMM...
LILLY'S THEORY
I KINDA HOPE IT'S A BOOK FAIR.
I LOVE LOOKING AT THE BOOKS WHILE AT SCHOOL.
IT'S SO MUCH FUN!
SKYLER? WHAT ABOUT YOU?
SKYLER'S THEORY
HMM...
SKYLER'S THEORY
I MIGHT NEED ANOTHER MINUTE TO THINK ON IT.
MAX, WHY DON'T YOU GO NEXT?

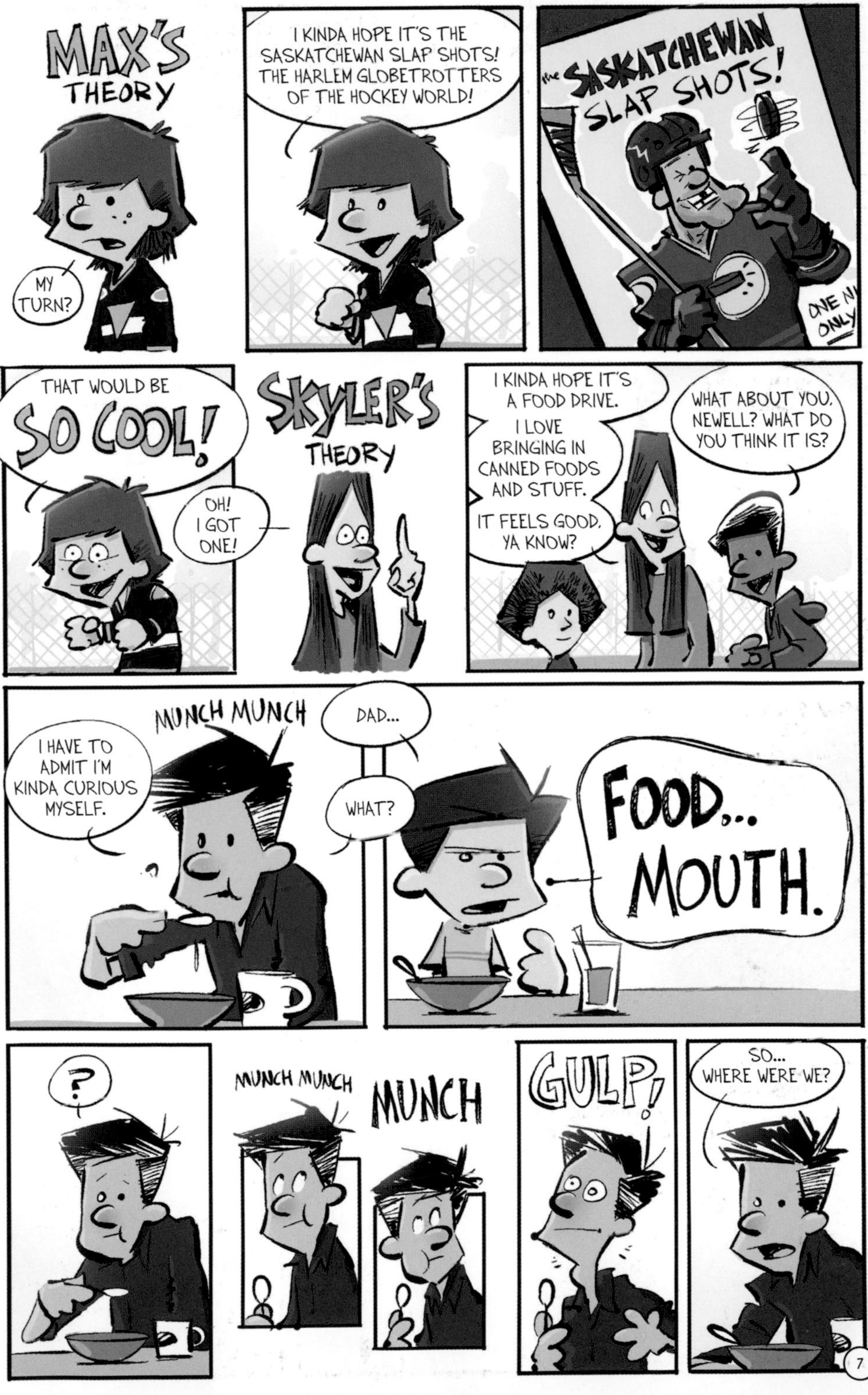

MAX'S THEORY
MY TURN?
I KINDA HOPE IT'S THE SASKATCHEWAN SLAP SHOTS! THE HARLEM GLOBETROTTERS OF THE HOCKEY WORLD!
the SASKATCHEWAN SLAP SHOTS!
ONE N ONLY
THAT WOULD BE SO COOL!
SKYLER'S THEORY
OH! I GOT ONE!
I KINDA HOPE IT'S A FOOD DRIVE.
I LOVE BRINGING IN CANNED FOODS AND STUFF.
IT FEELS GOOD, YA KNOW?
WHAT ABOUT YOU, NEWELL? WHAT DO YOU THINK IT IS?
I HAVE TO ADMIT I'M KINDA CURIOUS MYSELF.
MUNCH MUNCH
DAD...
WHAT?
FOOD... MOUTH.
?
MUNCH MUNCH
MUNCH
GULP!
SO... WHERE WERE WE?

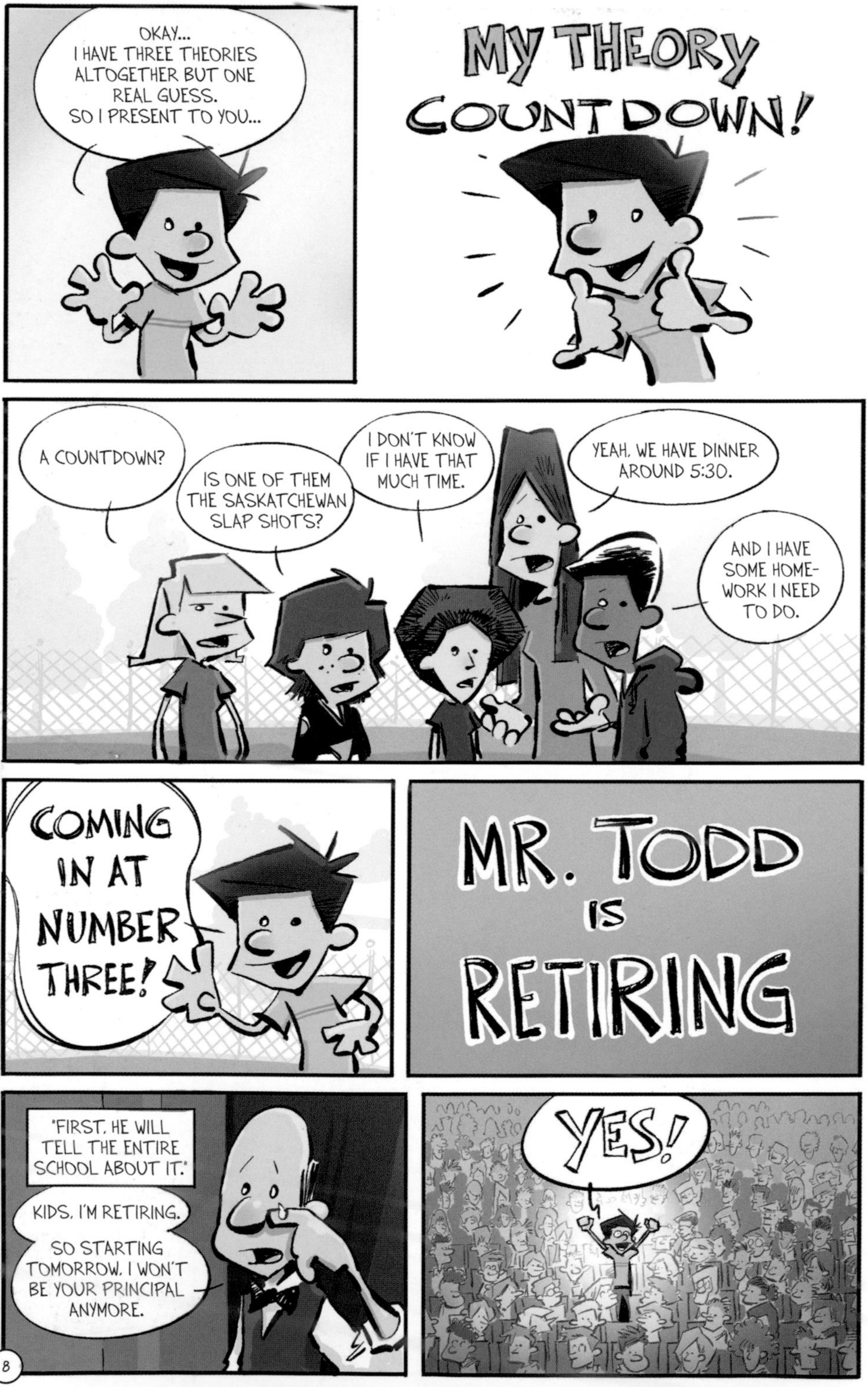
OKAY... I HAVE THREE THEORIES ALTOGETHER BUT ONE REAL GUESS. SO I PRESENT TO YOU...
MY THEORY COUNTDOWN!
A COUNTDOWN?
IS ONE OF THEM THE SASKATCHEWAN SLAP SHOTS?
I DON'T KNOW IF I HAVE THAT MUCH TIME.
YEAH, WE HAVE DINNER AROUND 5:30.
AND I HAVE SOME HOME-WORK I NEED TO DO.
COMING IN AT NUMBER THREE!
MR. TODD IS RETIRING
"FIRST, HE WILL TELL THE ENTIRE SCHOOL ABOUT IT."
KIDS, I'M RETIRING.
SO STARTING TOMORROW, I WON'T BE YOUR PRINCIPAL ANYMORE.
YES!

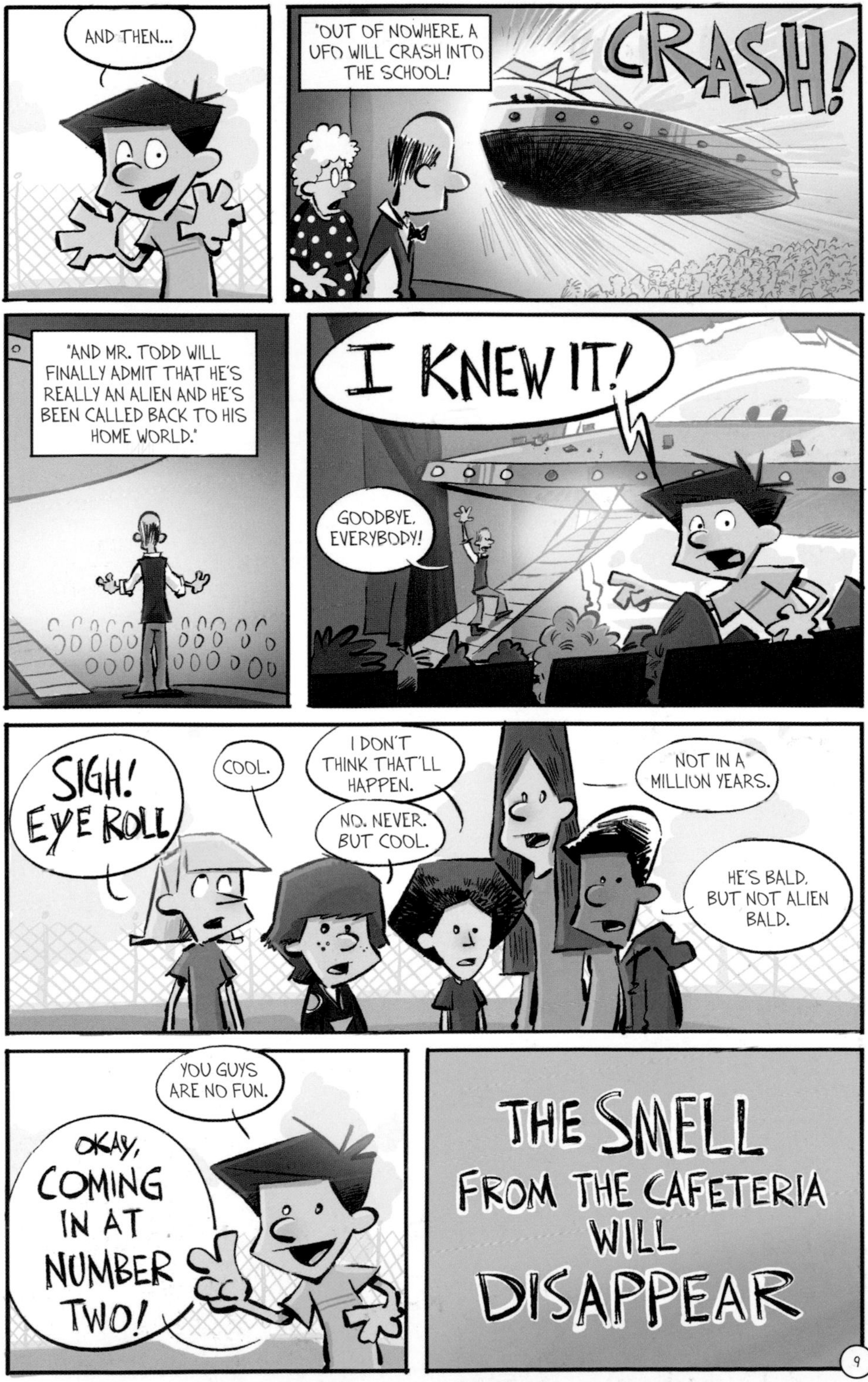
AND THEN...
"OUT OF NOWHERE, A UFO WILL CRASH INTO THE SCHOOL!
CRASH!
"AND MR. TODD WILL FINALLY ADMIT THAT HE'S REALLY AN ALIEN AND HE'S BEEN CALLED BACK TO HIS HOME WORLD."
I KNEW IT!
GOODBYE, EVERYBODY!
SIGH! EYE ROLL
COOL.
I DON'T THINK THAT'LL HAPPEN.
NO. NEVER. BUT COOL.
NOT IN A MILLION YEARS.
HE'S BALD, BUT NOT ALIEN BALD.
YOU GUYS ARE NO FUN.
OKAY, COMING IN AT NUMBER TWO!
THE SMELL FROM THE CAFETERIA WILL DISAPPEAR

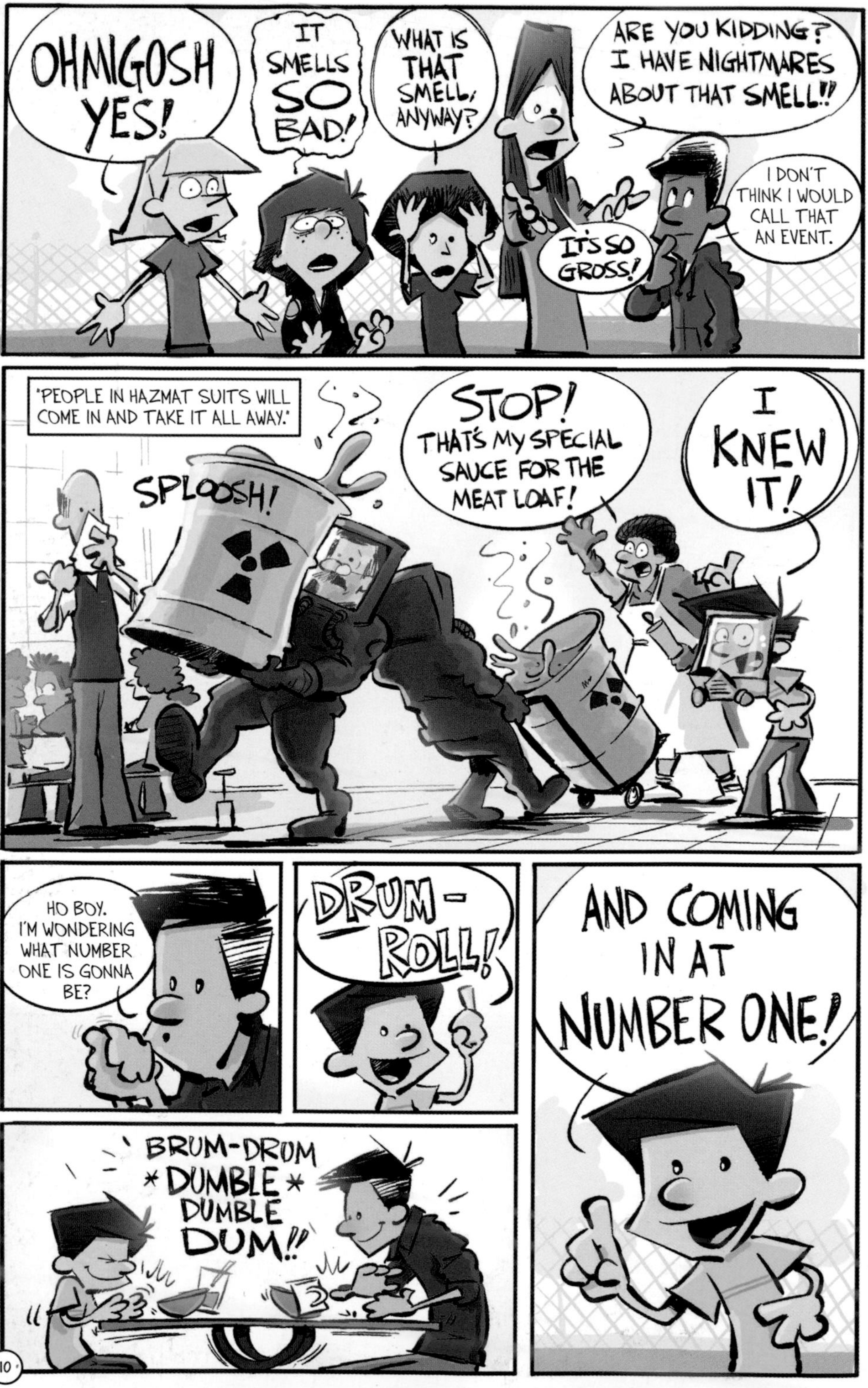
OHMIGOSH YES!
IT SMELLS SO BAD!
WHAT IS THAT SMELL, ANYWAY?
ARE YOU KIDDING? I HAVE NIGHTMARES ABOUT THAT SMELL!!
IT'S SO GROSS!
I DON'T THINK I WOULD CALL THAT AN EVENT.
"PEOPLE IN HAZMAT SUITS WILL COME IN AND TAKE IT ALL AWAY."
SPLOOSH!
STOP! THAT'S MY SPECIAL SAUCE FOR THE MEAT LOAF!
I KNEW IT!
HO BOY. I'M WONDERING WHAT NUMBER ONE IS GONNA BE?
DRUM-ROLL!
AND COMING IN AT NUMBER ONE!
BRUM-DROM *DUMBLE* DUMBLE DUM!!

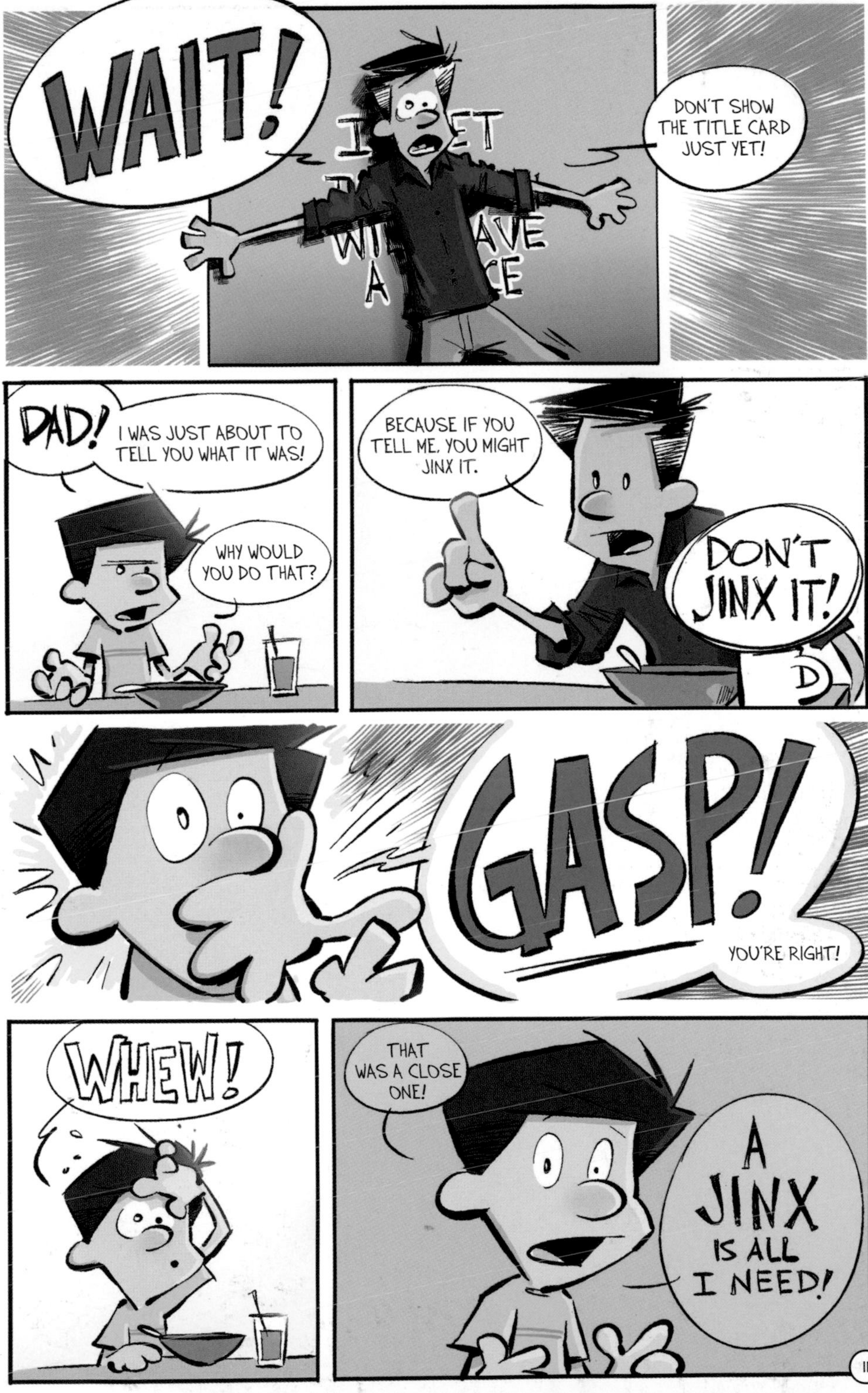
WAIT!
DON'T SHOW THE TITLE CARD JUST YET!
DAD! I WAS JUST ABOUT TO TELL YOU WHAT IT WAS!
WHY WOULD YOU DO THAT?
BECAUSE IF YOU TELL ME, YOU MIGHT JINX IT.
DON'T JINX IT!
GASP!
YOU'RE RIGHT!
WHEW!
THAT WAS A CLOSE ONE!
A JINX IS ALL I NEED!

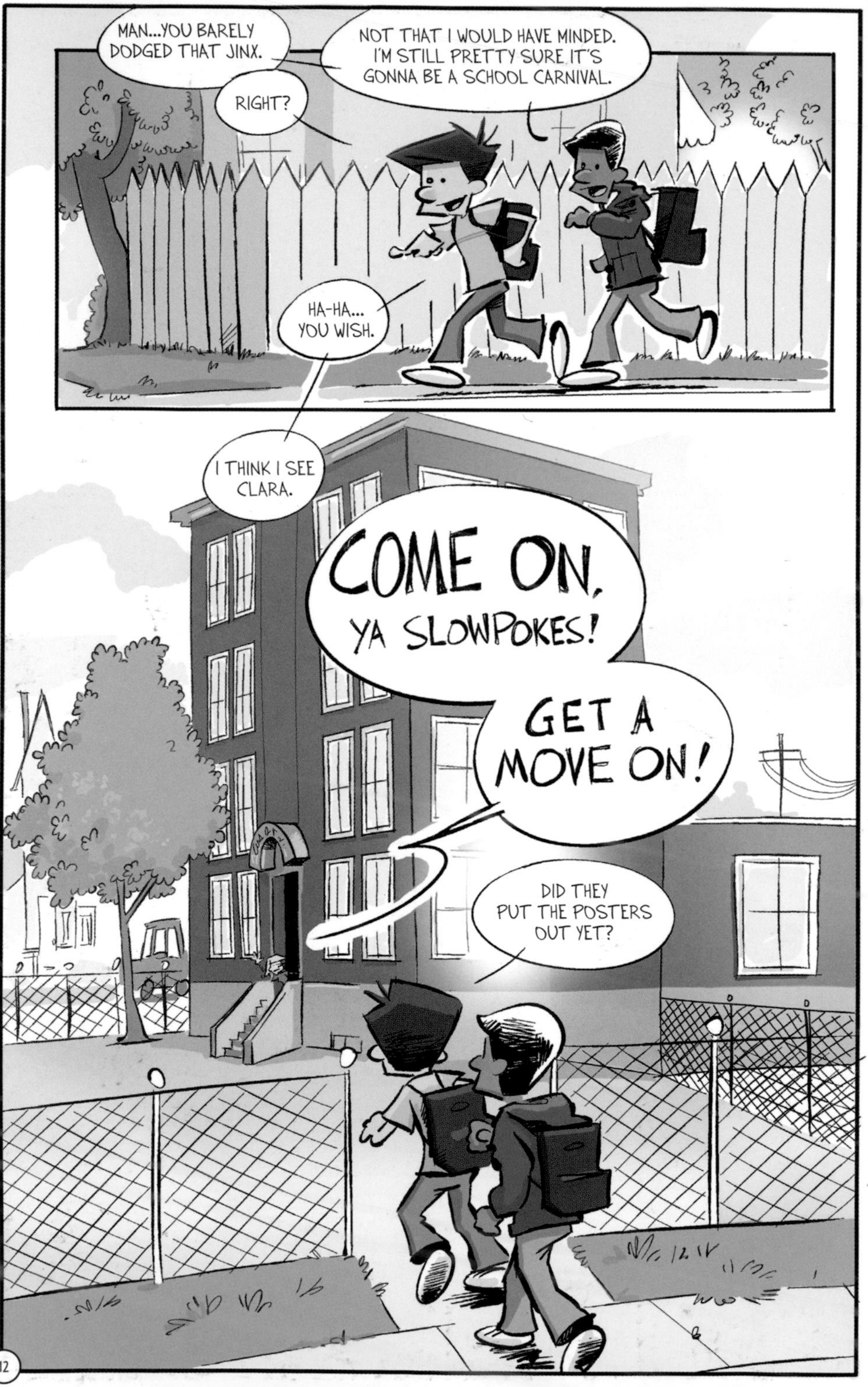
MAN...YOU BARELY DODGED THAT JINX.
NOT THAT I WOULD HAVE MINDED. I'M STILL PRETTY SURE IT'S GONNA BE A SCHOOL CARNIVAL.
RIGHT?
HA-HA... YOU WISH.
I THINK I SEE CLARA.
COME ON, YA SLOWPOKES!
GET A MOVE ON!
DID THEY PUT THE POSTERS OUT YET?

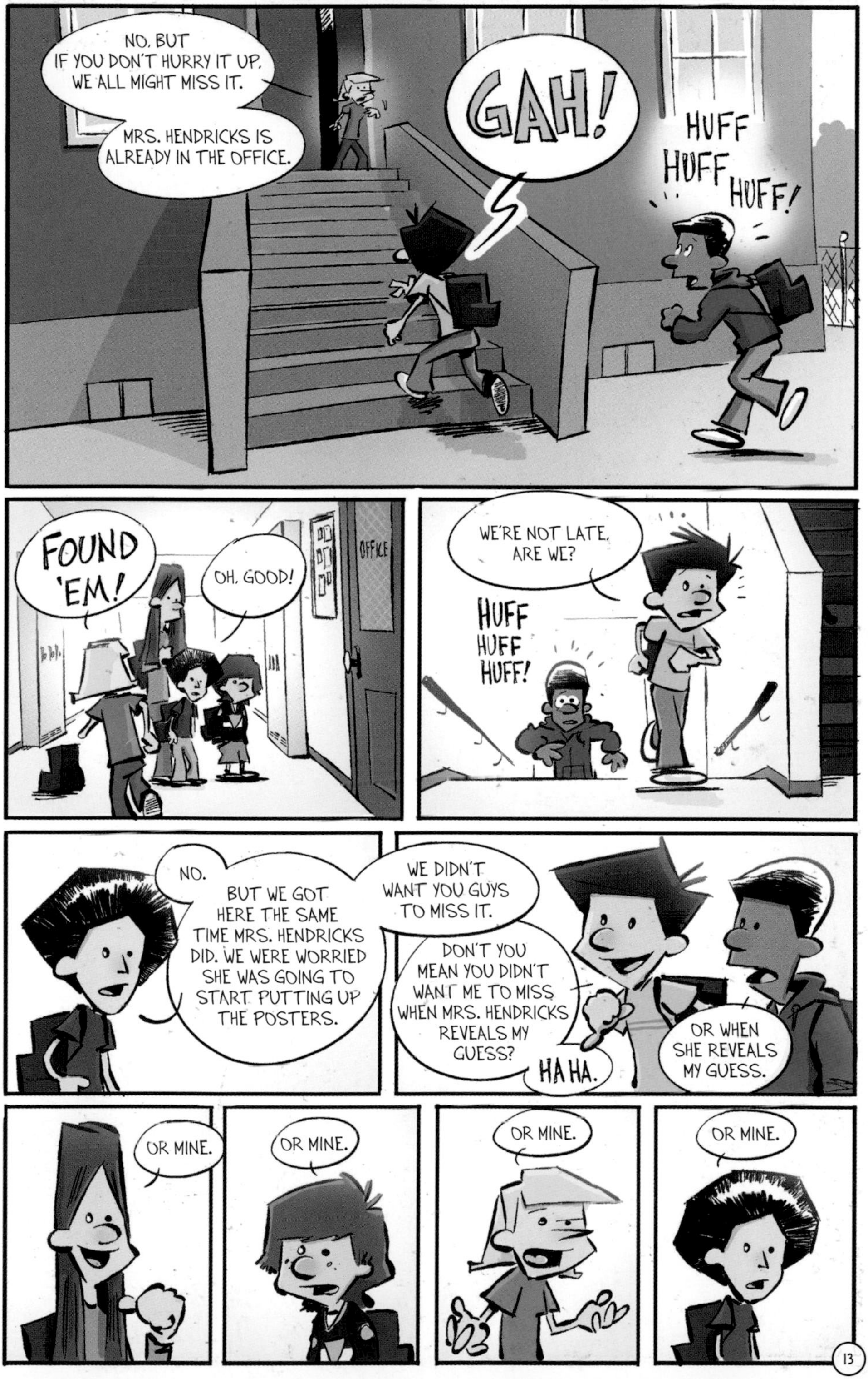
NO, BUT IF YOU DON'T HURRY IT UP, WE ALL MIGHT MISS IT.
MRS. HENDRICKS IS ALREADY IN THE OFFICE.
GAH!
HUFF HUFF HUFF!
FOUND 'EM!
OH, GOOD!
OFFICE
WE'RE NOT LATE, ARE WE?
HUFF HUFF HUFF!
NO.
BUT WE GOT HERE THE SAME TIME MRS. HENDRICKS DID. WE WERE WORRIED SHE WAS GOING TO START PUTTING UP THE POSTERS.
WE DIDN'T WANT YOU GUYS TO MISS IT.
DON'T YOU MEAN YOU DIDN'T WANT ME TO MISS WHEN MRS. HENDRICKS REVEALS MY GUESS?
HA HA.
OR WHEN SHE REVEALS MY GUESS.
OR MINE.
OR MINE.
OR MINE.
OR MINE.

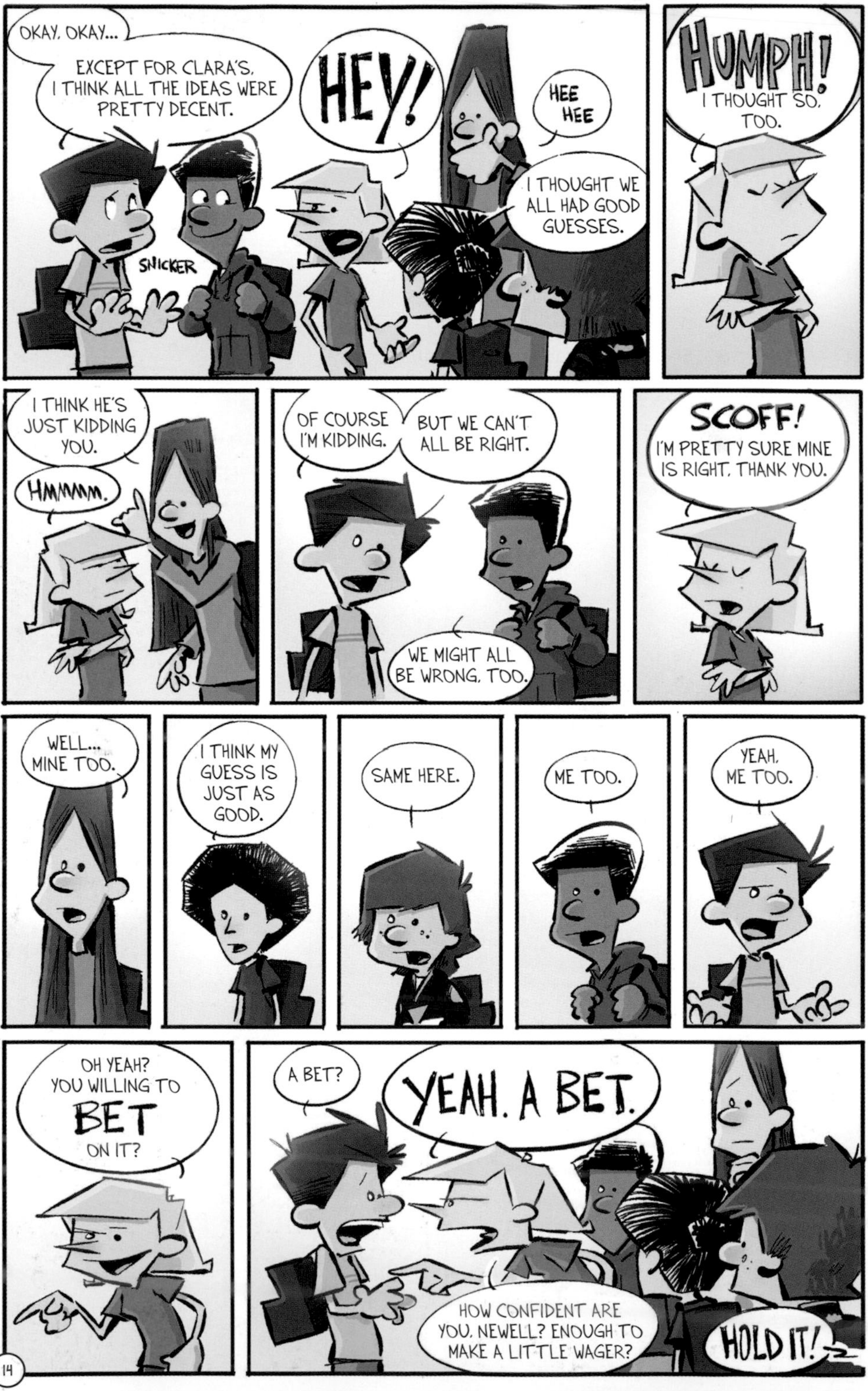
OKAY, OKAY...
EXCEPT FOR CLARA'S, I THINK ALL THE IDEAS WERE PRETTY DECENT.
HEY!
SNICKER
HEE HEE
I THOUGHT WE ALL HAD GOOD GUESSES.
HUMPH!
I THOUGHT SO, TOO.
I THINK HE'S JUST KIDDING YOU.
HMMMM.
OF COURSE I'M KIDDING.
BUT WE CAN'T ALL BE RIGHT.
WE MIGHT ALL BE WRONG, TOO.
SCOFF!
I'M PRETTY SURE MINE IS RIGHT, THANK YOU.
WELL... MINE TOO.
I THINK MY GUESS IS JUST AS GOOD.
SAME HERE.
ME TOO.
YEAH, ME TOO.
OH YEAH? YOU WILLING TO BET ON IT?
A BET?
YEAH. A BET.
HOW CONFIDENT ARE YOU, NEWELL? ENOUGH TO MAKE A LITTLE WAGER?
HOLD IT!

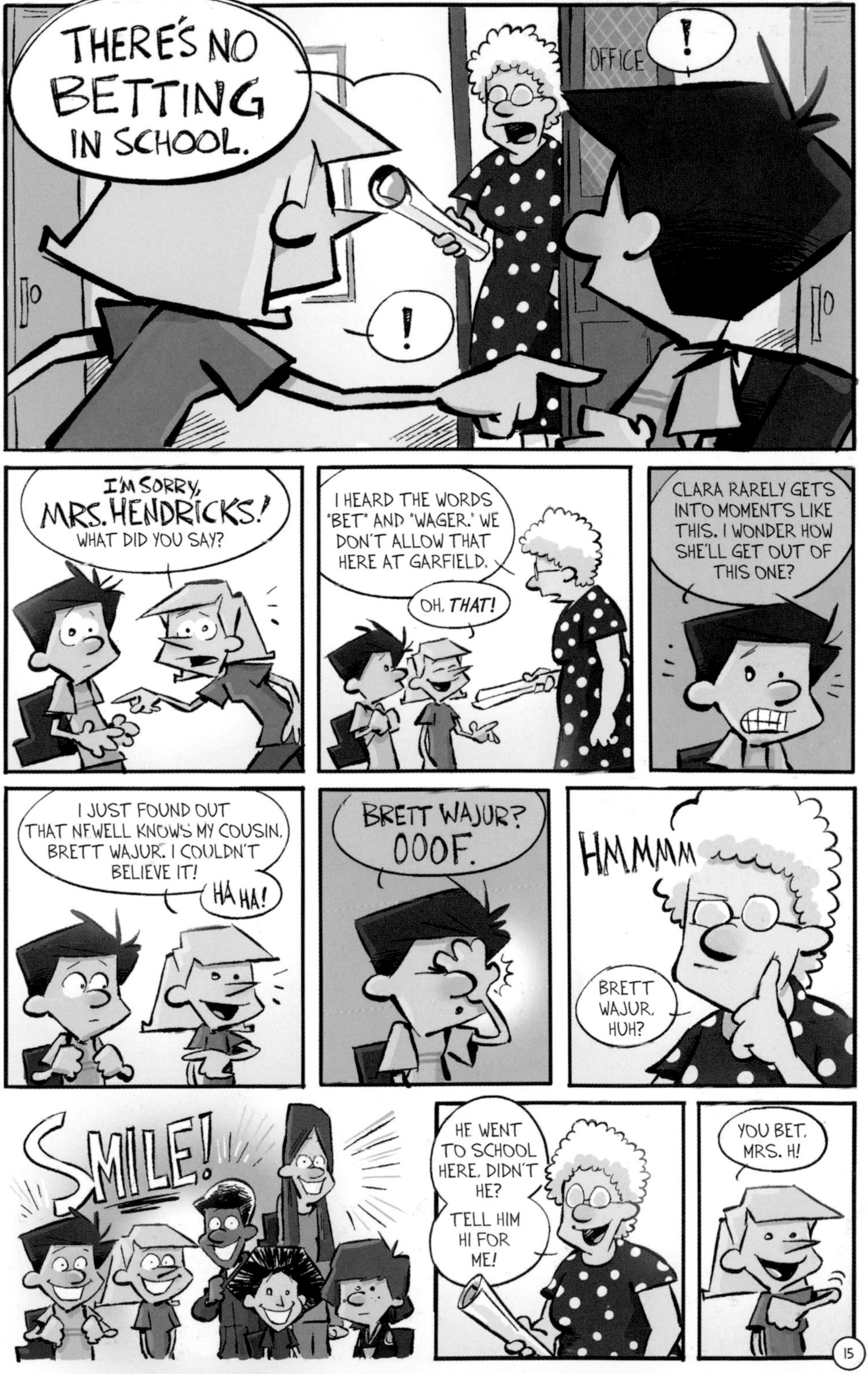
THERE'S NO BETTING IN SCHOOL.
!
OFFICE
!
I'M SORRY, MRS. HENDRICKS! WHAT DID YOU SAY?
I HEARD THE WORDS "BET" AND "WAGER." WE DON'T ALLOW THAT HERE AT GARFIELD.
OH, THAT!
CLARA RARELY GETS INTO MOMENTS LIKE THIS. I WONDER HOW SHE'LL GET OUT OF THIS ONE?
I JUST FOUND OUT THAT NEWELL KNOWS MY COUSIN, BRETT WAJUR. I COULDN'T BELIEVE IT!
HA HA!
BRETT WAJUR? OOOF.
HMMMM
BRETT WAJUR, HUH?
SMILE!
HE WENT TO SCHOOL HERE, DIDN'T HE?
TELL HIM HI FOR ME!
YOU BET, MRS. H!

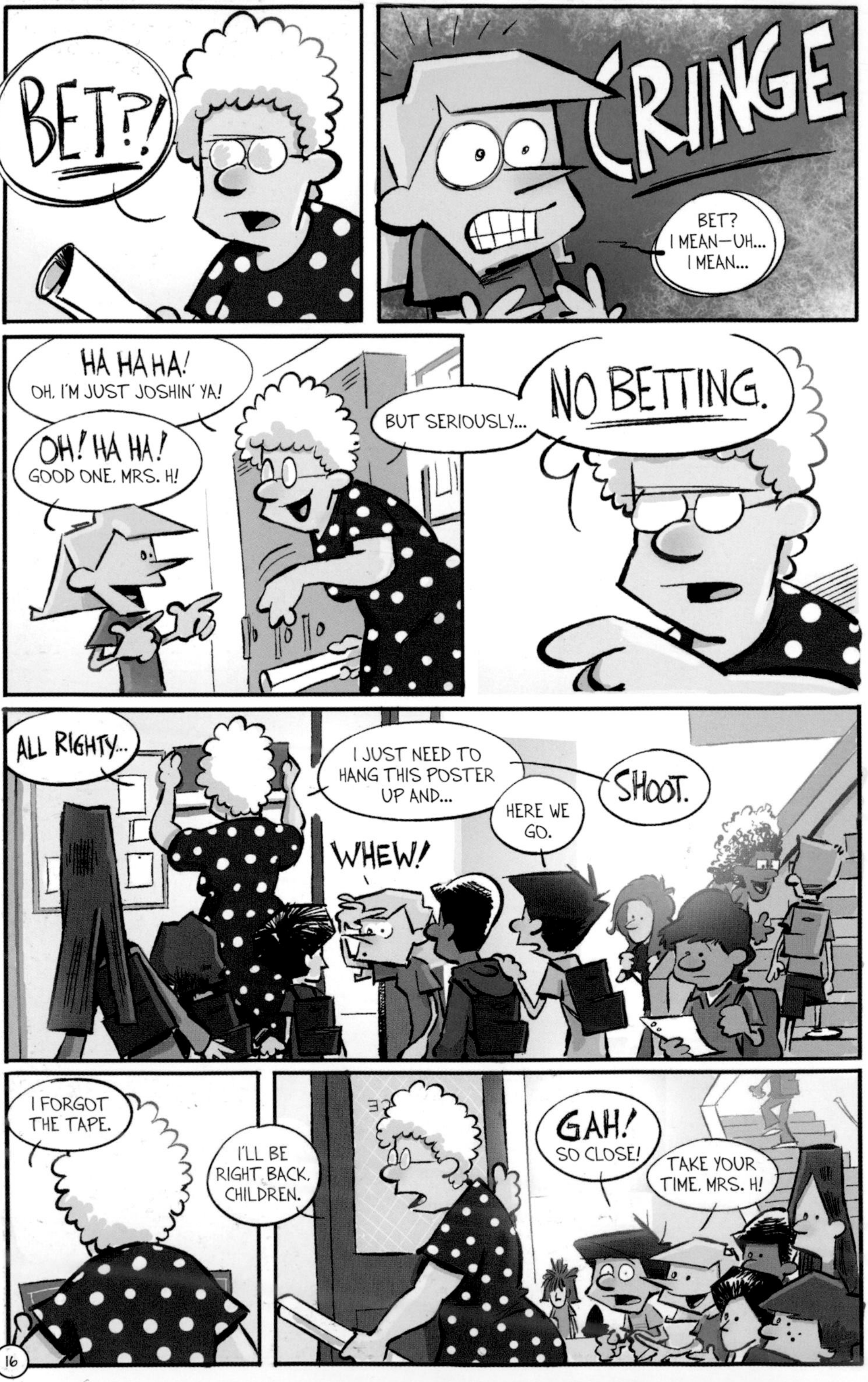
BET?!
CRINGE
BET? I MEAN—UH... I MEAN...
HA HA HA! OH, I'M JUST JOSHIN' YA!
OH! HA HA! GOOD ONE, MRS. H!
BUT SERIOUSLY...
NO BETTING.
ALL RIGHTY...
I JUST NEED TO HANG THIS POSTER UP AND...
SHOOT.
HERE WE GO.
WHEW!
I FORGOT THE TAPE.
I'LL BE RIGHT BACK, CHILDREN.
GAH! SO CLOSE!
TAKE YOUR TIME, MRS. H!

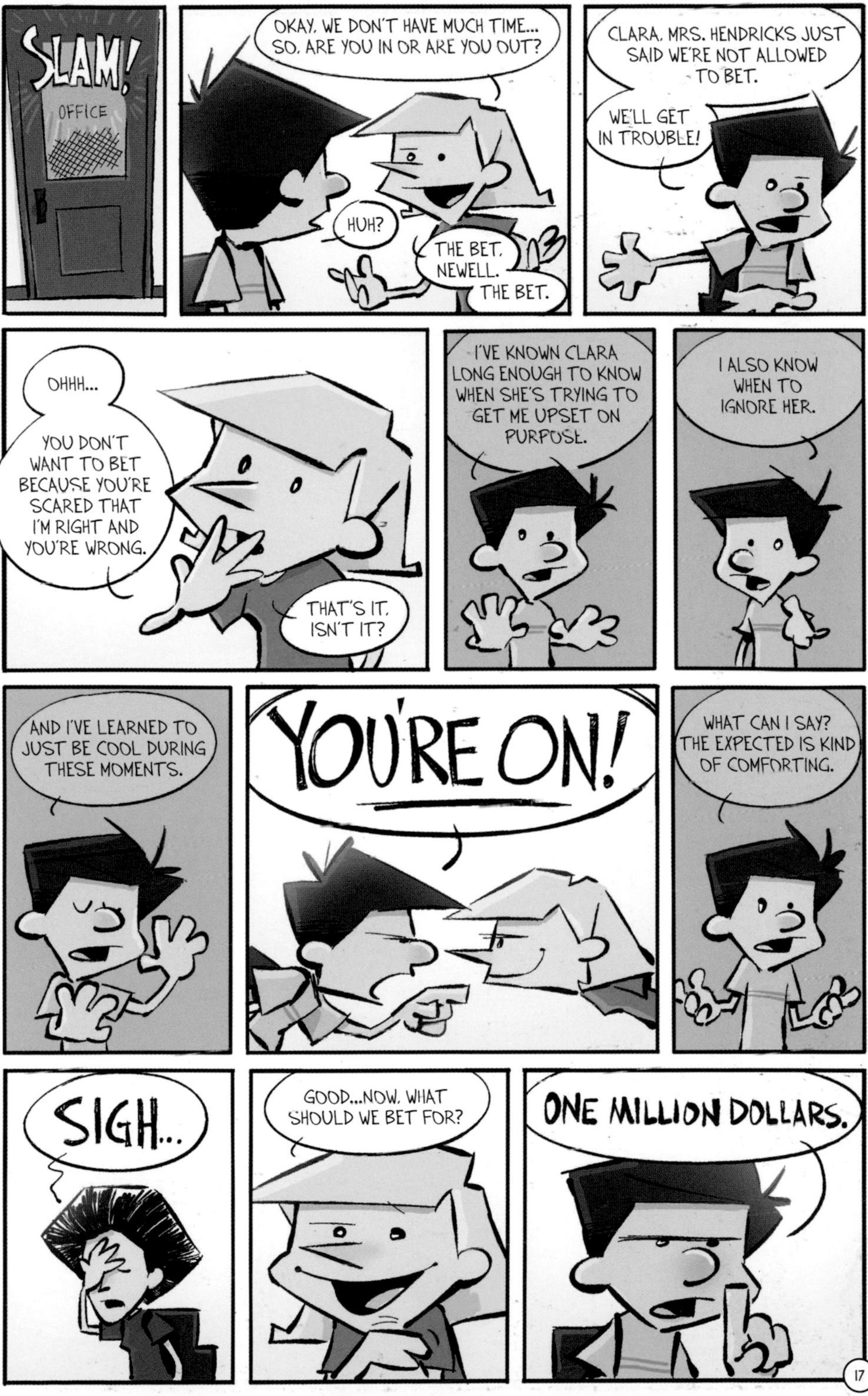
SLAM!
OFFICE
OKAY, WE DON'T HAVE MUCH TIME... SO, ARE YOU IN OR ARE YOU OUT?
HUH?
THE BET, NEWELL.
THE BET.
CLARA, MRS. HENDRICKS JUST SAID WE'RE NOT ALLOWED TO BET.
WE'LL GET IN TROUBLE!
OHHH...
YOU DON'T WANT TO BET BECAUSE YOU'RE SCARED THAT I'M RIGHT AND YOU'RE WRONG.
THAT'S IT, ISN'T IT?
I'VE KNOWN CLARA LONG ENOUGH TO KNOW WHEN SHE'S TRYING TO GET ME UPSET ON PURPOSE.
I ALSO KNOW WHEN TO IGNORE HER.
AND I'VE LEARNED TO JUST BE COOL DURING THESE MOMENTS.
YOU'RE ON!
WHAT CAN I SAY? THE EXPECTED IS KIND OF COMFORTING.
SIGH...
GOOD...NOW, WHAT SHOULD WE BET FOR?
ONE MILLION DOLLARS.

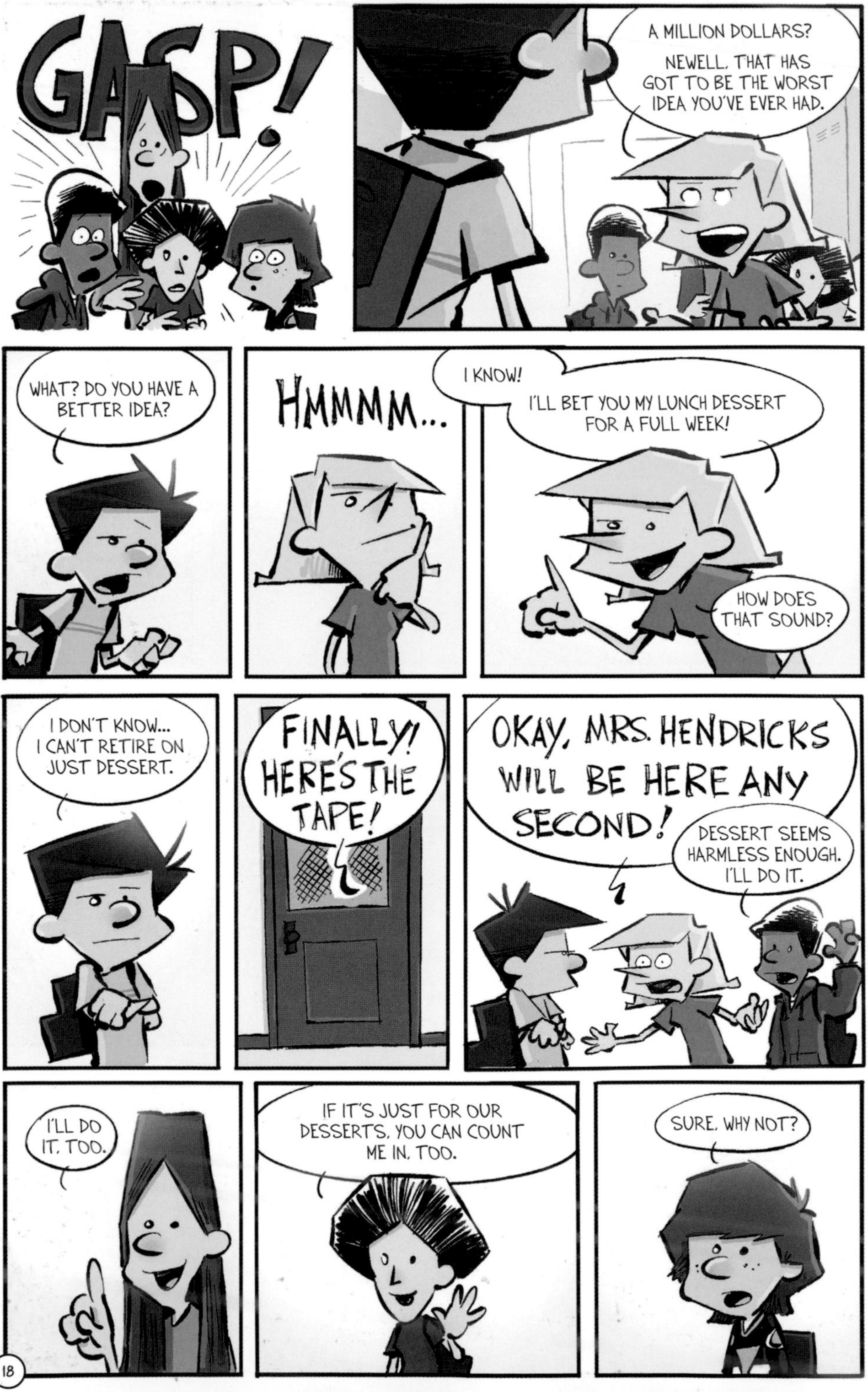
GASP!
A MILLION DOLLARS?
NEWELL, THAT HAS GOT TO BE THE WORST IDEA YOU'VE EVER HAD.
WHAT? DO YOU HAVE A BETTER IDEA?
HMMMM...
I KNOW!
I'LL BET YOU MY LUNCH DESSERT FOR A FULL WEEK!
HOW DOES THAT SOUND?
I DON'T KNOW... I CAN'T RETIRE ON JUST DESSERT.
FINALLY! HERE'S THE TAPE!
OKAY, MRS. HENDRICKS WILL BE HERE ANY SECOND!
DESSERT SEEMS HARMLESS ENOUGH. I'LL DO IT.
I'LL DO IT, TOO.
IF IT'S JUST FOR OUR DESSERTS, YOU CAN COUNT ME IN, TOO.
SURE, WHY NOT?

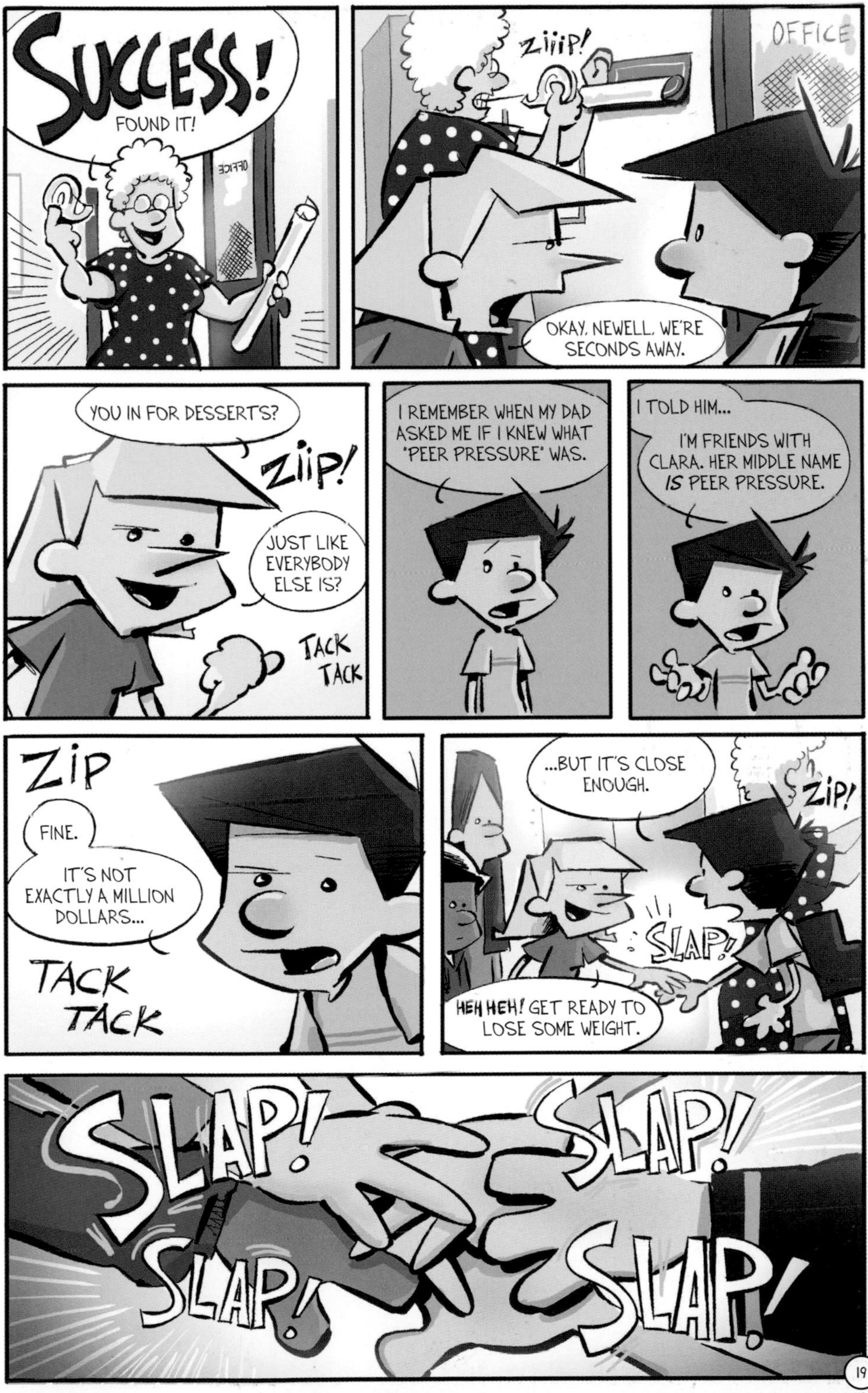
SUCCESS!
FOUND IT!
OFFICE
ZIIIP!
OFFICE
OKAY, NEWELL, WE'RE SECONDS AWAY.
YOU IN FOR DESSERTS?
ZIIP!
JUST LIKE EVERYBODY ELSE IS?
TACK TACK
I REMEMBER WHEN MY DAD ASKED ME IF I KNEW WHAT "PEER PRESSURE" WAS.
I TOLD HIM...
I'M FRIENDS WITH CLARA. HER MIDDLE NAME *IS* PEER PRESSURE.
ZIP
FINE.
IT'S NOT EXACTLY A MILLION DOLLARS...
TACK TACK
...BUT IT'S CLOSE ENOUGH.
ZIP!
SLAP!
HEH HEH! GET READY TO LOSE SOME WEIGHT.
SLAP!
SLAP!
SLAP!
SLAP!

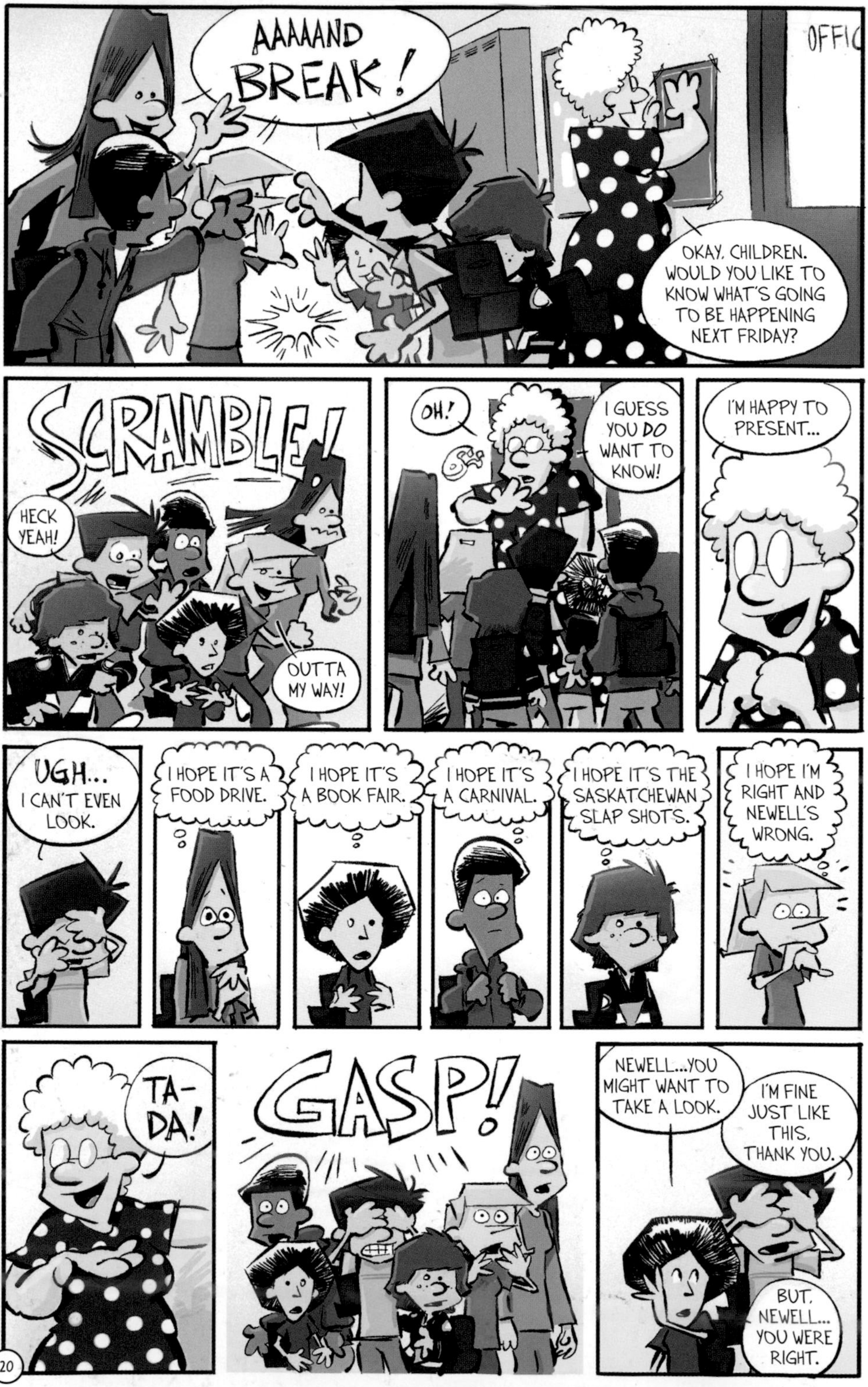
AAAAAND BREAK!
OFFIC
OKAY, CHILDREN. WOULD YOU LIKE TO KNOW WHAT'S GOING TO BE HAPPENING NEXT FRIDAY?
SCRAMBLE!
HECK YEAH!
OUTTA MY WAY!
OH!
I GUESS YOU DO WANT TO KNOW!
I'M HAPPY TO PRESENT...
UGH... I CAN'T EVEN LOOK.
I HOPE IT'S A FOOD DRIVE.
I HOPE IT'S A BOOK FAIR.
I HOPE IT'S A CARNIVAL.
I HOPE IT'S THE SASKATCHEWAN SLAP SHOTS.
I HOPE I'M RIGHT AND NEWELL'S WRONG.
TA-DA!
GASP!
NEWELL...YOU MIGHT WANT TO TAKE A LOOK.
I'M FINE JUST LIKE THIS, THANK YOU.
BUT, NEWELL... YOU WERE RIGHT.

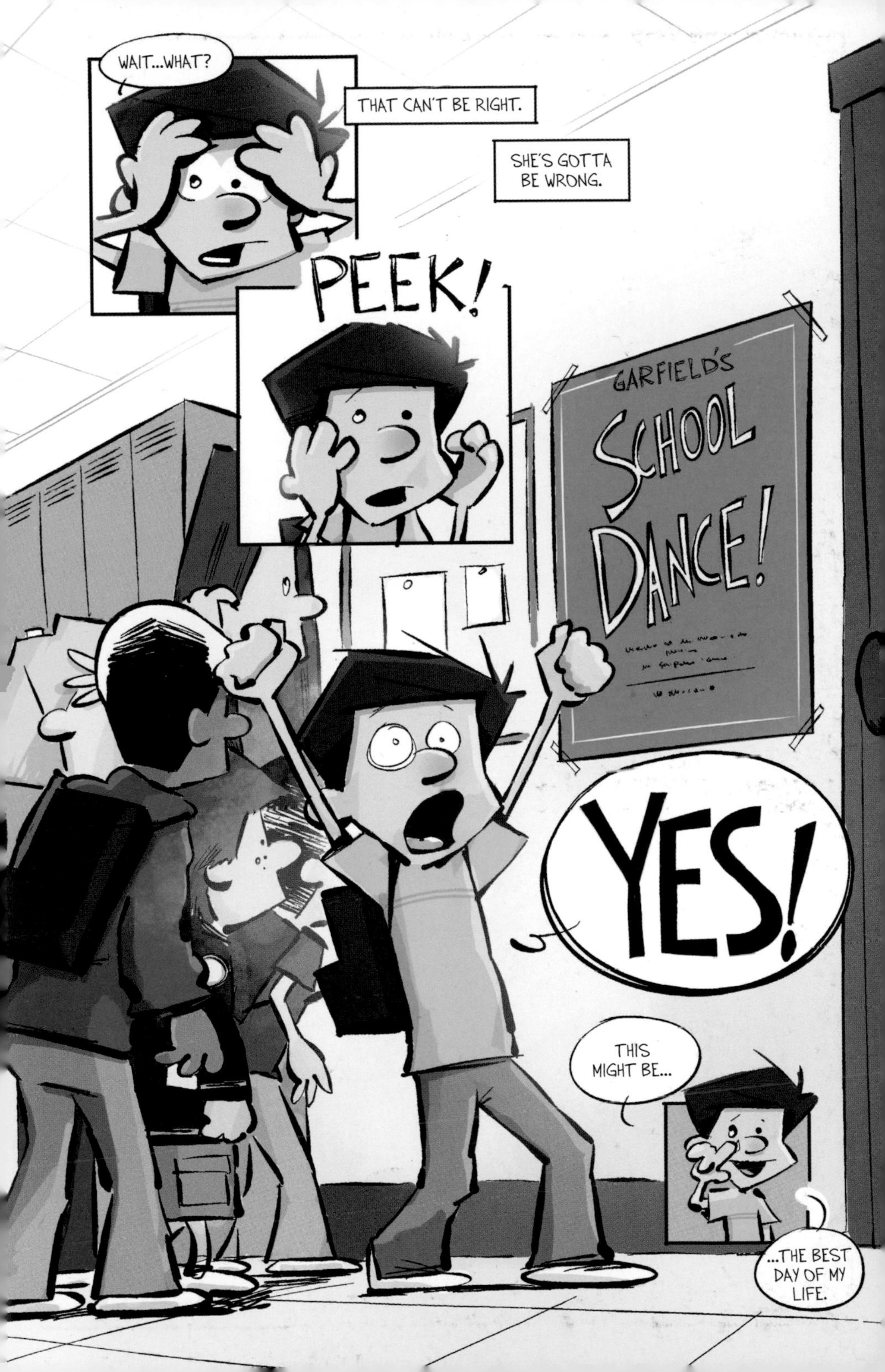
WAIT...WHAT?
THAT CAN'T BE RIGHT.
SHE'S GOTTA BE WRONG.
PEEK!
GARFIELD'S SCHOOL DANCE!
YES!
THIS MIGHT BE...
...THE BEST DAY OF MY LIFE.

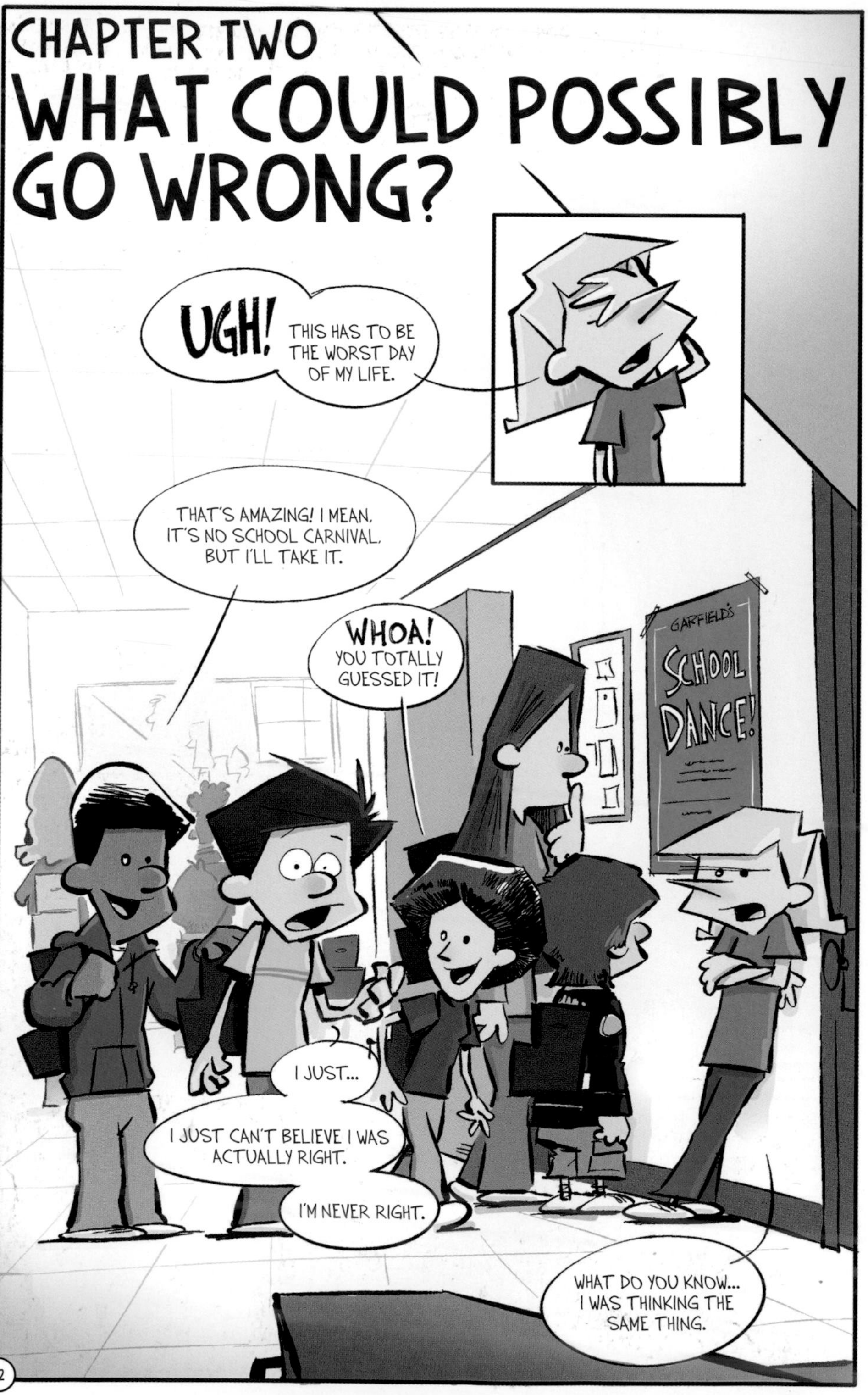
CHAPTER TWO
WHAT COULD POSSIBLY GO WRONG?
UGH! THIS HAS TO BE THE WORST DAY OF MY LIFE.
THAT'S AMAZING! I MEAN, IT'S NO SCHOOL CARNIVAL, BUT I'LL TAKE IT.
WHOA! YOU TOTALLY GUESSED IT!
GARFIELD'S SCHOOL DANCE!
I JUST...
I JUST CAN'T BELIEVE I WAS ACTUALLY RIGHT.
I'M NEVER RIGHT.
WHAT DO YOU KNOW... I WAS THINKING THE SAME THING.

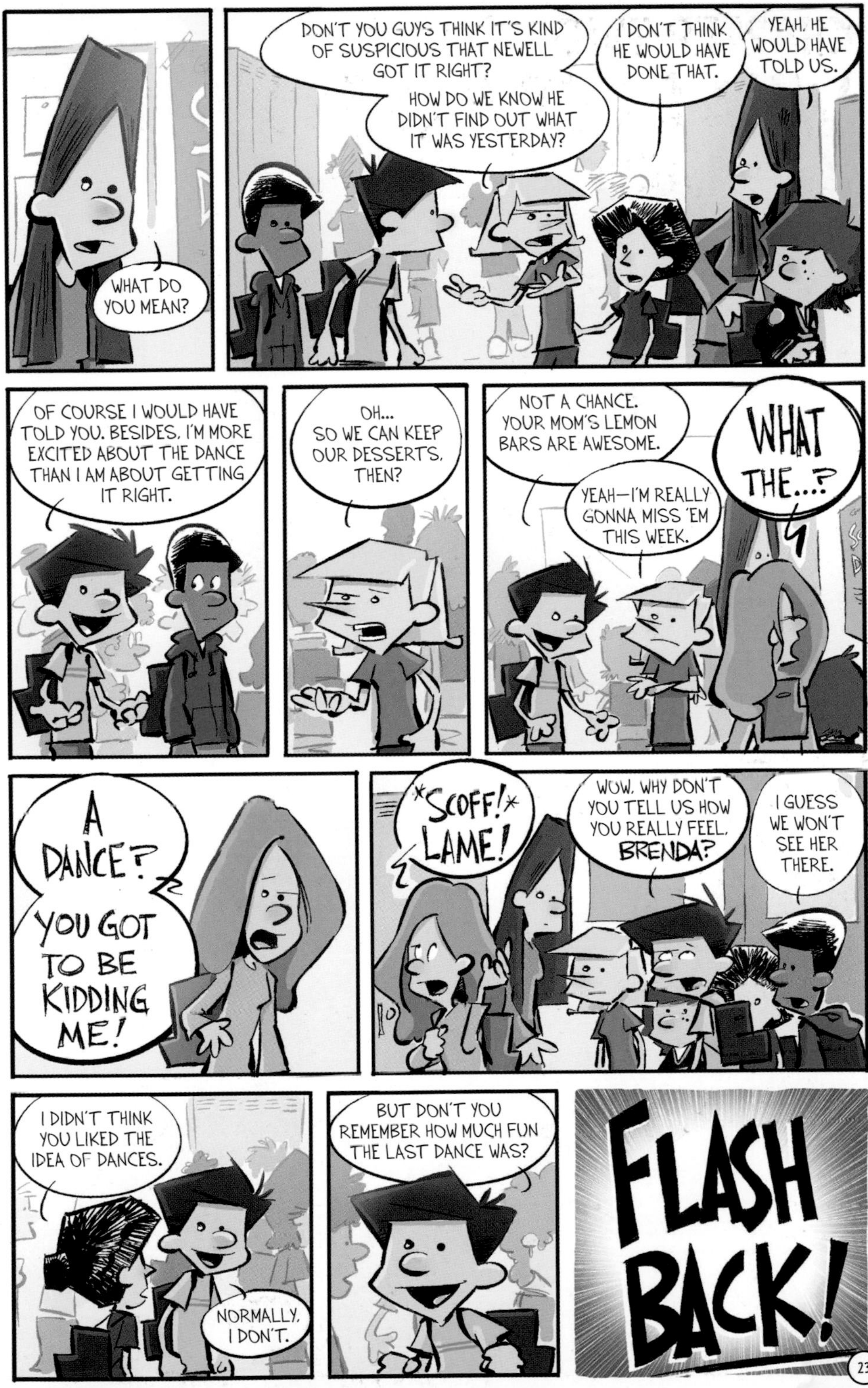
WHAT DO YOU MEAN?
DON'T YOU GUYS THINK IT'S KIND OF SUSPICIOUS THAT NEWELL GOT IT RIGHT?
HOW DO WE KNOW HE DIDN'T FIND OUT WHAT IT WAS YESTERDAY?
I DON'T THINK HE WOULD HAVE DONE THAT.
YEAH, HE WOULD HAVE TOLD US.
OF COURSE I WOULD HAVE TOLD YOU. BESIDES, I'M MORE EXCITED ABOUT THE DANCE THAN I AM ABOUT GETTING IT RIGHT.
OH... SO WE CAN KEEP OUR DESSERTS, THEN?
NOT A CHANCE. YOUR MOM'S LEMON BARS ARE AWESOME.
YEAH—I'M REALLY GONNA MISS 'EM THIS WEEK.
WHAT THE...?
A DANCE?
YOU GOT TO BE KIDDING ME!
SCOFF! LAME!
WOW, WHY DON'T YOU TELL US HOW YOU REALLY FEEL, BRENDA?
I GUESS WE WON'T SEE HER THERE.
I DIDN'T THINK YOU LIKED THE IDEA OF DANCES.
NORMALLY, I DON'T.
BUT DON'T YOU REMEMBER HOW MUCH FUN THE LAST DANCE WAS?
FLASH BACK!

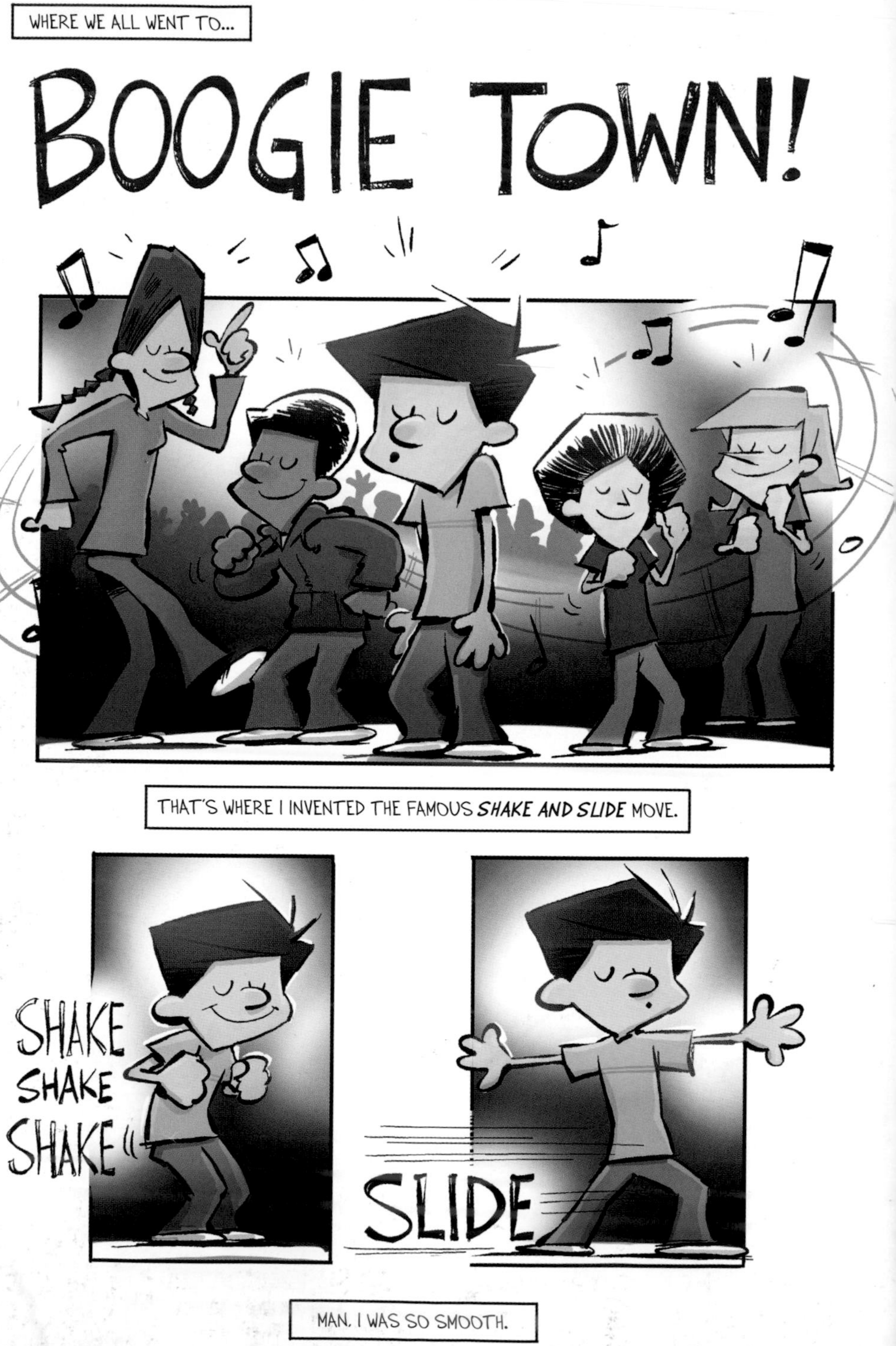
WHERE WE ALL WENT TO...
BOOGIE TOWN!
THAT'S WHERE I INVENTED THE FAMOUS SHAKE AND SLIDE MOVE.
SHAKE
SHAKE
SHAKE
SLIDE
MAN, I WAS SO SMOOTH.

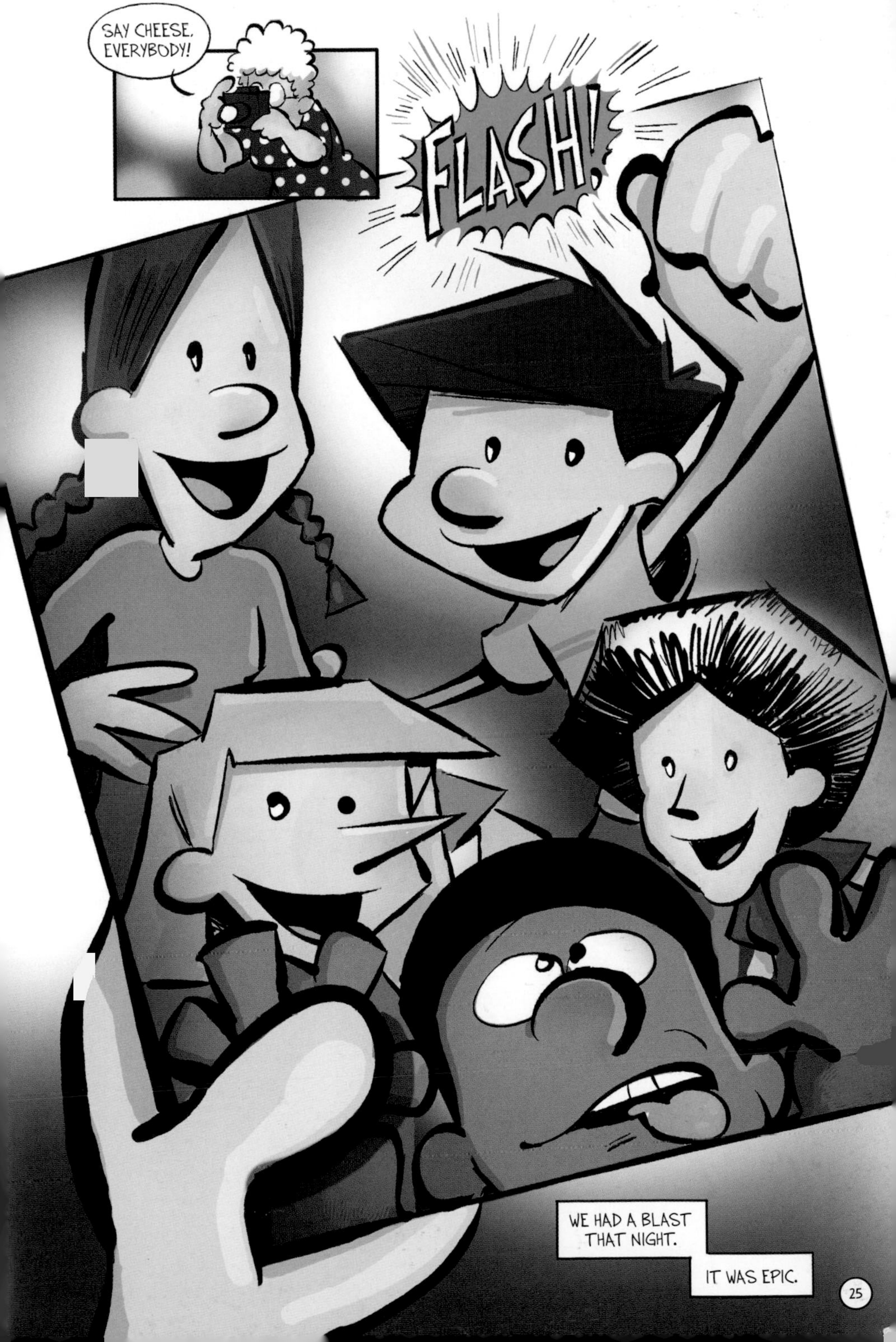
SAY CHEESE, EVERYBODY!
FLASH!
WE HAD A BLAST THAT NIGHT.
IT WAS EPIC.

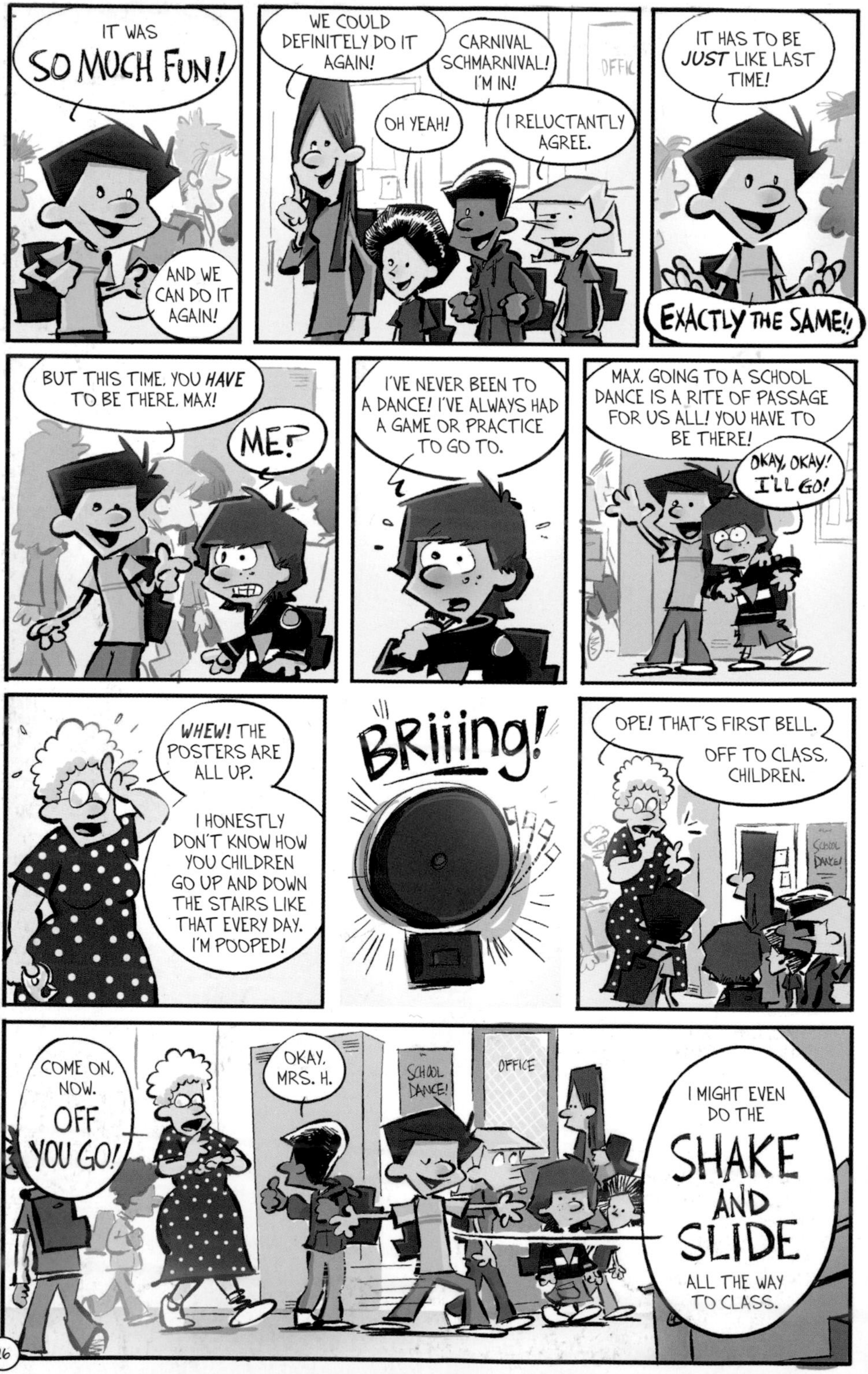
IT WAS SO MUCH FUN!
AND WE CAN DO IT AGAIN!
WE COULD DEFINITELY DO IT AGAIN!
CARNIVAL SCHMARNIVAL! I'M IN!
OH YEAH!
I RELUCTANTLY AGREE.
OFFIC
IT HAS TO BE JUST LIKE LAST TIME!
EXACTLY THE SAME!!
BUT THIS TIME, YOU HAVE TO BE THERE, MAX!
ME?
I'VE NEVER BEEN TO A DANCE! I'VE ALWAYS HAD A GAME OR PRACTICE TO GO TO.
MAX, GOING TO A SCHOOL DANCE IS A RITE OF PASSAGE FOR US ALL! YOU HAVE TO BE THERE!
OKAY, OKAY! I'LL GO!
WHEW! THE POSTERS ARE ALL UP.
I HONESTLY DON'T KNOW HOW YOU CHILDREN GO UP AND DOWN THE STAIRS LIKE THAT EVERY DAY. I'M POOPED!
BRiiing!
OPE! THAT'S FIRST BELL.
OFF TO CLASS, CHILDREN.
SCHOOL DANCE!
COME ON, NOW. OFF YOU GO!
OKAY, MRS. H.
SCHOOL DANCE!
OFFICE
I MIGHT EVEN DO THE SHAKE AND SLIDE ALL THE WAY TO CLASS.

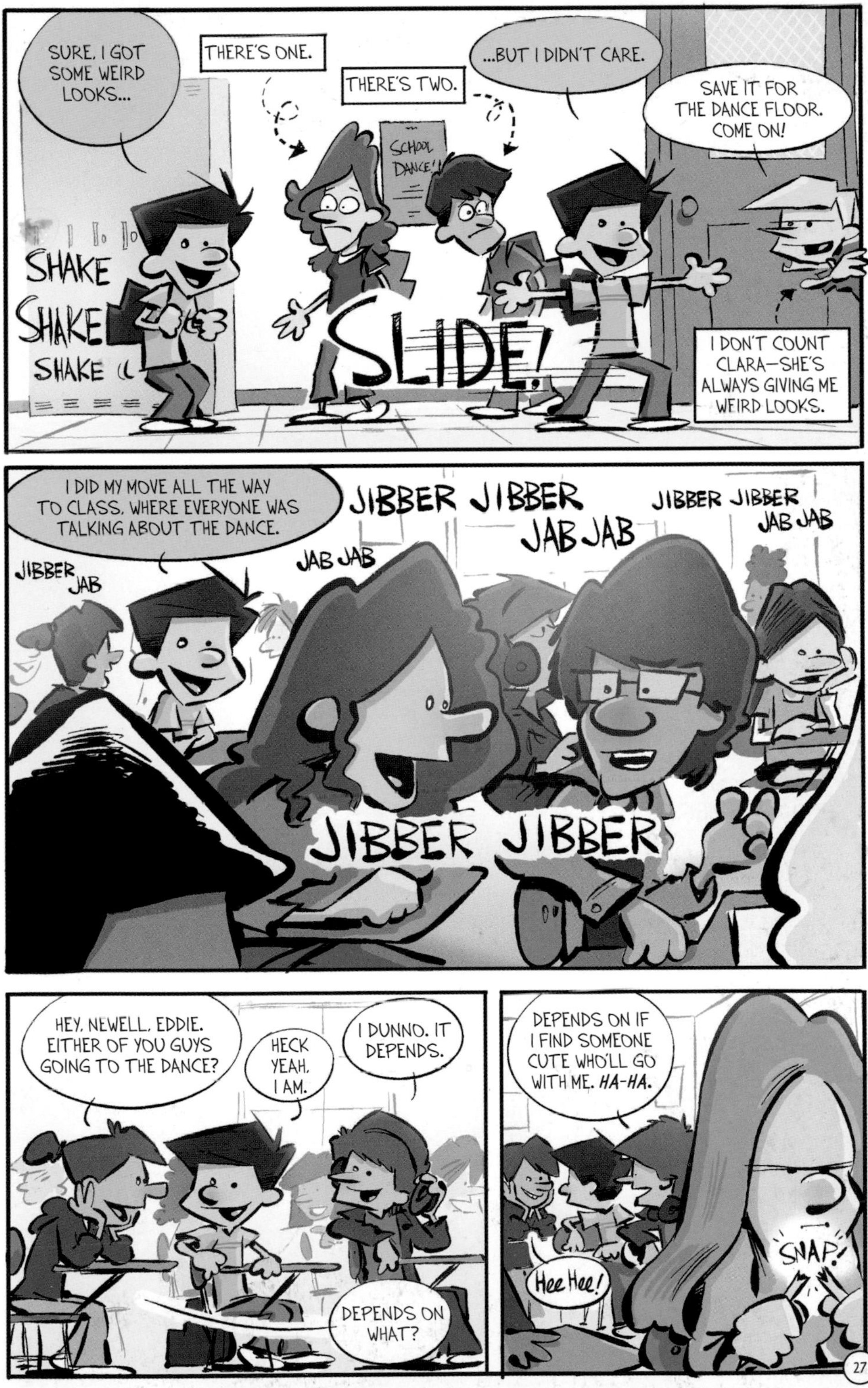

SURE, I GOT SOME WEIRD LOOKS...
THERE'S ONE.
THERE'S TWO.
...BUT I DIDN'T CARE.
SAVE IT FOR THE DANCE FLOOR. COME ON!
SCHOOL DANCE!
SHAKE
SHAKE
SHAKE
SLIDE!
I DON'T COUNT CLARA—SHE'S ALWAYS GIVING ME WEIRD LOOKS.
I DID MY MOVE ALL THE WAY TO CLASS, WHERE EVERYONE WAS TALKING ABOUT THE DANCE.
JIBBER JIBBER
JAB JAB
JIBBER JIBBER
JAB JAB
JIBBER JAB
JAB JAB
JIBBER JIBBER
HEY, NEWELL, EDDIE. EITHER OF YOU GUYS GOING TO THE DANCE?
HECK YEAH, I AM.
I DUNNO. IT DEPENDS.
DEPENDS ON WHAT?
DEPENDS ON IF I FIND SOMEONE CUTE WHO'LL GO WITH ME. HA-HA.
Hee Hee!
SNAP!

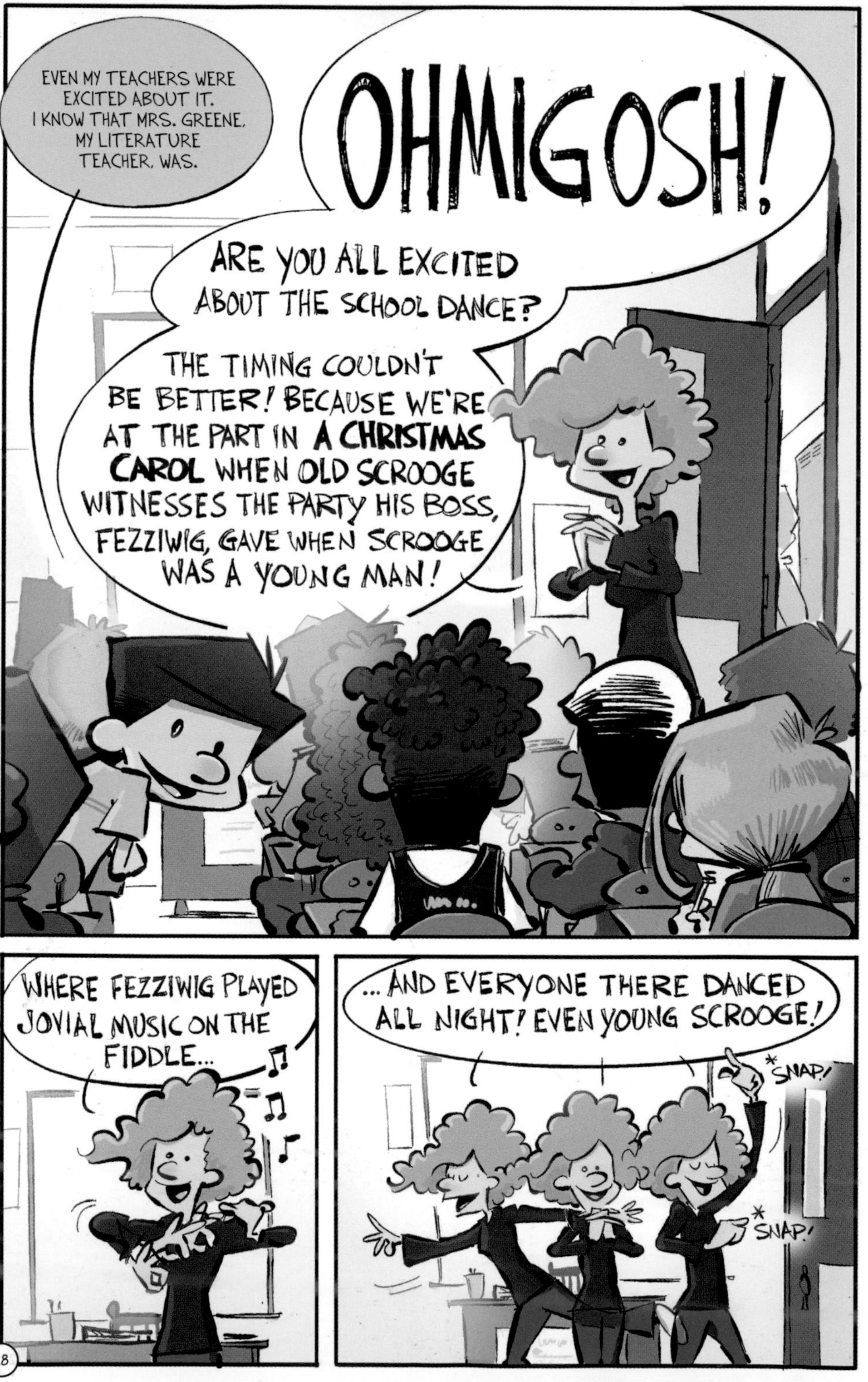
EVEN MY TEACHERS WERE EXCITED ABOUT IT. I KNOW THAT MRS. GREENE, MY LITERATURE TEACHER, WAS.
OHMIGOSH!
ARE YOU ALL EXCITED ABOUT THE SCHOOL DANCE?
THE TIMING COULDN'T BE BETTER! BECAUSE WE'RE AT THE PART IN A CHRISTMAS CAROL WHEN OLD SCROOGE WITNESSES THE PARTY HIS BOSS, FEZZIWIG, GAVE WHEN SCROOGE WAS A YOUNG MAN!
WHERE FEZZIWIG PLAYED JOVIAL MUSIC ON THE FIDDLE...
...AND EVERYONE THERE DANCED ALL NIGHT! EVEN YOUNG SCROOGE!
*SNAP!
*SNAP!

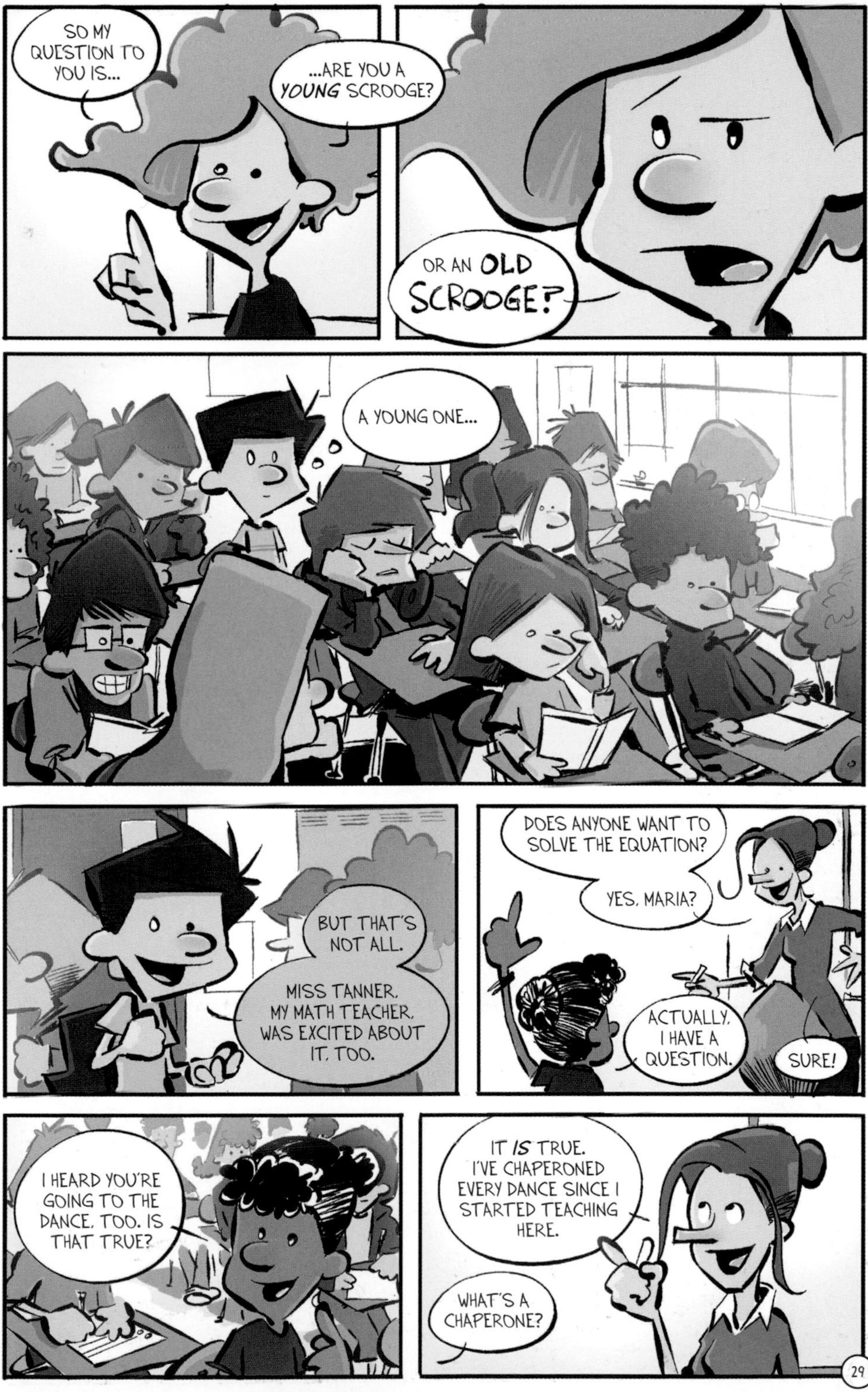
SO MY QUESTION TO YOU IS...
...ARE YOU A *YOUNG* SCROOGE?
OR AN **OLD SCROOGE?**
A YOUNG ONE...
BUT THAT'S NOT ALL.
MISS TANNER, MY MATH TEACHER, WAS EXCITED ABOUT IT, TOO.
DOES ANYONE WANT TO SOLVE THE EQUATION?
YES, MARIA?
ACTUALLY, I HAVE A QUESTION.
SURE!
I HEARD YOU'RE GOING TO THE DANCE, TOO. IS THAT TRUE?
IT *IS* TRUE. I'VE CHAPERONED EVERY DANCE SINCE I STARTED TEACHING HERE.
WHAT'S A CHAPERONE?

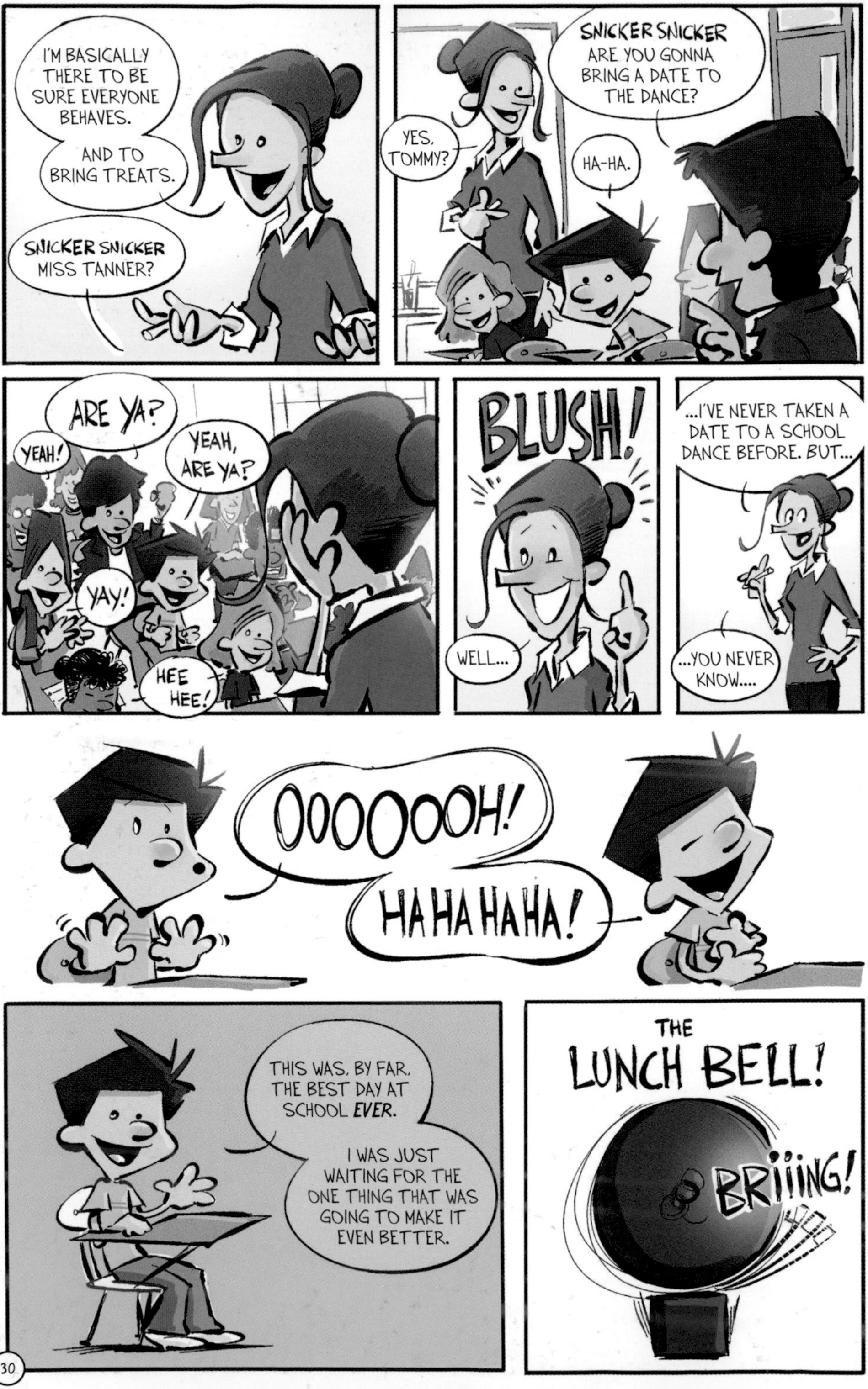
I'M BASICALLY THERE TO BE SURE EVERYONE BEHAVES.
AND TO BRING TREATS.
SNICKER SNICKER MISS TANNER?
YES, TOMMY?
SNICKER SNICKER ARE YOU GONNA BRING A DATE TO THE DANCE?
HA-HA.
YEAH!
ARE YA?
YEAH, ARE YA?
YAY!
HEE HEE!
BLUSH!
WELL...
...I'VE NEVER TAKEN A DATE TO A SCHOOL DANCE BEFORE. BUT...
...YOU NEVER KNOW....
OOOOOOH!
HAHAHAHA!
THIS WAS, BY FAR, THE BEST DAY AT SCHOOL EVER.
I WAS JUST WAITING FOR THE ONE THING THAT WAS GOING TO MAKE IT EVEN BETTER.
THE LUNCH BELL!
BRIiiNG!

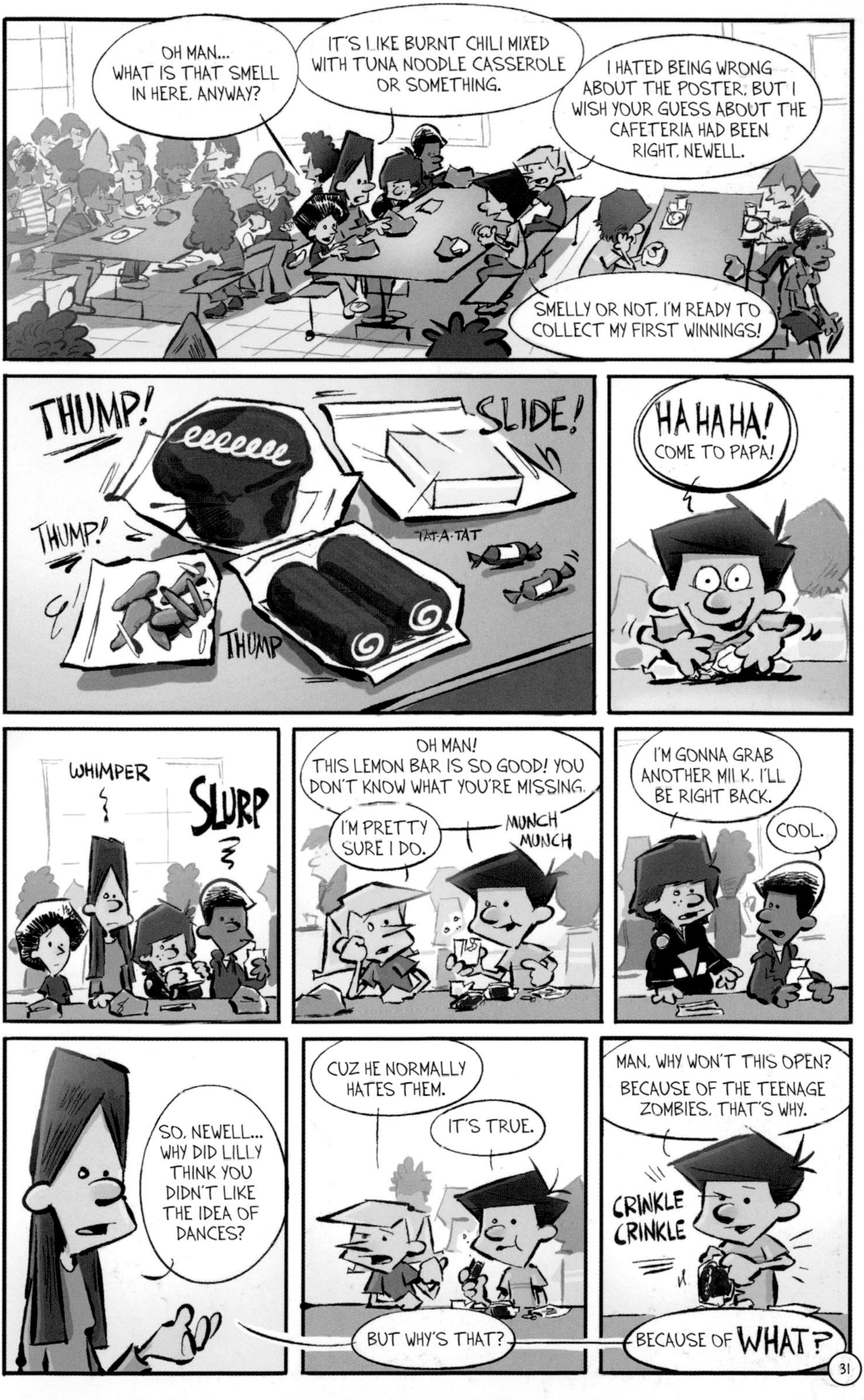
OH MAN... WHAT IS THAT SMELL IN HERE, ANYWAY?
IT'S LIKE BURNT CHILI MIXED WITH TUNA NOODLE CASSEROLE OR SOMETHING.
I HATED BEING WRONG ABOUT THE POSTER, BUT I WISH YOUR GUESS ABOUT THE CAFETERIA HAD BEEN RIGHT, NEWELL.
SMELLY OR NOT, I'M READY TO COLLECT MY FIRST WINNINGS!
THUMP!
SLIDE!
THUMP!
TAT-A-TAT
THUMP
HA HA HA! COME TO PAPA!
WHIMPER
SLURP
OH MAN! THIS LEMON BAR IS SO GOOD! YOU DON'T KNOW WHAT YOU'RE MISSING.
I'M PRETTY SURE I DO.
MUNCH MUNCH
I'M GONNA GRAB ANOTHER MILK. I'LL BE RIGHT BACK.
COOL.
SO, NEWELL... WHY DID LILLY THINK YOU DIDN'T LIKE THE IDEA OF DANCES?
CUZ HE NORMALLY HATES THEM.
IT'S TRUE.
BUT WHY'S THAT?
MAN, WHY WON'T THIS OPEN?
BECAUSE OF THE TEENAGE ZOMBIES, THAT'S WHY.
CRINKLE CRINKLE
BECAUSE OF WHAT?

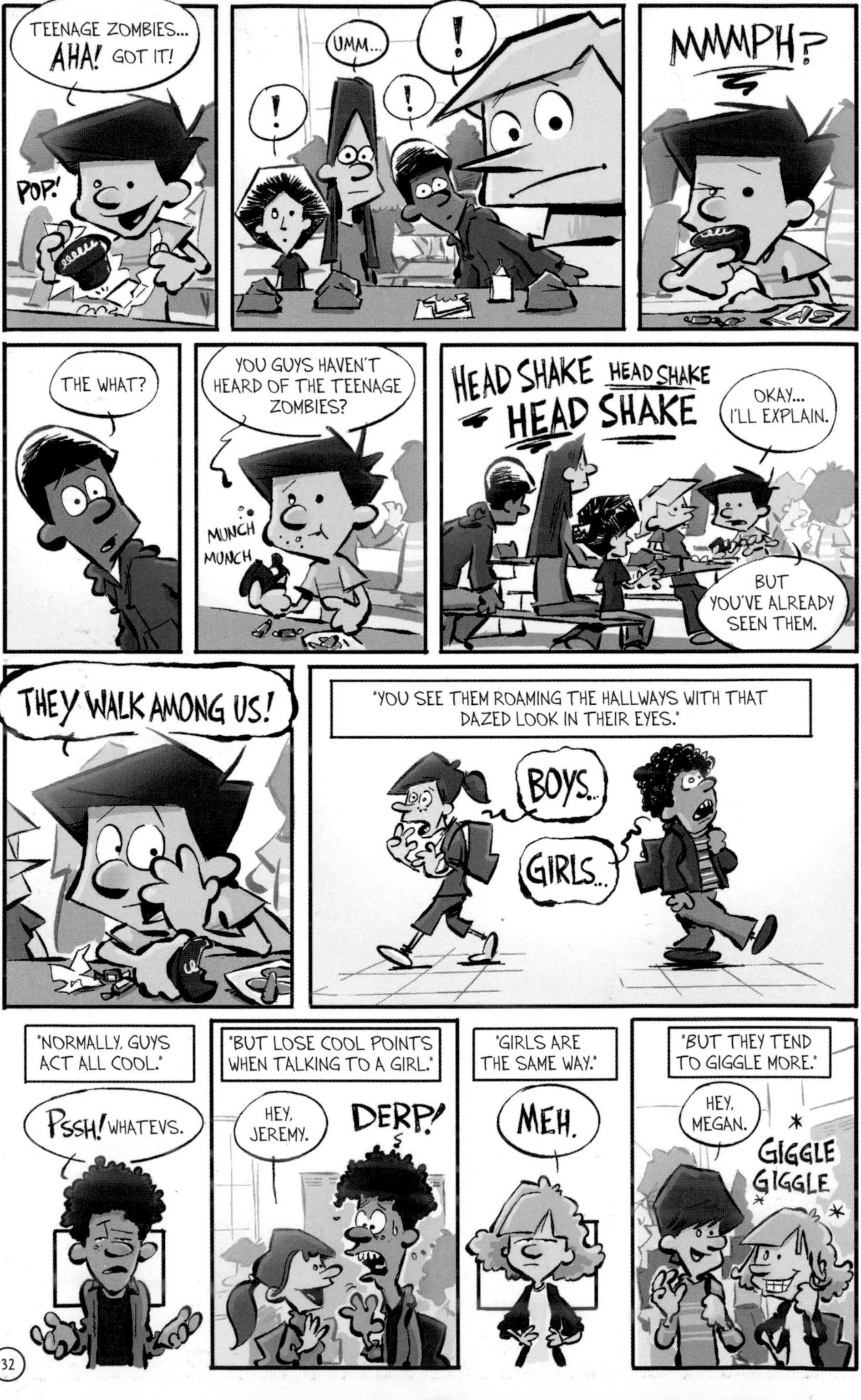

TEENAGE ZOMBIES... AHA! GOT IT!
POP!
UMM...
!
!
!
MMMPH?
THE WHAT?
YOU GUYS HAVEN'T HEARD OF THE TEENAGE ZOMBIES?
MUNCH
MUNCH
HEAD SHAKE HEAD SHAKE
HEAD SHAKE
OKAY... I'LL EXPLAIN.
BUT YOU'VE ALREADY SEEN THEM.
THEY WALK AMONG US!
"YOU SEE THEM ROAMING THE HALLWAYS WITH THAT DAZED LOOK IN THEIR EYES."
BOYS...
GIRLS...
"NORMALLY, GUYS ACT ALL COOL."
PSSH! WHATEVS.
"BUT LOSE COOL POINTS WHEN TALKING TO A GIRL."
HEY, JEREMY.
DERP!
"GIRLS ARE THE SAME WAY."
MEH.
"BUT THEY TEND TO GIGGLE MORE."
HEY, MEGAN.
GIGGLE
GIGGLE

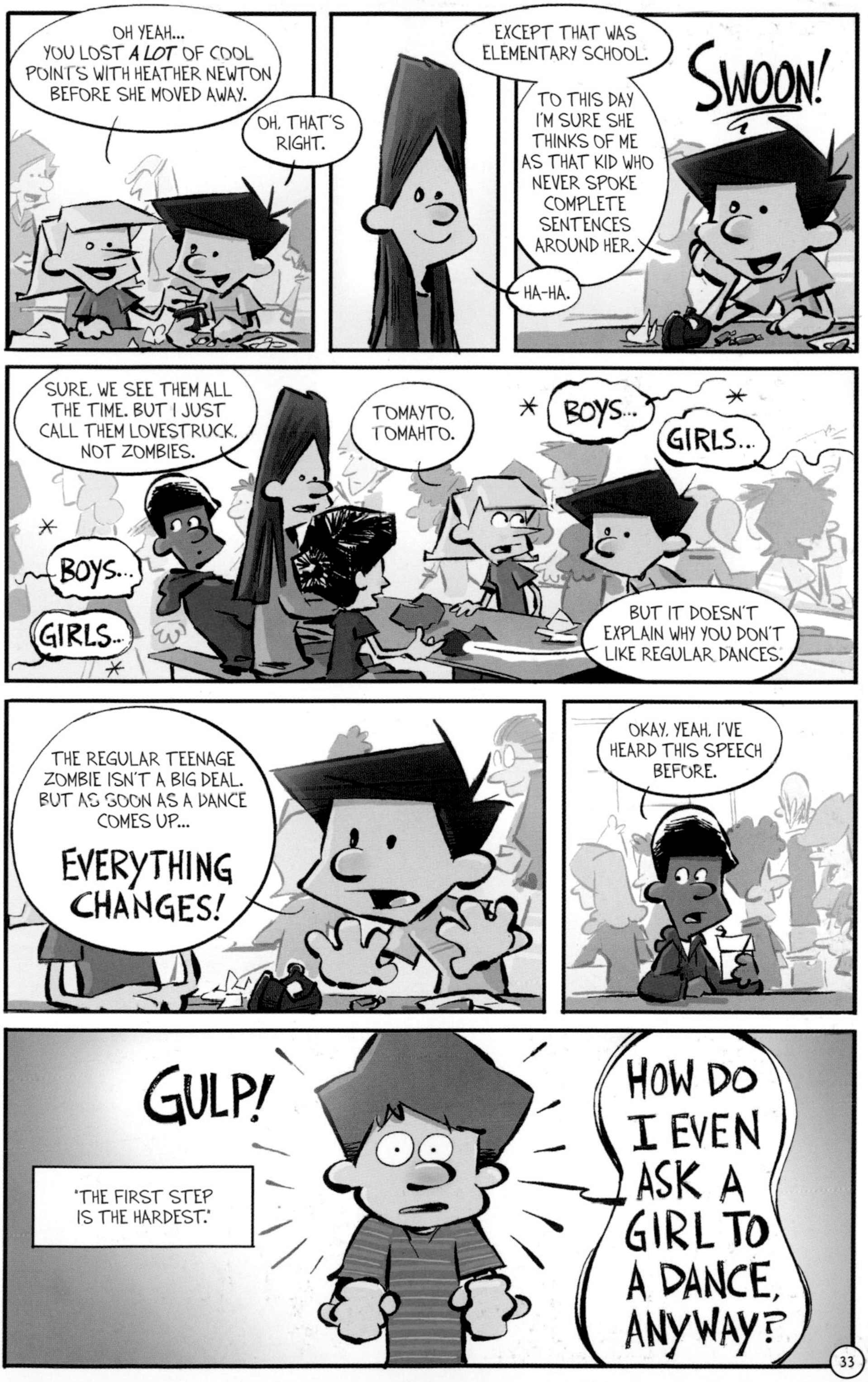

OH YEAH... YOU LOST A LOT OF COOL POINTS WITH HEATHER NEWTON BEFORE SHE MOVED AWAY.
OH, THAT'S RIGHT.
EXCEPT THAT WAS ELEMENTARY SCHOOL.
TO THIS DAY I'M SURE SHE THINKS OF ME AS THAT KID WHO NEVER SPOKE COMPLETE SENTENCES AROUND HER.
HA-HA.
SWOON!
SURE, WE SEE THEM ALL THE TIME. BUT I JUST CALL THEM LOVESTRUCK, NOT ZOMBIES.
TOMAYTO, TOMAHTO.
BOYS...
GIRLS...
BOYS...
GIRLS...
BUT IT DOESN'T EXPLAIN WHY YOU DON'T LIKE REGULAR DANCES.
THE REGULAR TEENAGE ZOMBIE ISN'T A BIG DEAL. BUT AS SOON AS A DANCE COMES UP...
EVERYTHING CHANGES!
OKAY, YEAH, I'VE HEARD THIS SPEECH BEFORE.
GULP!
"THE FIRST STEP IS THE HARDEST."
HOW DO I EVEN ASK A GIRL TO A DANCE, ANYWAY?

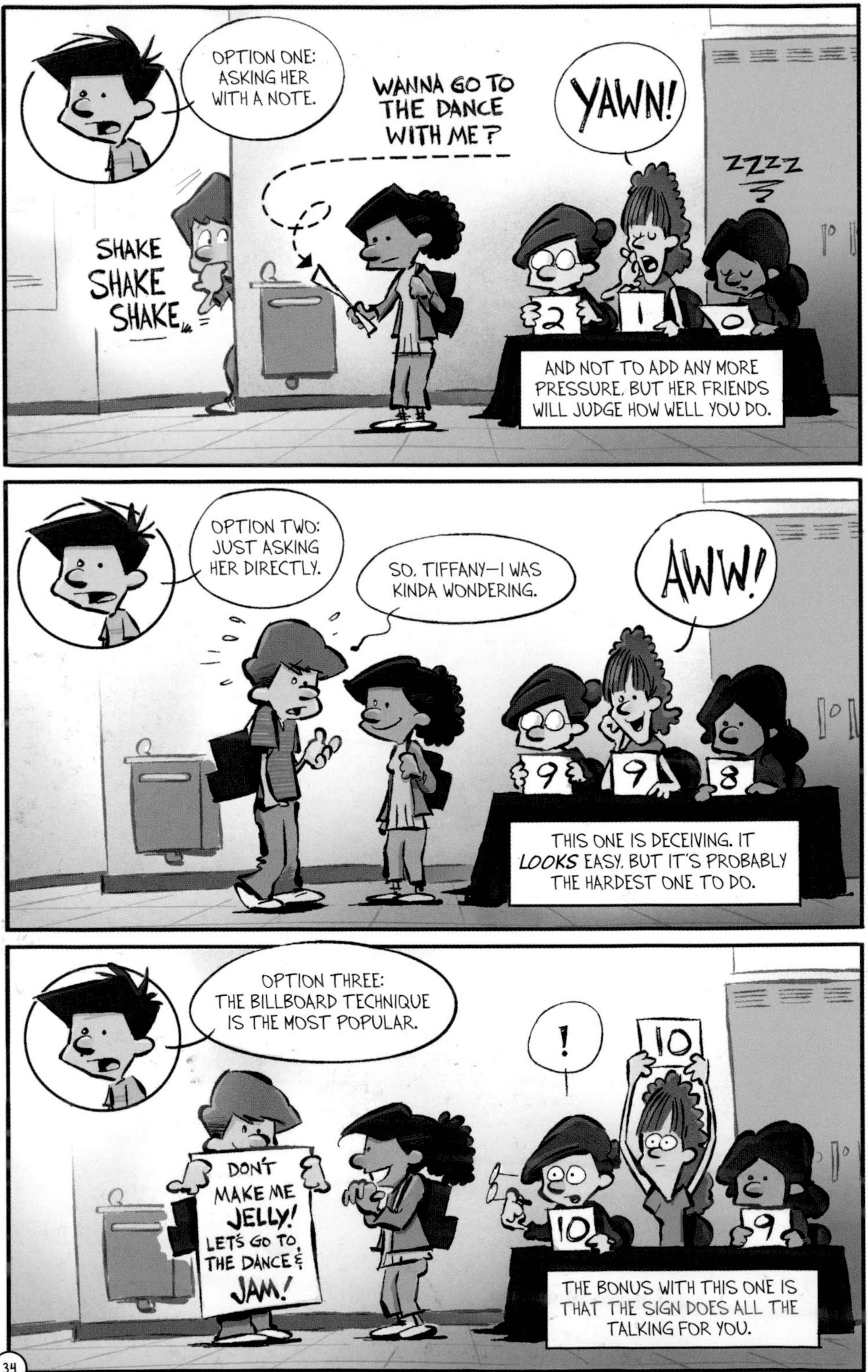

OPTION ONE: ASKING HER WITH A NOTE.
WANNA GO TO THE DANCE WITH ME?
YAWN!
ZZZZ
SHAKE SHAKE SHAKE
2
1
0
AND NOT TO ADD ANY MORE PRESSURE, BUT HER FRIENDS WILL JUDGE HOW WELL YOU DO.
OPTION TWO: JUST ASKING HER DIRECTLY.
SO, TIFFANY—I WAS KINDA WONDERING.
AWW!
9
9
8
THIS ONE IS DECEIVING. IT *LOOKS* EASY, BUT IT'S PROBABLY THE HARDEST ONE TO DO.
OPTION THREE: THE BILLBOARD TECHNIQUE IS THE MOST POPULAR.
!
10
DON'T MAKE ME JELLY! LET'S GO TO THE DANCE & JAM!
10
9
THE BONUS WITH THIS ONE IS THAT THE SIGN DOES ALL THE TALKING FOR YOU.

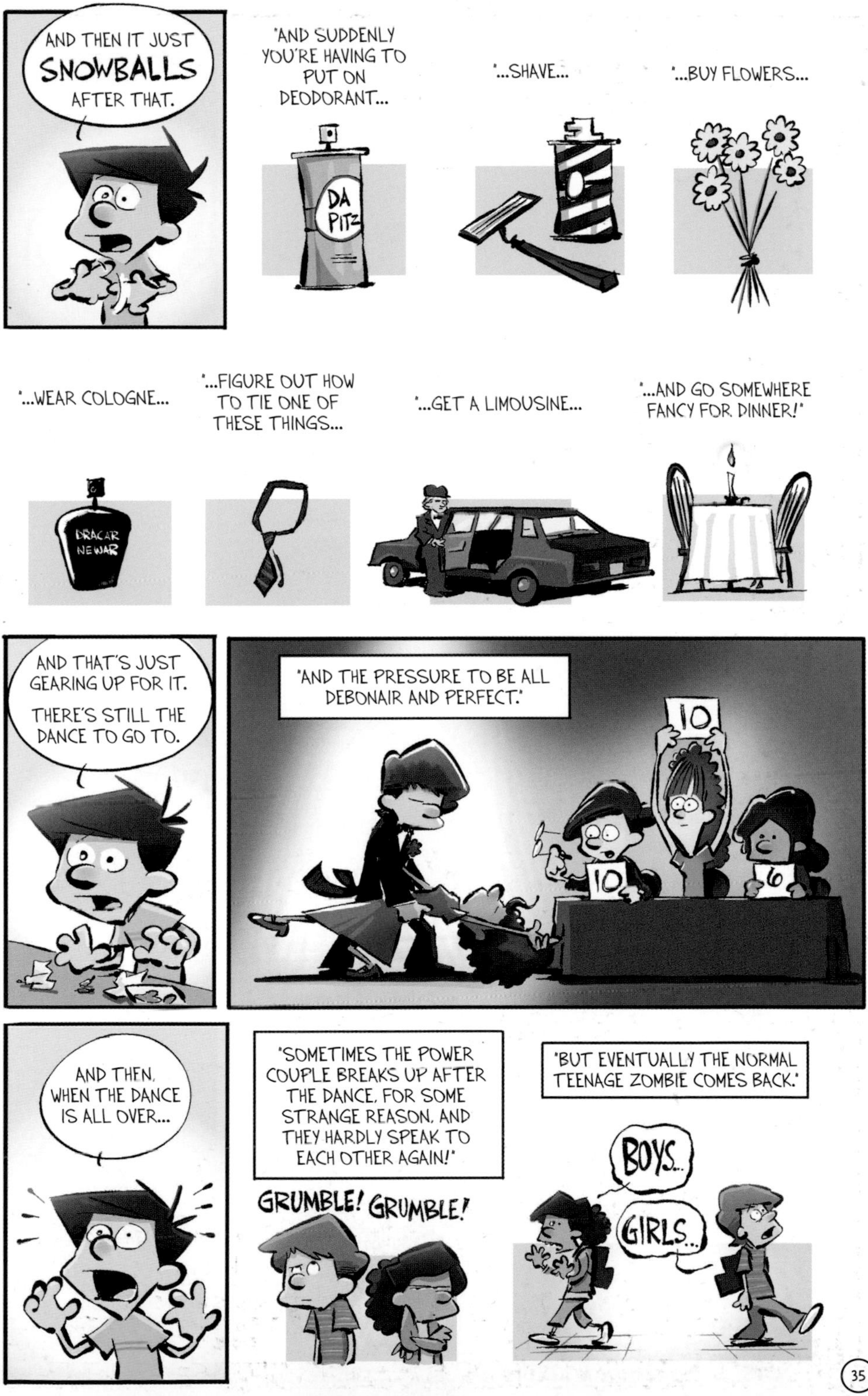

AND THEN IT JUST SNOWBALLS AFTER THAT.
"AND SUDDENLY YOU'RE HAVING TO PUT ON DEODORANT...
DA PITZ
"...SHAVE...
"...BUY FLOWERS...
"...WEAR COLOGNE...
DRACAR NEWAR
"...FIGURE OUT HOW TO TIE ONE OF THESE THINGS...
"...GET A LIMOUSINE...
"...AND GO SOMEWHERE FANCY FOR DINNER!"
AND THAT'S JUST GEARING UP FOR IT.
THERE'S STILL THE DANCE TO GO TO.
"AND THE PRESSURE TO BE ALL DEBONAIR AND PERFECT."
10
10
6
AND THEN, WHEN THE DANCE IS ALL OVER...
"SOMETIMES THE POWER COUPLE BREAKS UP AFTER THE DANCE, FOR SOME STRANGE REASON, AND THEY HARDLY SPEAK TO EACH OTHER AGAIN!"
GRUMBLE! GRUMBLE!
"BUT EVENTUALLY THE NORMAL TEENAGE ZOMBIE COMES BACK."
BOYS...
GIRLS...

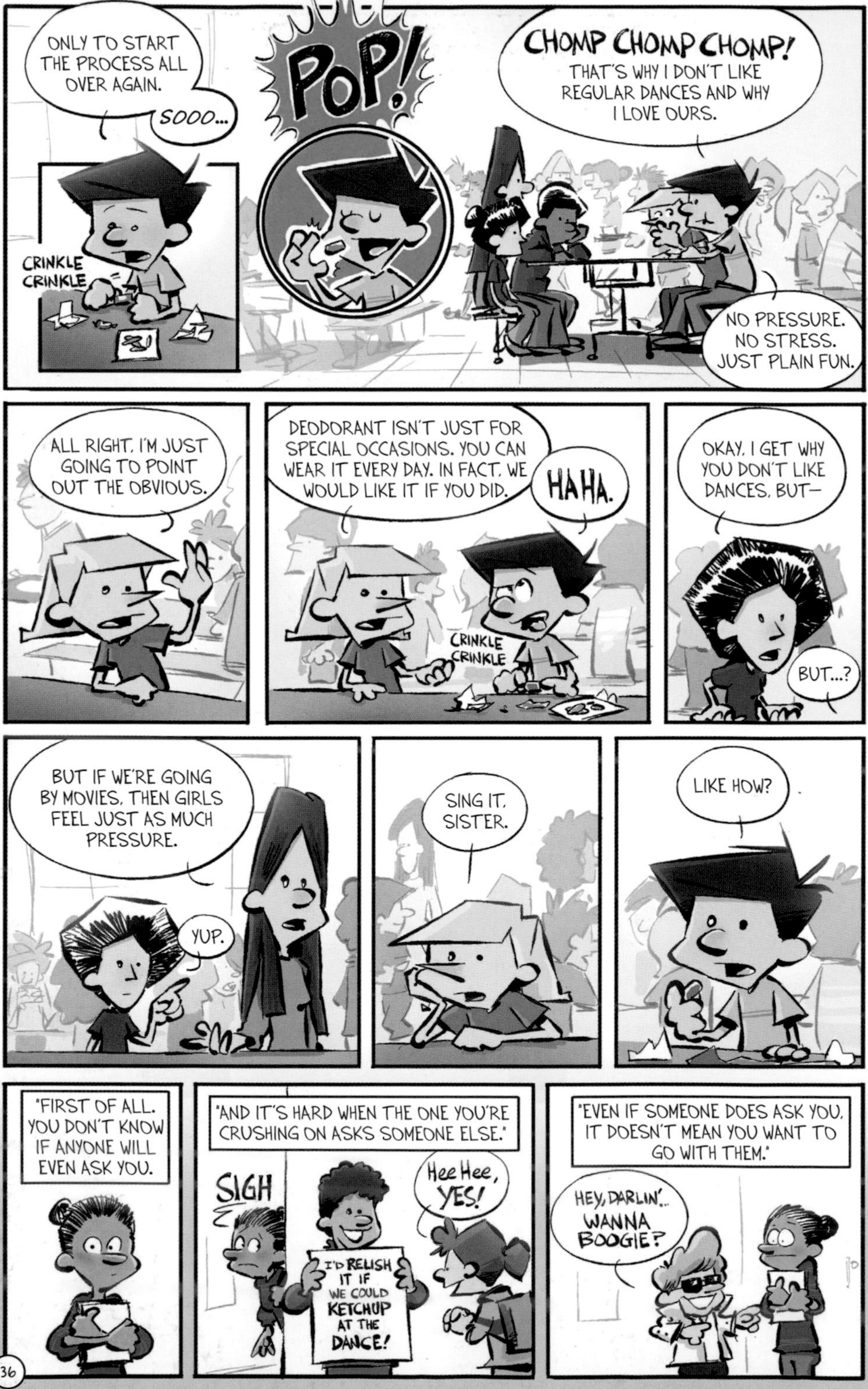

ONLY TO START THE PROCESS ALL OVER AGAIN.
SOOO...
CRINKLE CRINKLE
POP!
CHOMP CHOMP CHOMP! THAT'S WHY I DON'T LIKE REGULAR DANCES AND WHY I LOVE OURS.
NO PRESSURE. NO STRESS. JUST PLAIN FUN.
ALL RIGHT, I'M JUST GOING TO POINT OUT THE OBVIOUS.
DEODORANT ISN'T JUST FOR SPECIAL OCCASIONS. YOU CAN WEAR IT EVERY DAY. IN FACT, WE WOULD LIKE IT IF YOU DID.
HAHA.
CRINKLE CRINKLE
OKAY, I GET WHY YOU DON'T LIKE DANCES, BUT—
BUT...?
BUT IF WE'RE GOING BY MOVIES, THEN GIRLS FEEL JUST AS MUCH PRESSURE.
YUP.
SING IT, SISTER.
LIKE HOW?
"FIRST OF ALL, YOU DON'T KNOW IF ANYONE WILL EVEN ASK YOU.
"AND IT'S HARD WHEN THE ONE YOU'RE CRUSHING ON ASKS SOMEONE ELSE."
SIGH
I'D RELISH IT IF WE COULD KETCHUP AT THE DANCE!
Hee Hee, YES!
"EVEN IF SOMEONE DOES ASK YOU, IT DOESN'T MEAN YOU WANT TO GO WITH THEM."
HEY, DARLIN'... WANNA BOOGIE?

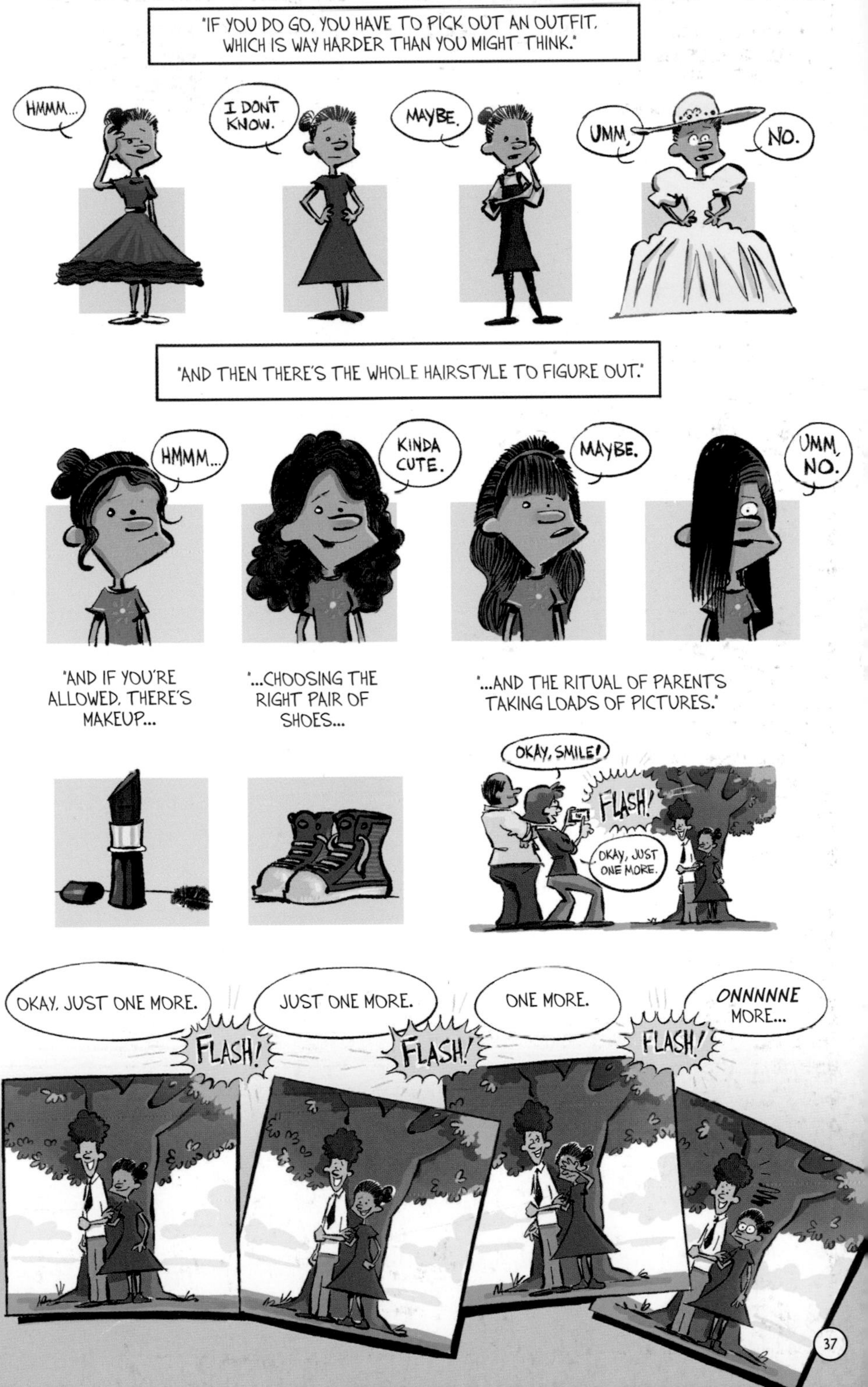
"IF YOU DO GO, YOU HAVE TO PICK OUT AN OUTFIT, WHICH IS WAY HARDER THAN YOU MIGHT THINK."
HMMM...
I DON'T KNOW.
MAYBE.
UMM,
NO.
"AND THEN THERE'S THE WHOLE HAIRSTYLE TO FIGURE OUT."
HMMM...
KINDA CUTE.
MAYBE.
UMM, NO.
"AND IF YOU'RE ALLOWED, THERE'S MAKEUP...
"...CHOOSING THE RIGHT PAIR OF SHOES...
"...AND THE RITUAL OF PARENTS TAKING LOADS OF PICTURES."
OKAY, SMILE!
FLASH!
OKAY, JUST ONE MORE.
OKAY, JUST ONE MORE.
FLASH!
JUST ONE MORE.
FLASH!
ONE MORE.
FLASH!
ONNNNNE MORE...

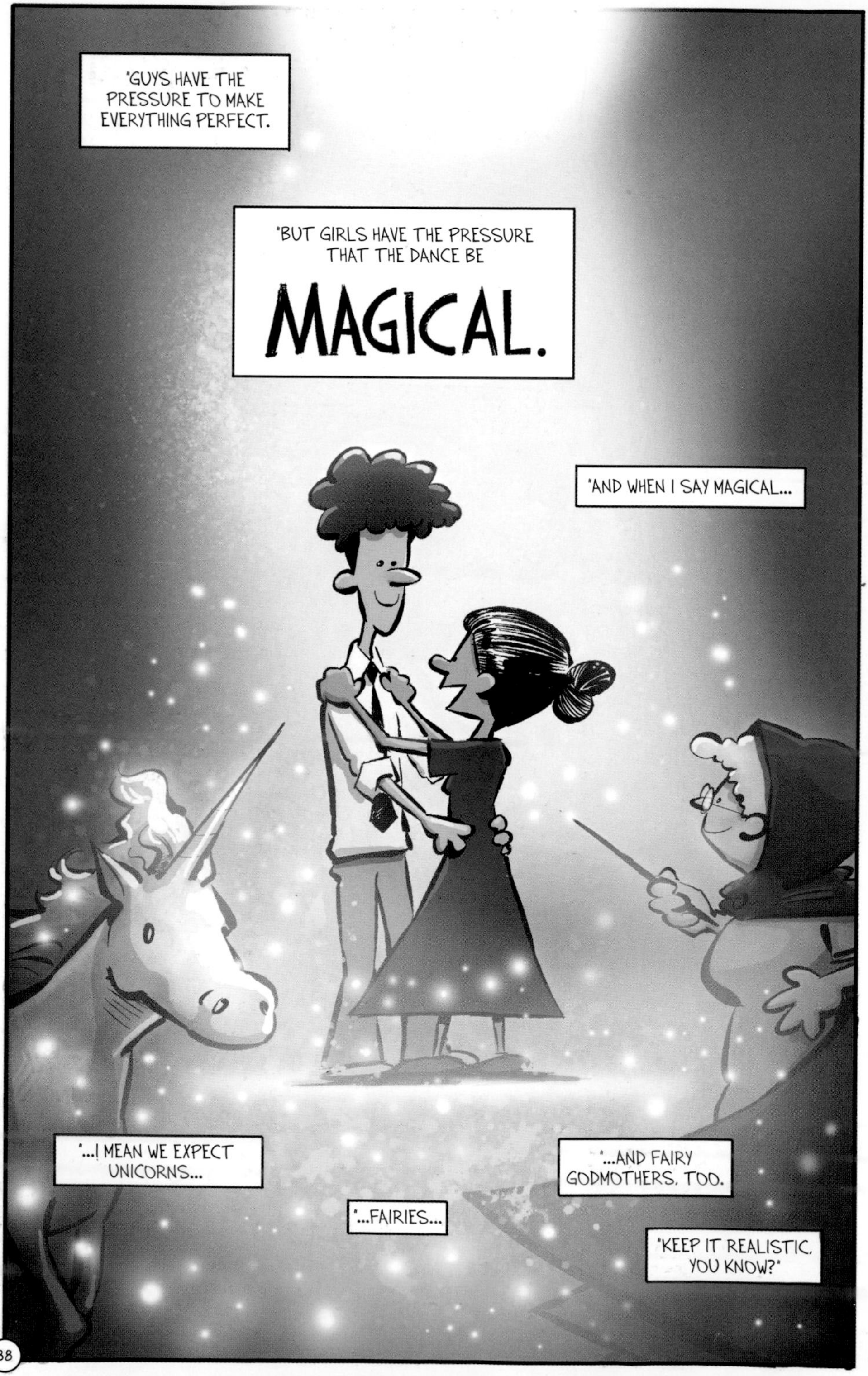
"GUYS HAVE THE PRESSURE TO MAKE EVERYTHING PERFECT.
"BUT GIRLS HAVE THE PRESSURE THAT THE DANCE BE
MAGICAL.
"AND WHEN I SAY MAGICAL...
"...I MEAN WE EXPECT UNICORNS...
"...FAIRIES...
"...AND FAIRY GODMOTHERS, TOO.
"KEEP IT REALISTIC, YOU KNOW?"

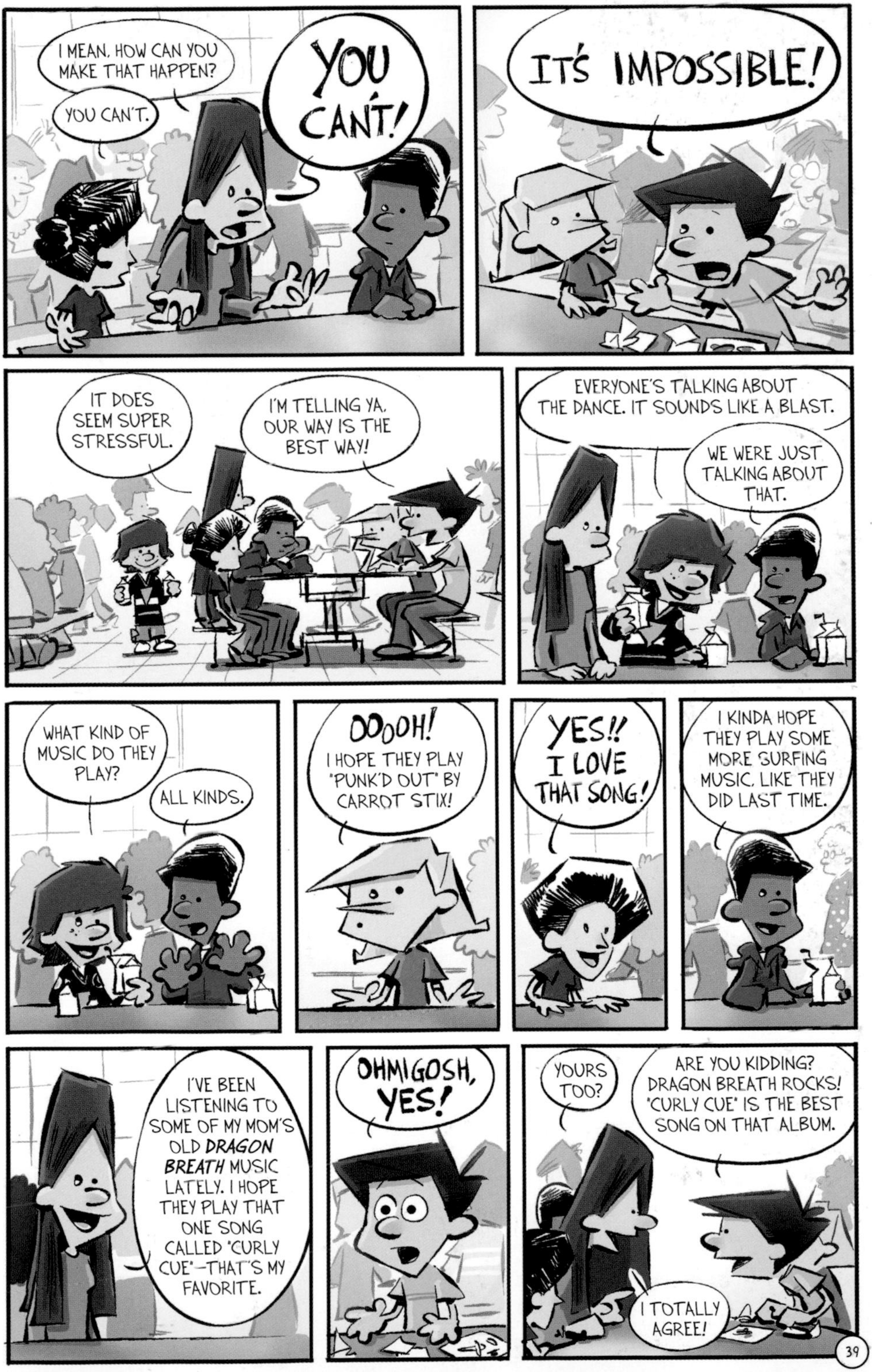
I MEAN, HOW CAN YOU MAKE THAT HAPPEN?
YOU CAN'T.
YOU CAN'T!
IT'S IMPOSSIBLE!
IT DOES SEEM SUPER STRESSFUL.
I'M TELLING YA, OUR WAY IS THE BEST WAY!
EVERYONE'S TALKING ABOUT THE DANCE. IT SOUNDS LIKE A BLAST.
WE WERE JUST TALKING ABOUT THAT.
WHAT KIND OF MUSIC DO THEY PLAY?
ALL KINDS.
OOOOH! I HOPE THEY PLAY "PUNK'D OUT" BY CARROT STIX!
YES!! I LOVE THAT SONG!
I KINDA HOPE THEY PLAY SOME MORE SURFING MUSIC, LIKE THEY DID LAST TIME.
I'VE BEEN LISTENING TO SOME OF MY MOM'S OLD DRAGON BREATH MUSIC LATELY. I HOPE THEY PLAY THAT ONE SONG CALLED "CURLY CUE"—THAT'S MY FAVORITE.
OHMIGOSH, YES!
YOURS TOO?
ARE YOU KIDDING? DRAGON BREATH ROCKS! "CURLY CUE" IS THE BEST SONG ON THAT ALBUM.
I TOTALLY AGREE!

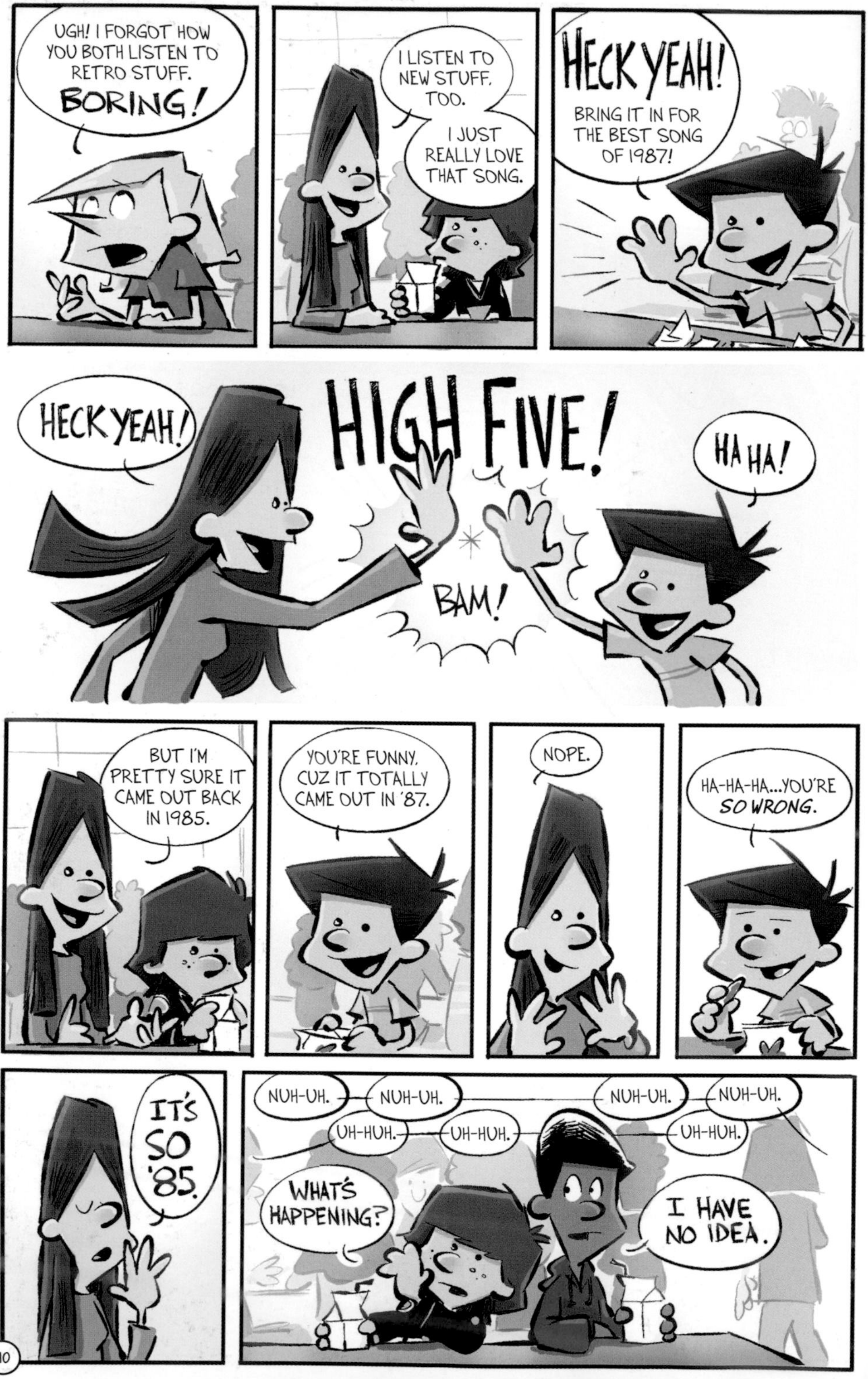

UGH! I FORGOT HOW YOU BOTH LISTEN TO RETRO STUFF.
BORING!
I LISTEN TO NEW STUFF, TOO.
I JUST REALLY LOVE THAT SONG.
HECK YEAH!
BRING IT IN FOR THE BEST SONG OF 1987!
HECK YEAH!
HIGH FIVE!
HA HA!
BAM!
BUT I'M PRETTY SURE IT CAME OUT BACK IN 1985.
YOU'RE FUNNY, CUZ IT TOTALLY CAME OUT IN '87.
NOPE.
HA-HA-HA...YOU'RE SO WRONG.
IT'S SO '85.
NUH-UH.
UH-HUH.
NUH-UH.
UH-HUH.
NUH-UH.
UH-HUH.
NUH-UH.
WHAT'S HAPPENING?
I HAVE NO IDEA.

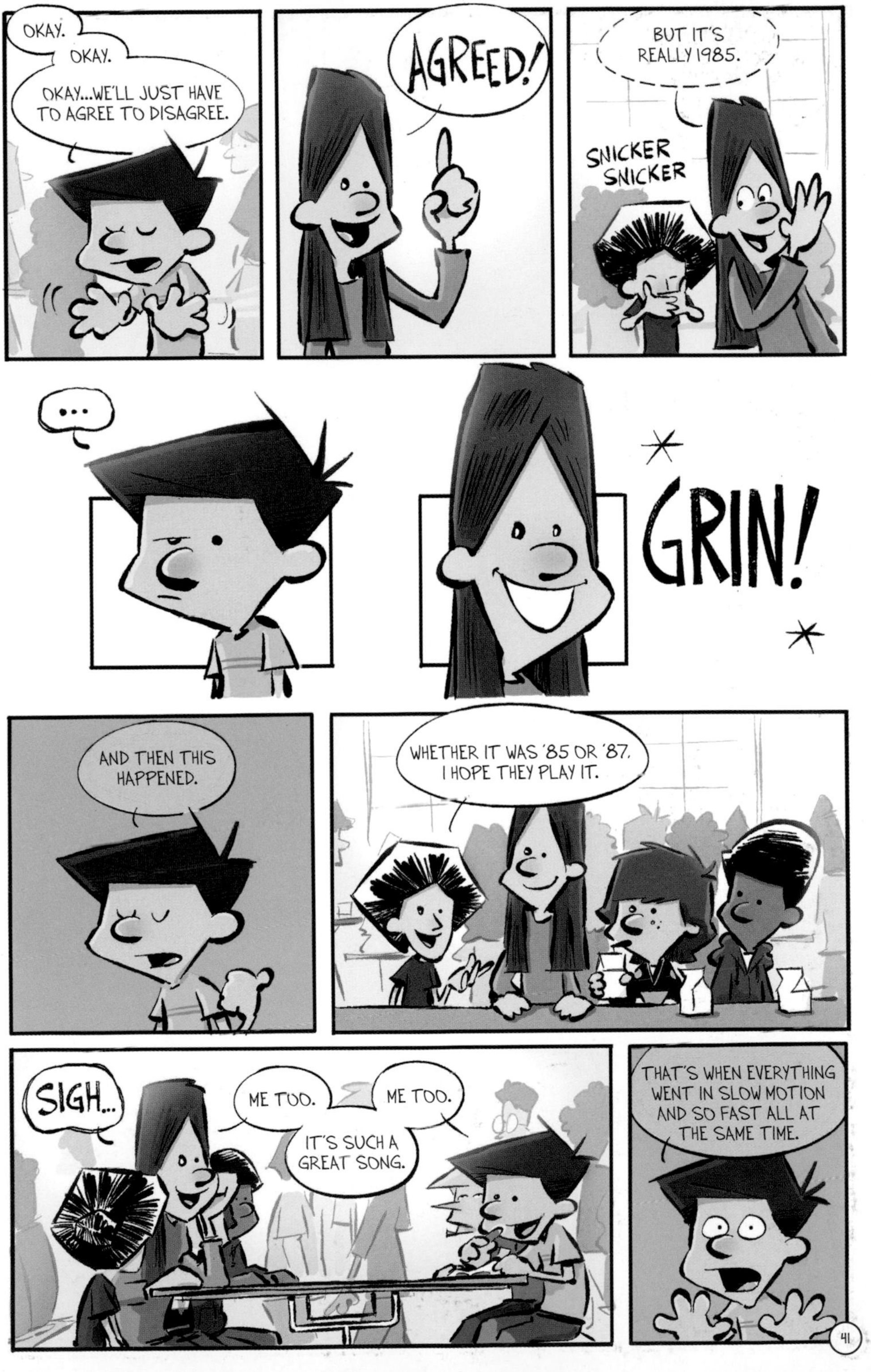
OKAY.
OKAY.
OKAY...WE'LL JUST HAVE TO AGREE TO DISAGREE.
AGREED!
BUT IT'S REALLY 1985.
SNICKER SNICKER
...
GRIN!
AND THEN THIS HAPPENED.
WHETHER IT WAS '85 OR '87, I HOPE THEY PLAY IT.
SIGH...
ME TOO.
ME TOO.
IT'S SUCH A GREAT SONG.
THAT'S WHEN EVERYTHING WENT IN SLOW MOTION AND SO FAST ALL AT THE SAME TIME.

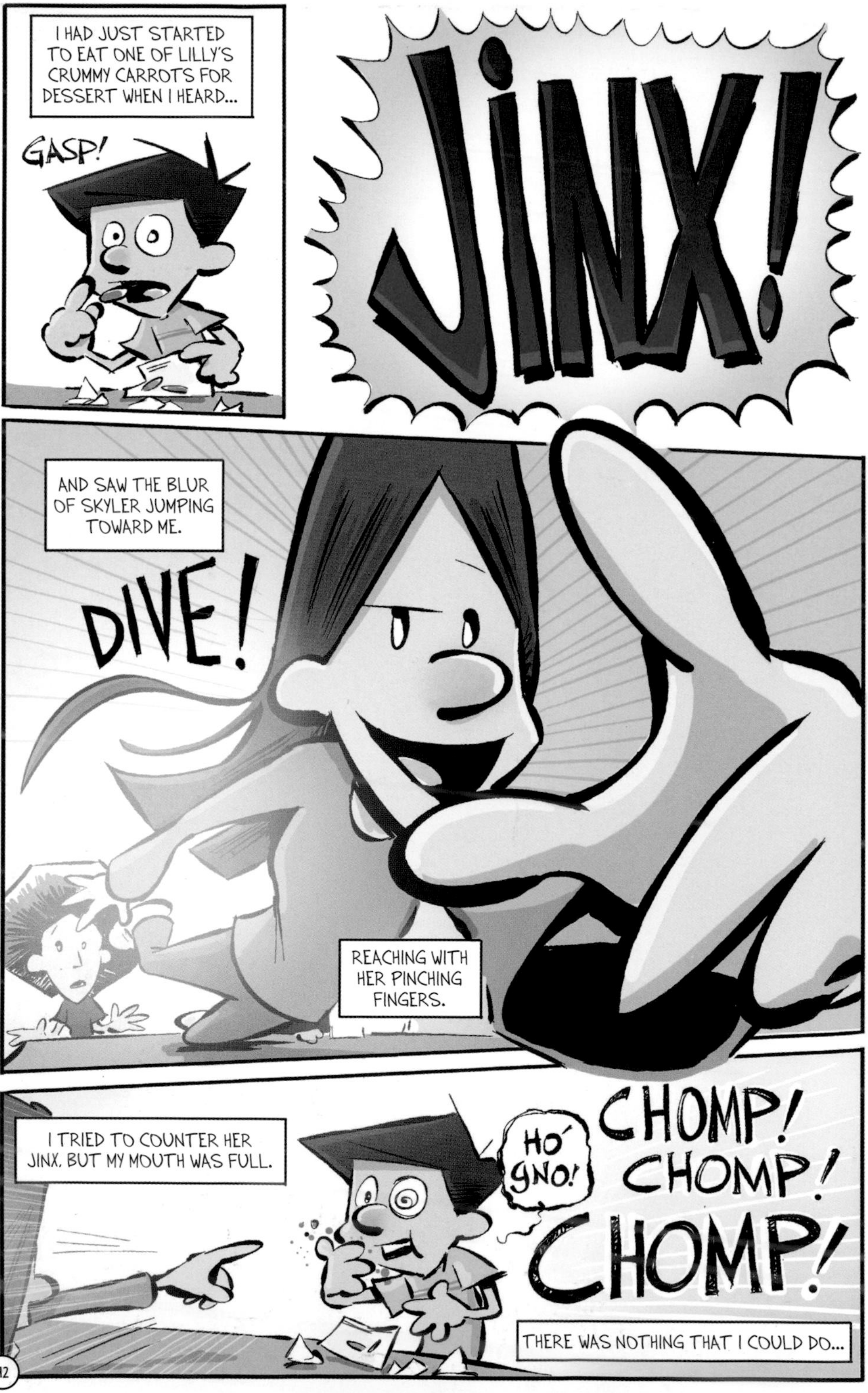
I HAD JUST STARTED TO EAT ONE OF LILLY'S CRUMMY CARROTS FOR DESSERT WHEN I HEARD...
GASP!
JINX!
AND SAW THE BLUR OF SKYLER JUMPING TOWARD ME.
DIVE!
REACHING WITH HER PINCHING FINGERS.
I TRIED TO COUNTER HER JINX, BUT MY MOUTH WAS FULL.
HO' GNO!
CHOMP! CHOMP! CHOMP!
THERE WAS NOTHING THAT I COULD DO...

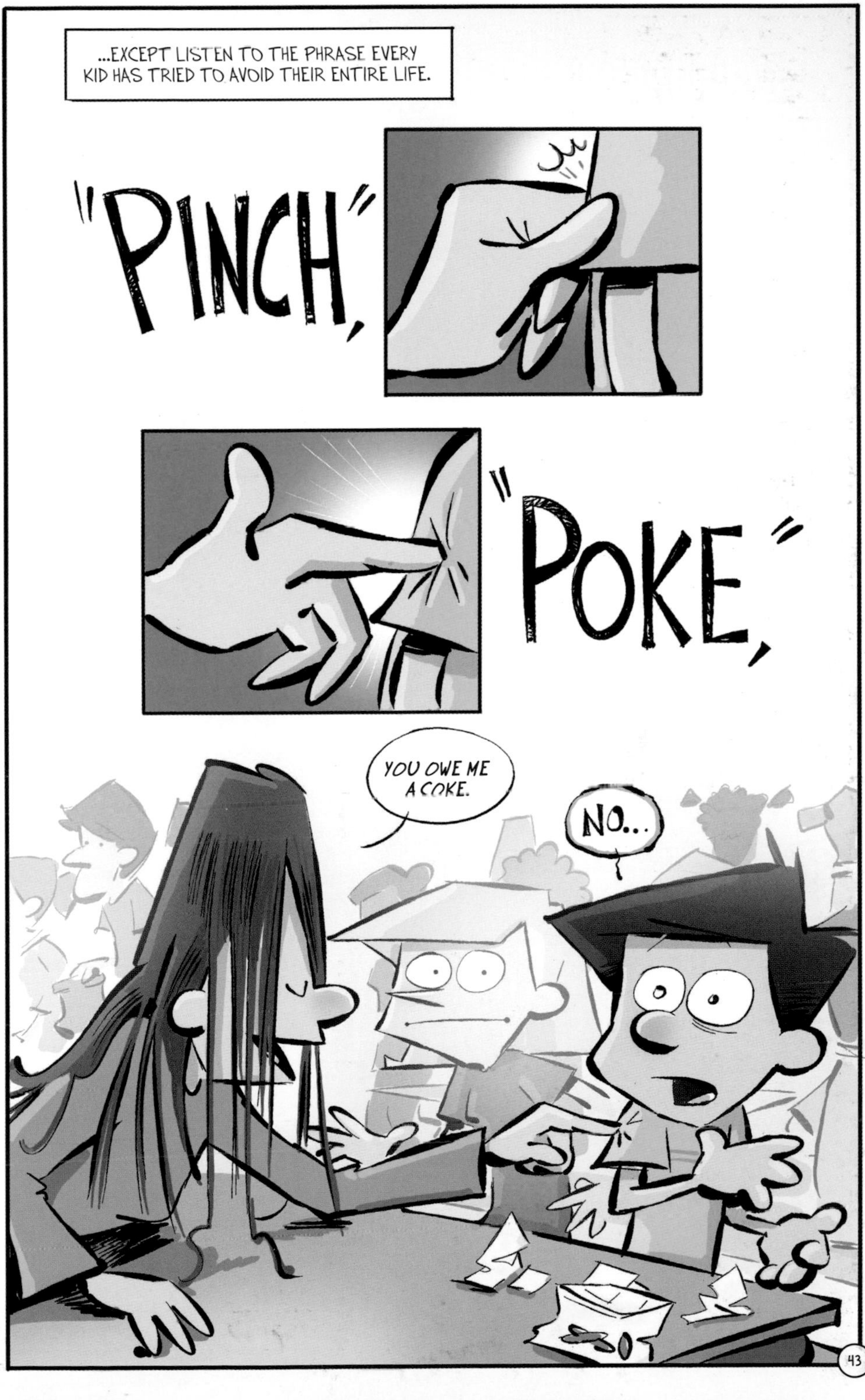
...EXCEPT LISTEN TO THE PHRASE EVERY KID HAS TRIED TO AVOID THEIR ENTIRE LIFE.
"PINCH,"
"POKE,"
YOU OWE ME A COKE.
NO...

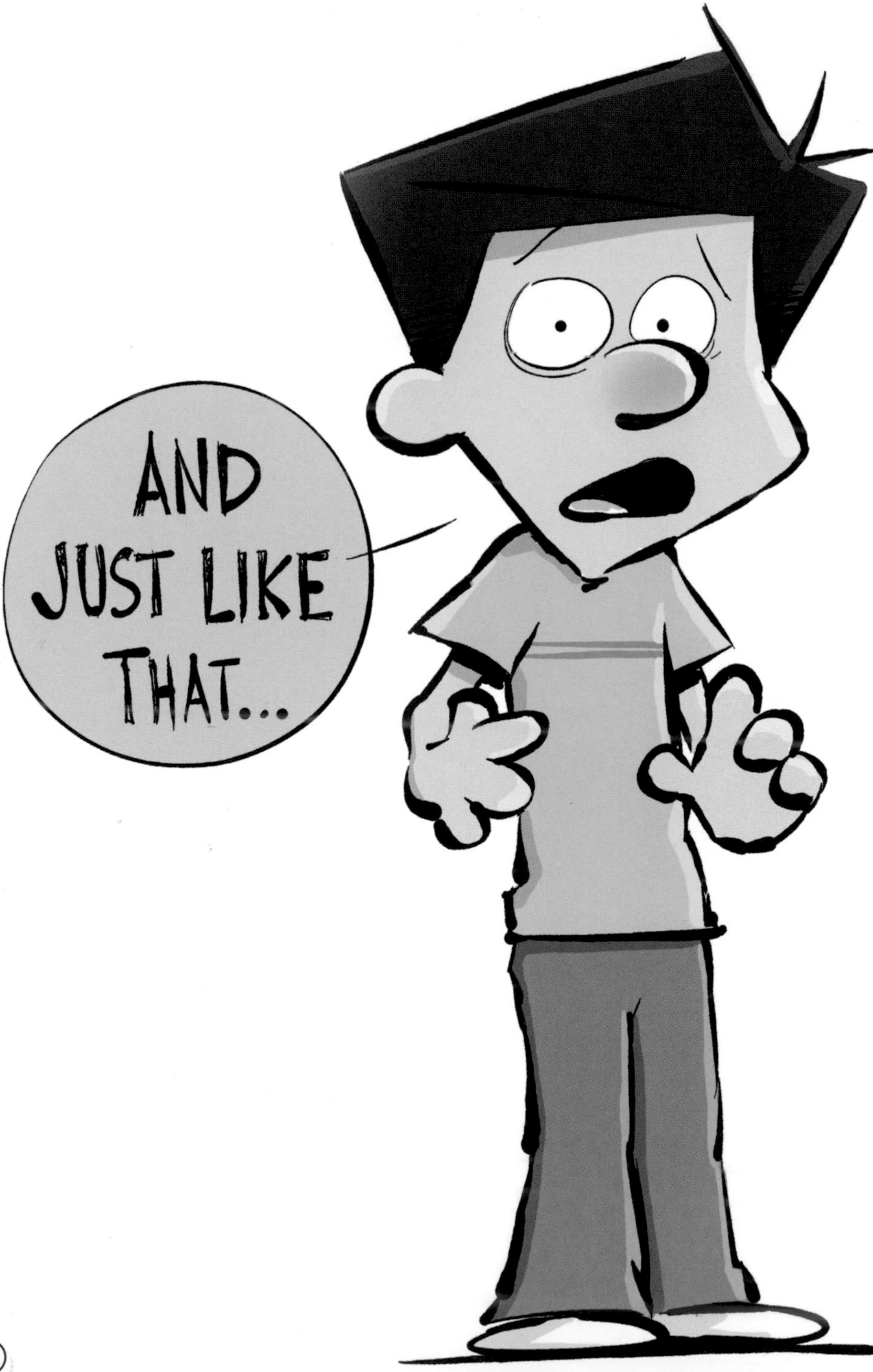
AND JUST LIKE THAT...

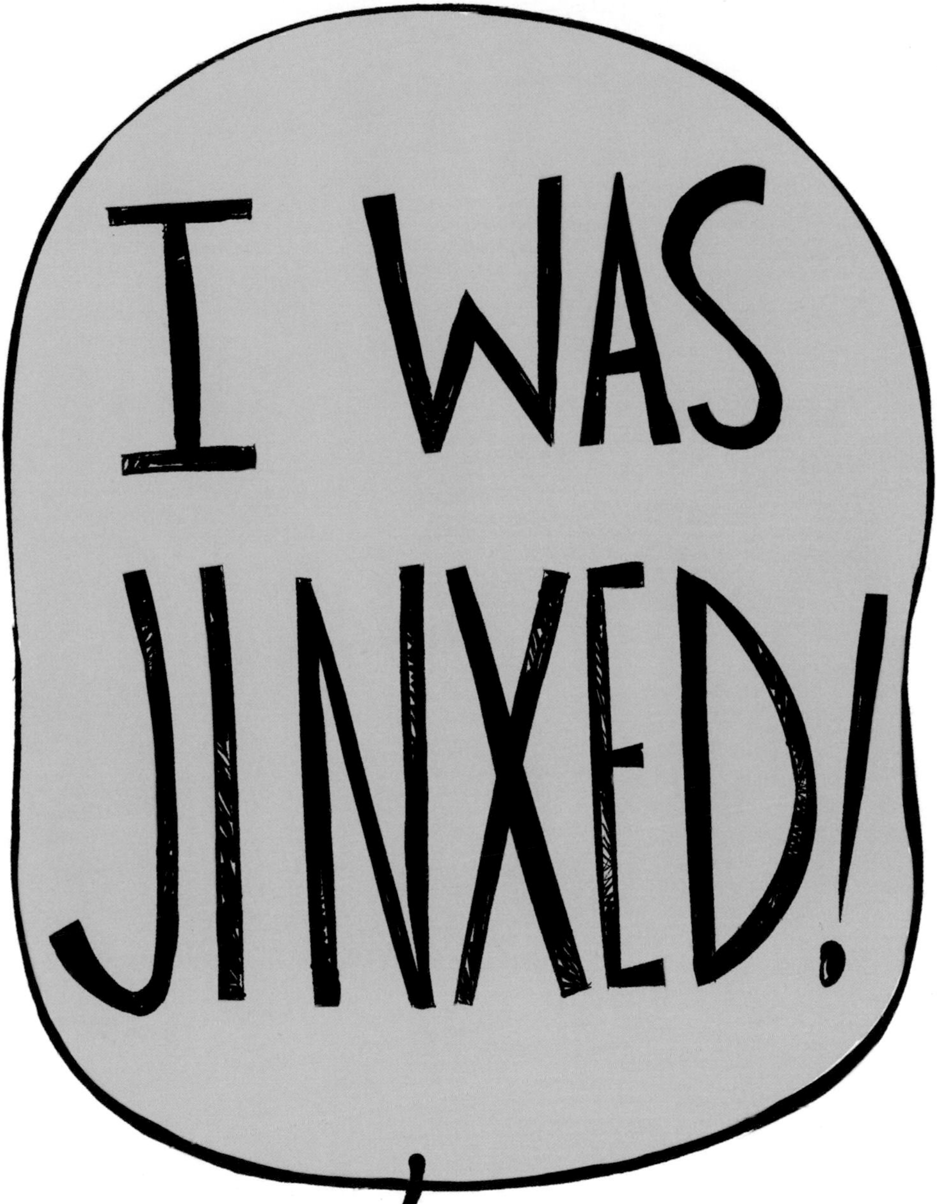
I WAS JINXED!

CHAPTER THREE
JINXED

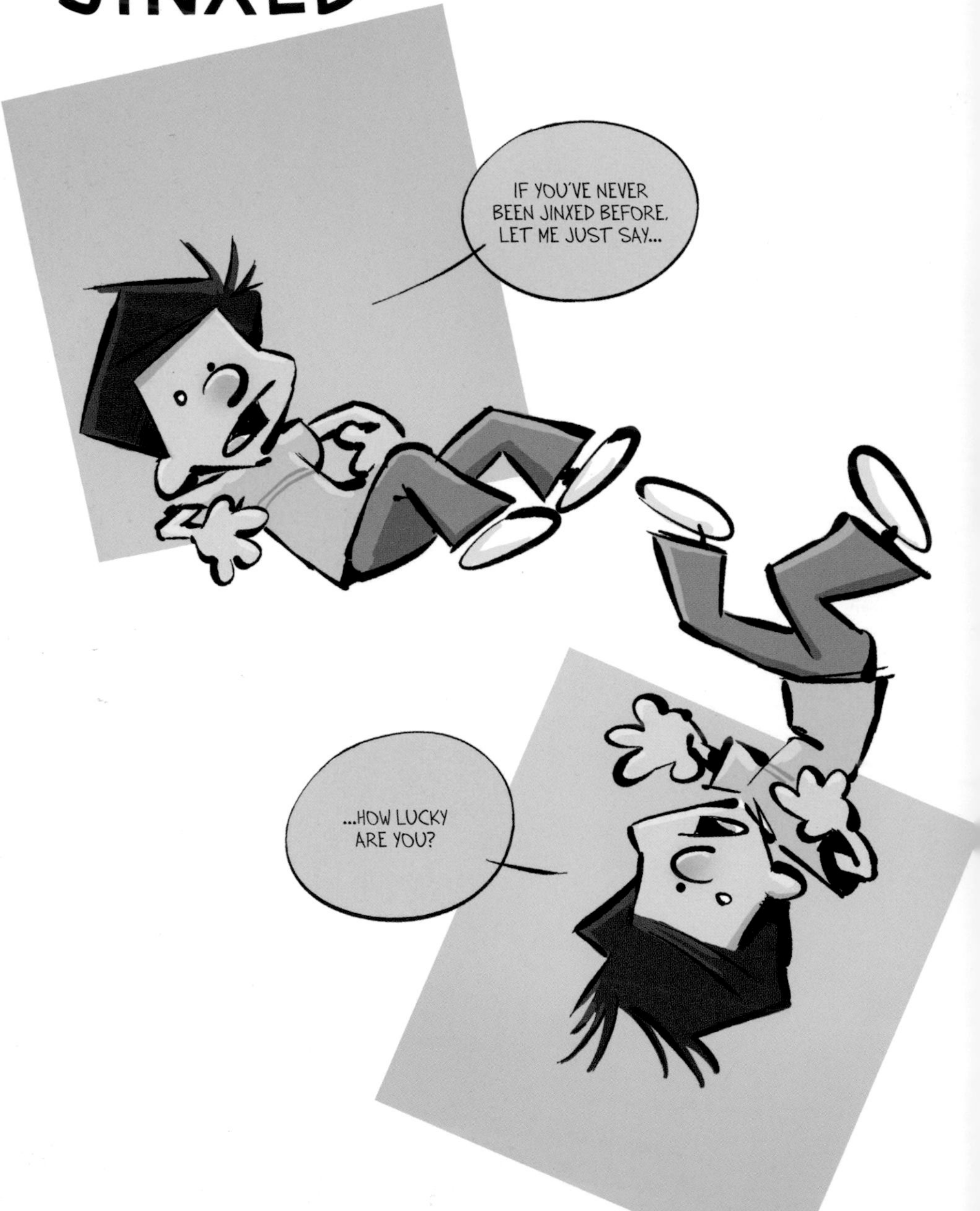
IF YOU'VE NEVER BEEN JINXED BEFORE, LET ME JUST SAY...
...HOW LUCKY ARE YOU?

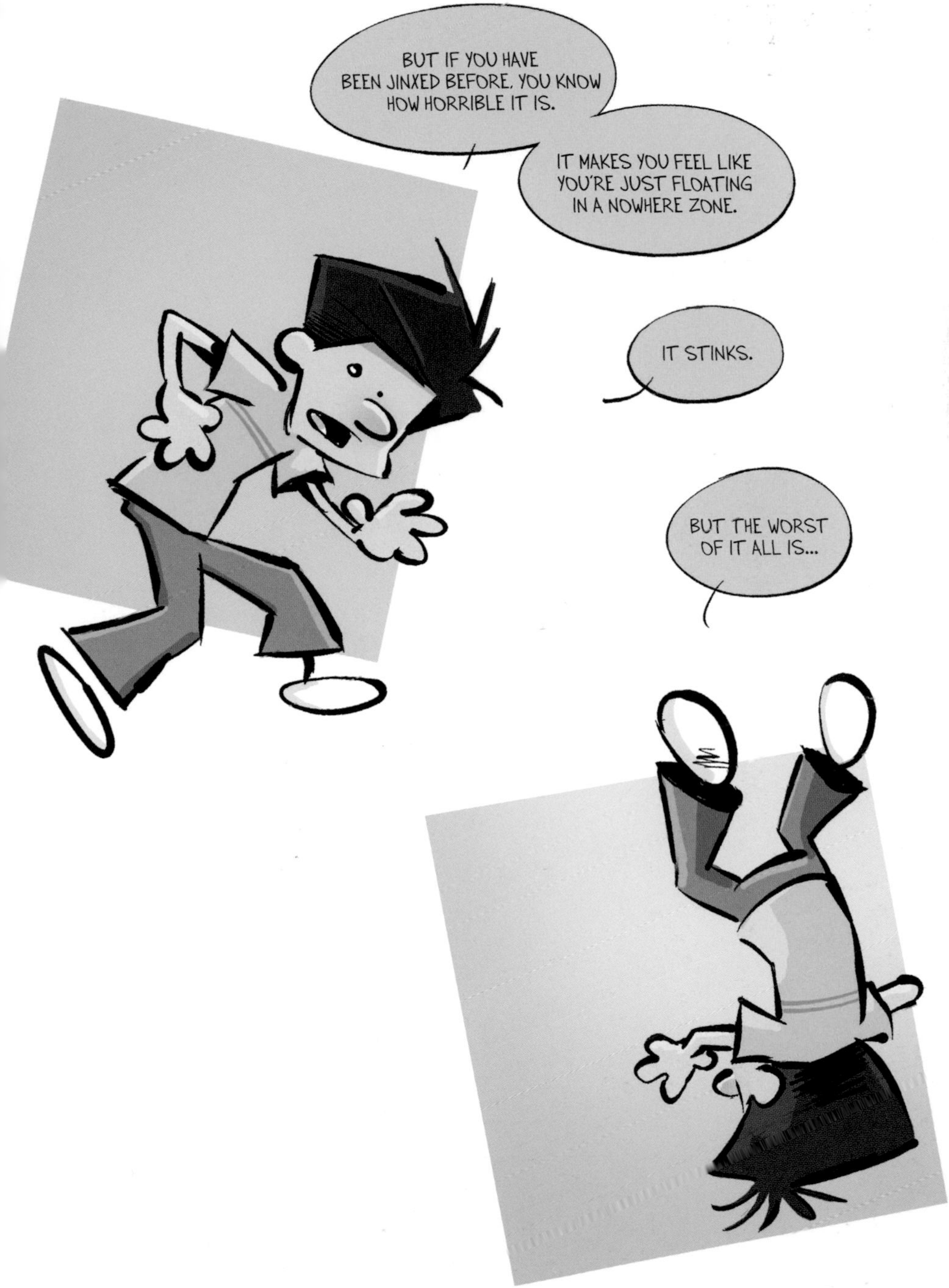
BUT IF YOU HAVE BEEN JINXED BEFORE, YOU KNOW HOW HORRIBLE IT IS.
IT MAKES YOU FEEL LIKE YOU'RE JUST FLOATING IN A NOWHERE ZONE.
IT STINKS.
BUT THE WORST OF IT ALL IS...

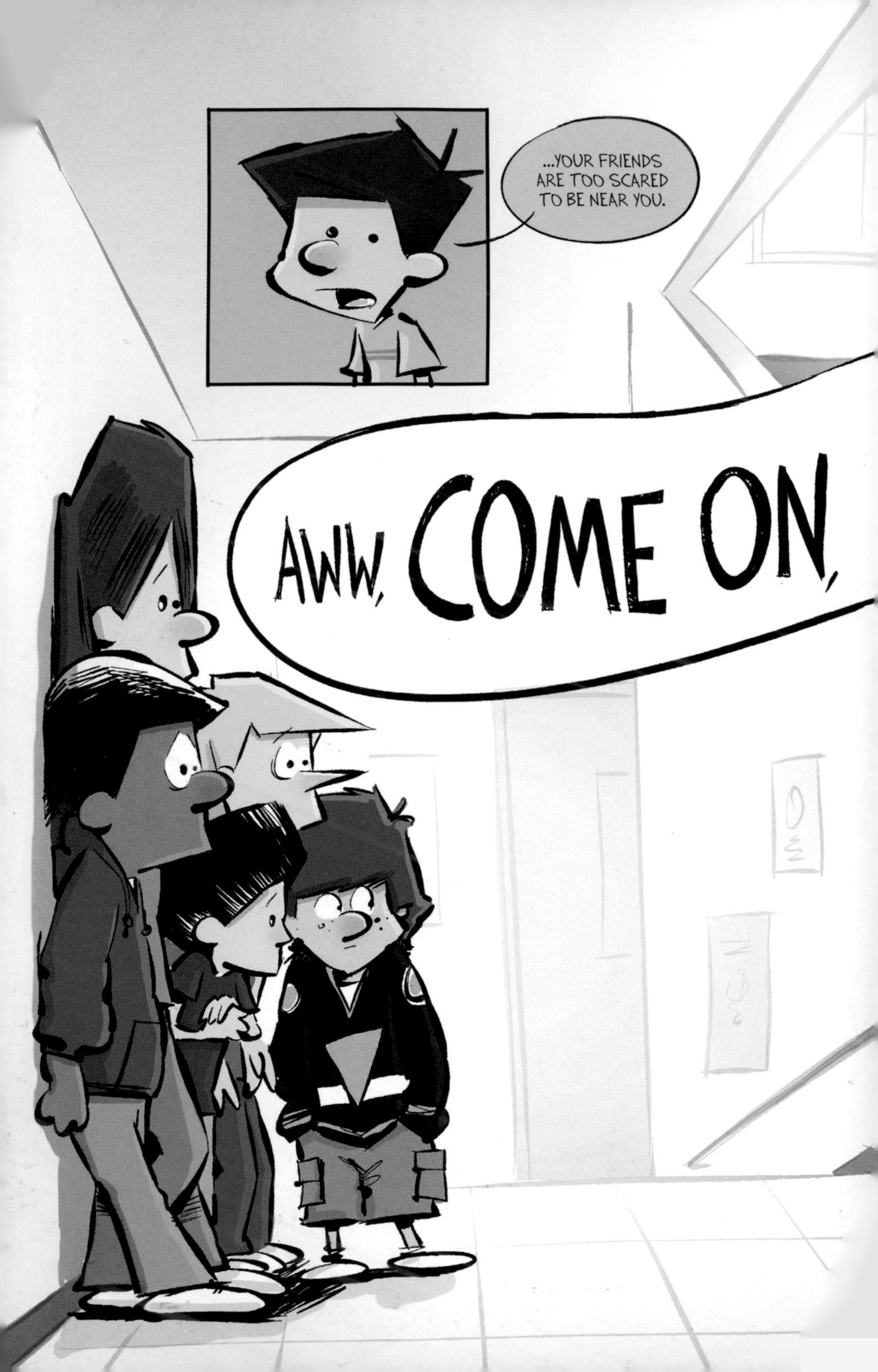
...YOUR FRIENDS ARE TOO SCARED TO BE NEAR YOU.
AWW, COME ON,

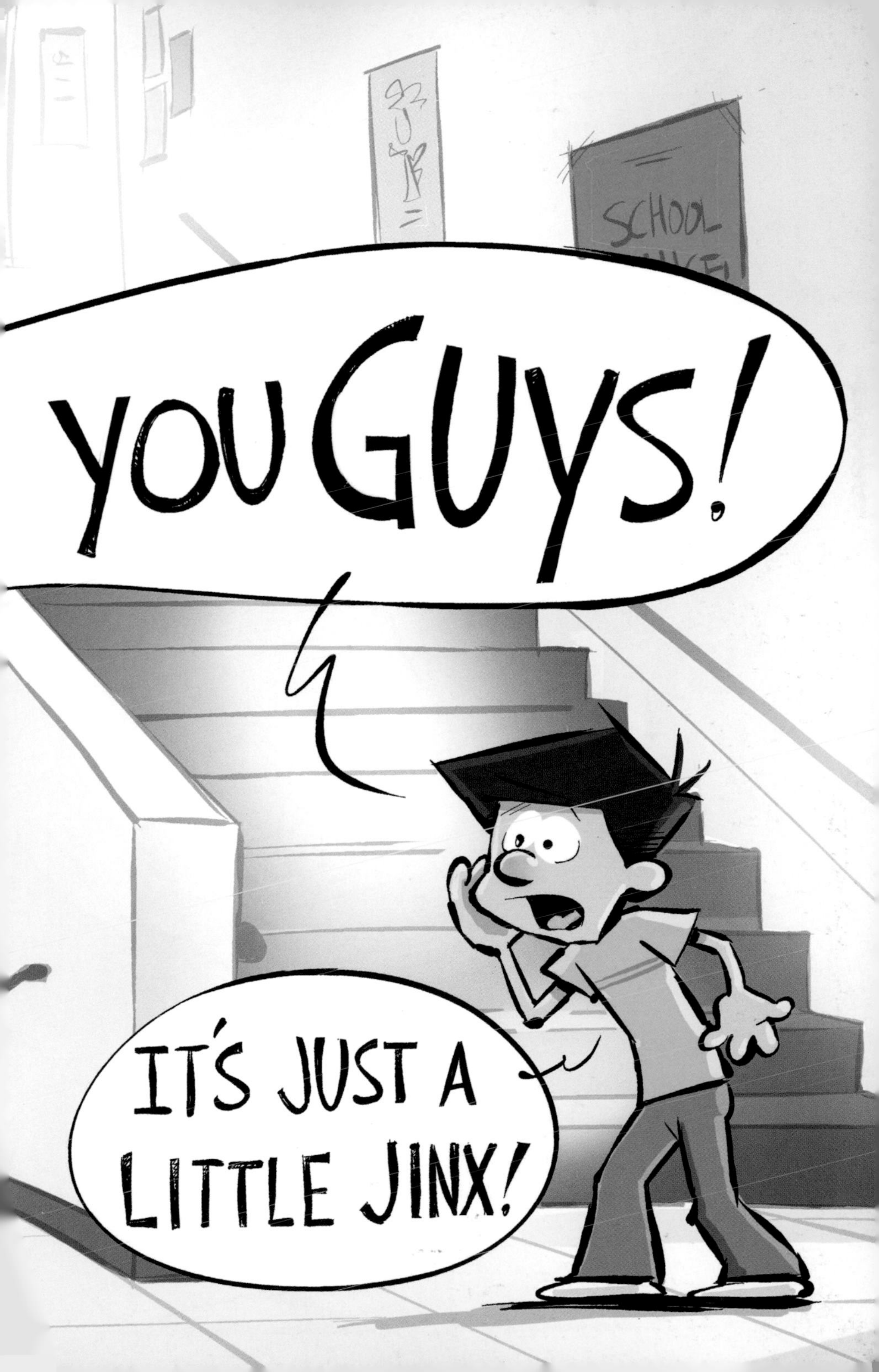
SCHOOL
YOU GUYS!
IT'S JUST A LITTLE JINX!

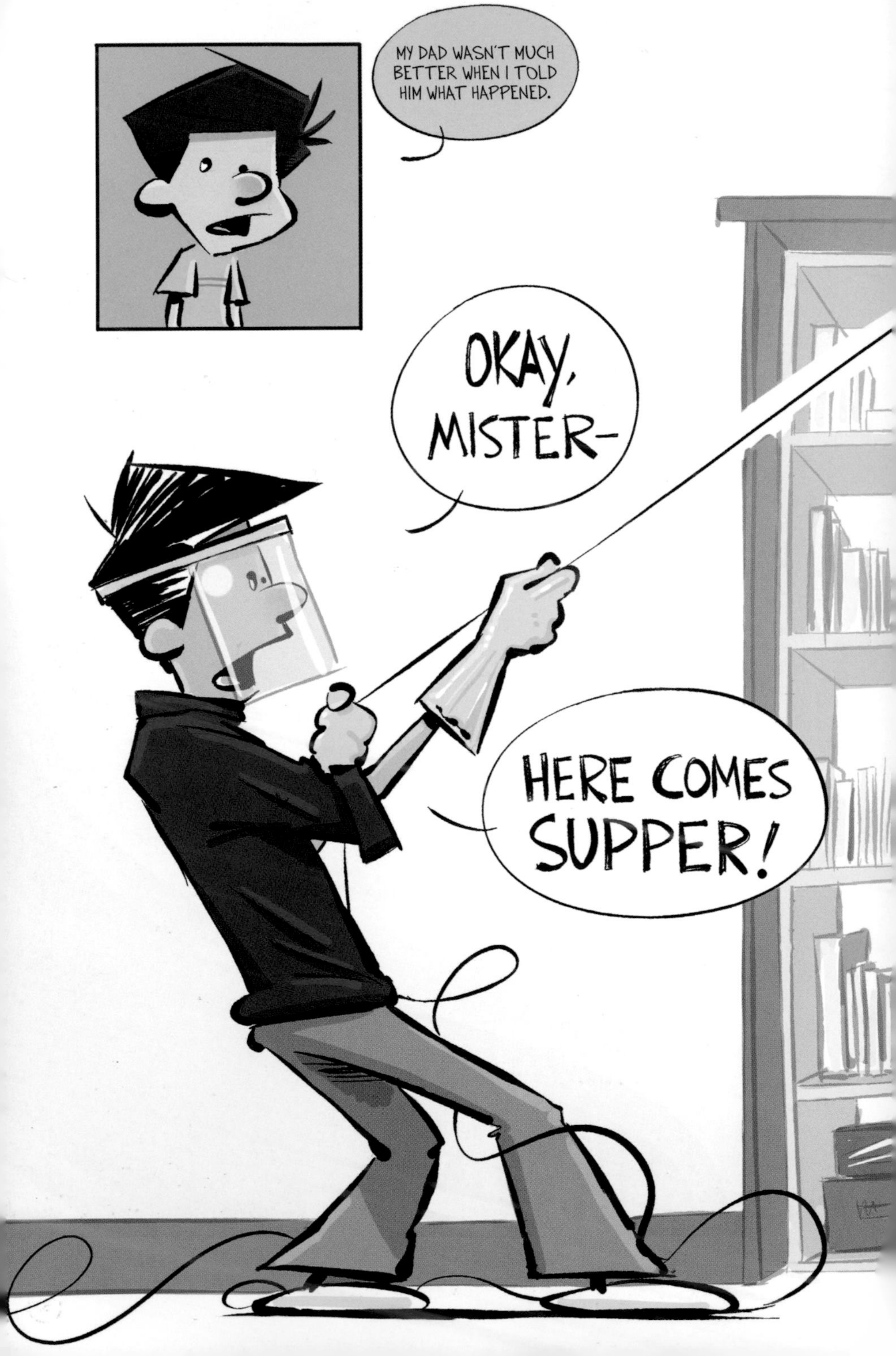
MY DAD WASN'T MUCH BETTER WHEN I TOLD HIM WHAT HAPPENED.
OKAY, MISTER-
HERE COMES SUPPER!

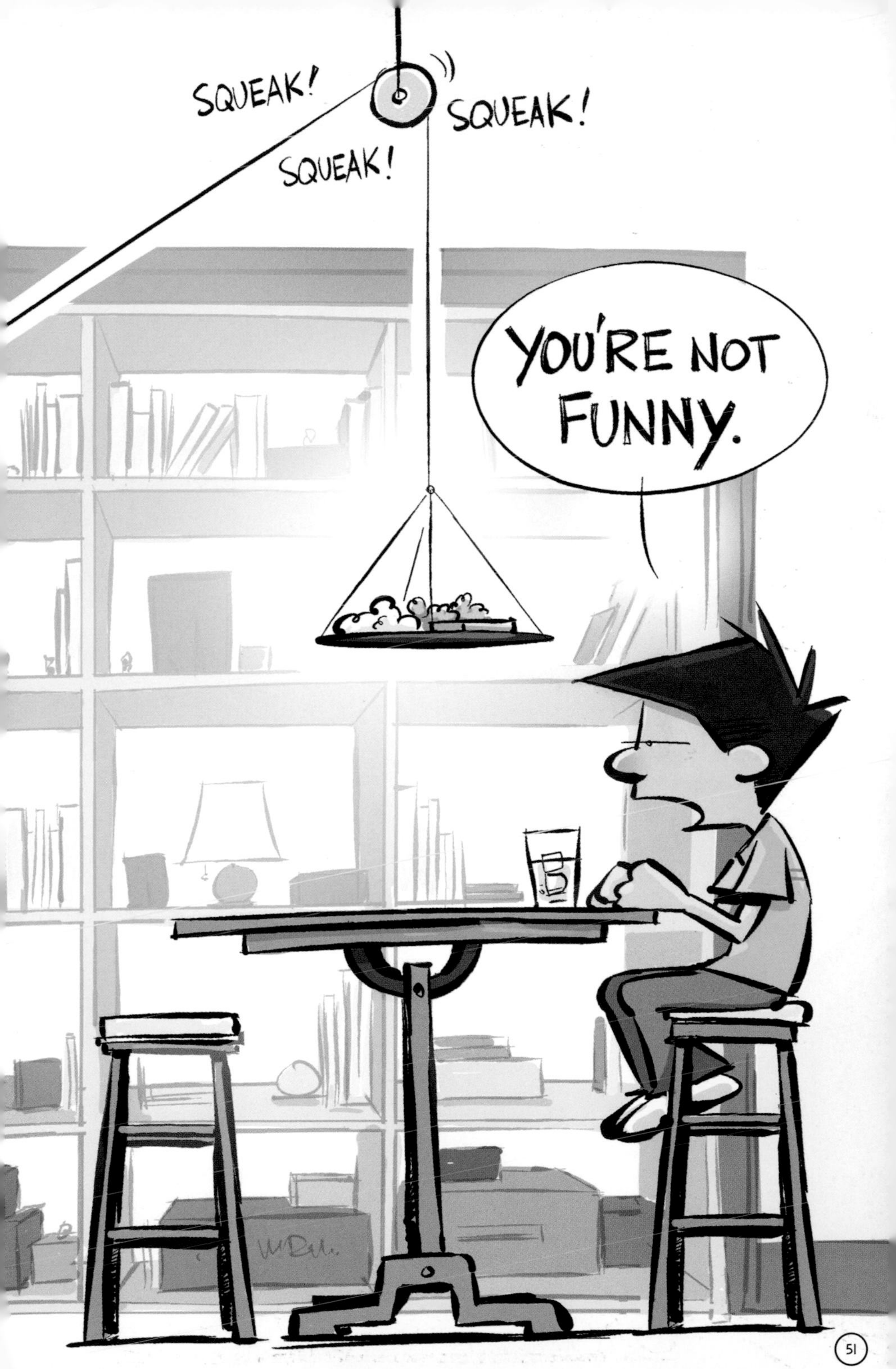
SQUEAK!
SQUEAK!
SQUEAK!
YOU'RE NOT FUNNY.

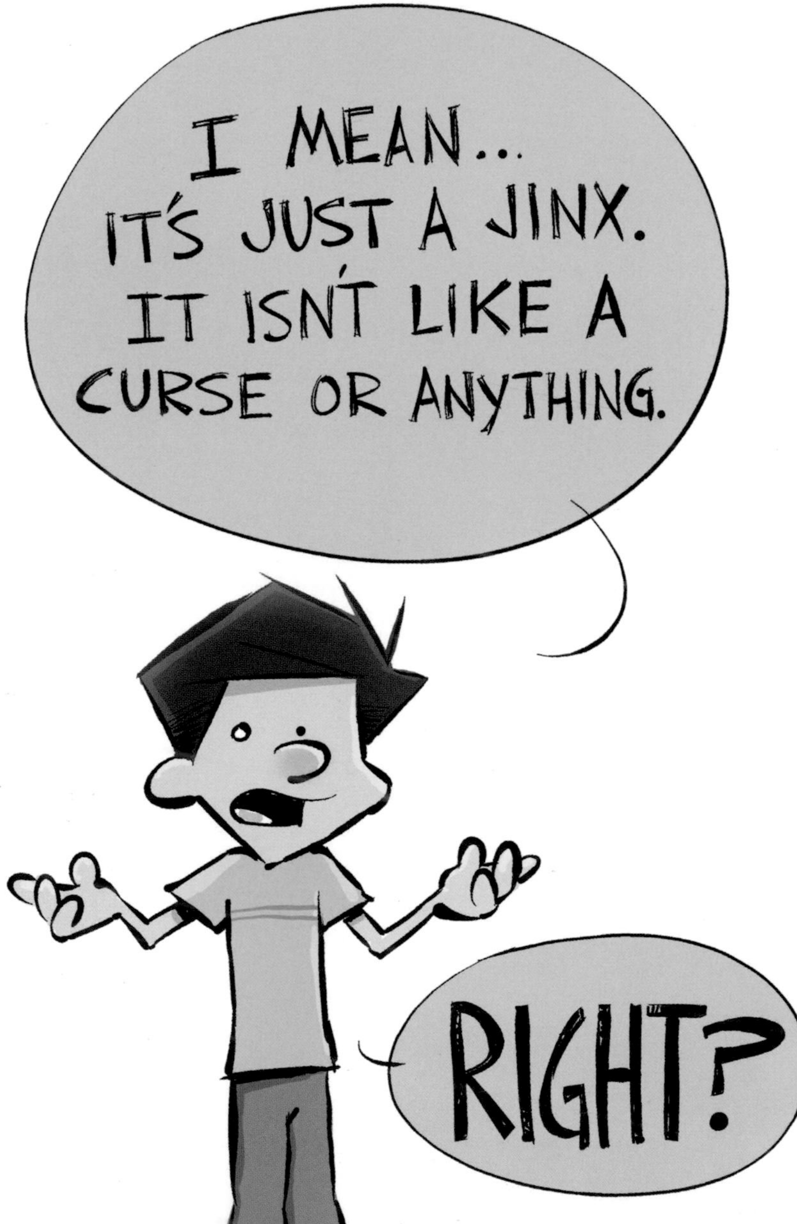
I MEAN... IT'S JUST A JINX. IT ISN'T LIKE A CURSE OR ANYTHING.
RIGHT?

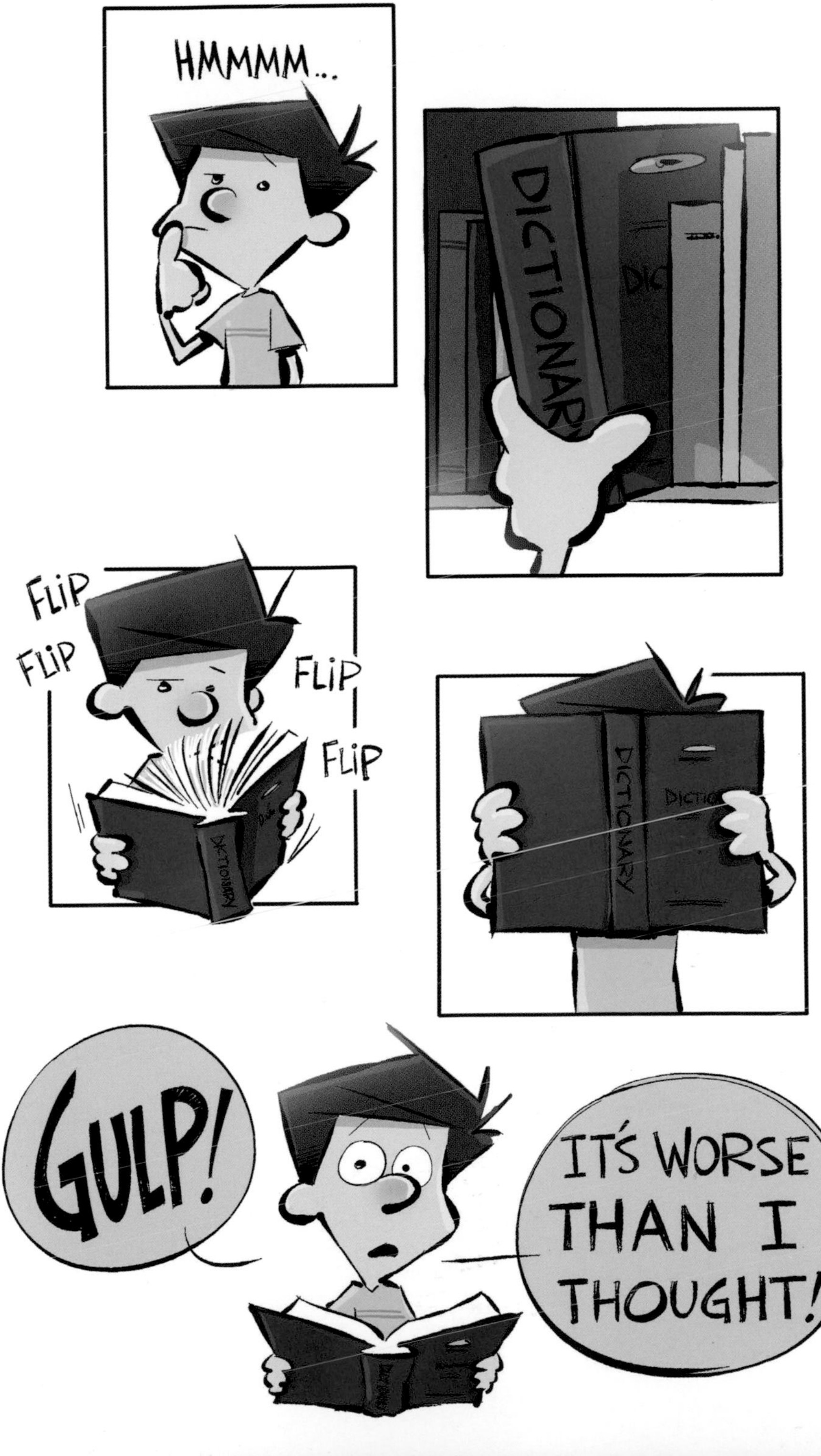
HMMMM...
DICTIONARY
FLIP
FLIP
FLIP
FLIP
DICTIONARY
DICTIONARY
GULP!
IT'S WORSE THAN I THOUGHT!

Jinx \'jiŋ(k)s\

(*n*) one that brings bad luck (see photo). (*v*) to foredoom to failure or misfortune; to bring bad luck to. Synonyms: curse, hex, spell, plague, Newell

EXAMPLE of one who is jinxed →

<u>WARNING!</u> STAY FAR AWAY FROM.

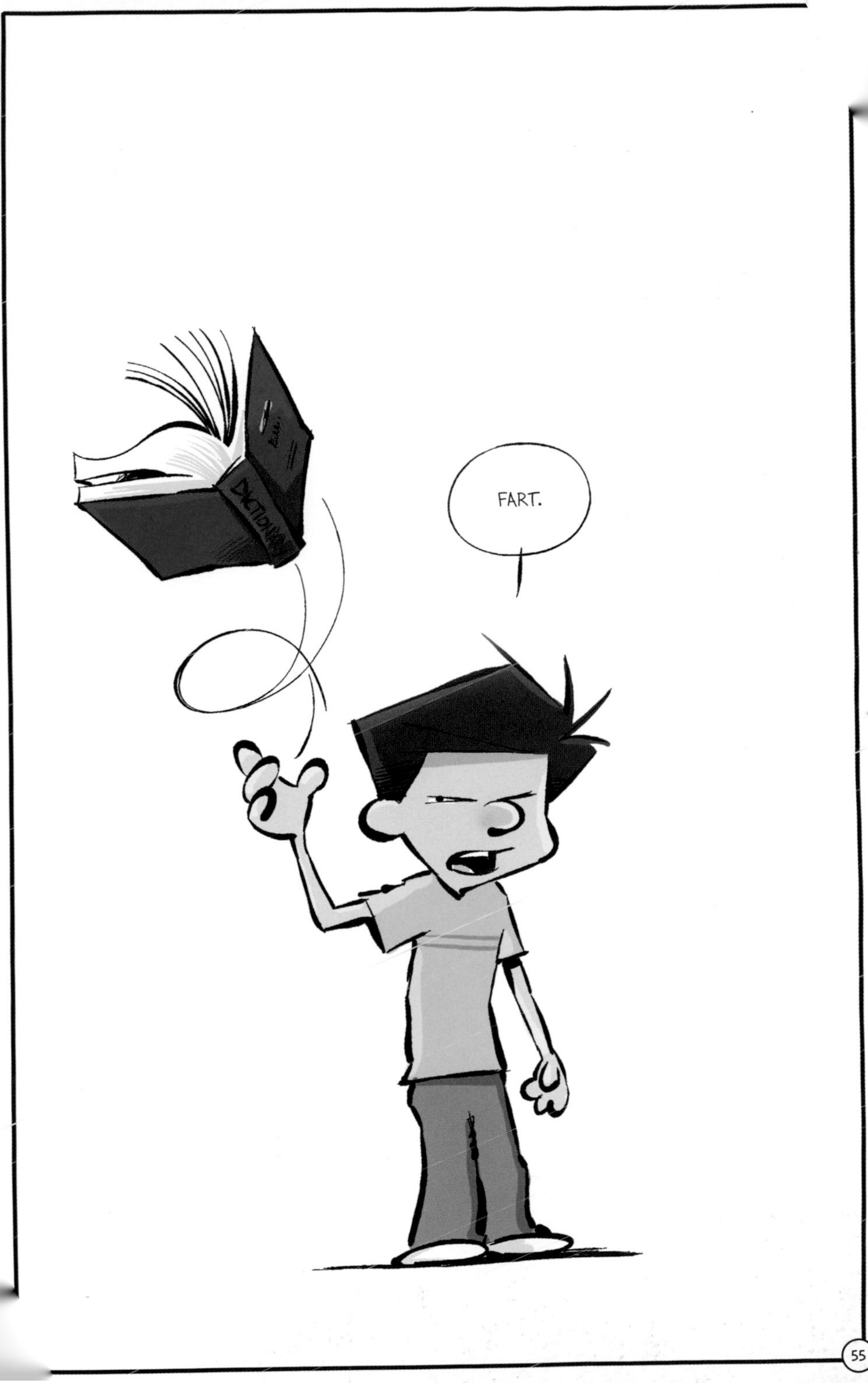
FART.

CHAPTER FOUR
IT DOESN'T GET ANY BETTER

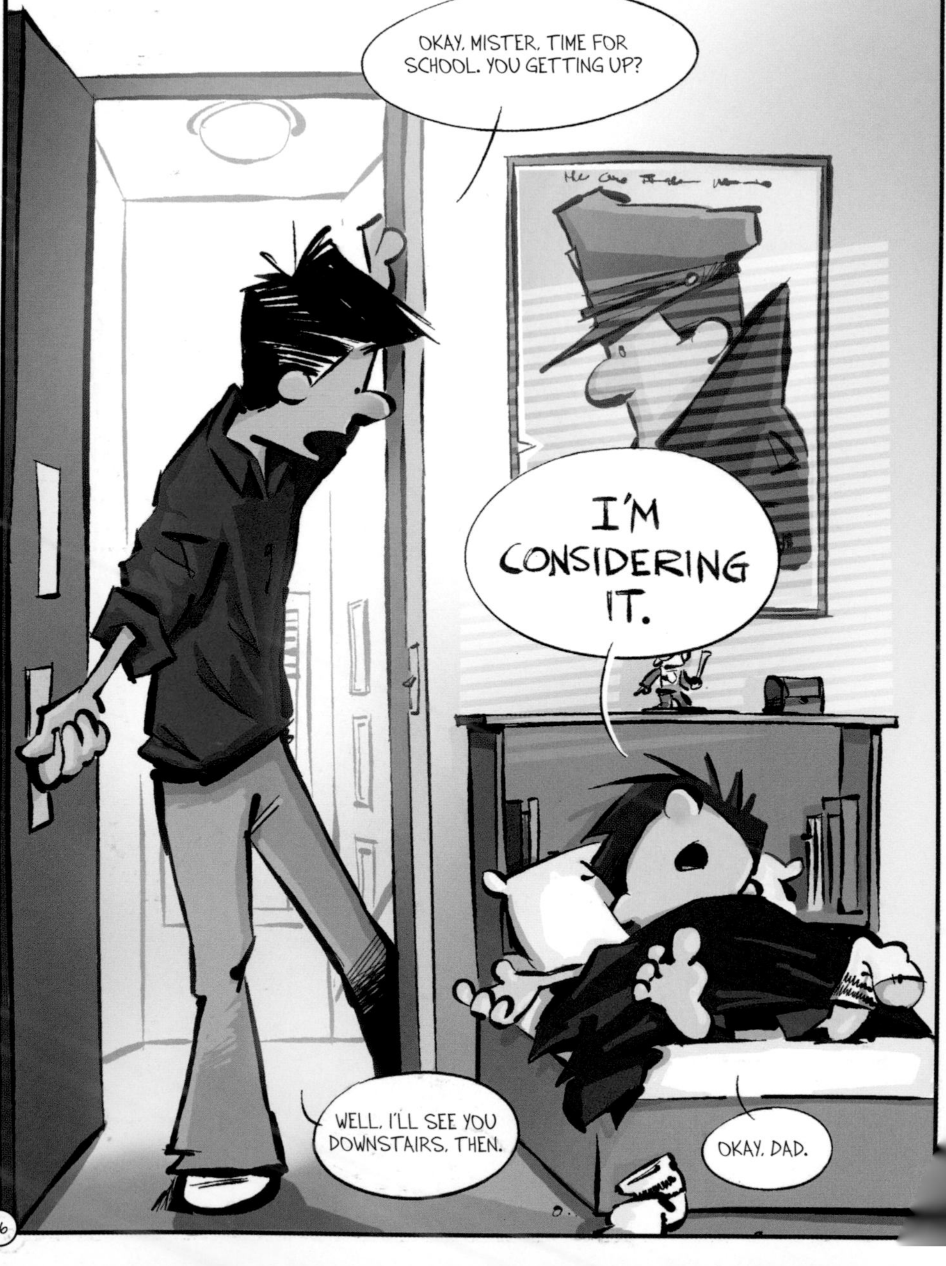
OKAY, MISTER, TIME FOR SCHOOL. YOU GETTING UP?
I'M CONSIDERING IT.
WELL, I'LL SEE YOU DOWNSTAIRS, THEN.
OKAY, DAD.

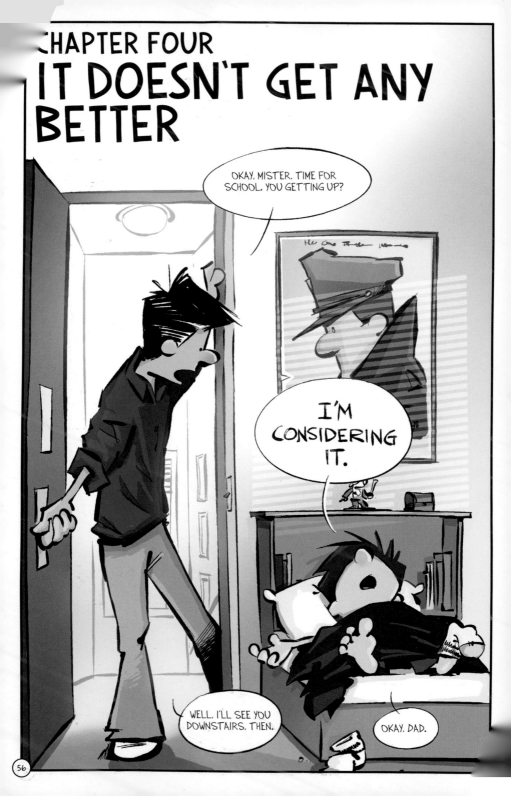

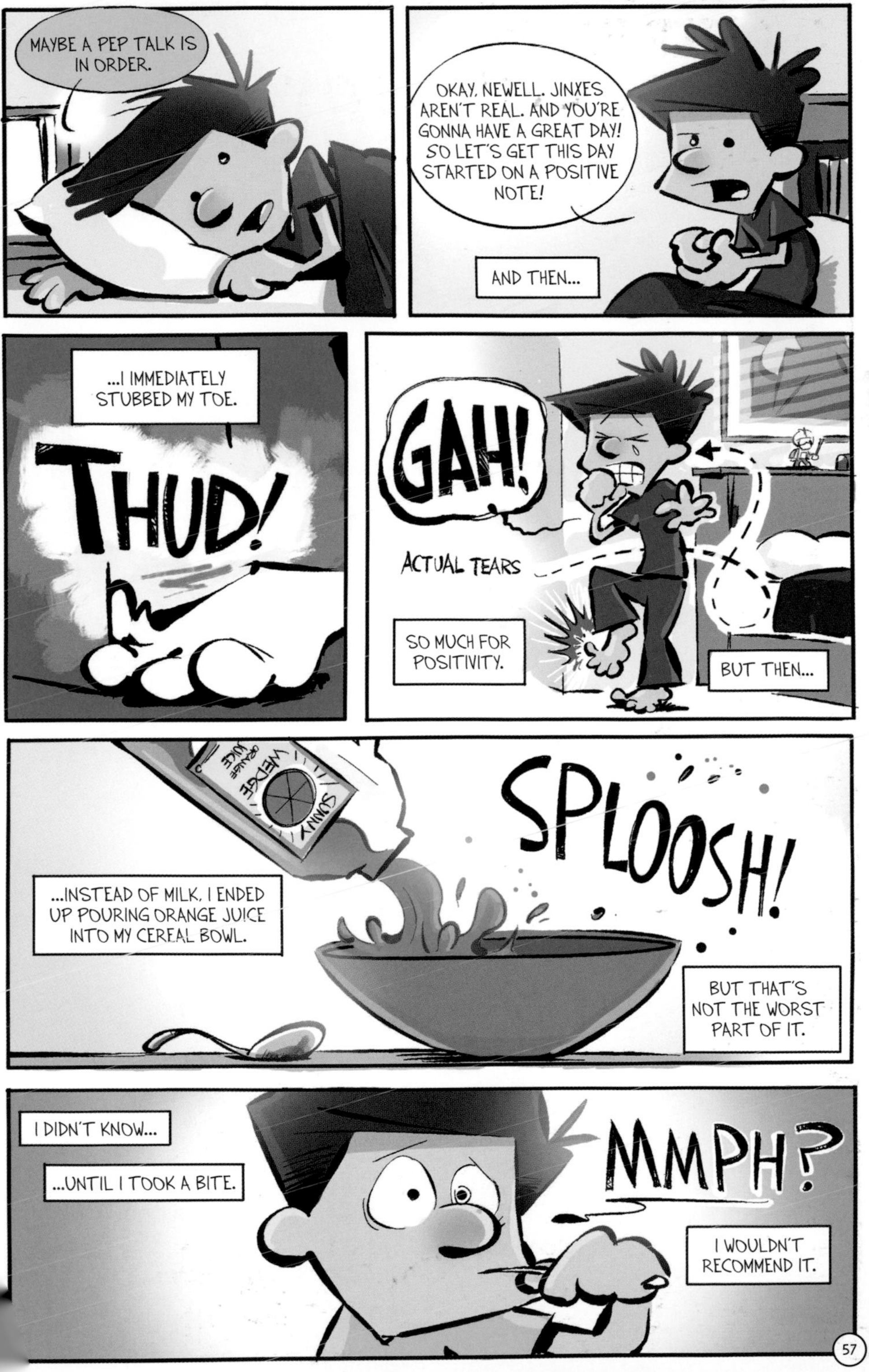
MAYBE A PEP TALK IS IN ORDER.
OKAY, NEWELL. JINXES AREN'T REAL. AND YOU'RE GONNA HAVE A GREAT DAY! SO LET'S GET THIS DAY STARTED ON A POSITIVE NOTE!
AND THEN...
...I IMMEDIATELY STUBBED MY TOE.
THUD!
GAH!
ACTUAL TEARS
SO MUCH FOR POSITIVITY.
BUT THEN...
SUNNY WEDGE ORANGE JUICE
SPLOOSH!
...INSTEAD OF MILK, I ENDED UP POURING ORANGE JUICE INTO MY CEREAL BOWL.
BUT THAT'S NOT THE WORST PART OF IT.
I DIDN'T KNOW...
...UNTIL I TOOK A BITE.
MMPH?
I WOULDN'T RECOMMEND IT.

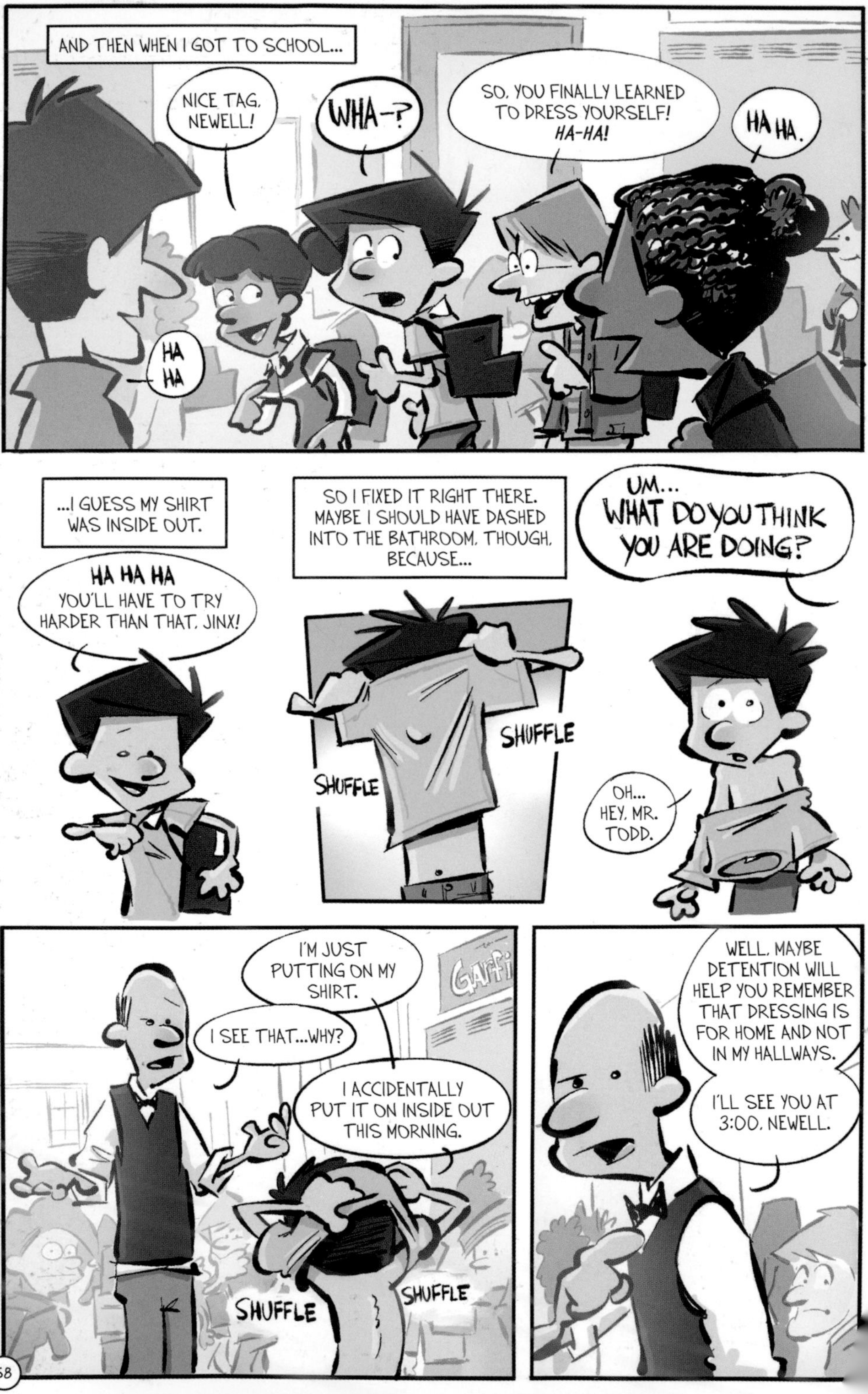
AND THEN WHEN I GOT TO SCHOOL...
NICE TAG, NEWELL!
WHA-?
SO, YOU FINALLY LEARNED TO DRESS YOURSELF! HA-HA!
HA HA.
HA HA
...I GUESS MY SHIRT WAS INSIDE OUT.
HA HA HA YOU'LL HAVE TO TRY HARDER THAN THAT, JINX!
SO I FIXED IT RIGHT THERE. MAYBE I SHOULD HAVE DASHED INTO THE BATHROOM, THOUGH, BECAUSE...
SHUFFLE
SHUFFLE
UM... WHAT DO YOU THINK YOU ARE DOING?
OH... HEY, MR. TODD.
I'M JUST PUTTING ON MY SHIRT.
I SEE THAT...WHY?
I ACCIDENTALLY PUT IT ON INSIDE OUT THIS MORNING.
SHUFFLE
SHUFFLE
WELL, MAYBE DETENTION WILL HELP YOU REMEMBER THAT DRESSING IS FOR HOME AND NOT IN MY HALLWAYS.
I'LL SEE YOU AT 3:00, NEWELL.

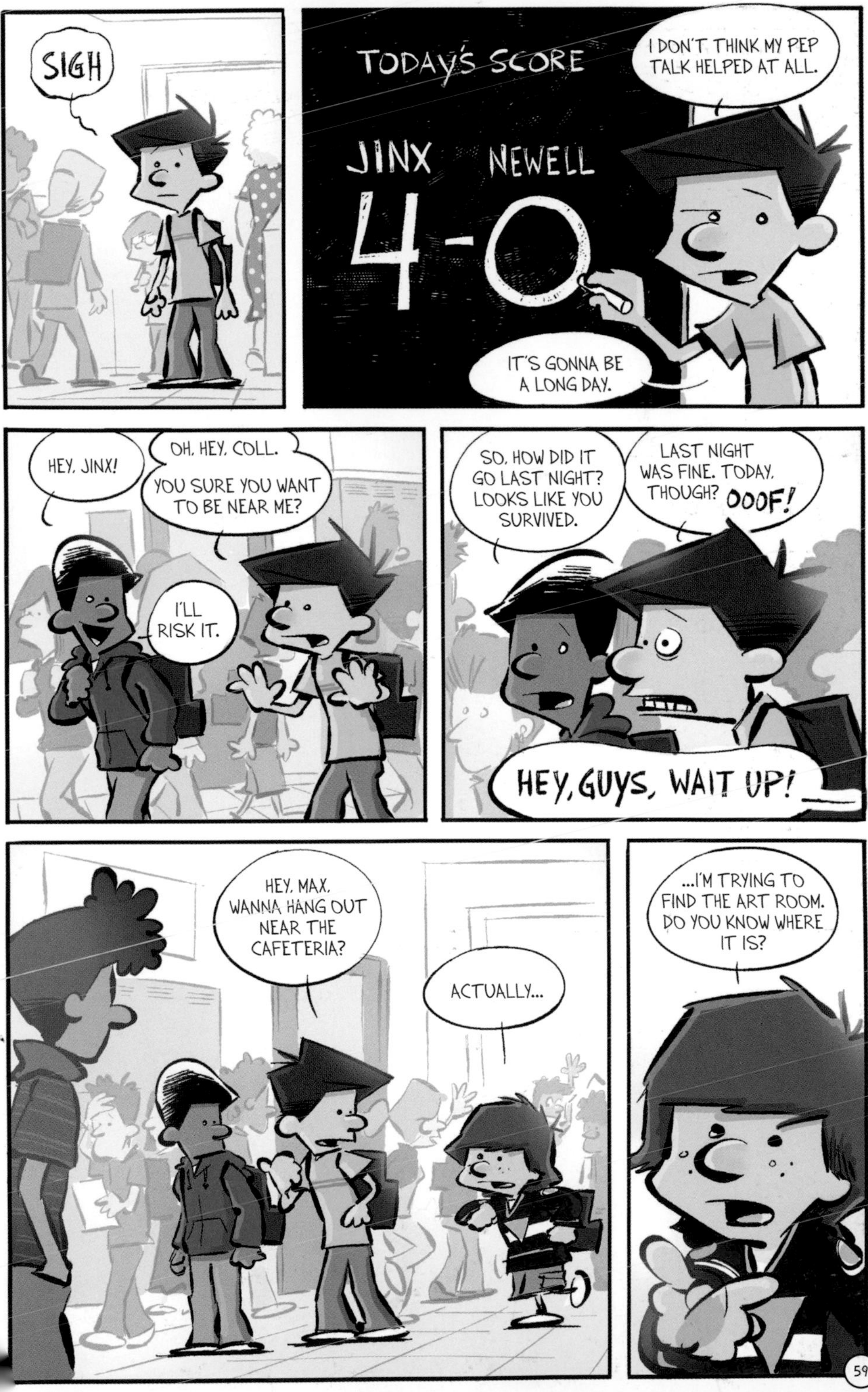
SIGH
TODAY'S SCORE
JINX NEWELL
4-0
I DON'T THINK MY PEP TALK HELPED AT ALL.
IT'S GONNA BE A LONG DAY.
HEY, JINX!
OH, HEY, COLL.
YOU SURE YOU WANT TO BE NEAR ME?
I'LL RISK IT.
SO, HOW DID IT GO LAST NIGHT? LOOKS LIKE YOU SURVIVED.
LAST NIGHT WAS FINE. TODAY, THOUGH? OOOF!
HEY, GUYS, WAIT UP!
HEY, MAX, WANNA HANG OUT NEAR THE CAFETERIA?
ACTUALLY...
...I'M TRYING TO FIND THE ART ROOM. DO YOU KNOW WHERE IT IS?

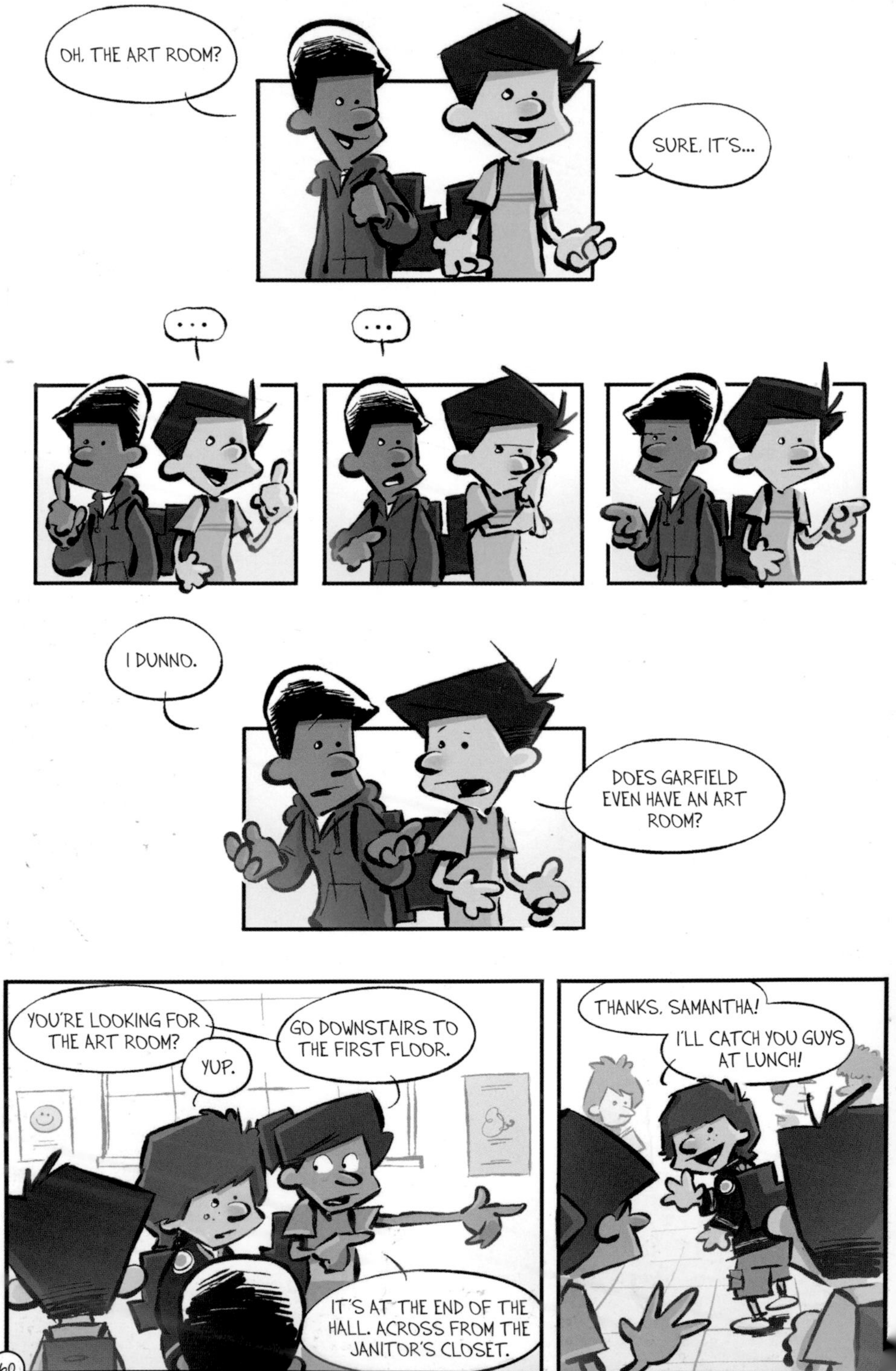
OH, THE ART ROOM?
SURE, IT'S...
...
...
I DUNNO.
DOES GARFIELD EVEN HAVE AN ART ROOM?
YOU'RE LOOKING FOR THE ART ROOM?
YUP.
GO DOWNSTAIRS TO THE FIRST FLOOR.
IT'S AT THE END OF THE HALL. ACROSS FROM THE JANITOR'S CLOSET.
THANKS, SAMANTHA!
I'LL CATCH YOU GUYS AT LUNCH!

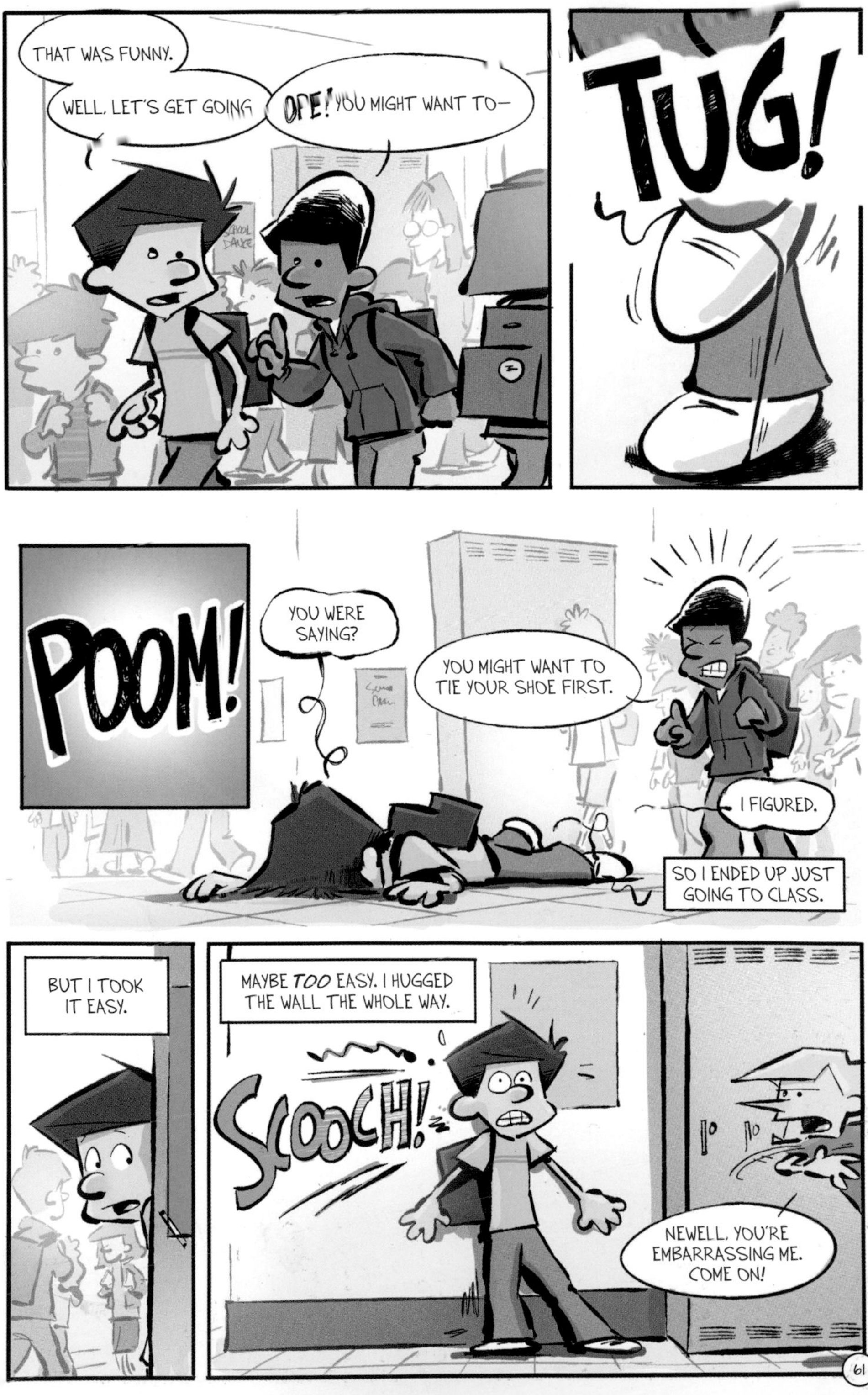
THAT WAS FUNNY.
WELL, LET'S GET GOING
OPE! YOU MIGHT WANT TO—
TUG!
POOM!
YOU WERE SAYING?
YOU MIGHT WANT TO TIE YOUR SHOE FIRST.
I FIGURED.
SO I ENDED UP JUST GOING TO CLASS.
BUT I TOOK IT EASY.
MAYBE *TOO* EASY. I HUGGED THE WALL THE WHOLE WAY.
SCOOCH!
NEWELL, YOU'RE EMBARRASSING ME. COME ON!

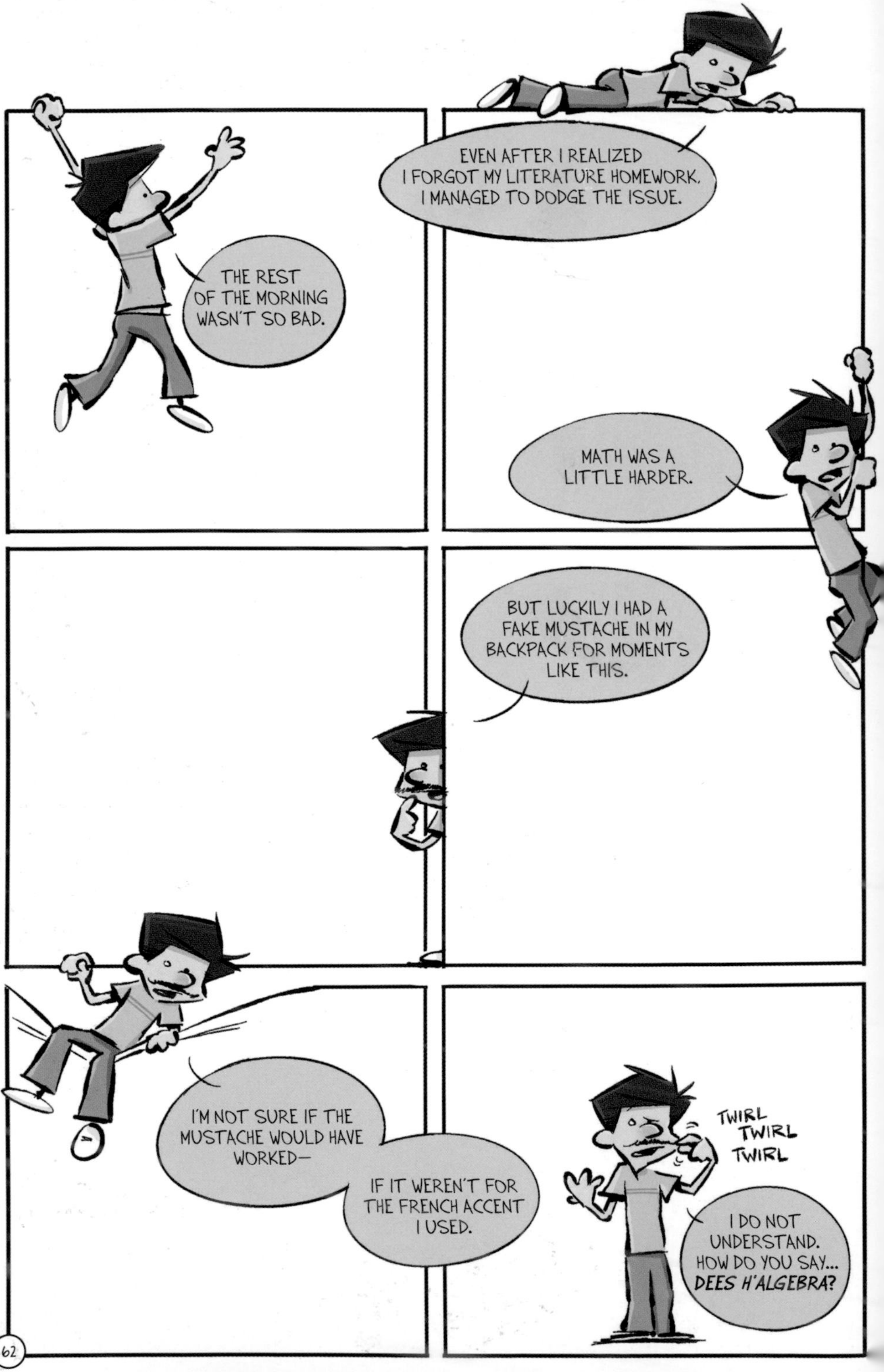
THE REST OF THE MORNING WASN'T SO BAD.
EVEN AFTER I REALIZED I FORGOT MY LITERATURE HOMEWORK, I MANAGED TO DODGE THE ISSUE.
MATH WAS A LITTLE HARDER.
BUT LUCKILY I HAD A FAKE MUSTACHE IN MY BACKPACK FOR MOMENTS LIKE THIS.
I'M NOT SURE IF THE MUSTACHE WOULD HAVE WORKED—
IF IT WEREN'T FOR THE FRENCH ACCENT I USED.
TWIRL TWIRL TWIRL
I DO NOT UNDERSTAND. HOW DO YOU SAY... ***DEES H'ALGEBRA?***

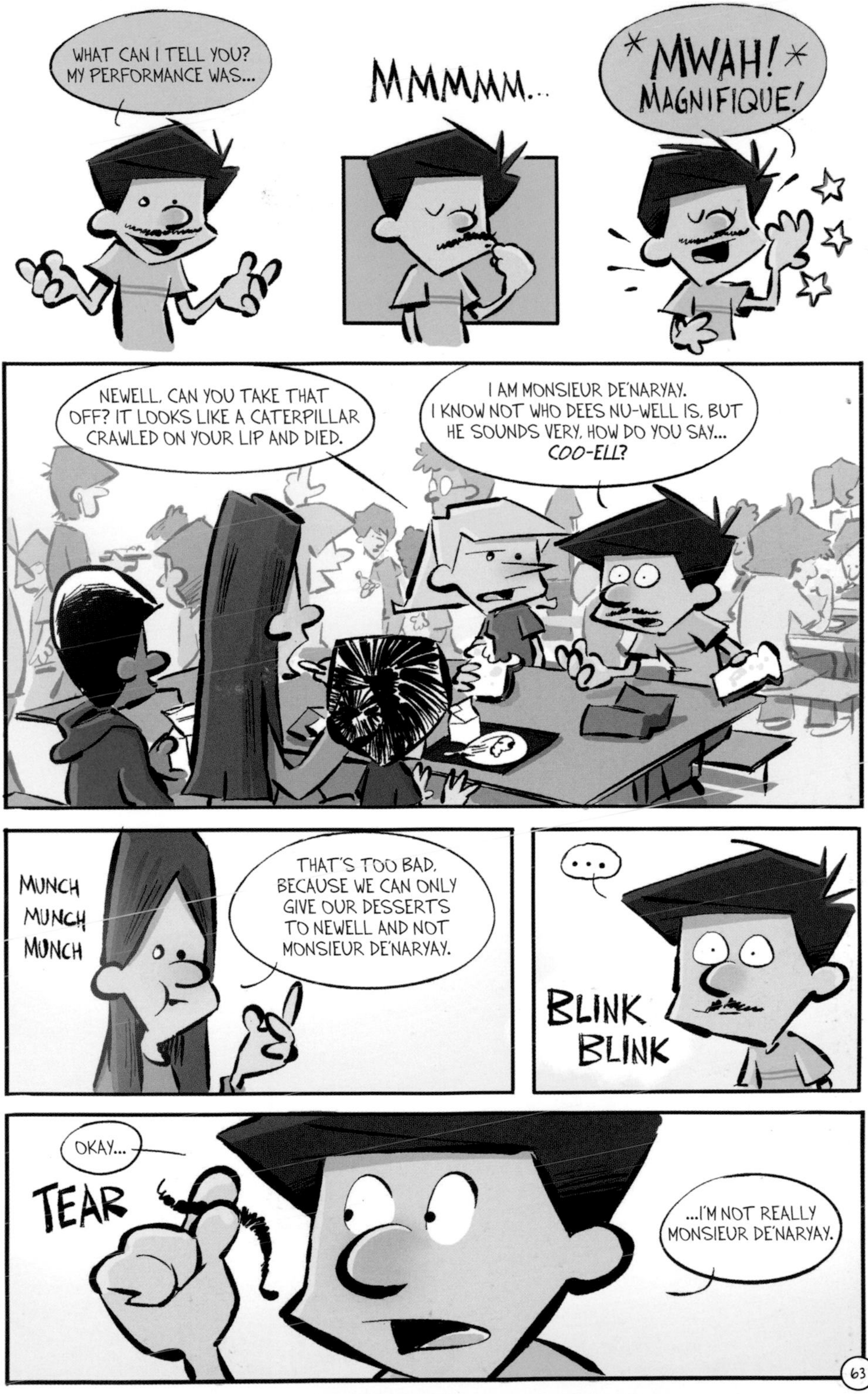

WHAT CAN I TELL YOU? MY PERFORMANCE WAS...
MMMMM...
MWAH! MAGNIFIQUE!
NEWELL, CAN YOU TAKE THAT OFF? IT LOOKS LIKE A CATERPILLAR CRAWLED ON YOUR LIP AND DIED.
I AM MONSIEUR DE'NARYAY. I KNOW NOT WHO DEES NU-WELL IS, BUT HE SOUNDS VERY, HOW DO YOU SAY... COO-ELL?
MUNCH MUNCH MUNCH
THAT'S TOO BAD, BECAUSE WE CAN ONLY GIVE OUR DESSERTS TO NEWELL AND NOT MONSIEUR DE'NARYAY.
...
BLINK BLINK
OKAY...
TEAR
...I'M NOT REALLY MONSIEUR DE'NARYAY.

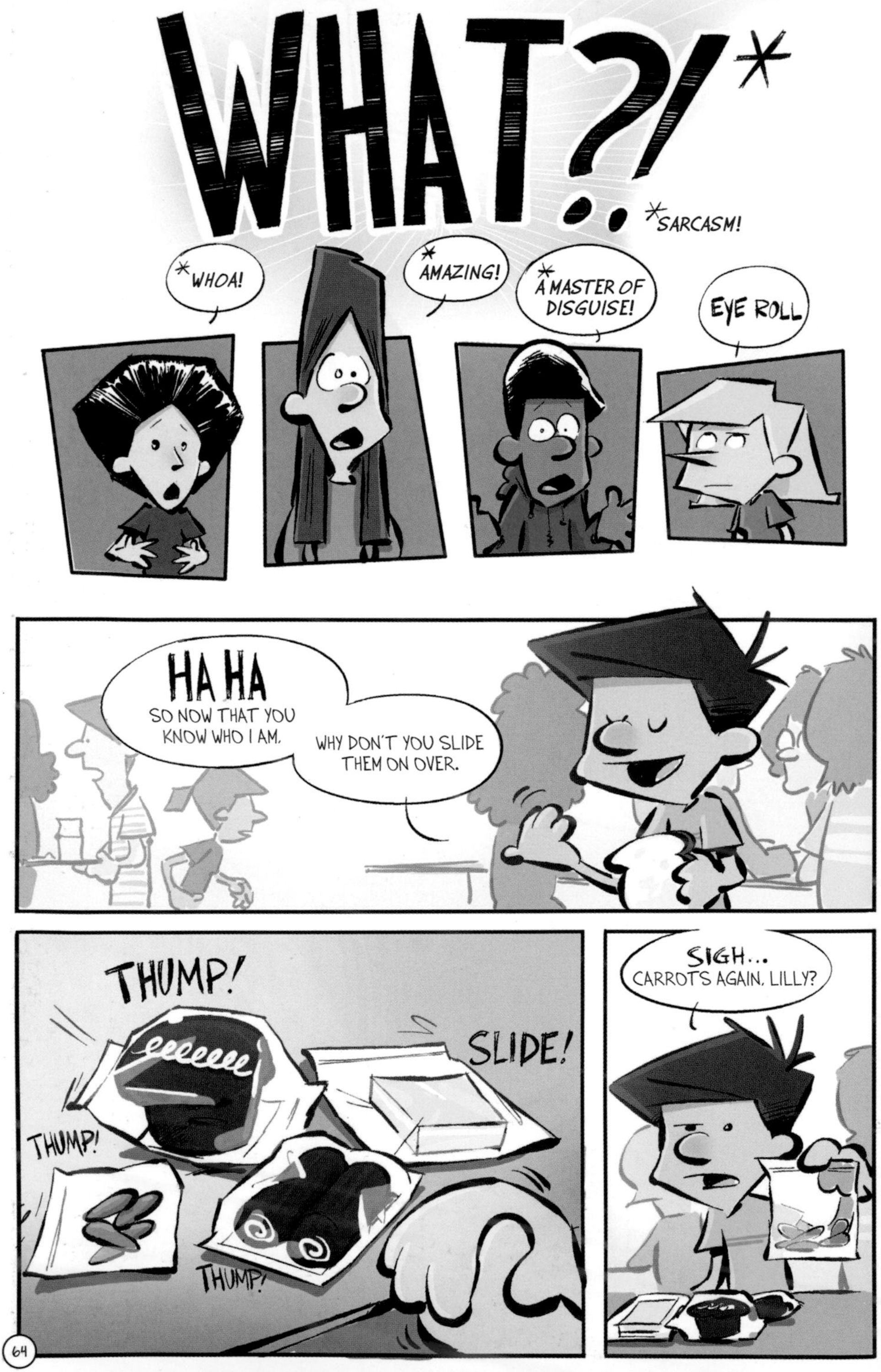

WHAT?!*
*SARCASM!
*WHOA!
*AMAZING!
*A MASTER OF DISGUISE!
EYE ROLL
HA HA
SO NOW THAT YOU KNOW WHO I AM,
WHY DON'T YOU SLIDE THEM ON OVER.
THUMP!
SLIDE!
THUMP!
THUMP!
SIGH...
CARROTS AGAIN, LILLY?

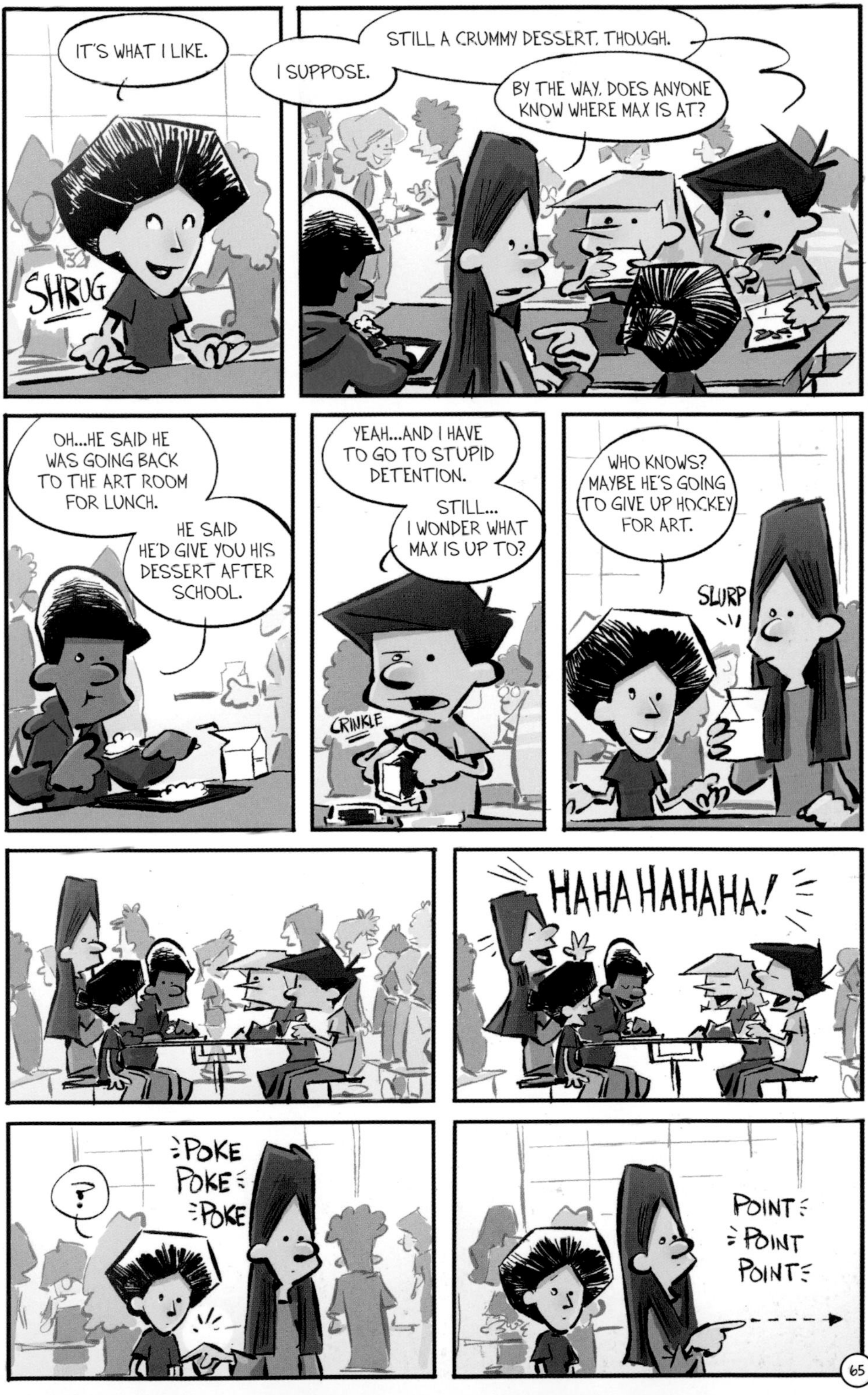
IT'S WHAT I LIKE.
SHRUG
I SUPPOSE.
STILL A CRUMMY DESSERT, THOUGH.
BY THE WAY, DOES ANYONE KNOW WHERE MAX IS AT?
OH...HE SAID HE WAS GOING BACK TO THE ART ROOM FOR LUNCH.
HE SAID HE'D GIVE YOU HIS DESSERT AFTER SCHOOL.
YEAH...AND I HAVE TO GO TO STUPID DETENTION.
STILL... I WONDER WHAT MAX IS UP TO?
CRINKLE
WHO KNOWS? MAYBE HE'S GOING TO GIVE UP HOCKEY FOR ART.
SLURP
HAHAHAHAHA!
?
POKE
POKE
POKE
POINT
POINT
POINT

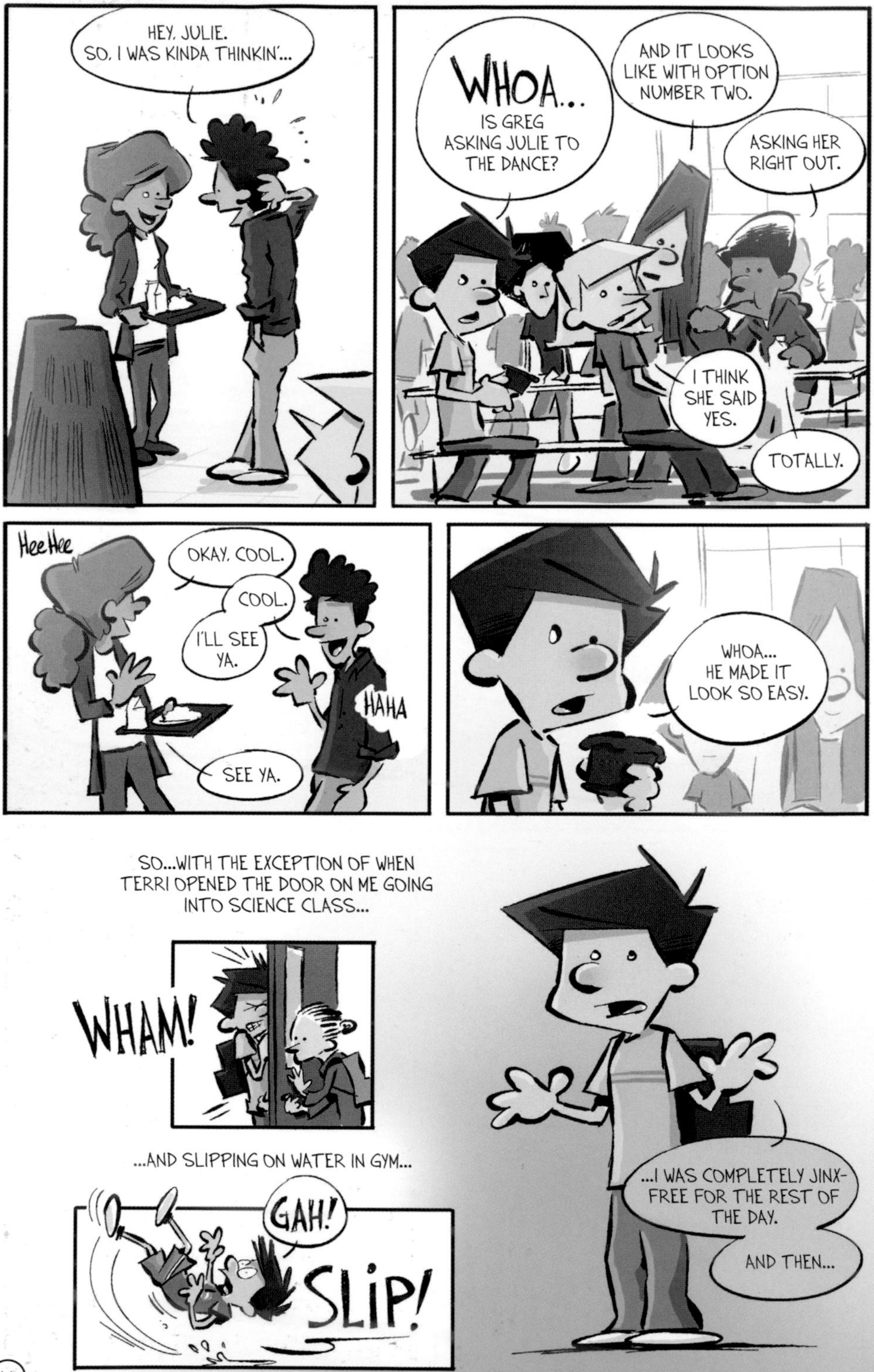
HEY, JULIE.
SO, I WAS KINDA THINKIN'...
WHOA...
IS GREG ASKING JULIE TO THE DANCE?
AND IT LOOKS LIKE WITH OPTION NUMBER TWO.
ASKING HER RIGHT OUT.
I THINK SHE SAID YES.
TOTALLY.
Hee Hee
OKAY, COOL.
COOL.
I'LL SEE YA.
HAHA
SEE YA.
WHOA...
HE MADE IT LOOK SO EASY.
SO...WITH THE EXCEPTION OF WHEN TERRI OPENED THE DOOR ON ME GOING INTO SCIENCE CLASS...
WHAM!
...AND SLIPPING ON WATER IN GYM...
GAH!
SLIP!
...I WAS COMPLETELY JINX-FREE FOR THE REST OF THE DAY.
AND THEN...

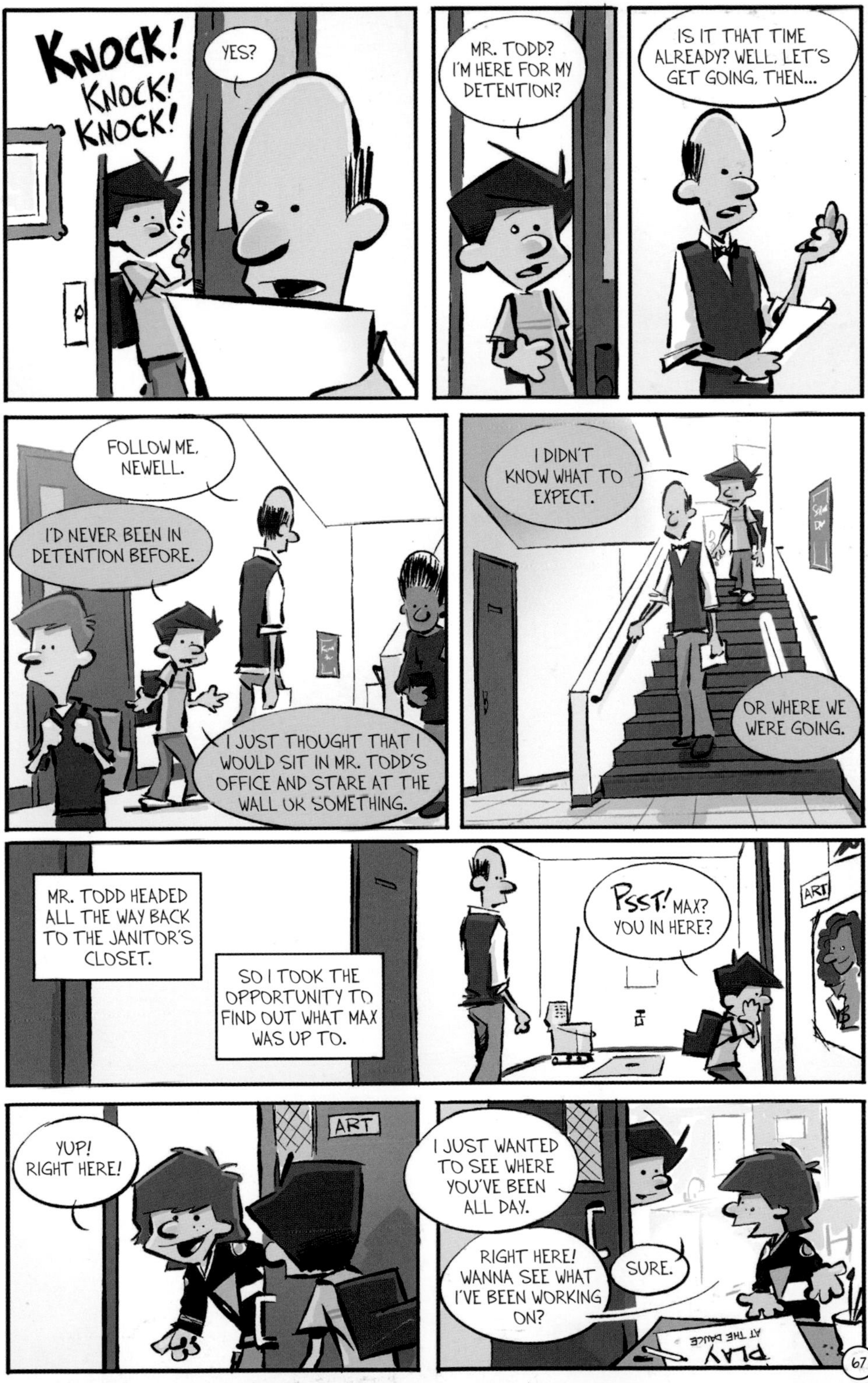
KNOCK! KNOCK! KNOCK!
YES?
MR. TODD? I'M HERE FOR MY DETENTION?
IS IT THAT TIME ALREADY? WELL, LET'S GET GOING, THEN...
FOLLOW ME, NEWELL.
I'D NEVER BEEN IN DETENTION BEFORE.
I JUST THOUGHT THAT I WOULD SIT IN MR. TODD'S OFFICE AND STARE AT THE WALL OR SOMETHING.
I DIDN'T KNOW WHAT TO EXPECT.
OR WHERE WE WERE GOING.
MR. TODD HEADED ALL THE WAY BACK TO THE JANITOR'S CLOSET.
SO I TOOK THE OPPORTUNITY TO FIND OUT WHAT MAX WAS UP TO.
PSST! MAX? YOU IN HERE?
ART
YUP! RIGHT HERE!
ART
I JUST WANTED TO SEE WHERE YOU'VE BEEN ALL DAY.
RIGHT HERE! WANNA SEE WHAT I'VE BEEN WORKING ON?
SURE.
PLAY AT THE DANCE

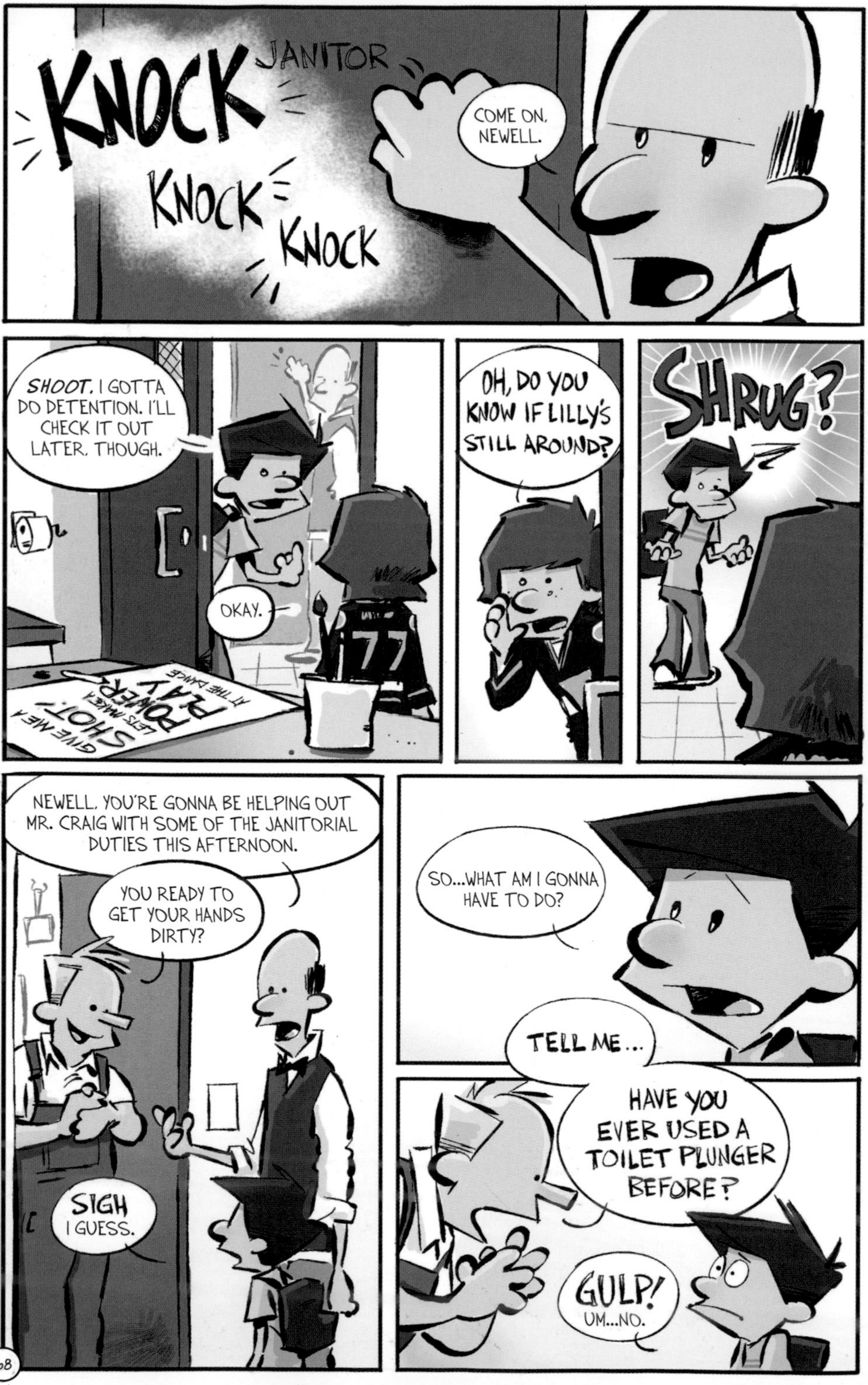
KNOCK
JANITOR
KNOCK
KNOCK
COME ON, NEWELL.
SHOOT. I GOTTA DO DETENTION. I'LL CHECK IT OUT LATER, THOUGH.
OKAY.
GIVE ME A SHOT - LET'S MAKE A POWER PLAY AT THE DANCE
...
OH, DO YOU KNOW IF LILLY'S STILL AROUND?
SHRUG?
NEWELL, YOU'RE GONNA BE HELPING OUT MR. CRAIG WITH SOME OF THE JANITORIAL DUTIES THIS AFTERNOON.
YOU READY TO GET YOUR HANDS DIRTY?
SIGH
I GUESS.
SO...WHAT AM I GONNA HAVE TO DO?
TELL ME...
HAVE YOU EVER USED A TOILET PLUNGER BEFORE?
GULP!
UM...NO.

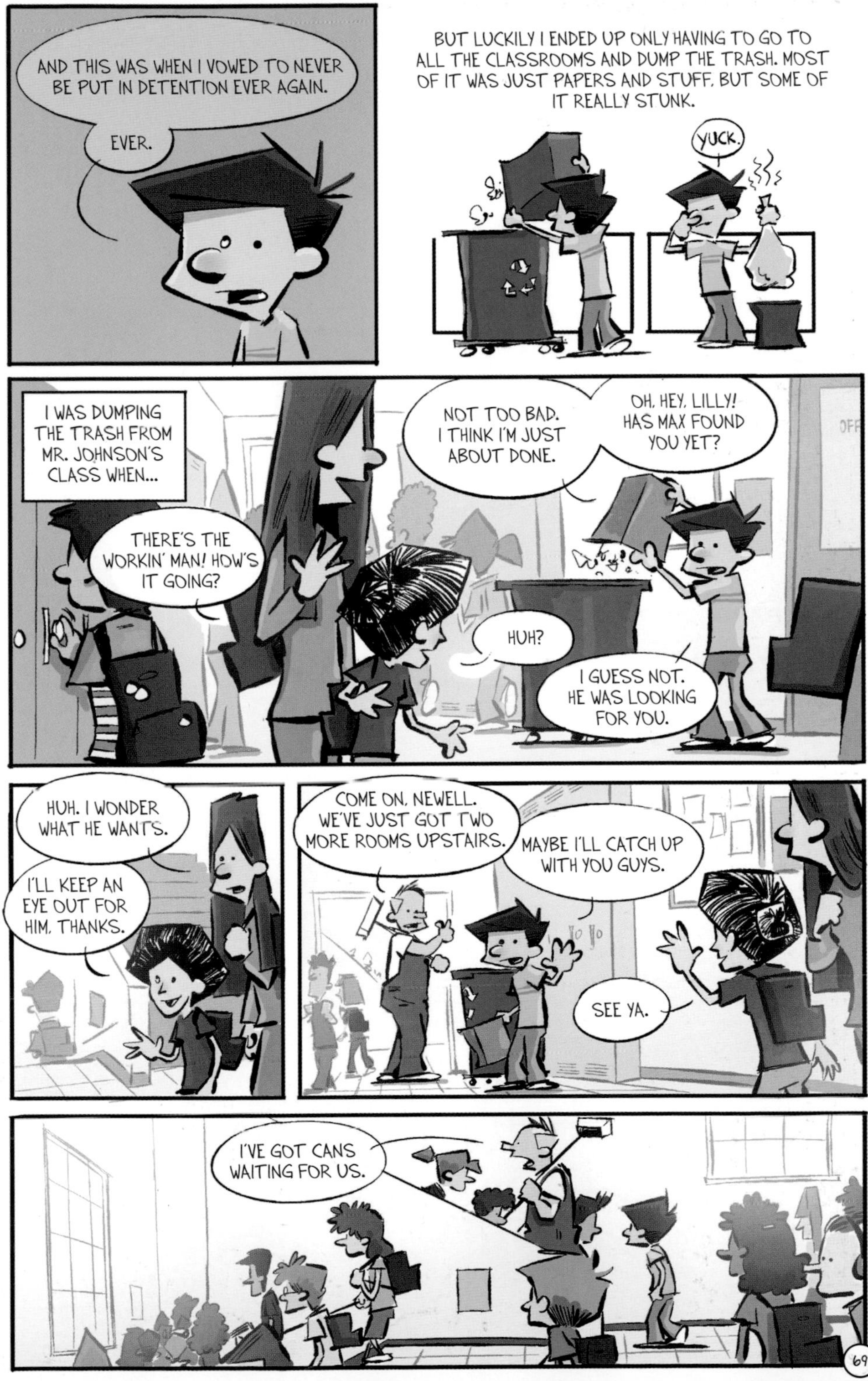
AND THIS WAS WHEN I VOWED TO NEVER BE PUT IN DETENTION EVER AGAIN.
EVER.
BUT LUCKILY I ENDED UP ONLY HAVING TO GO TO ALL THE CLASSROOMS AND DUMP THE TRASH. MOST OF IT WAS JUST PAPERS AND STUFF, BUT SOME OF IT REALLY STUNK.
YUCK.
I WAS DUMPING THE TRASH FROM MR. JOHNSON'S CLASS WHEN...
THERE'S THE WORKIN' MAN! HOW'S IT GOING?
NOT TOO BAD. I THINK I'M JUST ABOUT DONE.
OH, HEY, LILLY! HAS MAX FOUND YOU YET?
HUH?
I GUESS NOT. HE WAS LOOKING FOR YOU.
HUH. I WONDER WHAT HE WANTS.
I'LL KEEP AN EYE OUT FOR HIM, THANKS.
COME ON, NEWELL. WE'VE JUST GOT TWO MORE ROOMS UPSTAIRS.
MAYBE I'LL CATCH UP WITH YOU GUYS.
SEE YA.
I'VE GOT CANS WAITING FOR US.

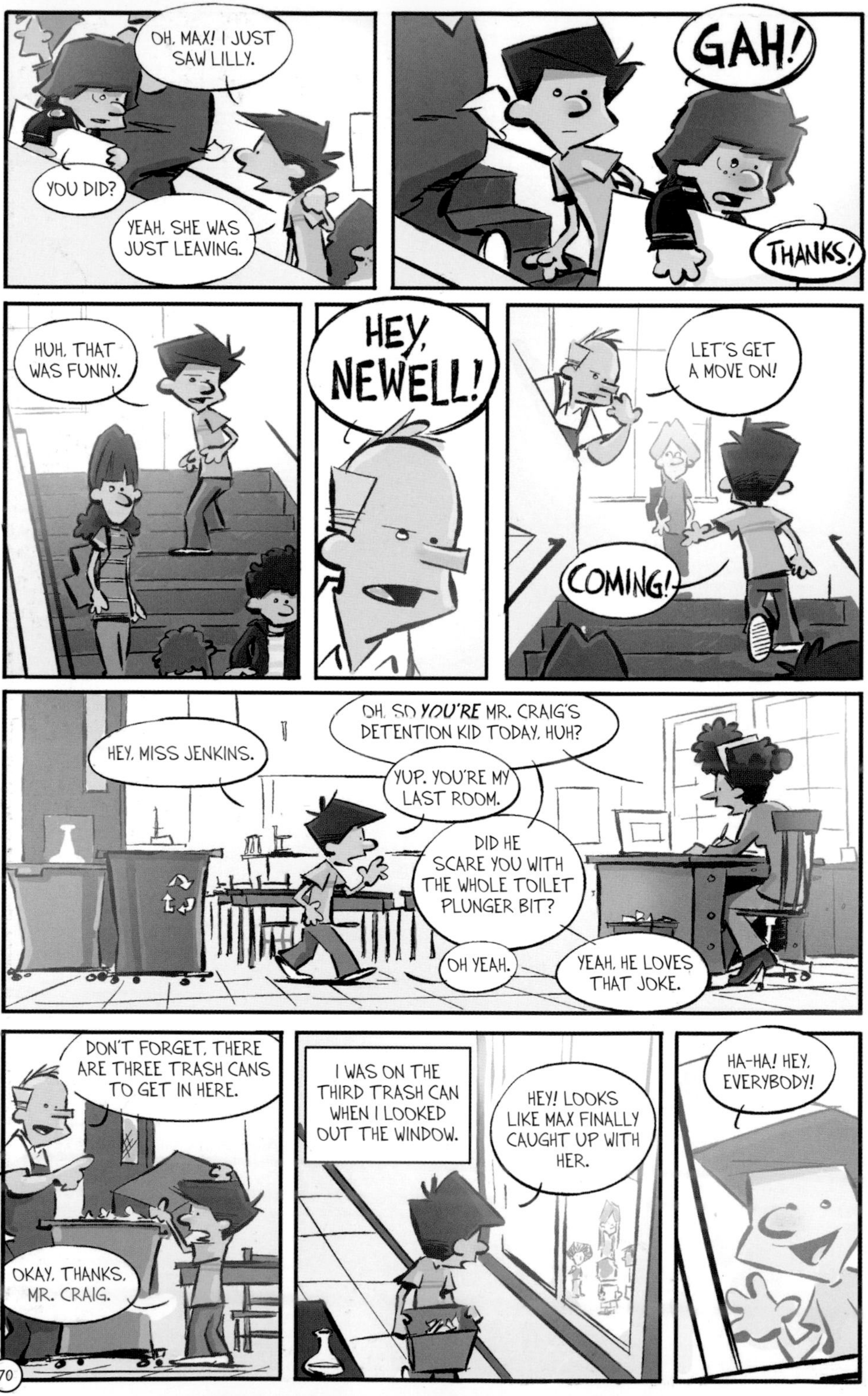

OH, MAX! I JUST SAW LILLY.
YOU DID?
YEAH, SHE WAS JUST LEAVING.
GAH!
THANKS!
HUH, THAT WAS FUNNY.
HEY, NEWELL!
LET'S GET A MOVE ON!
COMING!
HEY, MISS JENKINS.
OH, SO *YOU'RE* MR. CRAIG'S DETENTION KID TODAY, HUH?
YUP. YOU'RE MY LAST ROOM.
DID HE SCARE YOU WITH THE WHOLE TOILET PLUNGER BIT?
OH YEAH.
YEAH, HE LOVES THAT JOKE.
DON'T FORGET, THERE ARE THREE TRASH CANS TO GET IN HERE.
OKAY, THANKS, MR. CRAIG.
I WAS ON THE THIRD TRASH CAN WHEN I LOOKED OUT THE WINDOW.
HEY! LOOKS LIKE MAX FINALLY CAUGHT UP WITH HER.
HA-HA! HEY, EVERYBODY!

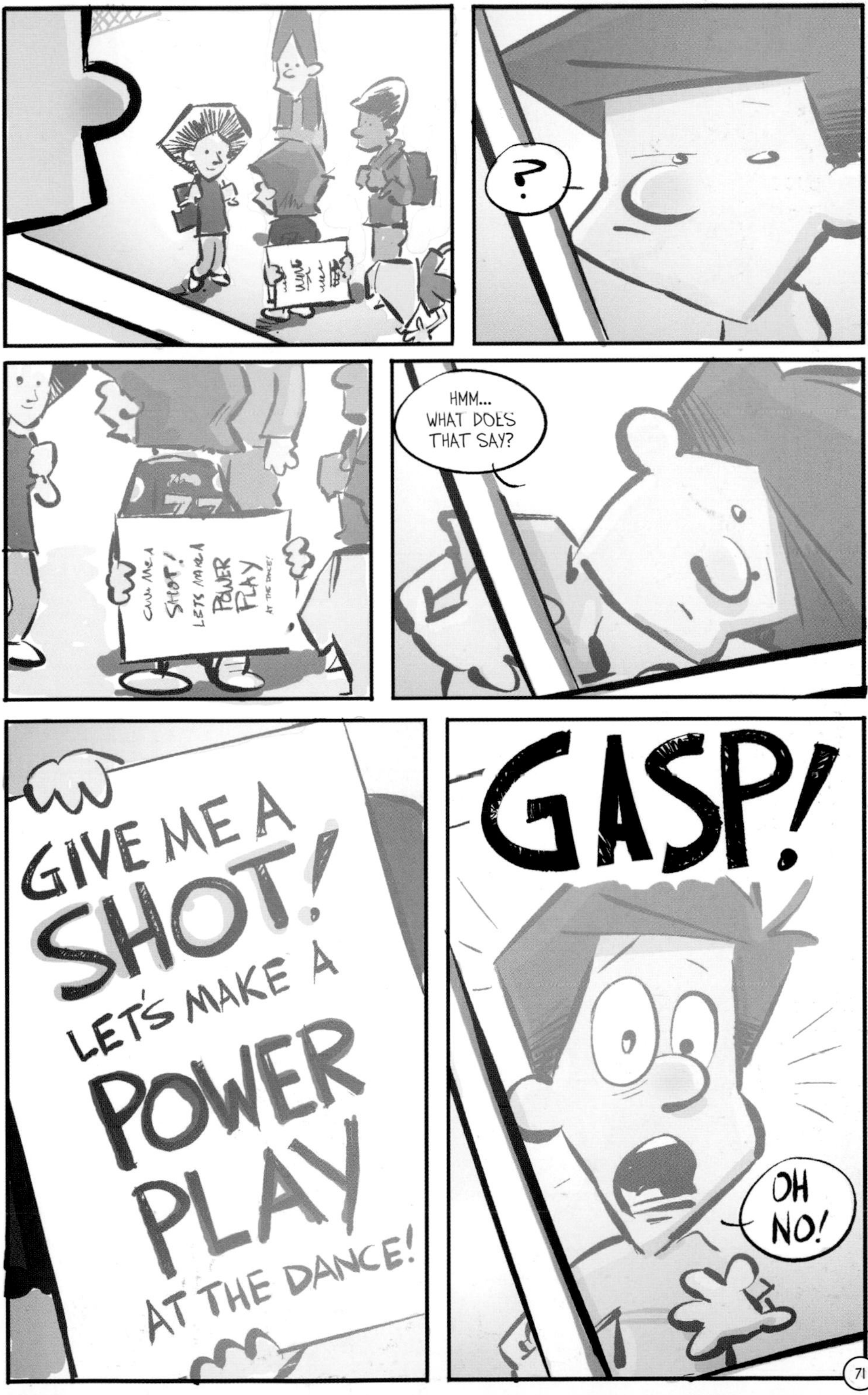
?
HMM... WHAT DOES THAT SAY?
GIVE ME A SHOT! LET'S MAKE A POWER PLAY AT THE DANCE!
GASP!
OH NO!

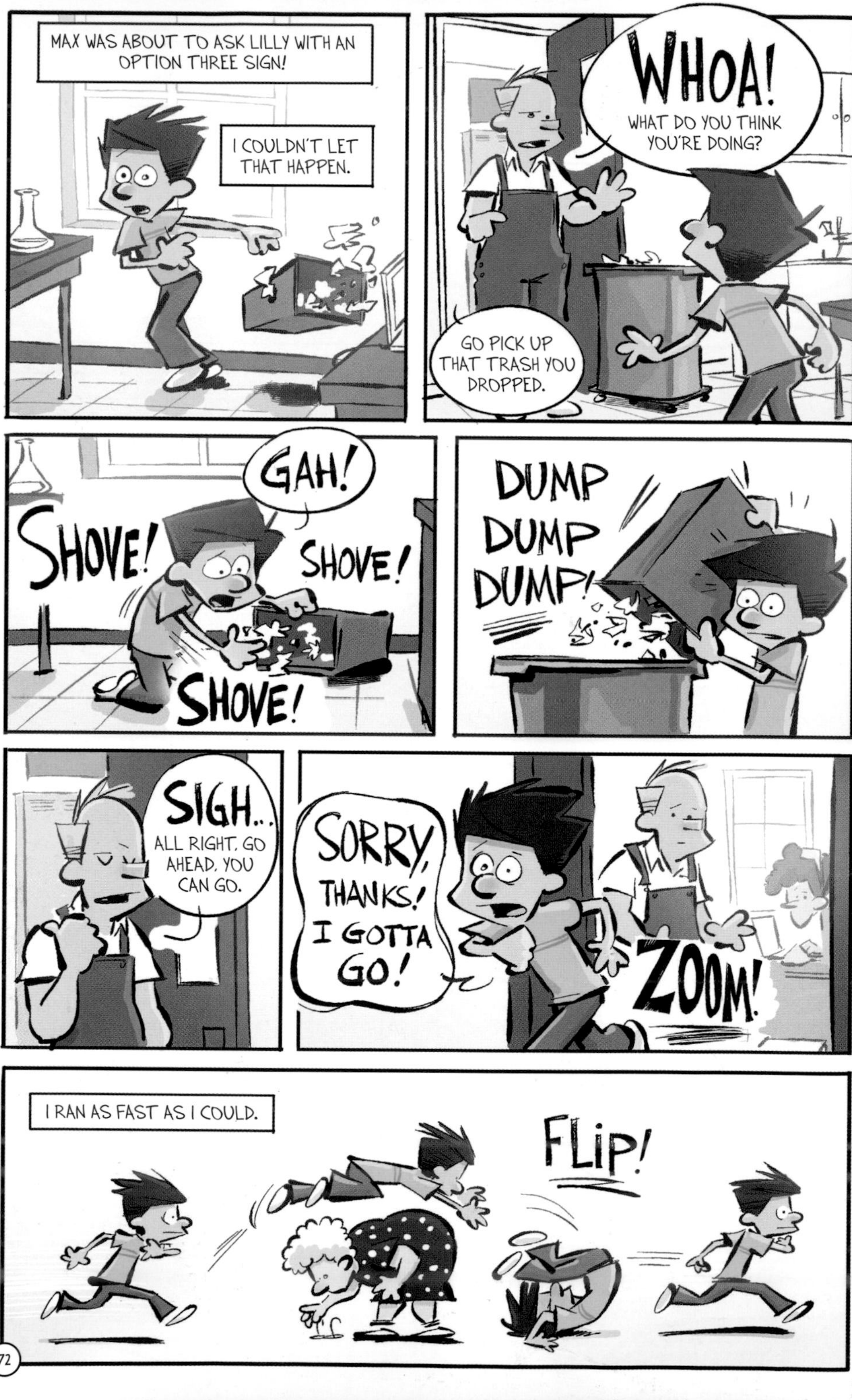
MAX WAS ABOUT TO ASK LILLY WITH AN OPTION THREE SIGN!
I COULDN'T LET THAT HAPPEN.
WHOA! WHAT DO YOU THINK YOU'RE DOING?
GO PICK UP THAT TRASH YOU DROPPED.
GAH!
SHOVE! SHOVE! SHOVE!
DUMP DUMP DUMP!
SIGH... ALL RIGHT, GO AHEAD, YOU CAN GO.
SORRY, THANKS! I GOTTA GO!
ZOOM!
I RAN AS FAST AS I COULD.
FLIP!

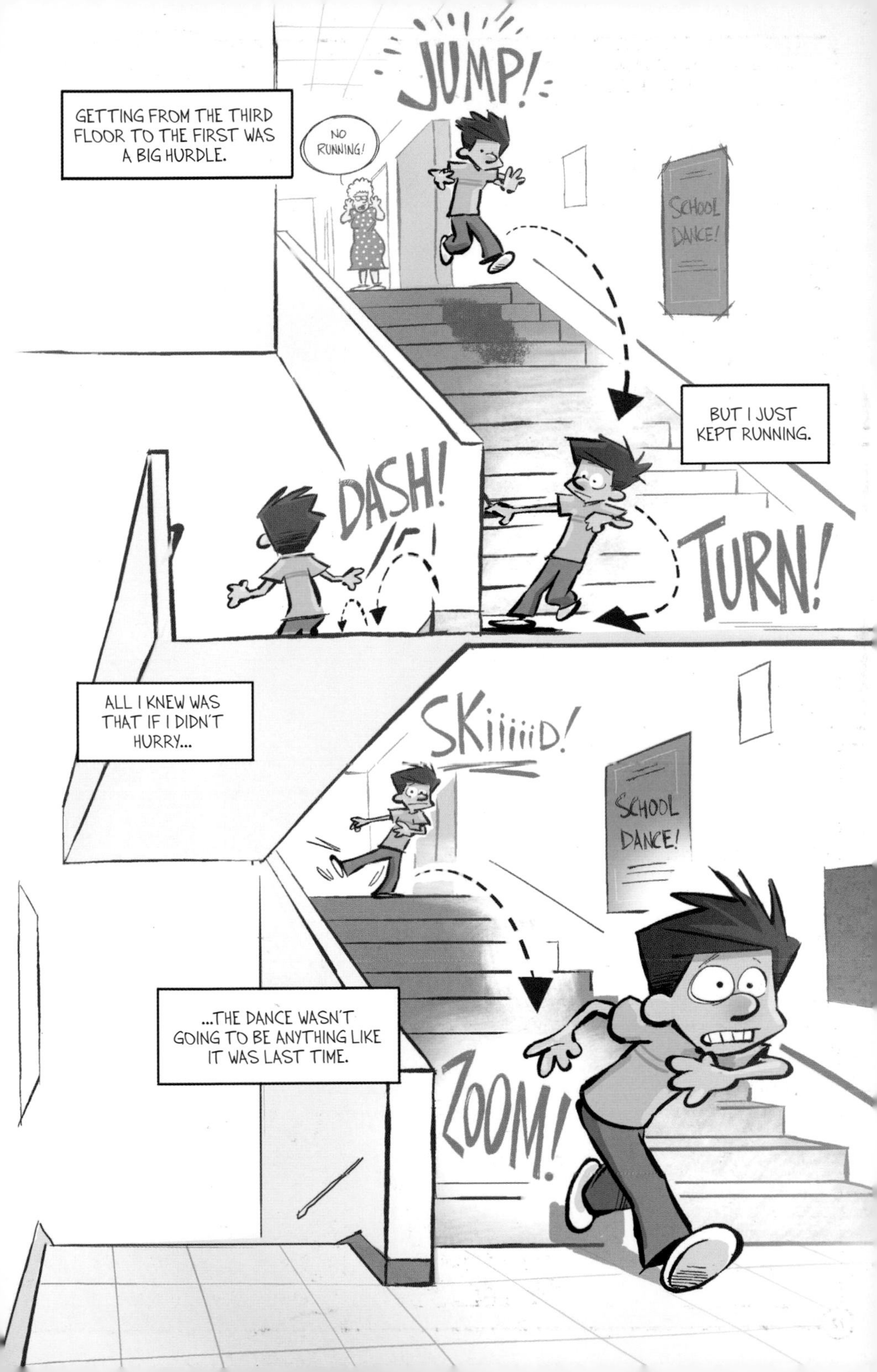
GETTING FROM THE THIRD FLOOR TO THE FIRST WAS A BIG HURDLE.
NO RUNNING!
JUMP!
SCHOOL DANCE!
BUT I JUST KEPT RUNNING.
DASH!
TURN!
ALL I KNEW WAS THAT IF I DIDN'T HURRY...
SKiiiiiD!
SCHOOL DANCE!
...THE DANCE WASN'T GOING TO BE ANYTHING LIKE IT WAS LAST TIME.
ZOOM!

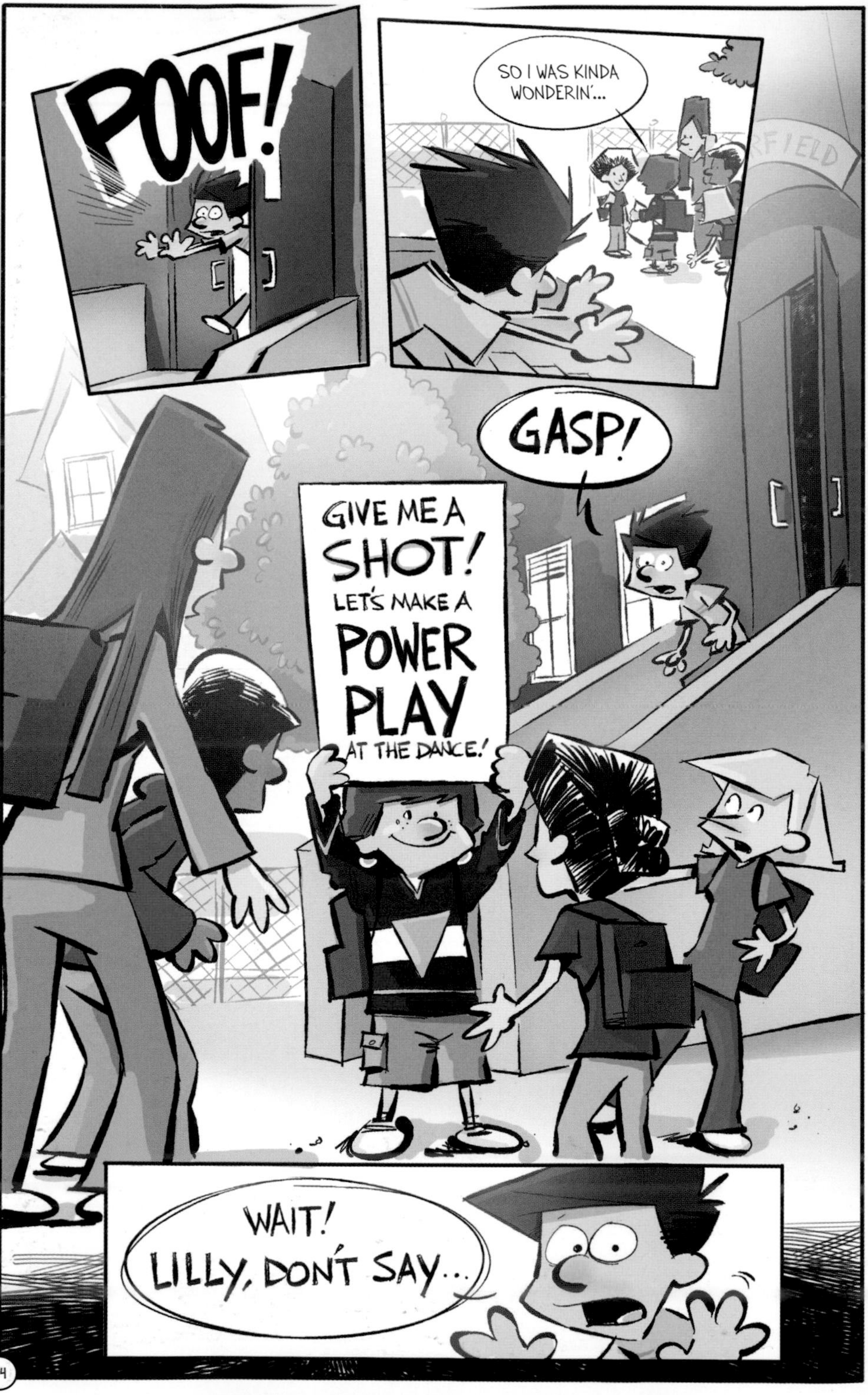
POOF!
SO I WAS KINDA WONDERIN'...
RFIELD
GASP!
GIVE ME A SHOT! LET'S MAKE A POWER PLAY AT THE DANCE!
WAIT! LILLY, DON'T SAY...

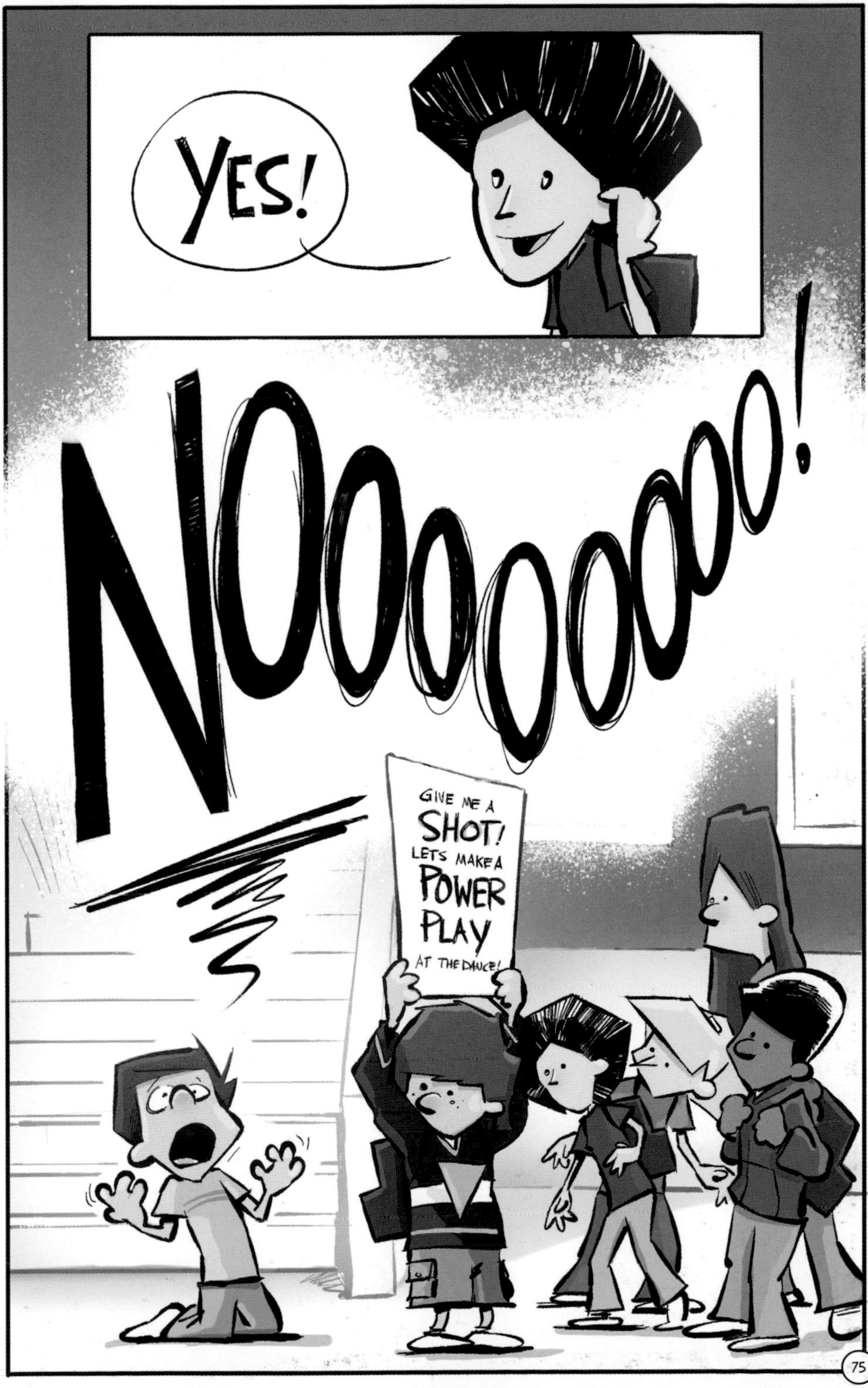
YES!
NOOOOOOOOO!
GIVE ME A SHOT! LETS MAKE A POWER PLAY AT THE DANCE!

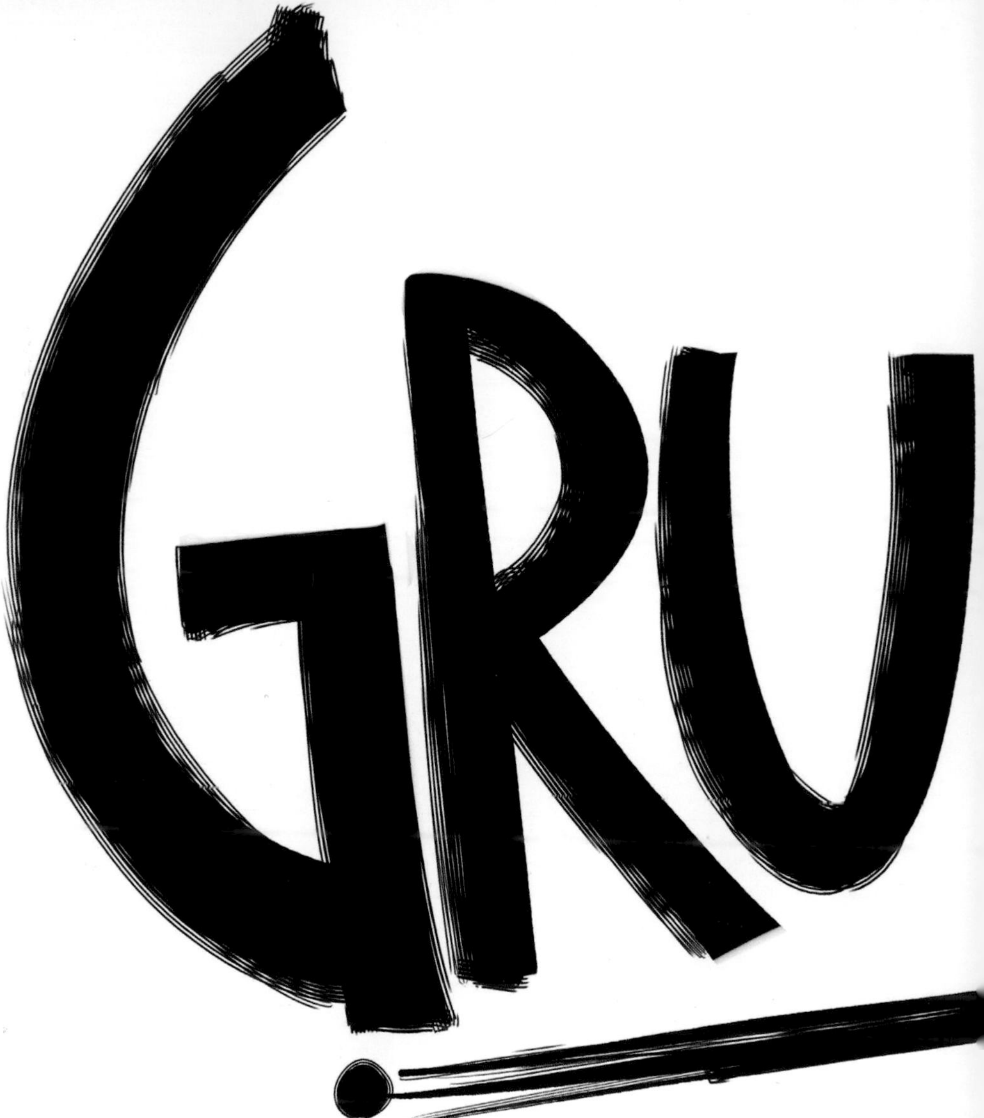
GRU

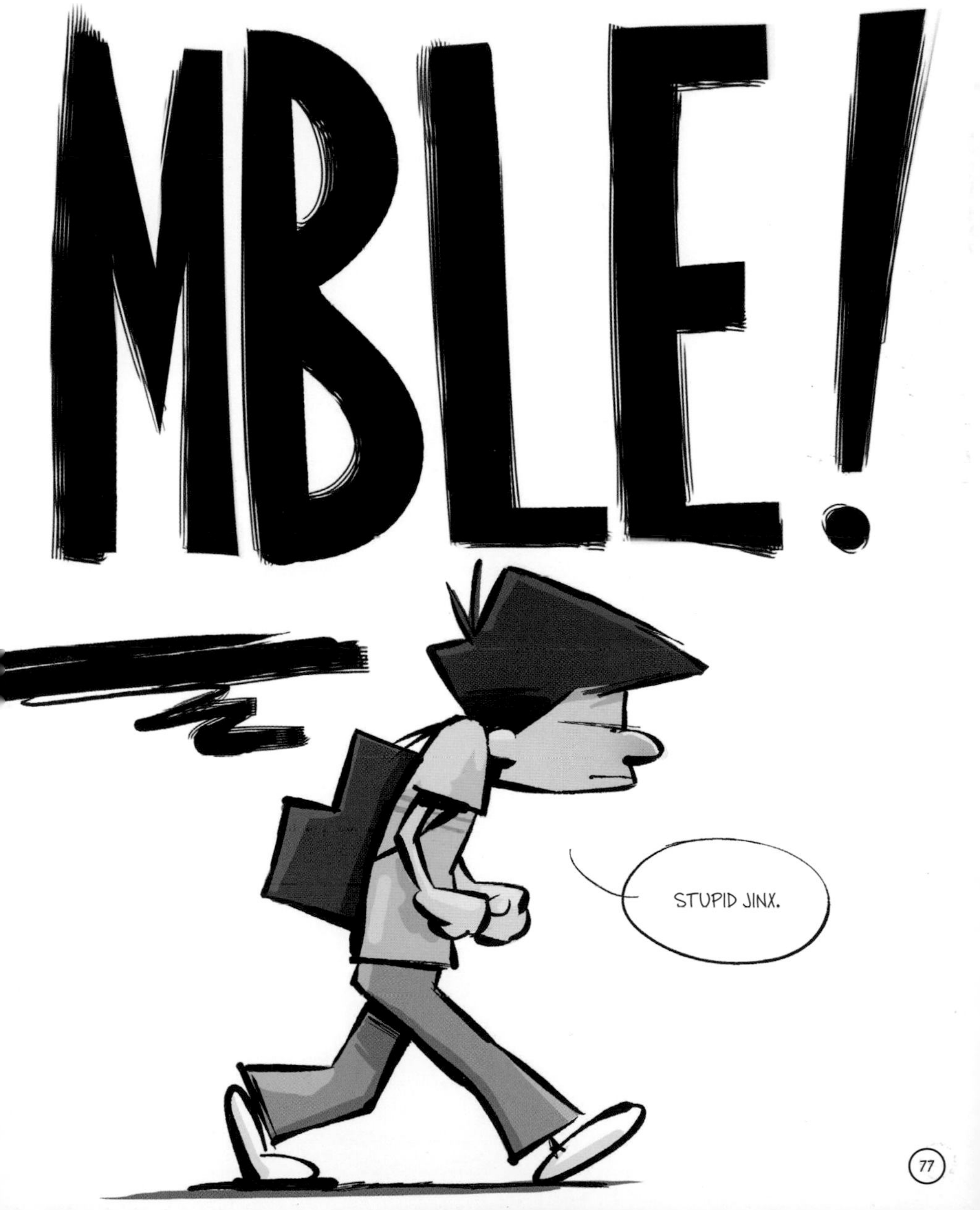
MBLE!
STUPID JINX.

CHAPTER FIVE
THE JINX BREAKER

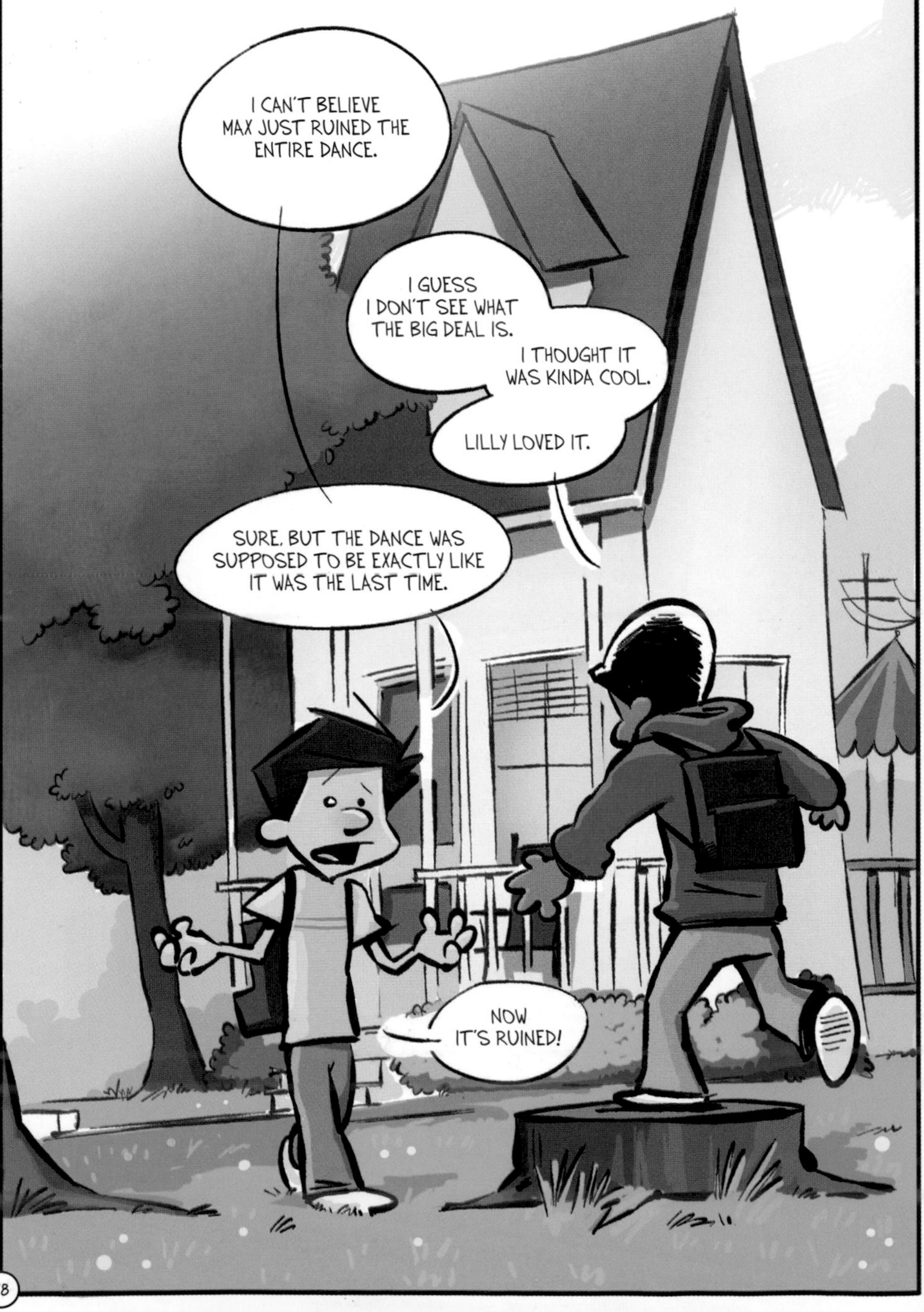
I CAN'T BELIEVE MAX JUST RUINED THE ENTIRE DANCE.
I GUESS I DON'T SEE WHAT THE BIG DEAL IS.
I THOUGHT IT WAS KINDA COOL.
LILLY LOVED IT.
SURE, BUT THE DANCE WAS SUPPOSED TO BE EXACTLY LIKE IT WAS THE LAST TIME.
NOW IT'S RUINED!

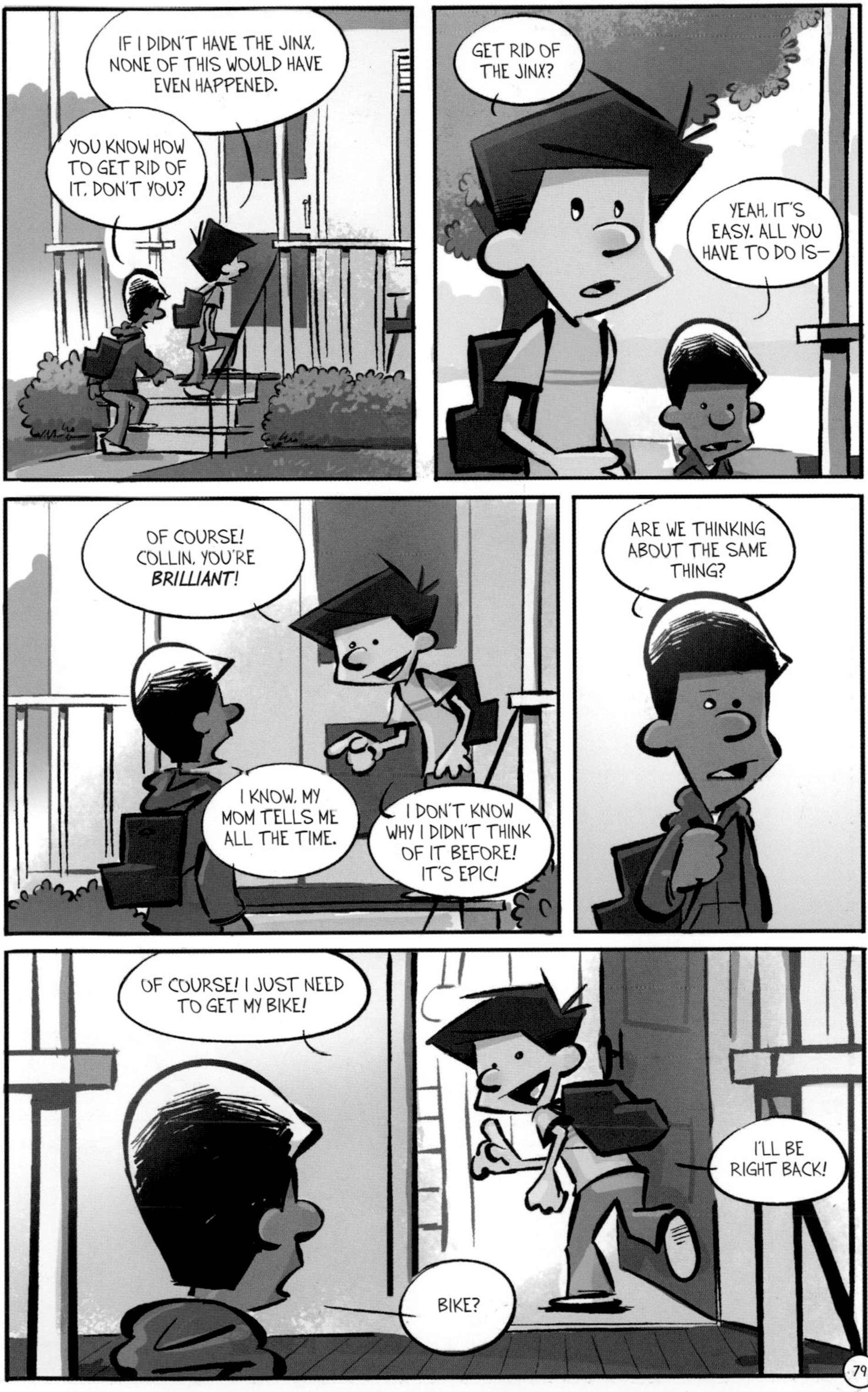

IF I DIDN'T HAVE THE JINX, NONE OF THIS WOULD HAVE EVEN HAPPENED.
YOU KNOW HOW TO GET RID OF IT, DON'T YOU?
GET RID OF THE JINX?
YEAH, IT'S EASY. ALL YOU HAVE TO DO IS—
OF COURSE! COLLIN, YOU'RE *BRILLIANT*!
I KNOW, MY MOM TELLS ME ALL THE TIME.
I DON'T KNOW WHY I DIDN'T THINK OF IT BEFORE! IT'S EPIC!
ARE WE THINKING ABOUT THE SAME THING?
OF COURSE! I JUST NEED TO GET MY BIKE!
I'LL BE RIGHT BACK!
BIKE?

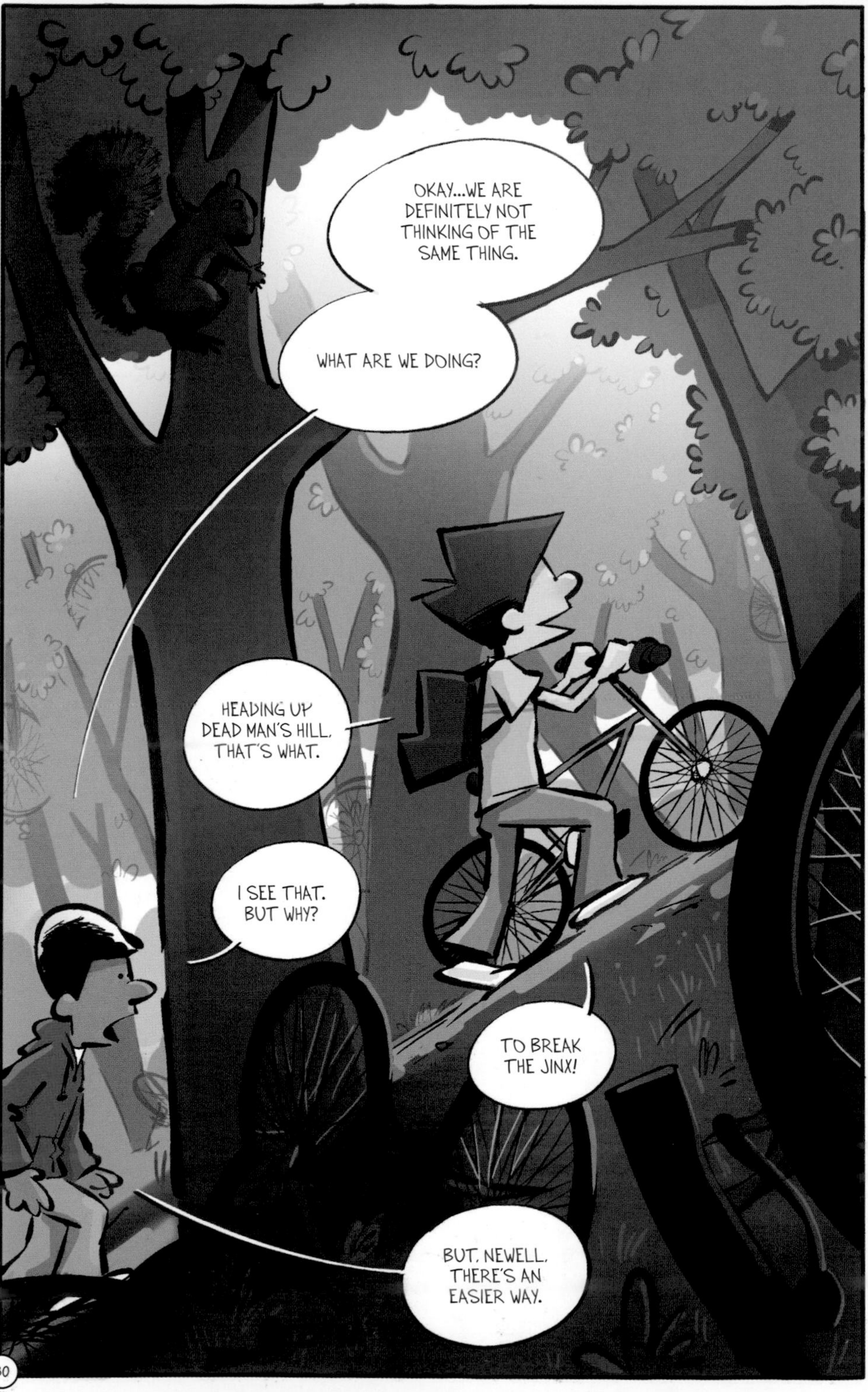
OKAY...WE ARE DEFINITELY NOT THINKING OF THE SAME THING.
WHAT ARE WE DOING?
HEADING UP DEAD MAN'S HILL, THAT'S WHAT.
I SEE THAT. BUT WHY?
TO BREAK THE JINX!
BUT, NEWELL, THERE'S AN EASIER WAY.

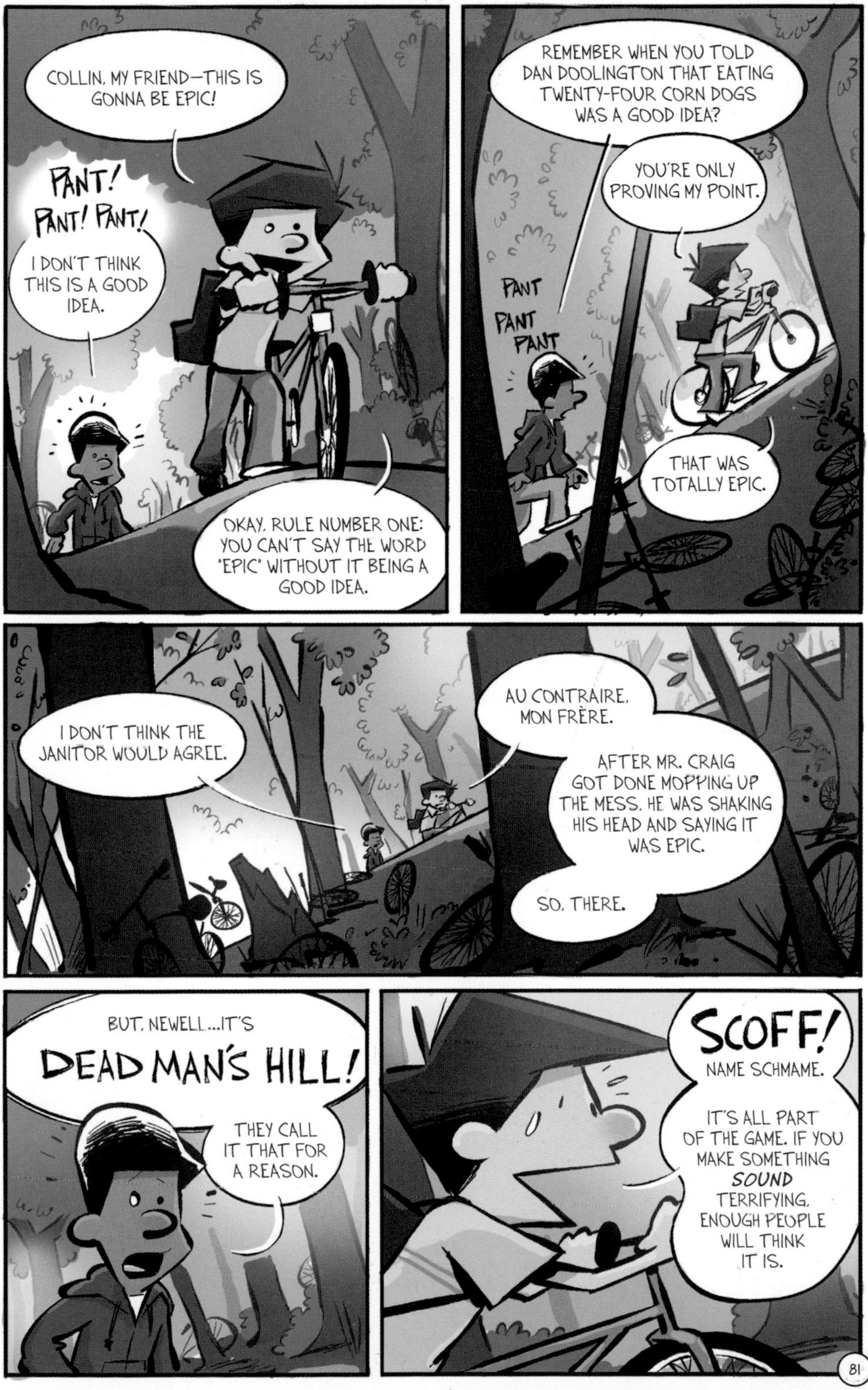

COLLIN, MY FRIEND—THIS IS GONNA BE EPIC!
PANT! PANT! PANT!
I DON'T THINK THIS IS A GOOD IDEA.
OKAY, RULE NUMBER ONE: YOU CAN'T SAY THE WORD "EPIC" WITHOUT IT BEING A GOOD IDEA.
REMEMBER WHEN YOU TOLD DAN DOOLINGTON THAT EATING TWENTY-FOUR CORN DOGS WAS A GOOD IDEA?
YOU'RE ONLY PROVING MY POINT.
PANT PANT PANT
THAT WAS TOTALLY EPIC.
I DON'T THINK THE JANITOR WOULD AGREE.
AU CONTRAIRE, MON FRÈRE.
AFTER MR. CRAIG GOT DONE MOPPING UP THE MESS, HE WAS SHAKING HIS HEAD AND SAYING IT WAS EPIC.
SO, THERE.
BUT, NEWELL...IT'S DEAD MAN'S HILL!
THEY CALL IT THAT FOR A REASON.
SCOFF! NAME SCHMAME.
IT'S ALL PART OF THE GAME. IF YOU MAKE SOMETHING *SOUND* TERRIFYING, ENOUGH PEOPLE WILL THINK IT IS.

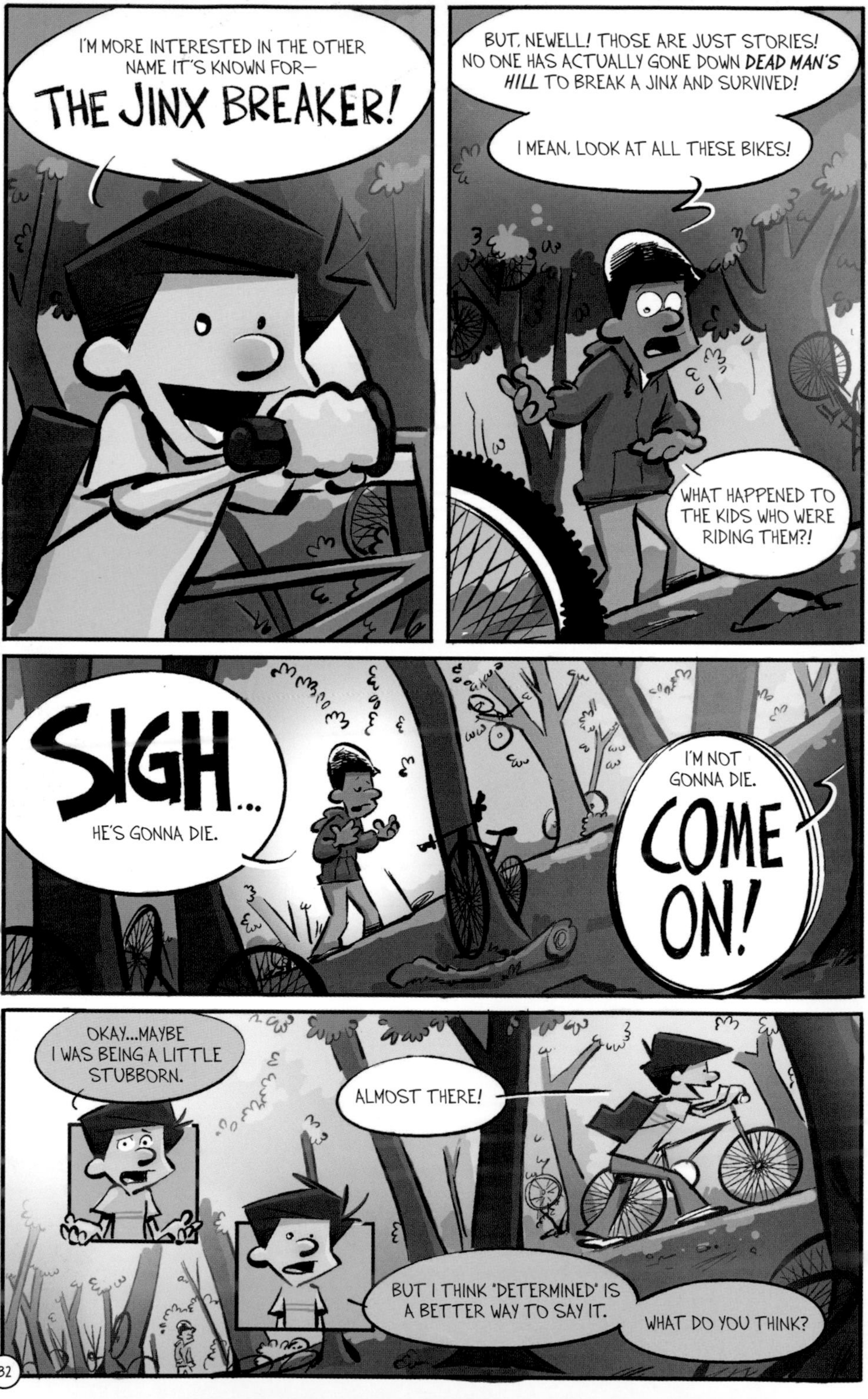
I'M MORE INTERESTED IN THE OTHER NAME IT'S KNOWN FOR—
THE JINX BREAKER!
BUT, NEWELL! THOSE ARE JUST STORIES! NO ONE HAS ACTUALLY GONE DOWN DEAD MAN'S HILL TO BREAK A JINX AND SURVIVED!
I MEAN, LOOK AT ALL THESE BIKES!
WHAT HAPPENED TO THE KIDS WHO WERE RIDING THEM?!
SIGH...
HE'S GONNA DIE.
I'M NOT GONNA DIE.
COME ON!
OKAY...MAYBE I WAS BEING A LITTLE STUBBORN.
ALMOST THERE!
BUT I THINK "DETERMINED" IS A BETTER WAY TO SAY IT.
WHAT DO YOU THINK?

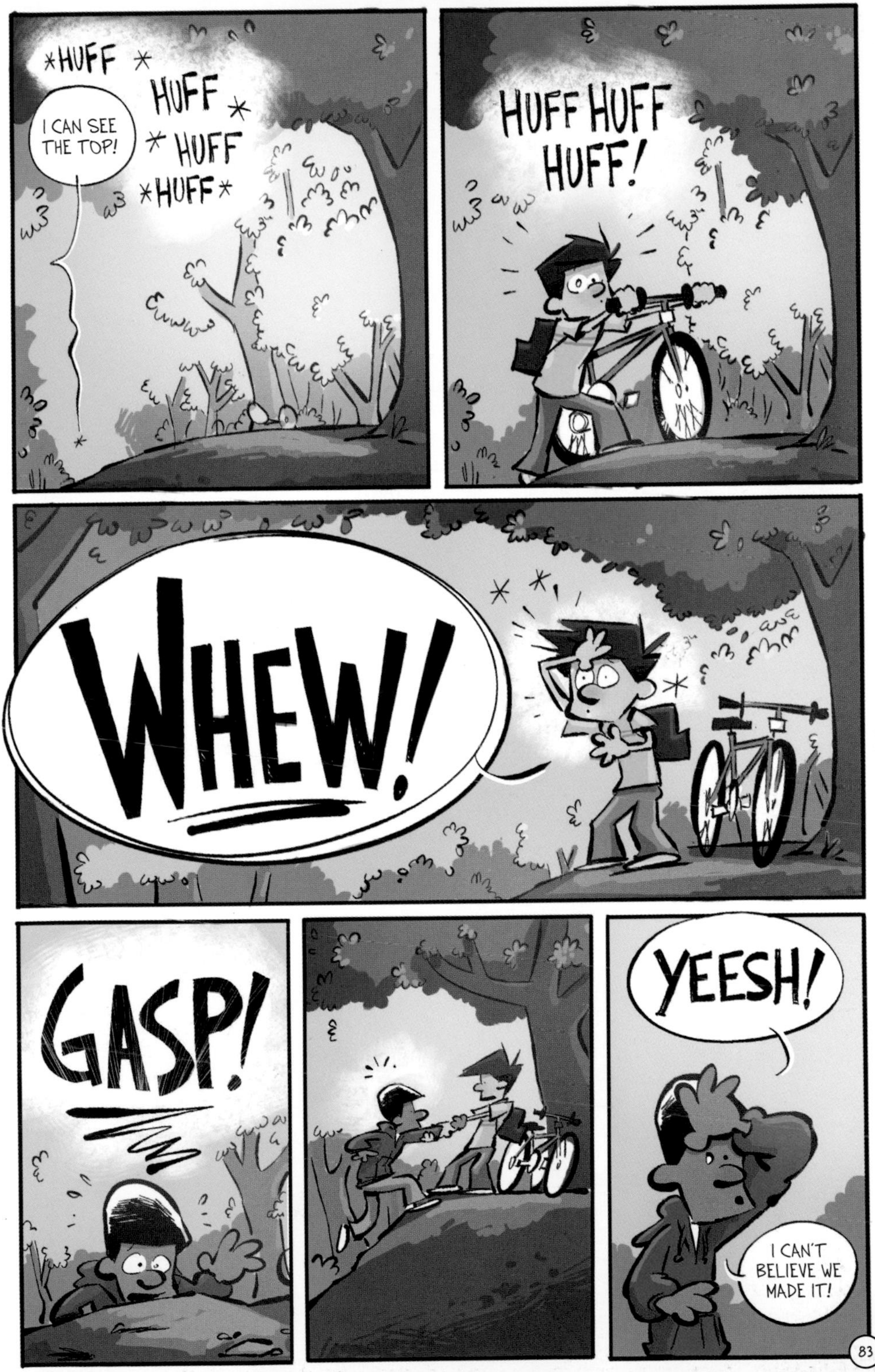
*HUFF * HUFF * *HUFF *HUFF*
I CAN SEE THE TOP!
HUFF HUFF HUFF!
WHEW!
GASP!
YEESH!
I CAN'T BELIEVE WE MADE IT!

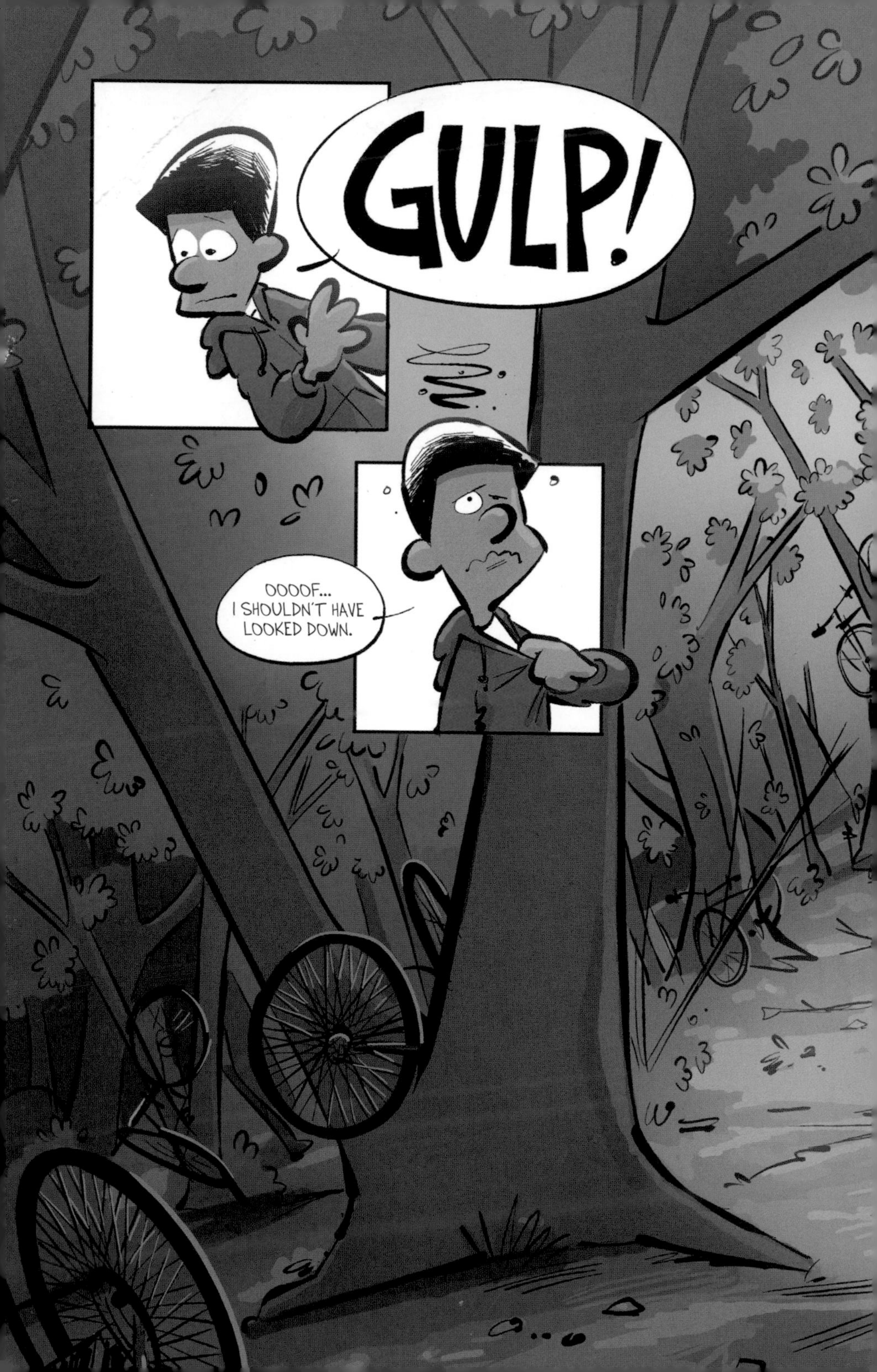
GULP!
OOOOF... I SHOULDN'T HAVE LOOKED DOWN.

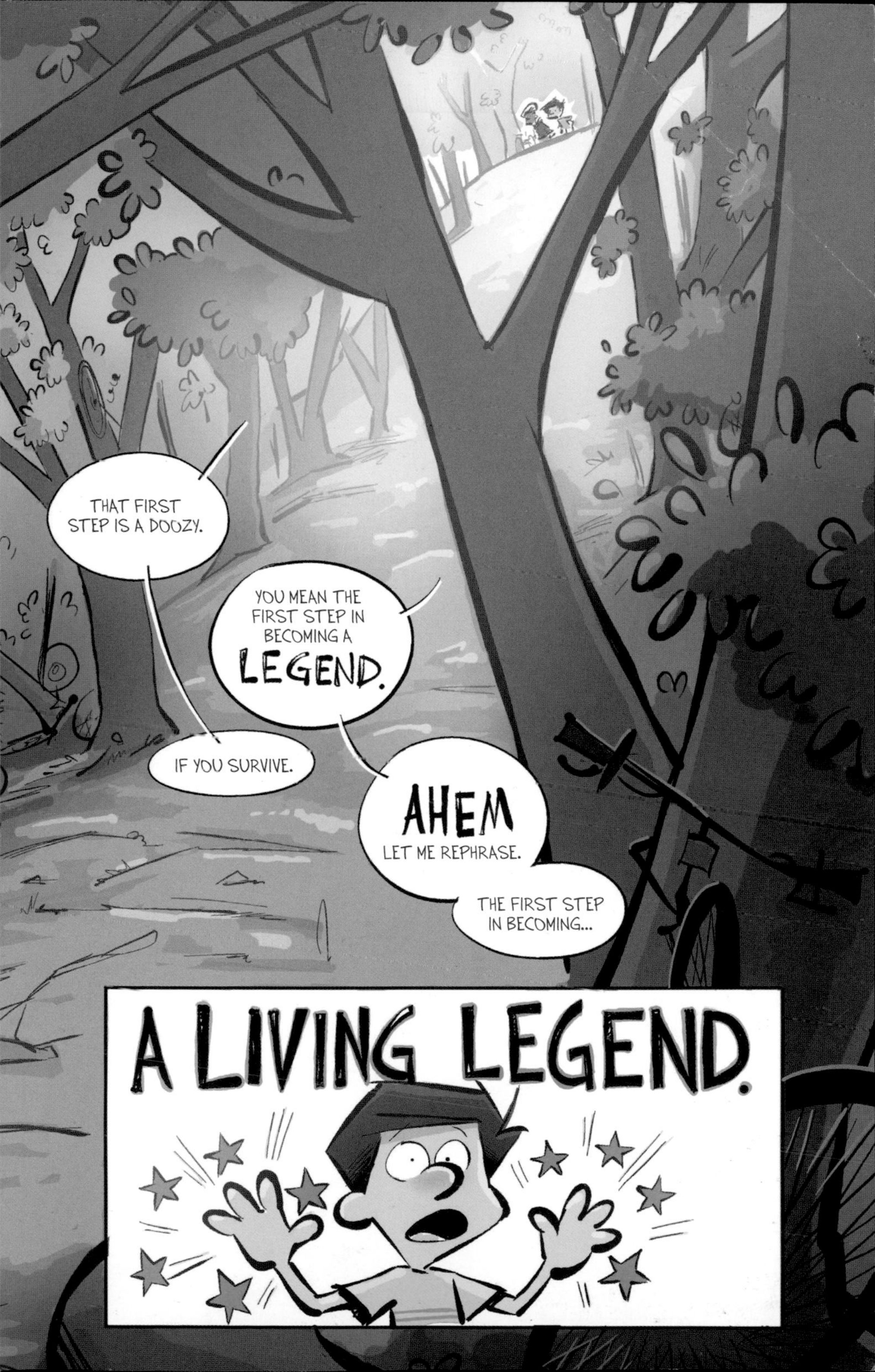
THAT FIRST STEP IS A DOOZY.
YOU MEAN THE FIRST STEP IN BECOMING A LEGEND.
IF YOU SURVIVE.
AHEM
LET ME REPHRASE.
THE FIRST STEP IN BECOMING...
A LIVING LEGEND.

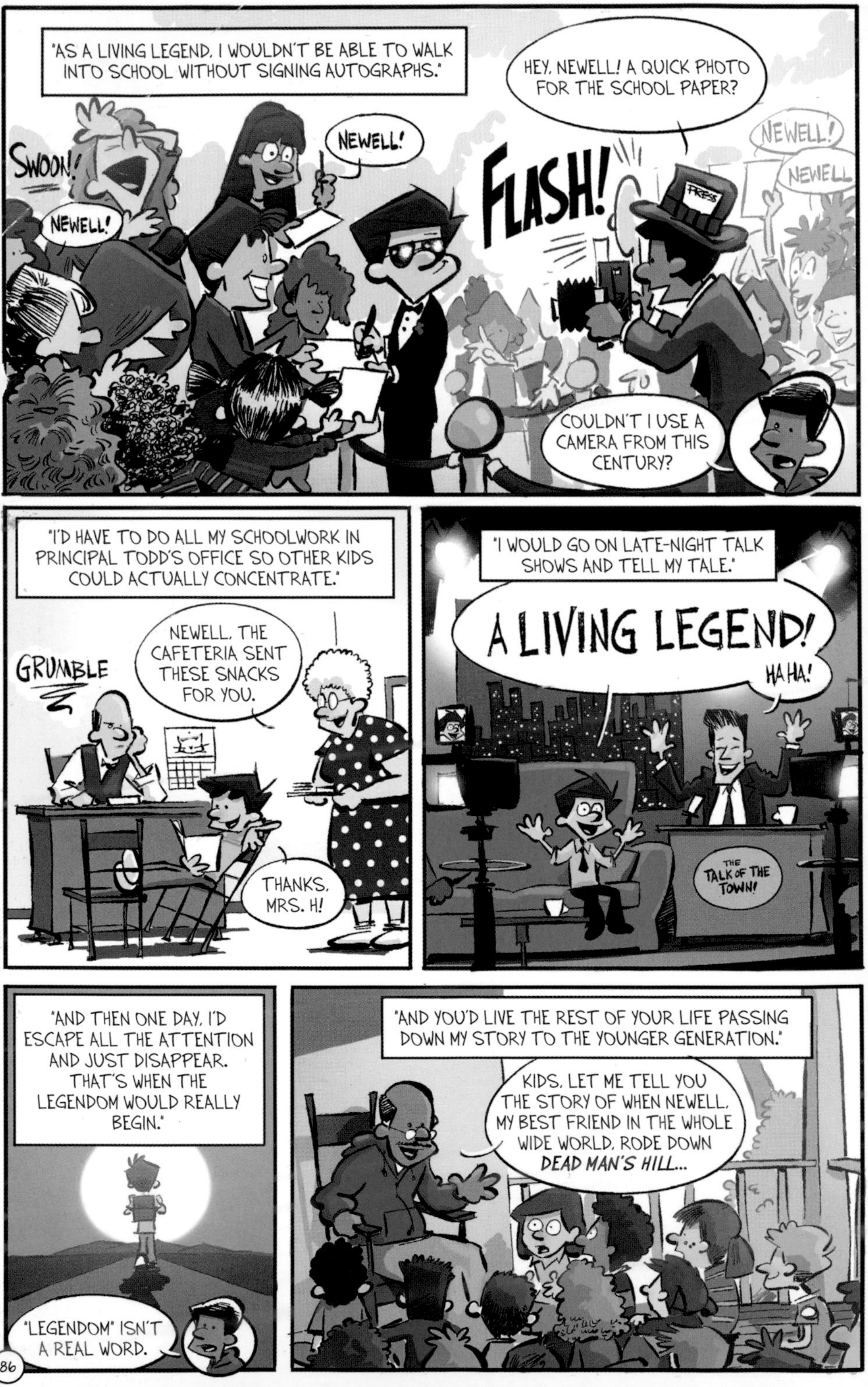
"AS A LIVING LEGEND, I WOULDN'T BE ABLE TO WALK INTO SCHOOL WITHOUT SIGNING AUTOGRAPHS."
SWOON!
NEWELL!
NEWELL!
FLASH!
HEY, NEWELL! A QUICK PHOTO FOR THE SCHOOL PAPER?
NEWELL!
NEWELL
PRESS
COULDN'T I USE A CAMERA FROM THIS CENTURY?
"I'D HAVE TO DO ALL MY SCHOOLWORK IN PRINCIPAL TODD'S OFFICE SO OTHER KIDS COULD ACTUALLY CONCENTRATE."
GRUMBLE
NEWELL, THE CAFETERIA SENT THESE SNACKS FOR YOU.
THANKS, MRS. H!
"I WOULD GO ON LATE-NIGHT TALK SHOWS AND TELL MY TALE."
A LIVING LEGEND!
HA HA!
THE TALK OF THE TOWN!
"AND THEN ONE DAY, I'D ESCAPE ALL THE ATTENTION AND JUST DISAPPEAR. THAT'S WHEN THE LEGENDOM WOULD REALLY BEGIN."
"LEGENDOM" ISN'T A REAL WORD.
"AND YOU'D LIVE THE REST OF YOUR LIFE PASSING DOWN MY STORY TO THE YOUNGER GENERATION."
KIDS, LET ME TELL YOU THE STORY OF WHEN NEWELL, MY BEST FRIEND IN THE WHOLE WIDE WORLD, RODE DOWN DEAD MAN'S HILL...

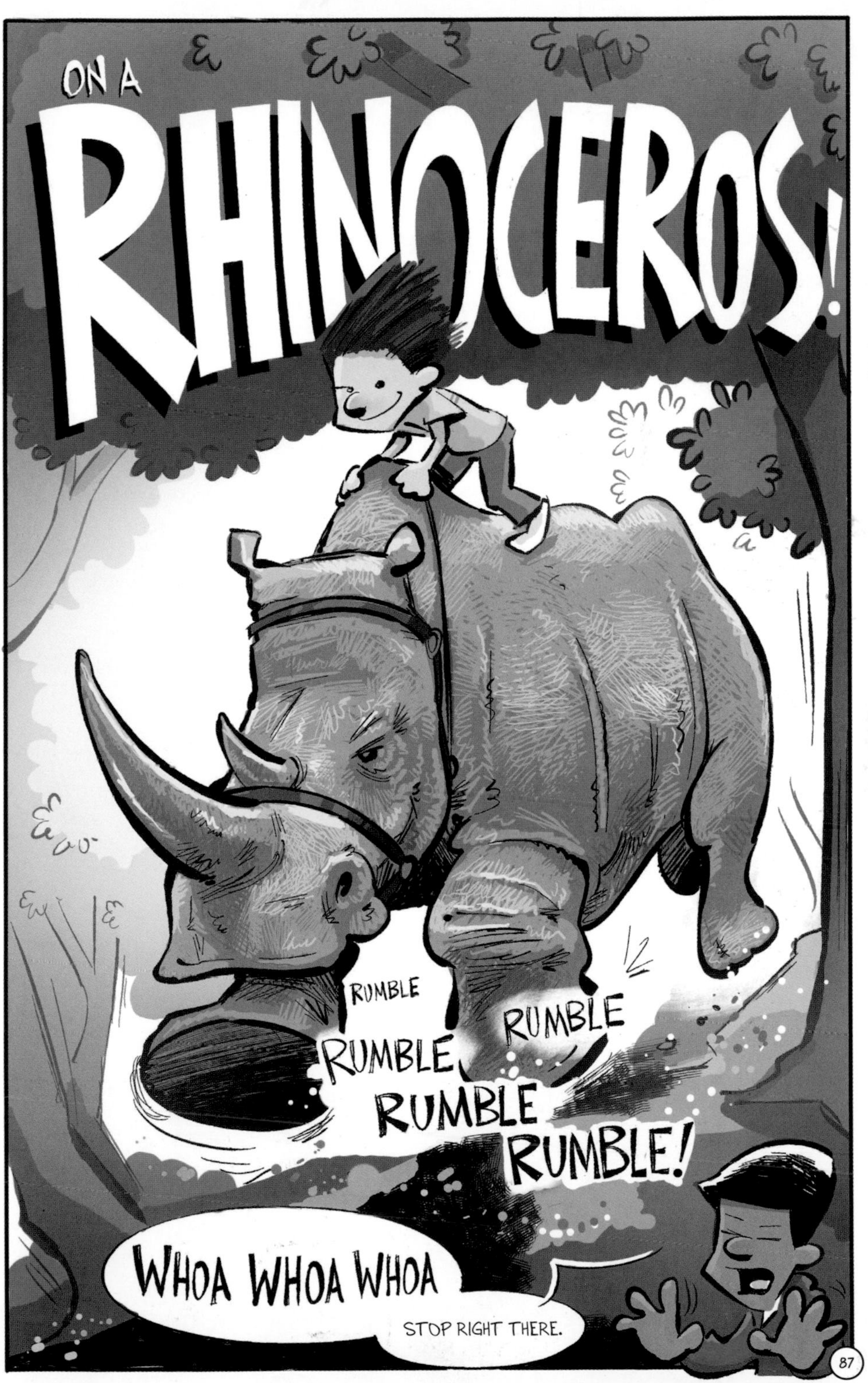
ON A
RHINOCEROS!
RUMBLE
RUMBLE
RUMBLE
RUMBLE
RUMBLE!
WHOA WHOA WHOA
STOP RIGHT THERE.

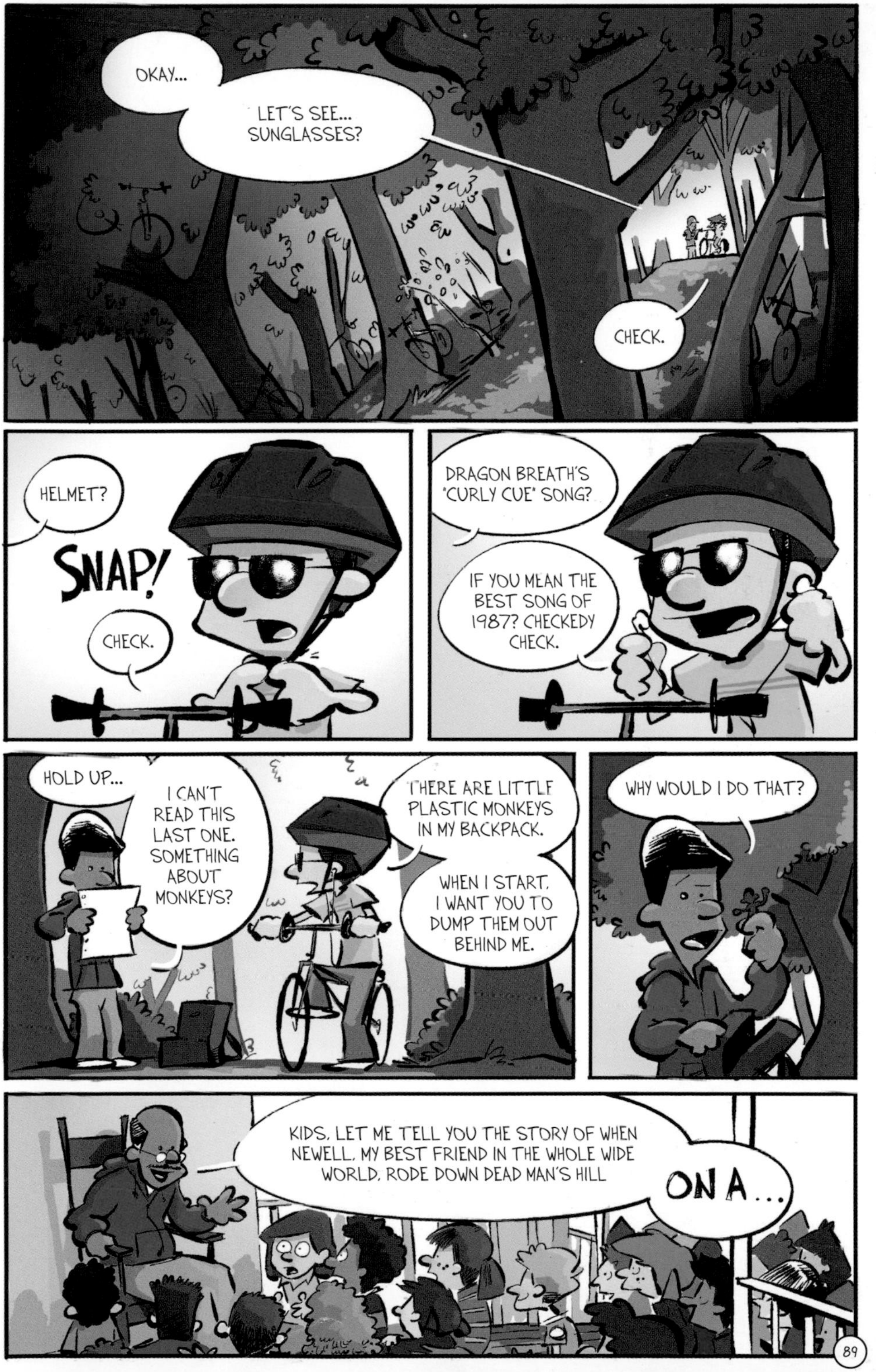
OKAY...
LET'S SEE... SUNGLASSES?
CHECK.
HELMET?
SNAP!
CHECK.
DRAGON BREATH'S "CURLY CUE" SONG?
IF YOU MEAN THE BEST SONG OF 1987? CHECKEDY CHECK.
HOLD UP...
I CAN'T READ THIS LAST ONE. SOMETHING ABOUT MONKEYS?
THERE ARE LITTLE PLASTIC MONKEYS IN MY BACKPACK.
WHEN I START, I WANT YOU TO DUMP THEM OUT BEHIND ME.
WHY WOULD I DO THAT?
KIDS, LET ME TELL YOU THE STORY OF WHEN NEWELL, MY BEST FRIEND IN THE WHOLE WIDE WORLD, RODE DOWN DEAD MAN'S HILL
ON A...

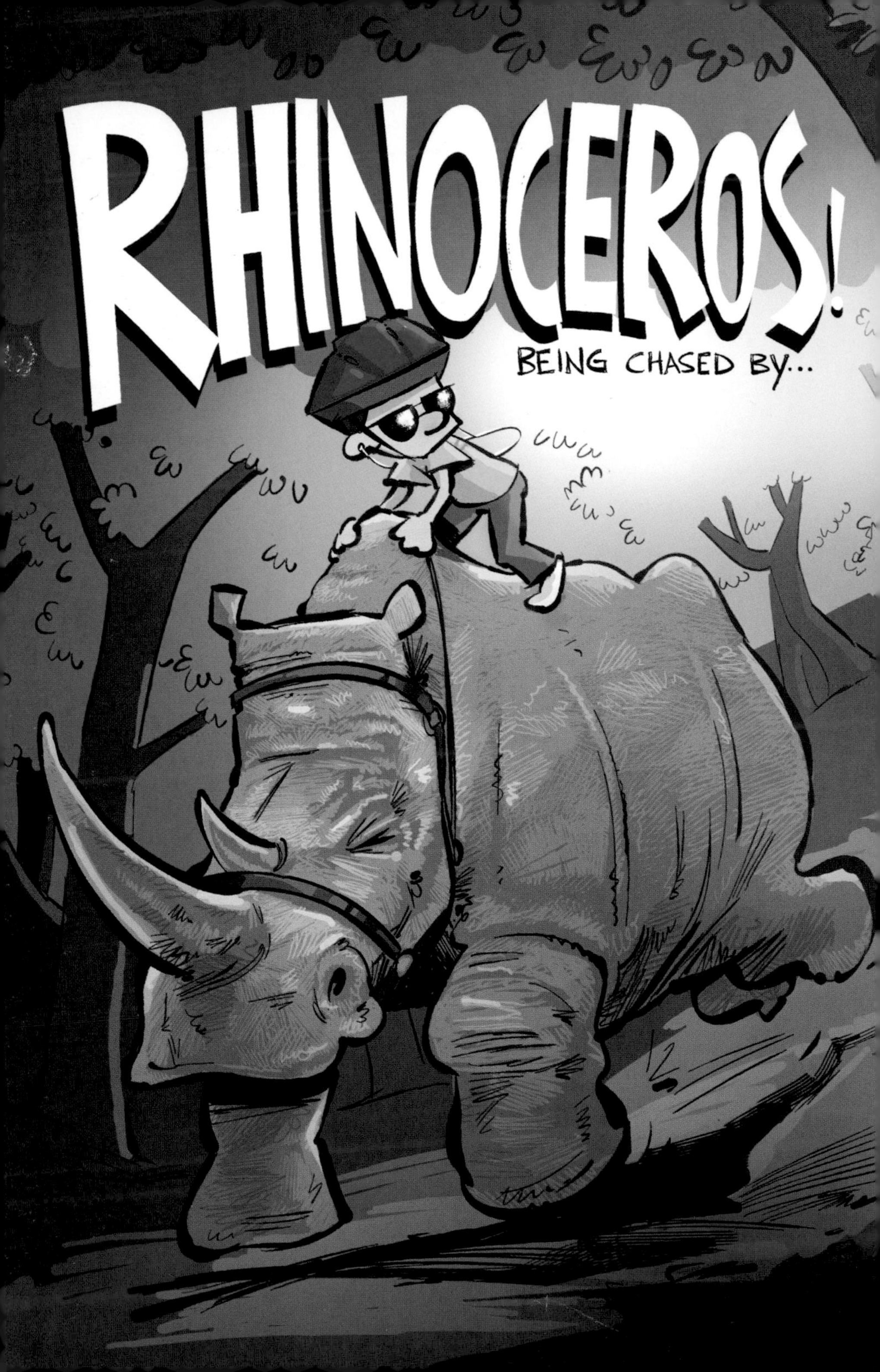
RHINOCEROS!
BEING CHASED BY...

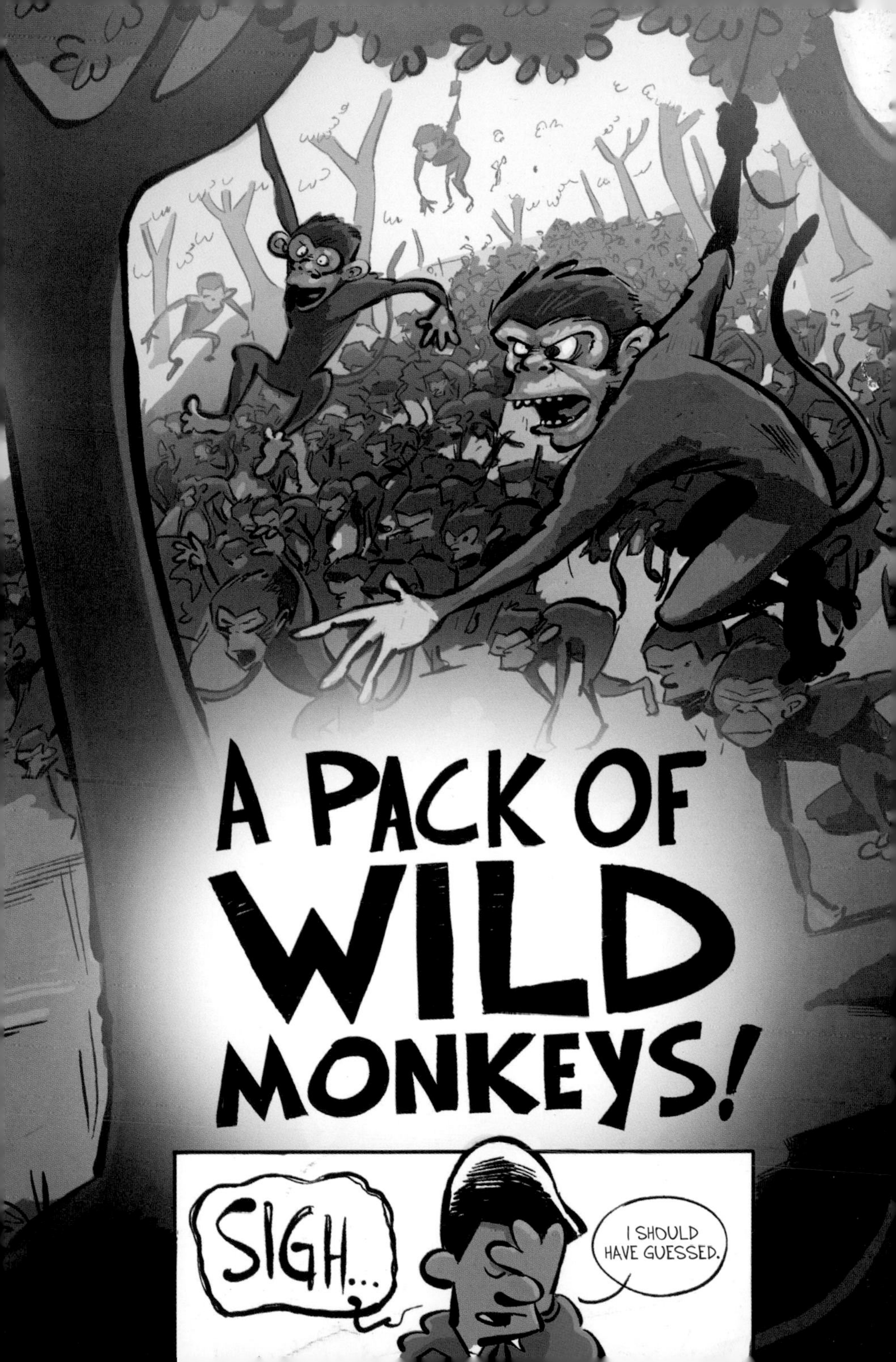
A PACK OF
WILD
MONKEYS!
SIGH...
I SHOULD HAVE GUESSED.

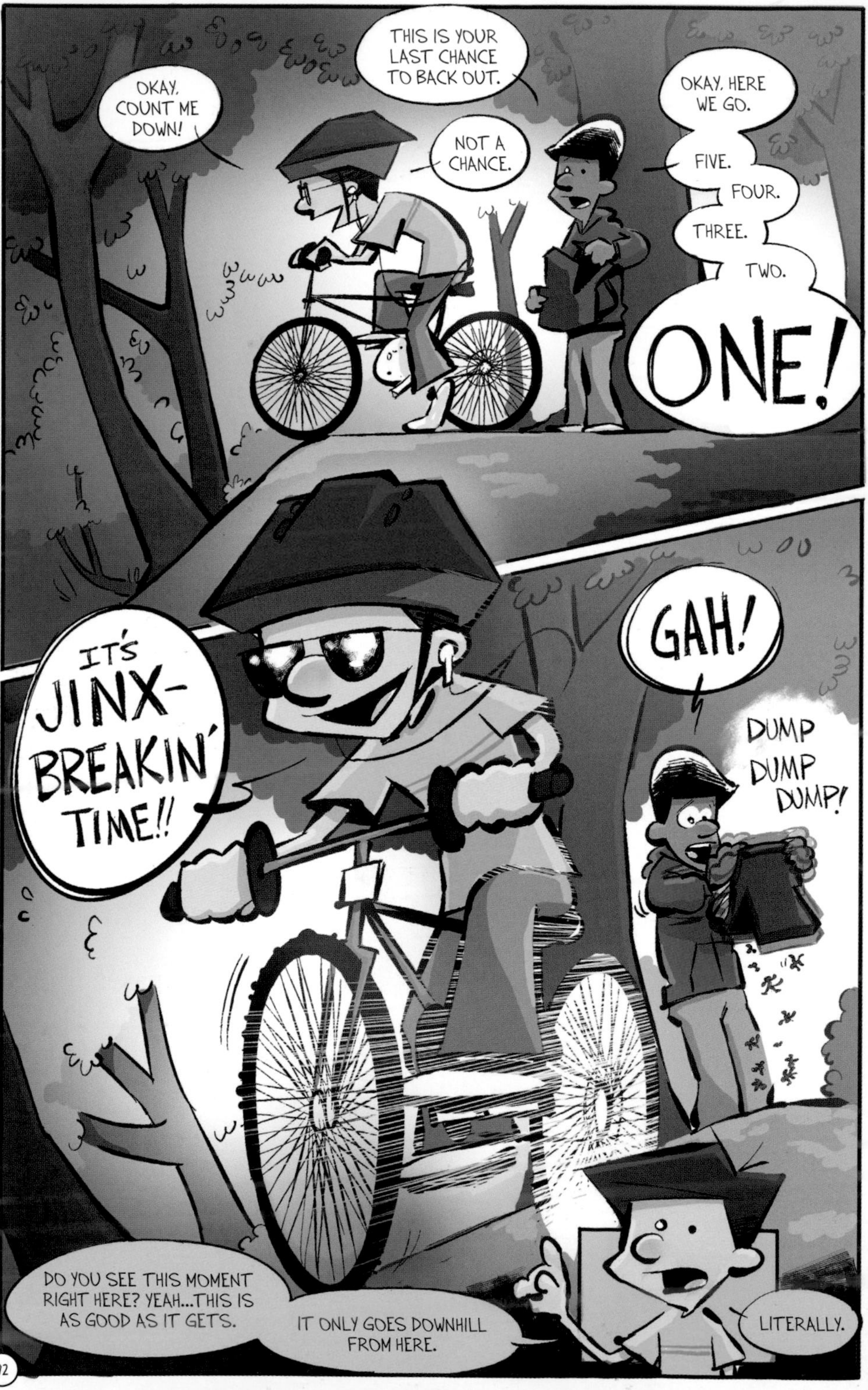
OKAY, COUNT ME DOWN!
THIS IS YOUR LAST CHANCE TO BACK OUT.
NOT A CHANCE.
OKAY, HERE WE GO.
FIVE.
FOUR.
THREE.
TWO.
ONE!
IT'S JINX-BREAKIN' TIME!!
GAH!
DUMP DUMP DUMP!
DO YOU SEE THIS MOMENT RIGHT HERE? YEAH...THIS IS AS GOOD AS IT GETS.
IT ONLY GOES DOWNHILL FROM HERE.
LITERALLY.

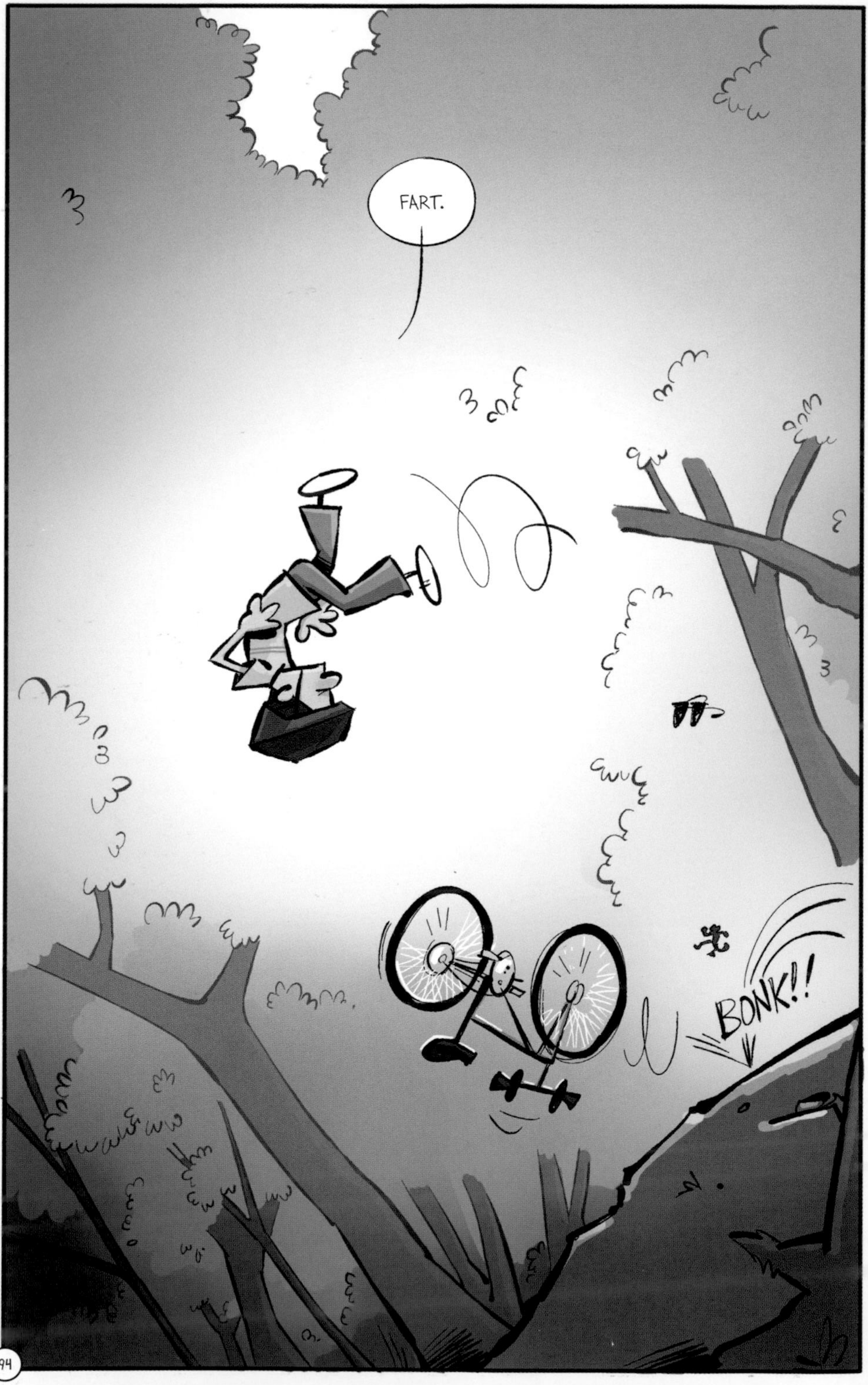
FART.
BONK!!

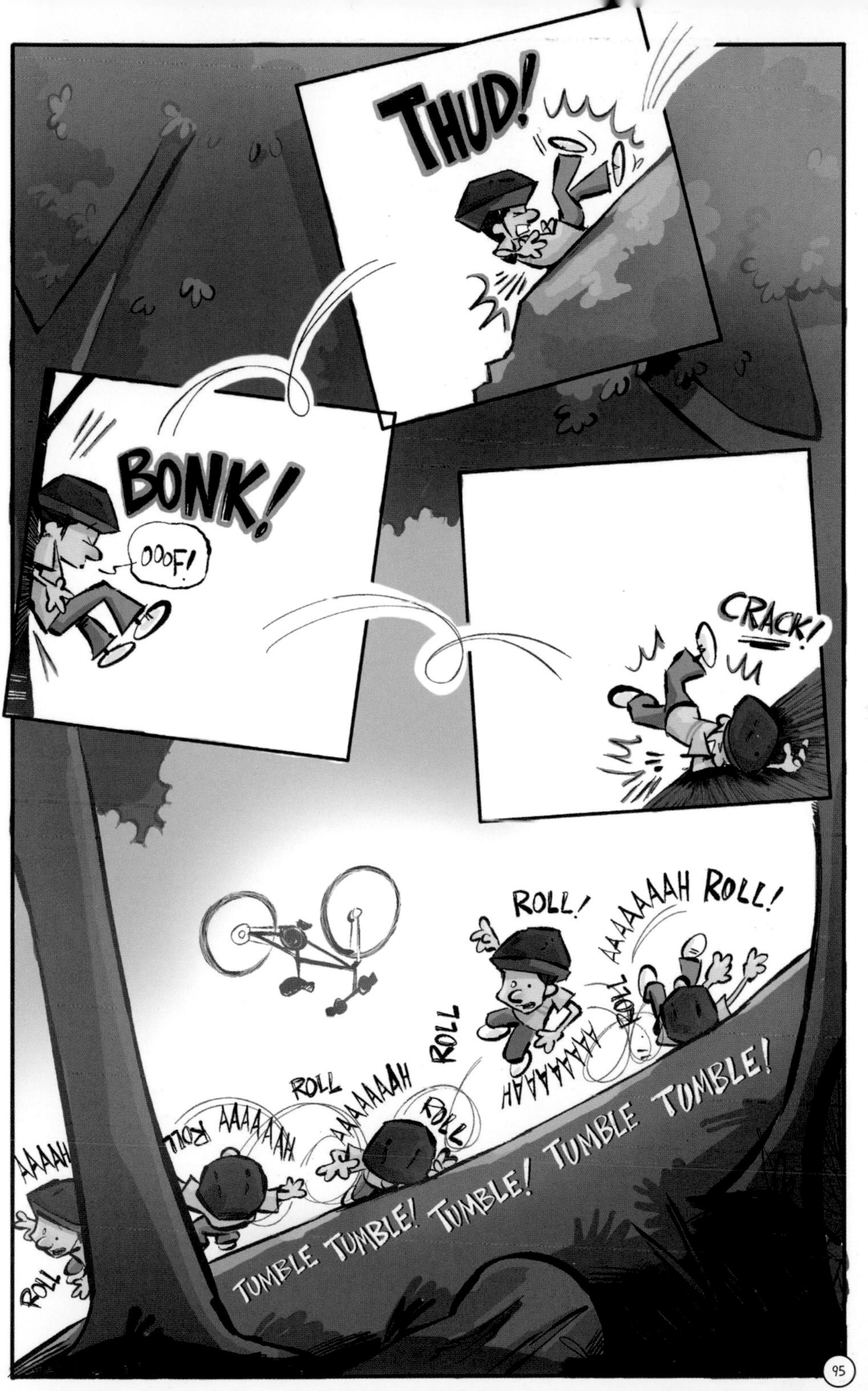
THUD!
BONK!
OOOF!
CRACK!
ROLL!
AAAAAAAH ROLL!
ROLL
AAAAAAAH
ROLL
AAAAAAAH
ROLL
ROLL
AAAAAH
ROLL
AAAAAH
ROLL
TUMBLE TUMBLE! TUMBLE! TUMBLE TUMBLE!

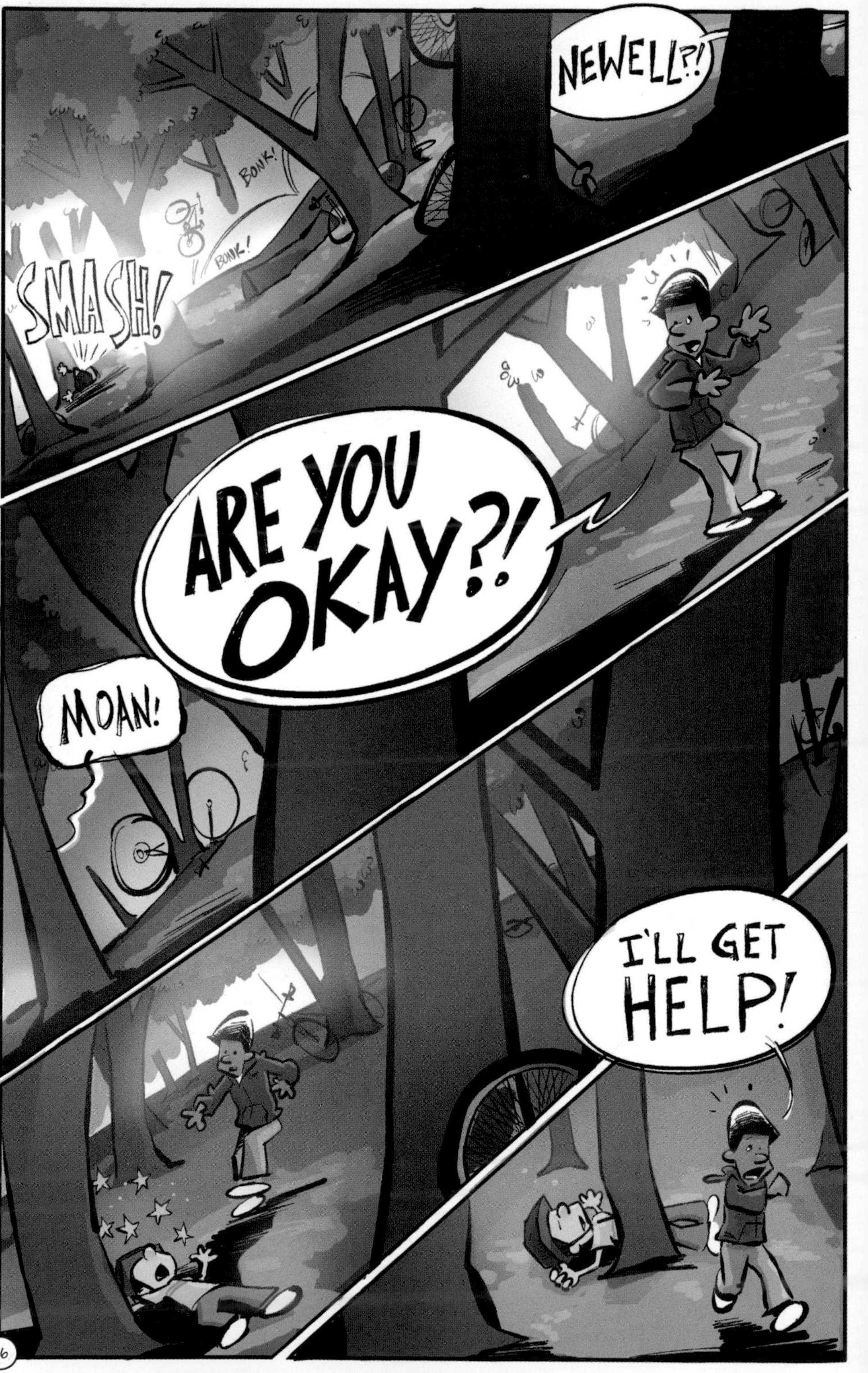
NEWELL?!
BONK!
BONK!
SMASH!
ARE YOU OKAY?!
MOAN!
I'LL GET HELP!

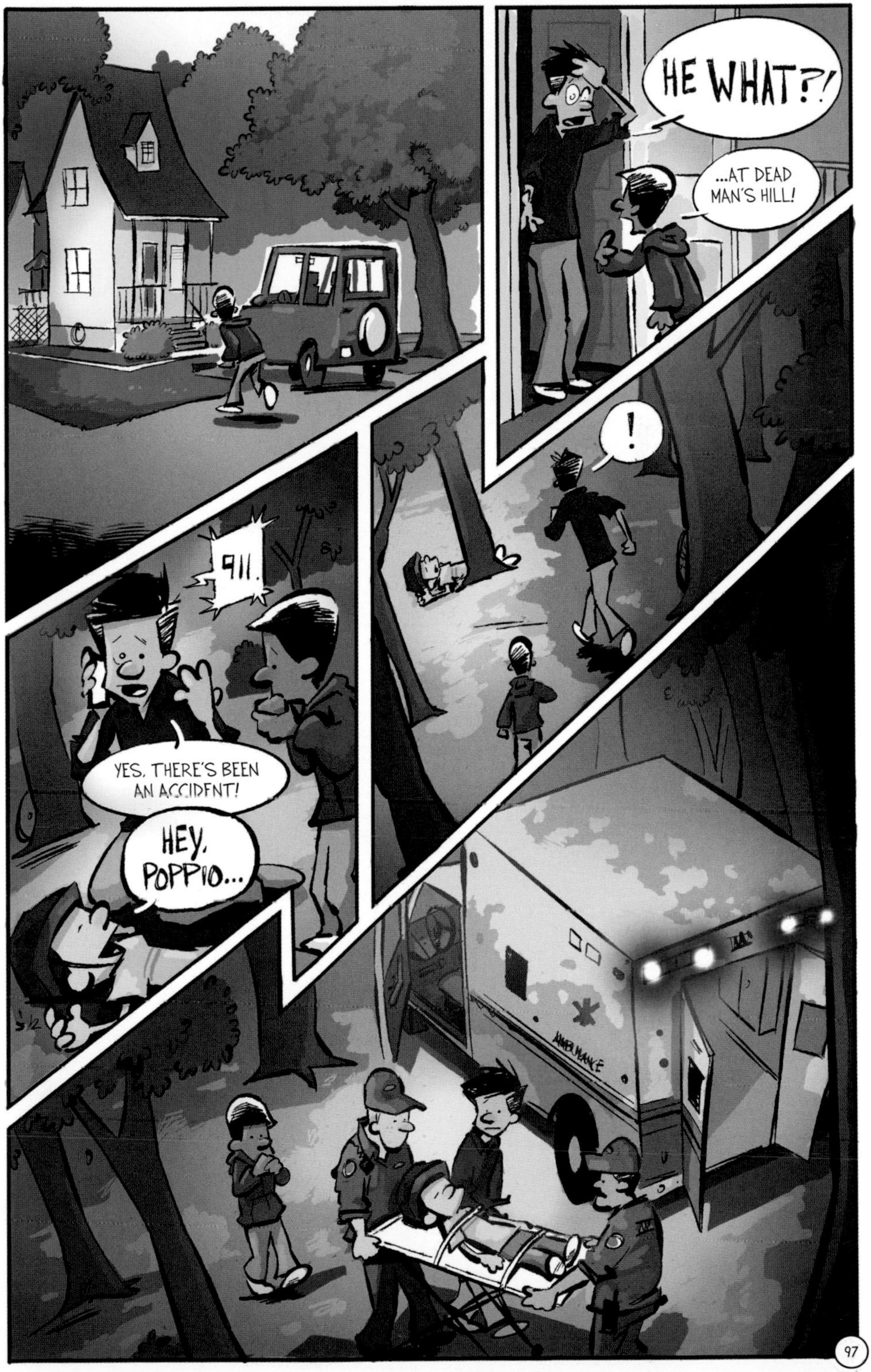
HE WHAT?!
...AT DEAD MAN'S HILL!
!
911.
YES, THERE'S BEEN AN ACCIDENT!
HEY, POPPIO...
AMBULANCE

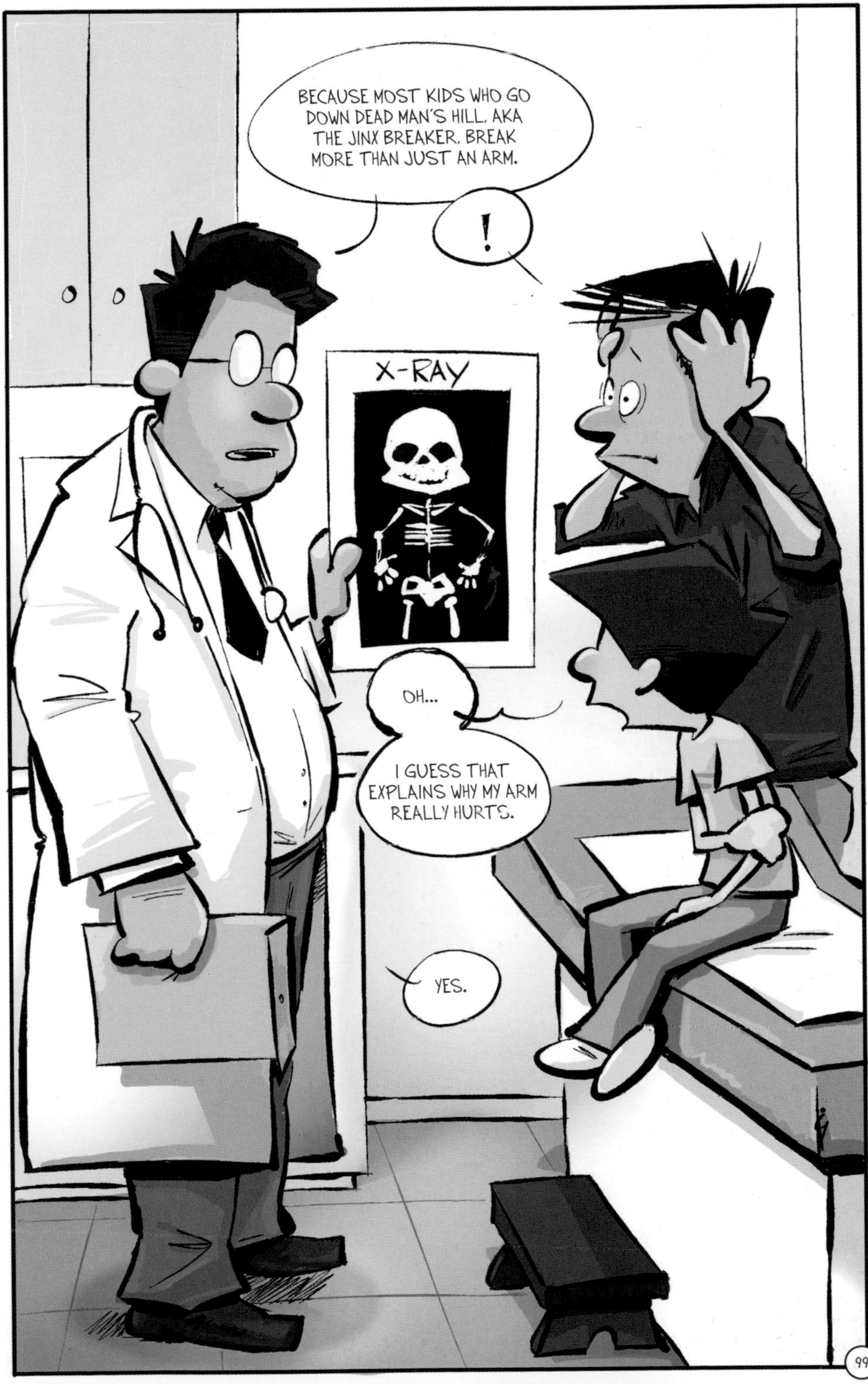
BECAUSE MOST KIDS WHO GO DOWN DEAD MAN'S HILL, AKA THE JINX BREAKER, BREAK MORE THAN JUST AN ARM.
!
X-RAY
OH...
I GUESS THAT EXPLAINS WHY MY ARM REALLY HURTS.
YES.

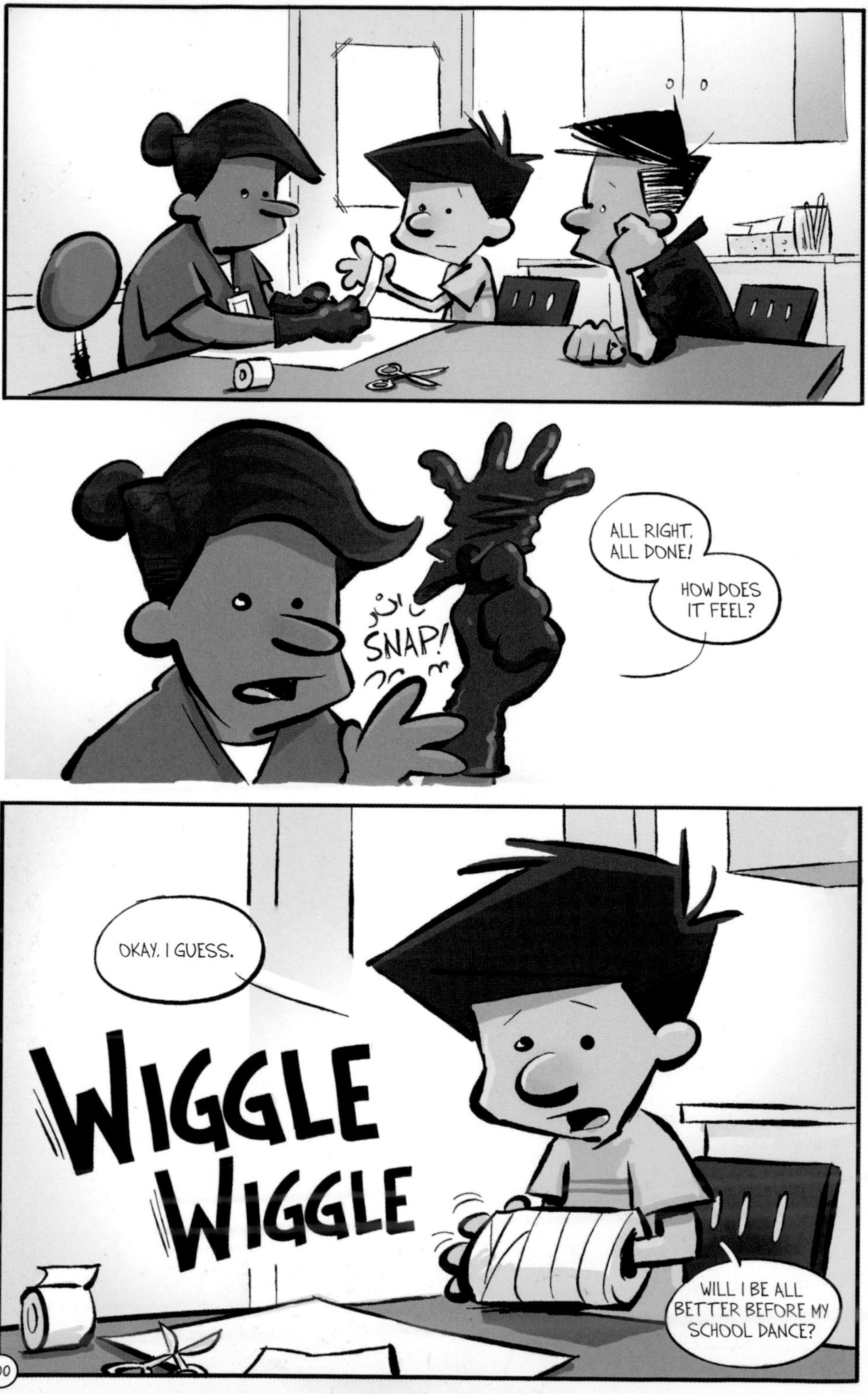
SNAP!
ALL RIGHT, ALL DONE!
HOW DOES IT FEEL?
OKAY, I GUESS.
WIGGLE WIGGLE
WILL I BE ALL BETTER BEFORE MY SCHOOL DANCE?

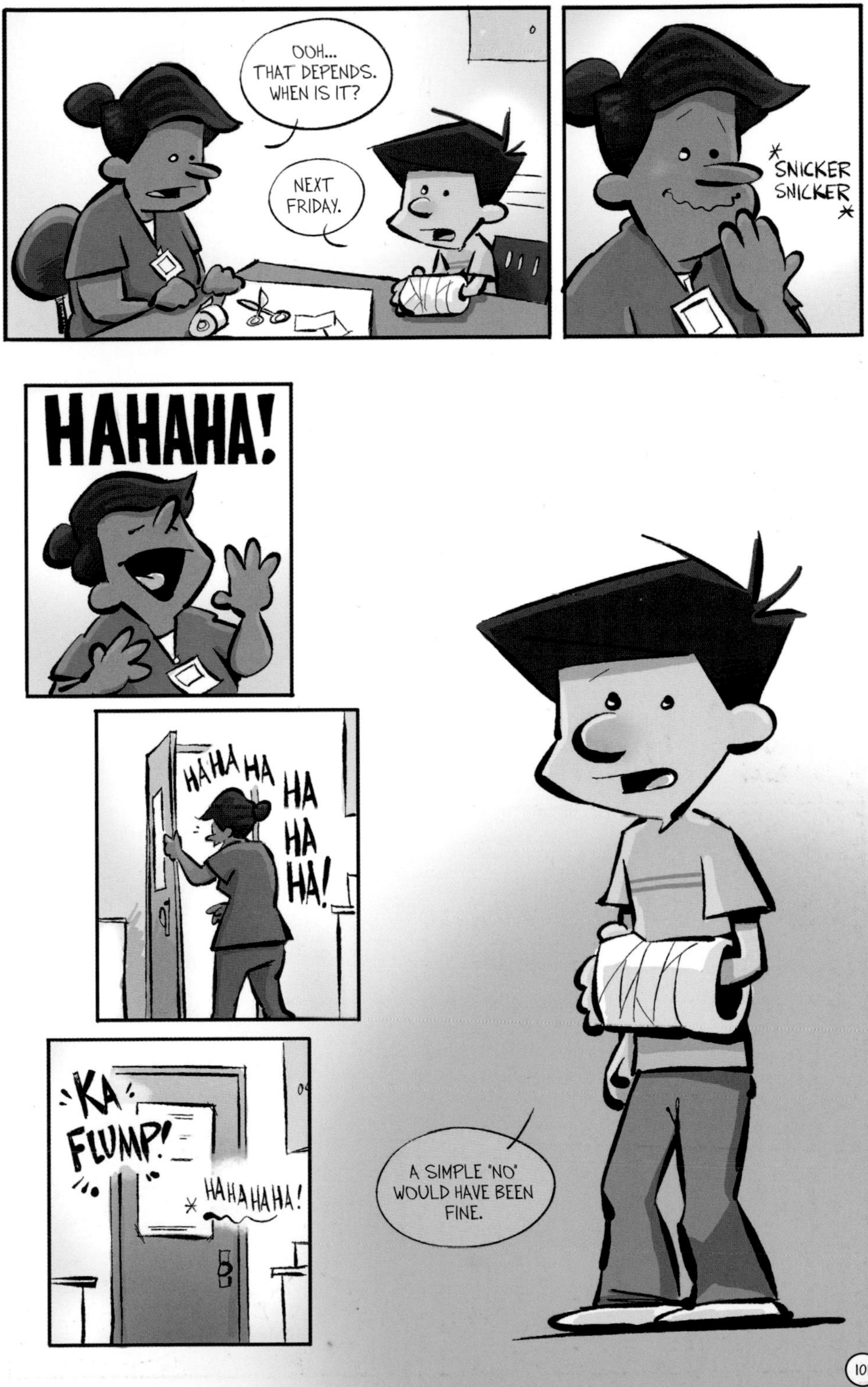
OOH... THAT DEPENDS. WHEN IS IT?
NEXT FRIDAY.
SNICKER SNICKER
HAHAHA!
HA HA HA HA HA HA HA!
KA FLUMP!
*HAHAHAHA!
A SIMPLE "NO" WOULD HAVE BEEN FINE.

CHAPTER SIX
BROKEN

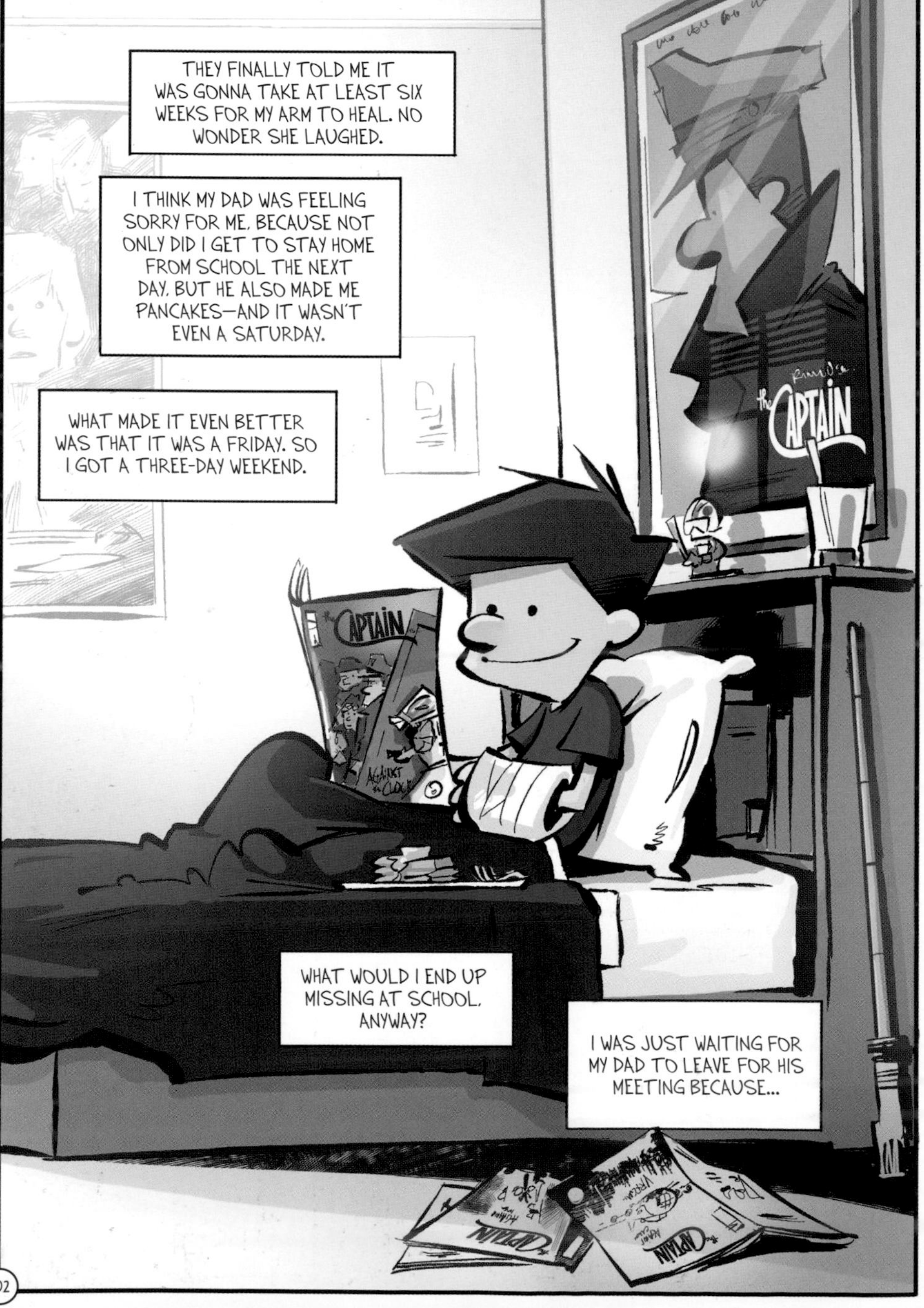
THEY FINALLY TOLD ME IT WAS GONNA TAKE AT LEAST SIX WEEKS FOR MY ARM TO HEAL. NO WONDER SHE LAUGHED.
I THINK MY DAD WAS FEELING SORRY FOR ME, BECAUSE NOT ONLY DID I GET TO STAY HOME FROM SCHOOL THE NEXT DAY, BUT HE ALSO MADE ME PANCAKES—AND IT WASN'T EVEN A SATURDAY.
WHAT MADE IT EVEN BETTER WAS THAT IT WAS A FRIDAY. SO I GOT A THREE-DAY WEEKEND.
the CAPTAIN
CAPTAIN
WHAT WOULD I END UP MISSING AT SCHOOL, ANYWAY?
I WAS JUST WAITING FOR MY DAD TO LEAVE FOR HIS MEETING BECAUSE...

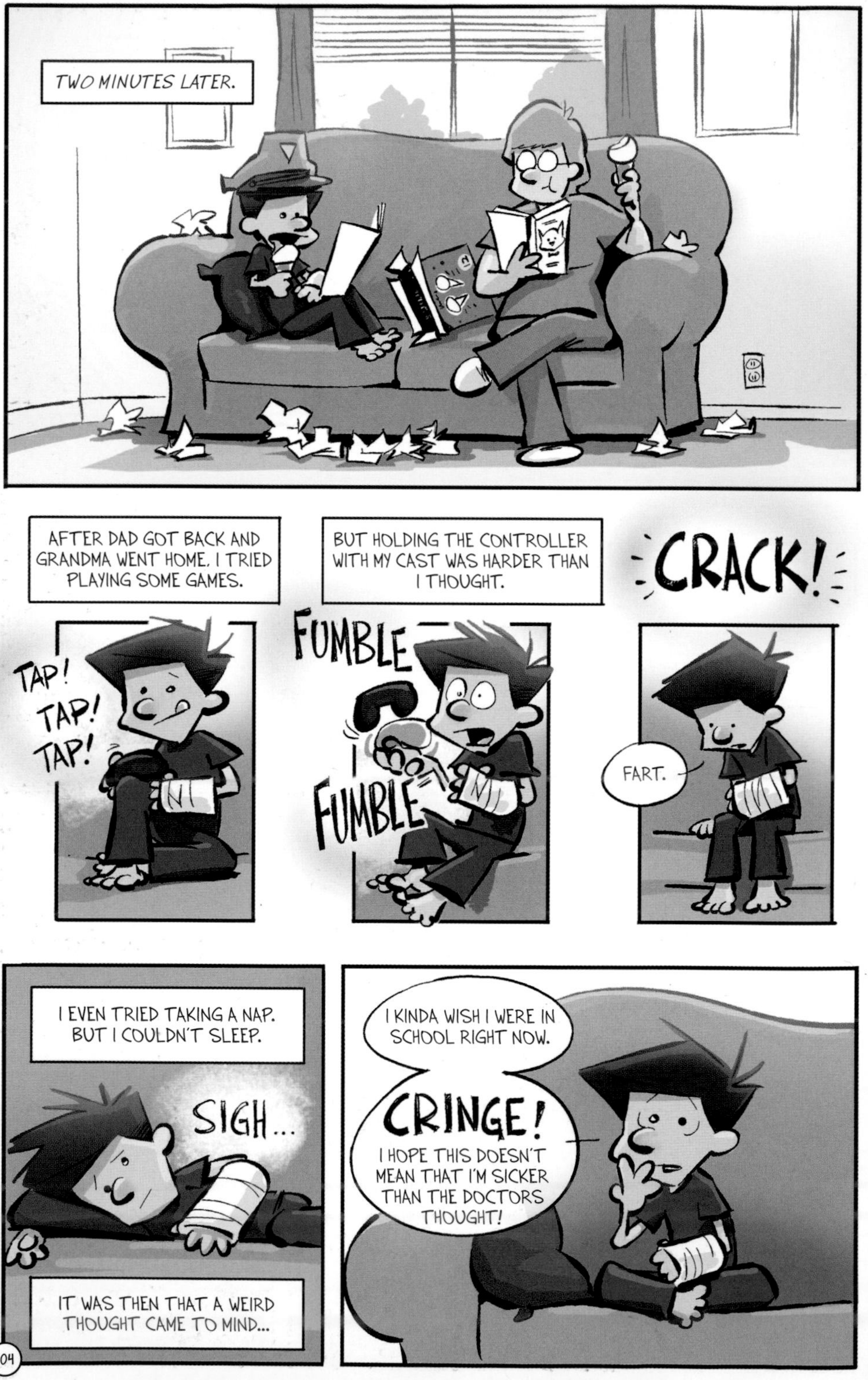
TWO MINUTES LATER.
AFTER DAD GOT BACK AND GRANDMA WENT HOME, I TRIED PLAYING SOME GAMES.
TAP! TAP! TAP!
BUT HOLDING THE CONTROLLER WITH MY CAST WAS HARDER THAN I THOUGHT.
FUMBLE FUMBLE
CRACK!
FART.
I EVEN TRIED TAKING A NAP. BUT I COULDN'T SLEEP.
SIGH...
IT WAS THEN THAT A WEIRD THOUGHT CAME TO MIND...
I KINDA WISH I WERE IN SCHOOL RIGHT NOW.
CRINGE! I HOPE THIS DOESN'T MEAN THAT I'M SICKER THAN THE DOCTORS THOUGHT!

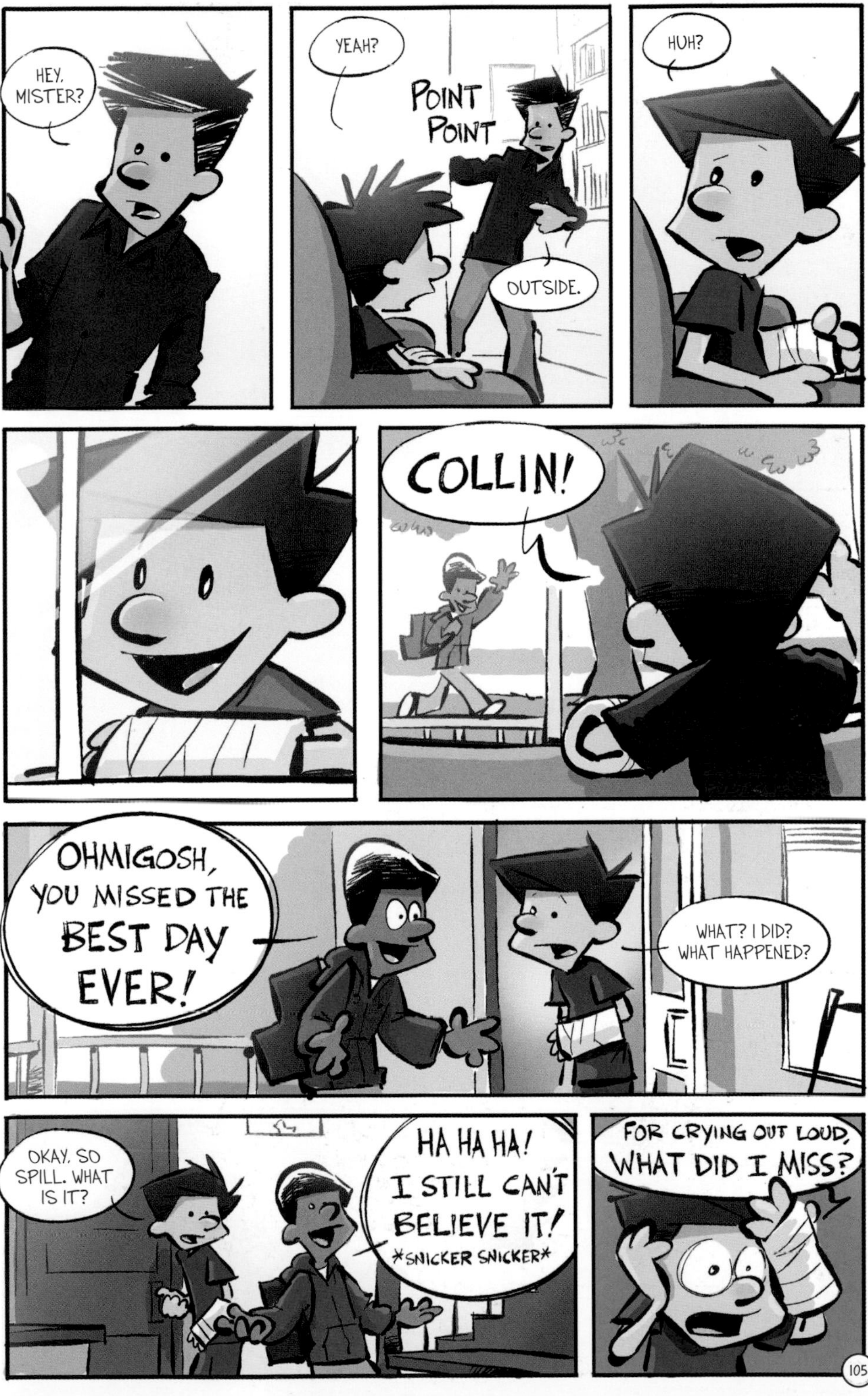
HEY, MISTER?
YEAH?
POINT POINT
OUTSIDE.
HUH?
COLLIN!
OHMIGOSH, YOU MISSED THE BEST DAY EVER!
WHAT? I DID? WHAT HAPPENED?
OKAY, SO SPILL. WHAT IS IT?
HA HA HA! I STILL CAN'T BELIEVE IT!
SNICKER SNICKER
FOR CRYING OUT LOUD, WHAT DID I MISS?

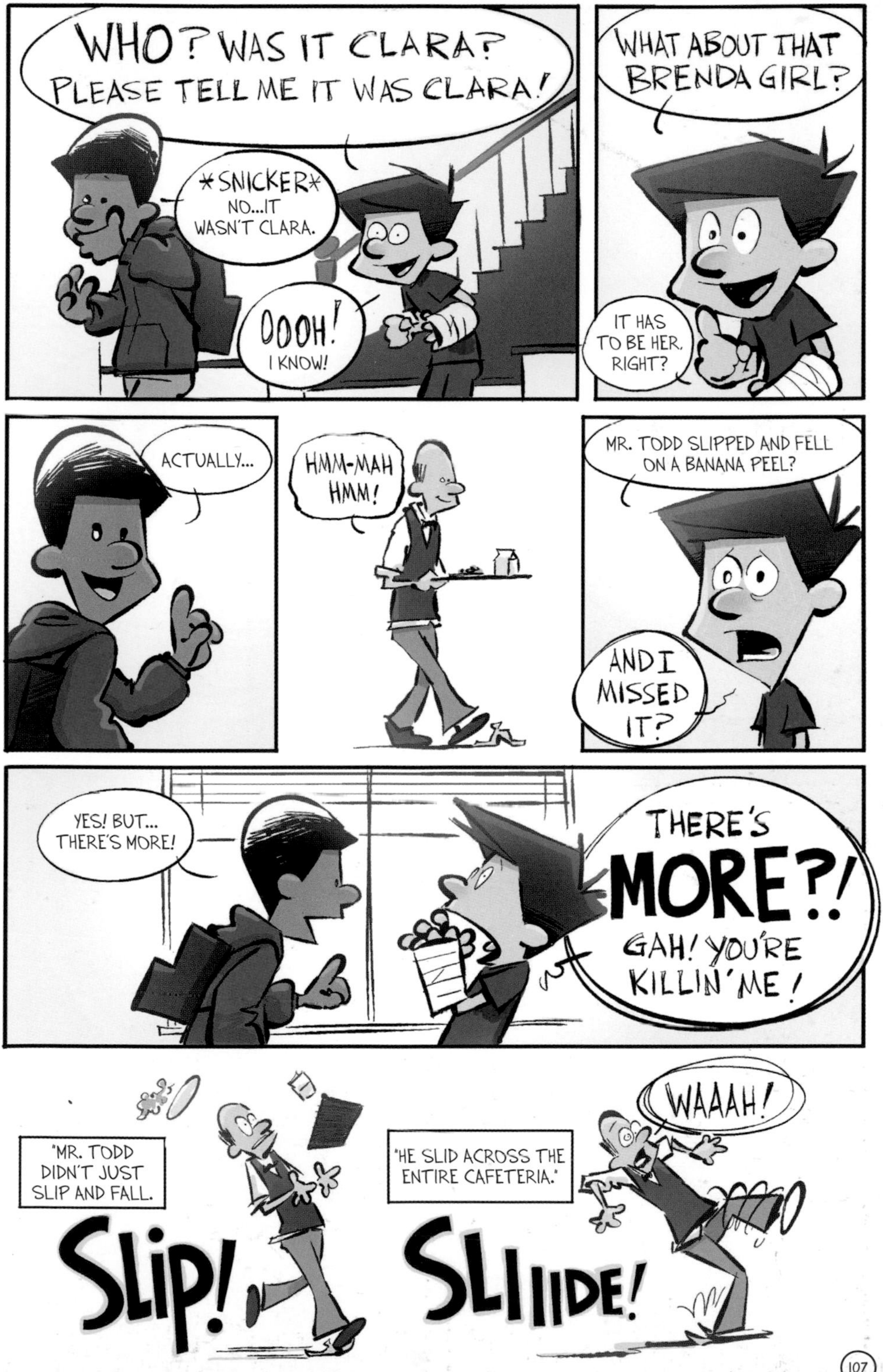
WHO? WAS IT CLARA? PLEASE TELL ME IT WAS CLARA!
SNICKER NO...IT WASN'T CLARA.
OOOH! I KNOW!
WHAT ABOUT THAT BRENDA GIRL?
IT HAS TO BE HER, RIGHT?
ACTUALLY...
HMM-MAH HMM!
MR. TODD SLIPPED AND FELL ON A BANANA PEEL?
AND I MISSED IT?
YES! BUT... THERE'S MORE!
THERE'S MORE?! GAH! YOU'RE KILLIN' ME!
"MR. TODD DIDN'T JUST SLIP AND FALL.
SLIP!
"HE SLID ACROSS THE ENTIRE CAFETERIA."
WAAAH!
SLIIIIDE!

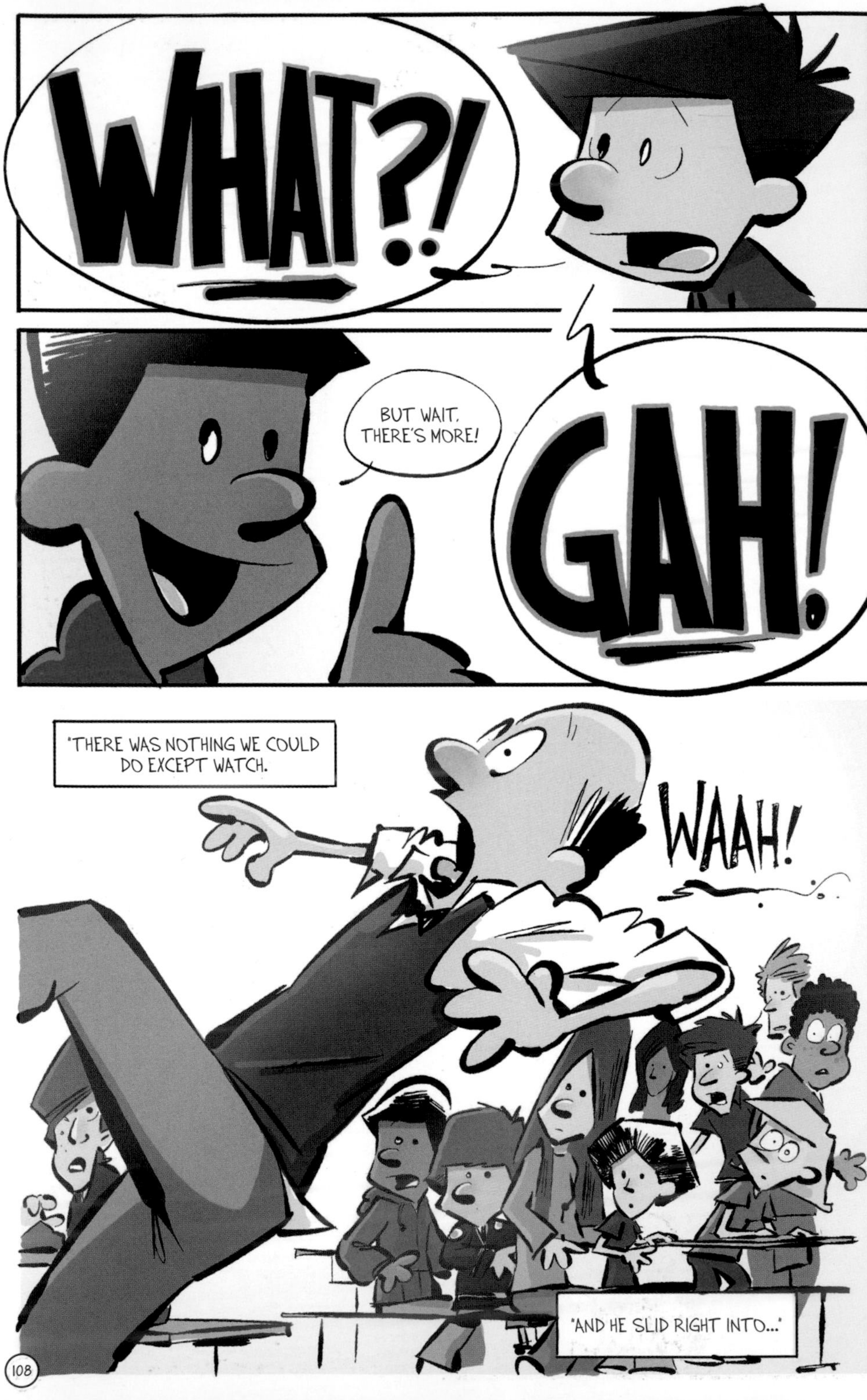
WHAT?!
GAH!
BUT WAIT. THERE'S MORE!
"THERE WAS NOTHING WE COULD DO EXCEPT WATCH.
WAAH!
"AND HE SLID RIGHT INTO..."

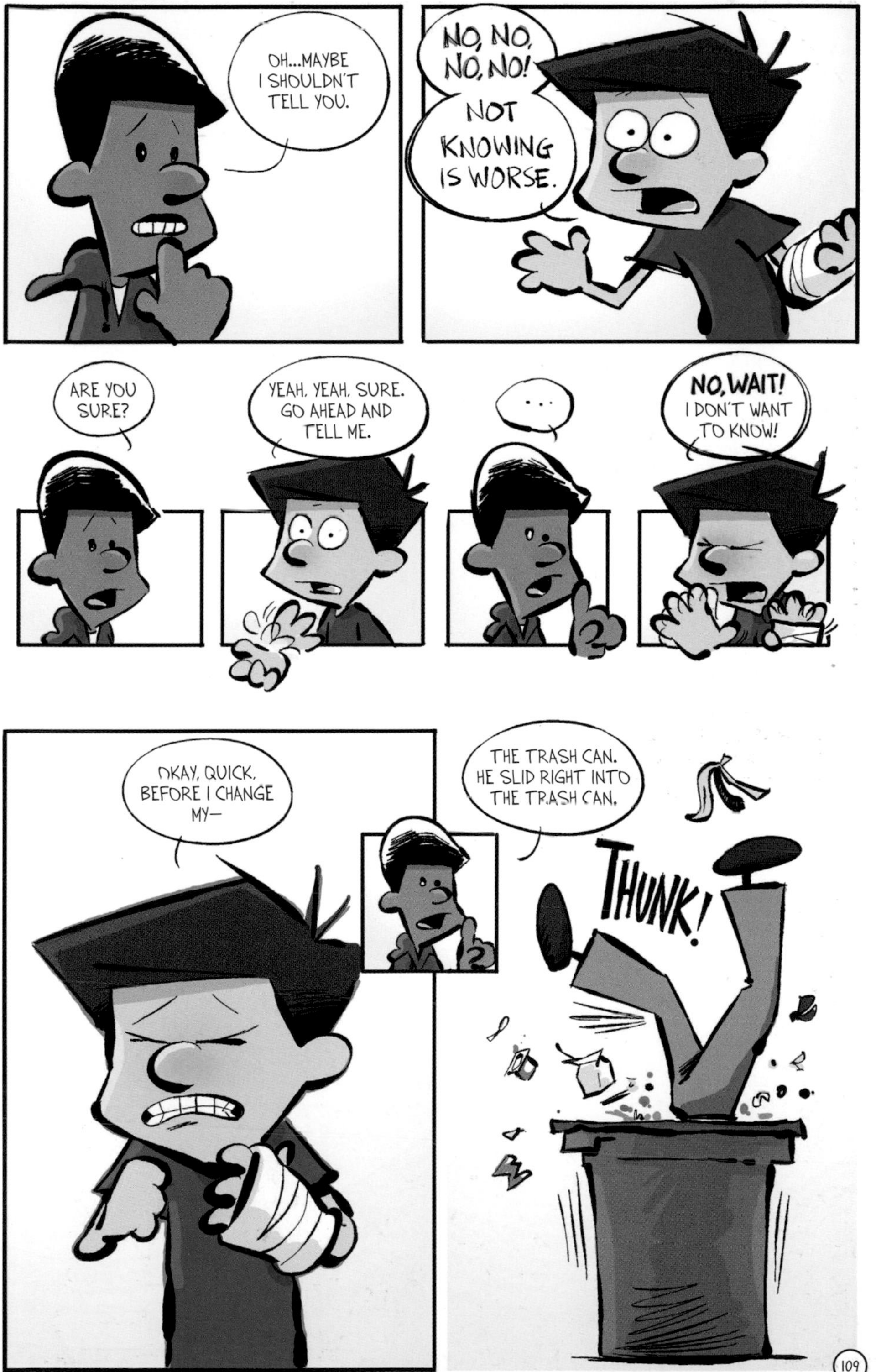
OH...MAYBE I SHOULDN'T TELL YOU.
NO, NO, NO, NO!
NOT KNOWING IS WORSE.
ARE YOU SURE?
YEAH, YEAH, SURE. GO AHEAD AND TELL ME.
...
NO, WAIT! I DON'T WANT TO KNOW!
OKAY, QUICK, BEFORE I CHANGE MY—
THE TRASH CAN. HE SLID RIGHT INTO THE TRASH CAN.
THUNK!

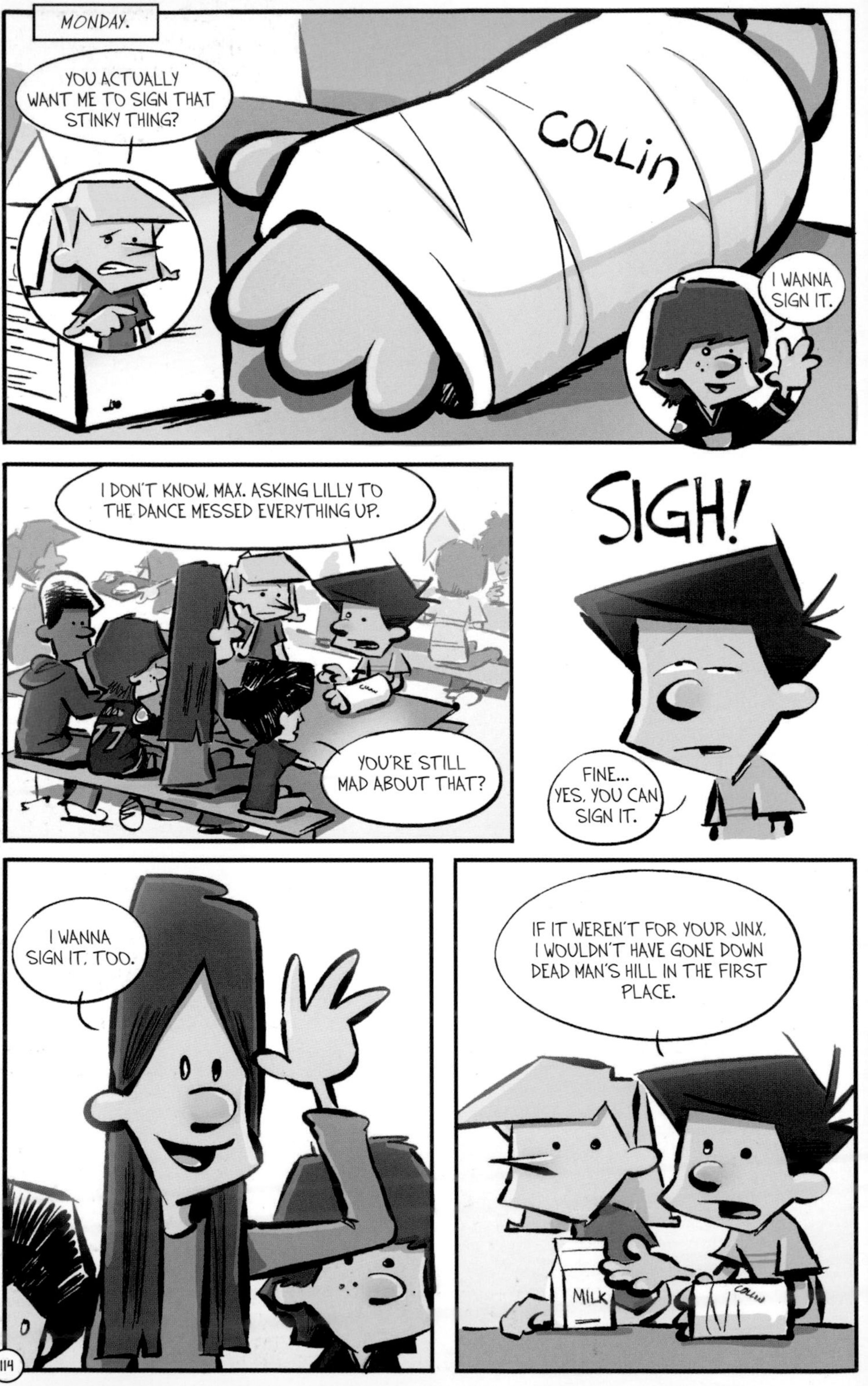
MONDAY.
YOU ACTUALLY WANT ME TO SIGN THAT STINKY THING?
COLLIN
I WANNA SIGN IT.
I DON'T KNOW, MAX. ASKING LILLY TO THE DANCE MESSED EVERYTHING UP.
YOU'RE STILL MAD ABOUT THAT?
SIGH!
FINE... YES, YOU CAN SIGN IT.
I WANNA SIGN IT, TOO.
IF IT WEREN'T FOR YOUR JINX, I WOULDN'T HAVE GONE DOWN DEAD MAN'S HILL IN THE FIRST PLACE.
MILK

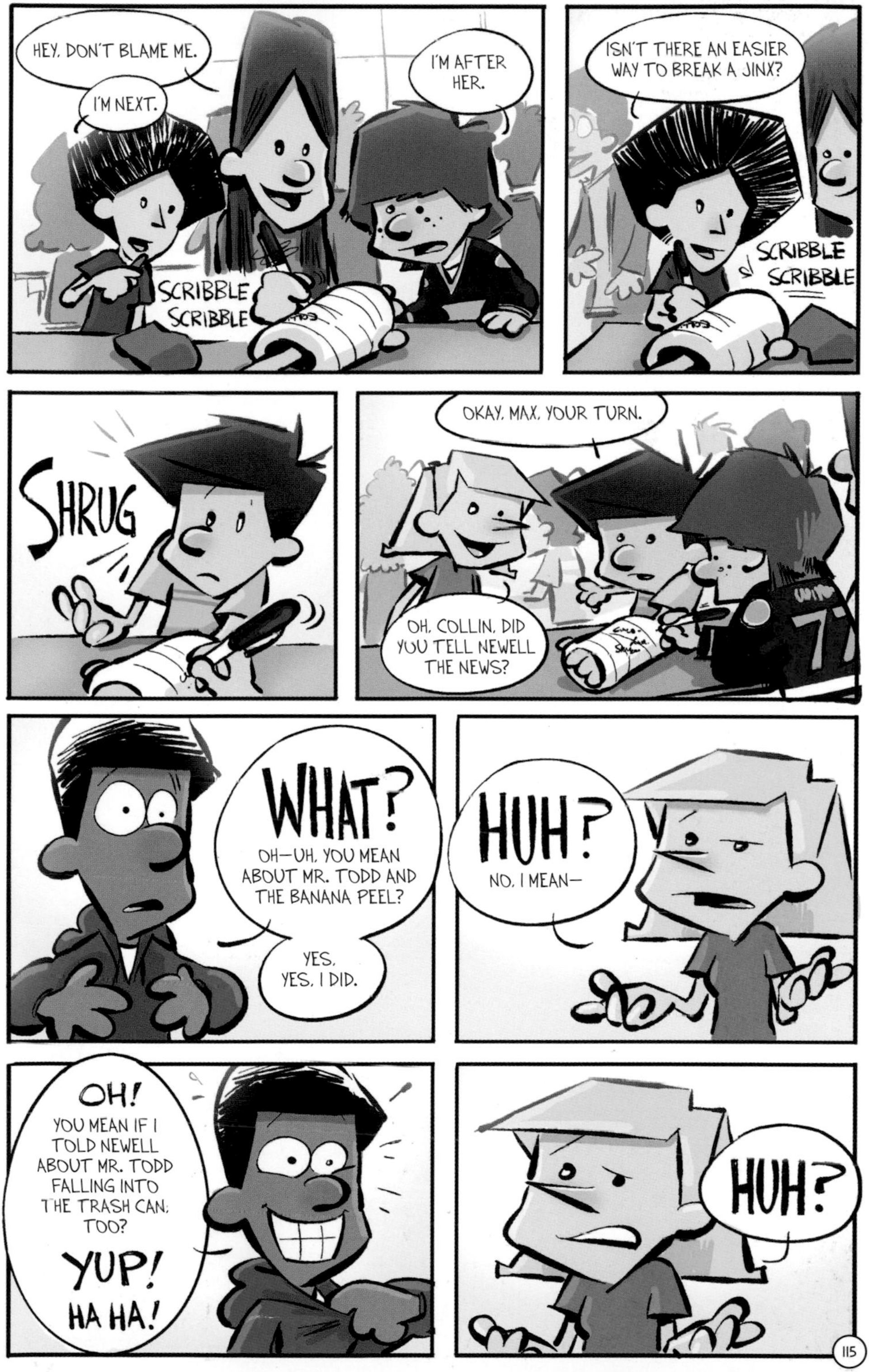
HEY, DON'T BLAME ME.
I'M NEXT.
SCRIBBLE SCRIBBLE
I'M AFTER HER.
ISN'T THERE AN EASIER WAY TO BREAK A JINX?
SCRIBBLE SCRIBBLE
SHRUG
OKAY, MAX, YOUR TURN.
OH, COLLIN, DID YOU TELL NEWELL THE NEWS?
WHAT?
OH—UH, YOU MEAN ABOUT MR. TODD AND THE BANANA PEEL?
YES, YES, I DID.
HUH?
NO, I MEAN—
OH!
YOU MEAN IF I TOLD NEWELL ABOUT MR. TODD FALLING INTO THE TRASH CAN, TOO?
YUP!
HA HA!
HUH?

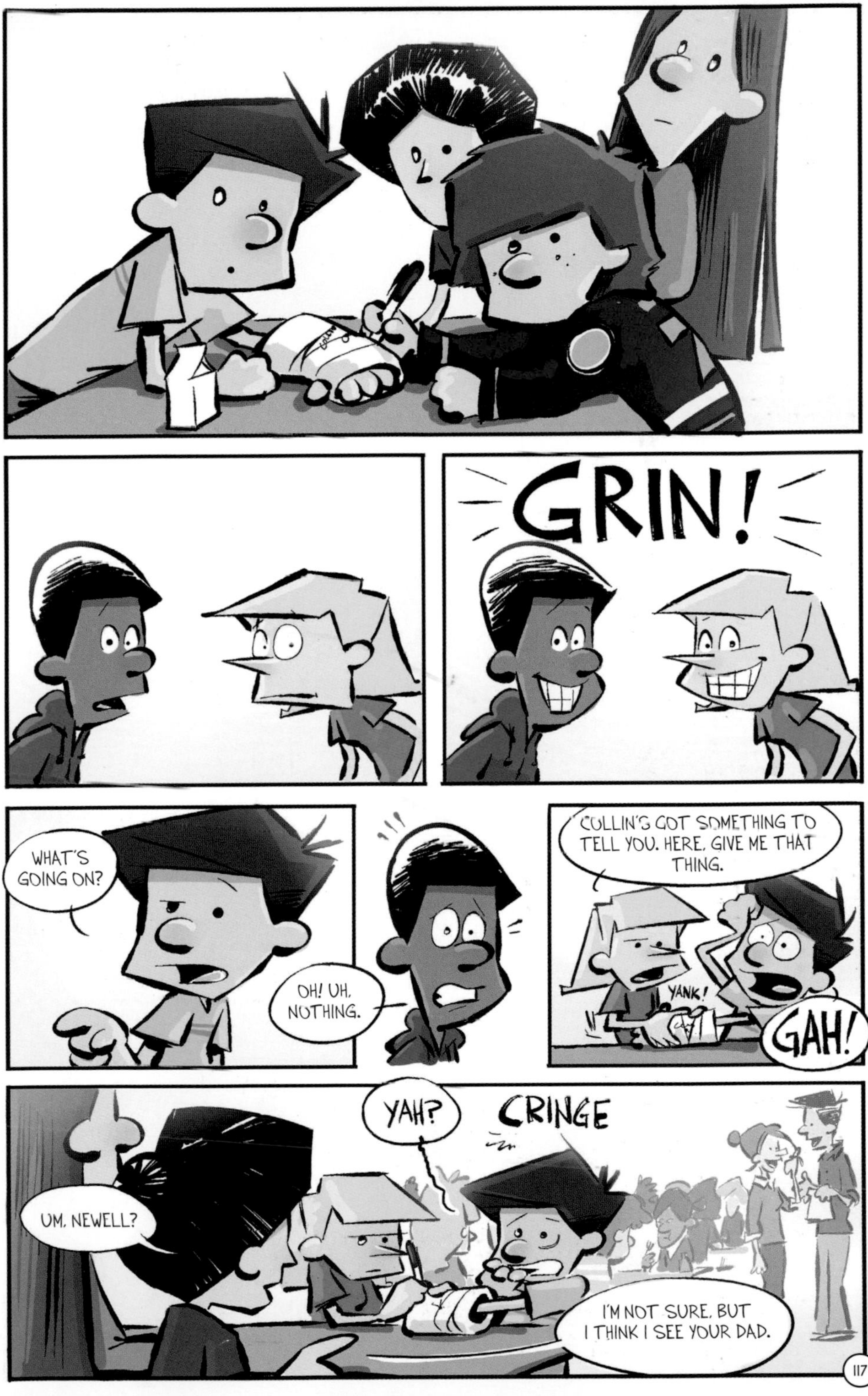
GRIN!
WHAT'S GOING ON?
OH! UH, NOTHING.
COLLIN'S GOT SOMETHING TO TELL YOU. HERE, GIVE ME THAT THING.
YANK!
GAH!
UM, NEWELL?
YAH?
CRINGE
I'M NOT SURE, BUT I THINK I SEE YOUR DAD.

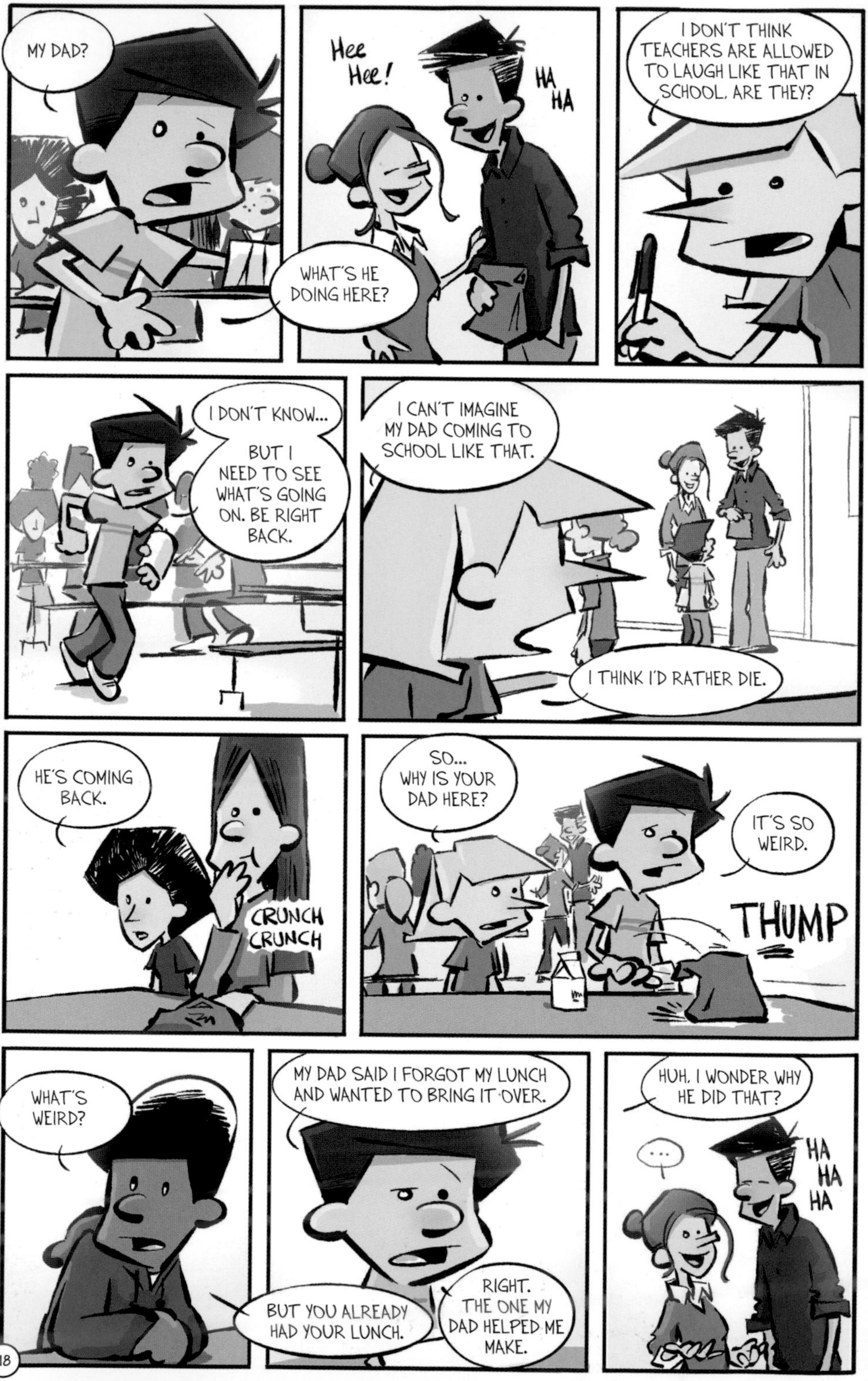
MY DAD?
Hee Hee!
HA HA
WHAT'S HE DOING HERE?
I DON'T THINK TEACHERS ARE ALLOWED TO LAUGH LIKE THAT IN SCHOOL, ARE THEY?
I DON'T KNOW...
BUT I NEED TO SEE WHAT'S GOING ON. BE RIGHT BACK.
I CAN'T IMAGINE MY DAD COMING TO SCHOOL LIKE THAT.
I THINK I'D RATHER DIE.
HE'S COMING BACK.
CRUNCH CRUNCH
SO... WHY IS YOUR DAD HERE?
IT'S SO WEIRD.
THUMP
WHAT'S WEIRD?
MY DAD SAID I FORGOT MY LUNCH AND WANTED TO BRING IT OVER.
BUT YOU ALREADY HAD YOUR LUNCH.
RIGHT. THE ONE MY DAD HELPED ME MAKE.
HUH, I WONDER WHY HE DID THAT?
...
HA HA HA

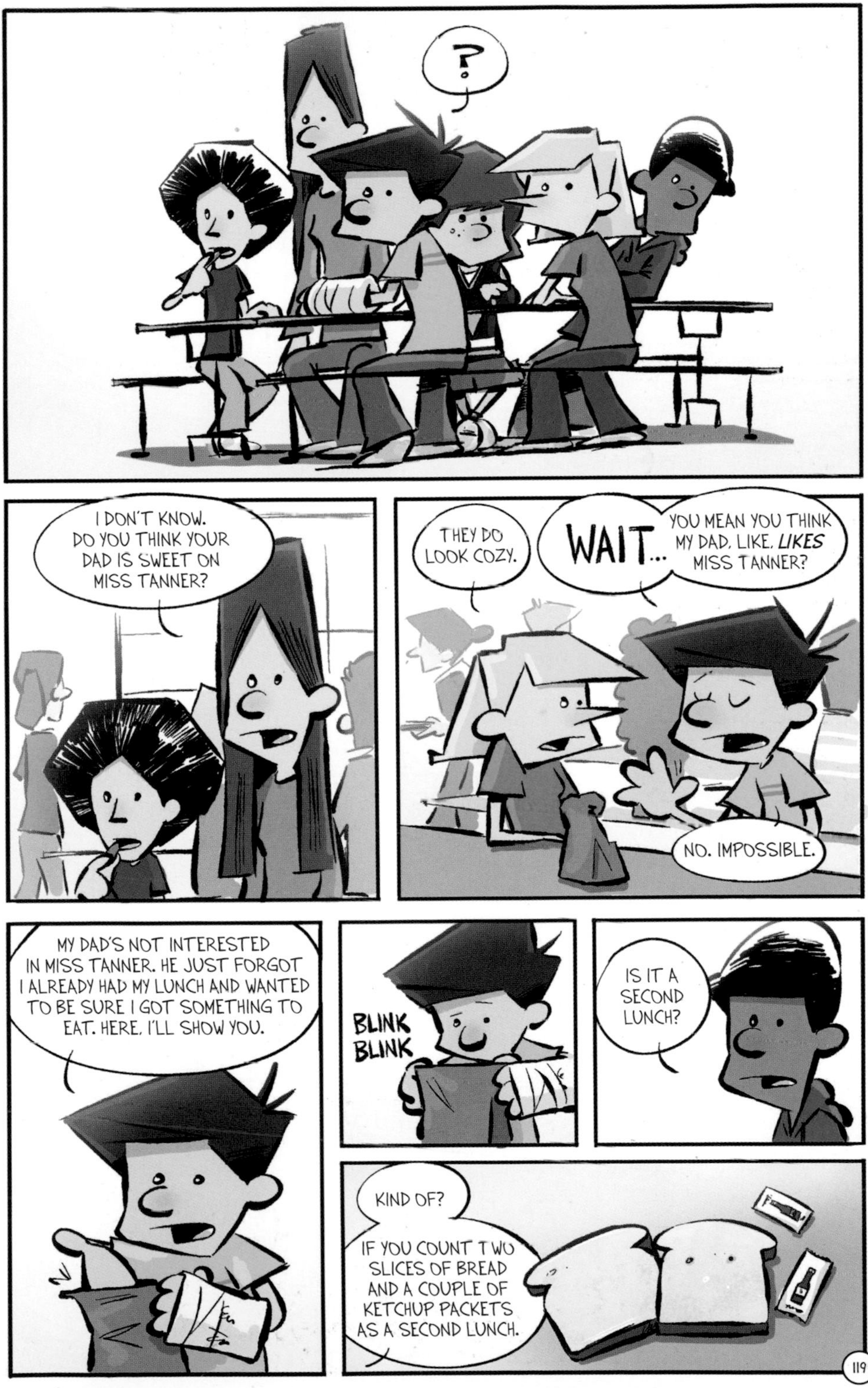
?
I DON'T KNOW. DO YOU THINK YOUR DAD IS SWEET ON MISS TANNER?
THEY DO LOOK COZY.
WAIT...
YOU MEAN YOU THINK MY DAD, LIKE, *LIKES* MISS TANNER?
NO. IMPOSSIBLE.
MY DAD'S NOT INTERESTED IN MISS TANNER. HE JUST FORGOT I ALREADY HAD MY LUNCH AND WANTED TO BE SURE I GOT SOMETHING TO EAT. HERE, I'LL SHOW YOU.
BLINK BLINK
IS IT A SECOND LUNCH?
KIND OF?
IF YOU COUNT TWO SLICES OF BREAD AND A COUPLE OF KETCHUP PACKETS AS A SECOND LUNCH.

121

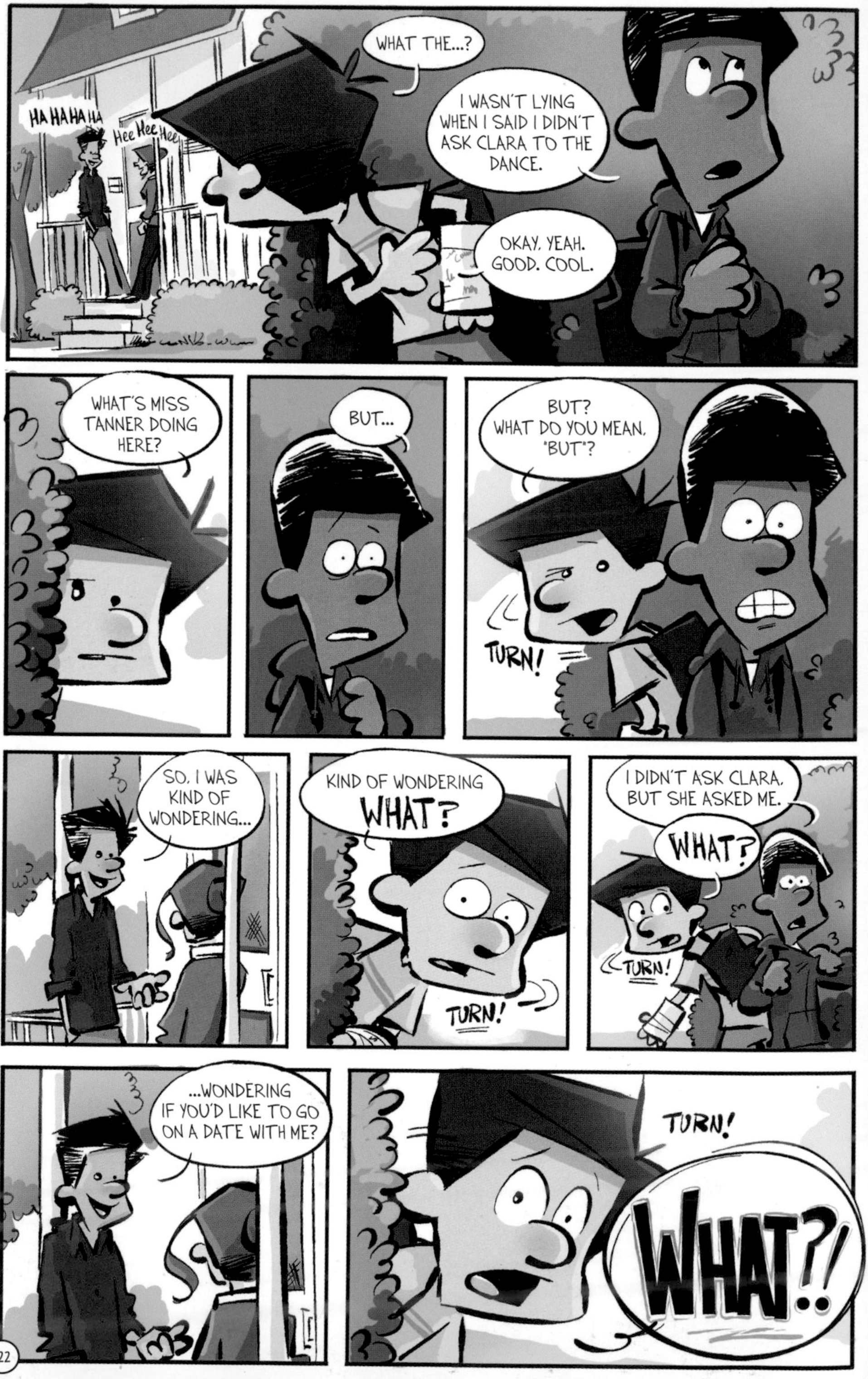

HA HA HA HA HA
Hee Hee Hee
WHAT THE...?
I WASN'T LYING WHEN I SAID I DIDN'T ASK CLARA TO THE DANCE.
OKAY. YEAH. GOOD. COOL.
WHAT'S MISS TANNER DOING HERE?
BUT...
BUT? WHAT DO YOU MEAN, "BUT"?
TURN!
SO, I WAS KIND OF WONDERING...
KIND OF WONDERING WHAT?
TURN!
I DIDN'T ASK CLARA, BUT SHE ASKED ME.
WHAT?
TURN!
...WONDERING IF YOU'D LIKE TO GO ON A DATE WITH ME?
TURN!
WHAT?!

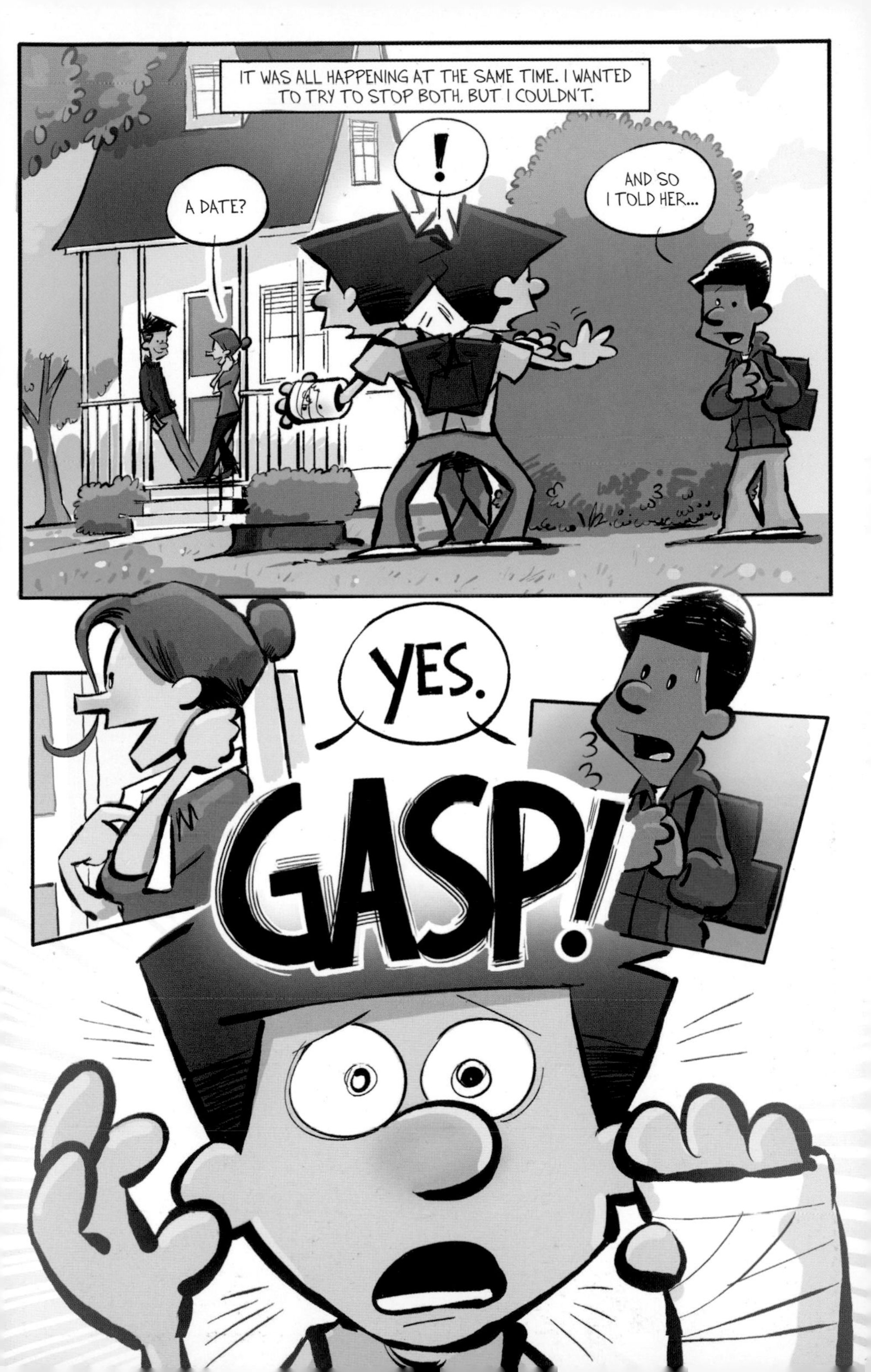
IT WAS ALL HAPPENING AT THE SAME TIME. I WANTED TO TRY TO STOP BOTH, BUT I COULDN'T.
A DATE?
!
AND SO I TOLD HER...
YES.
GASP!

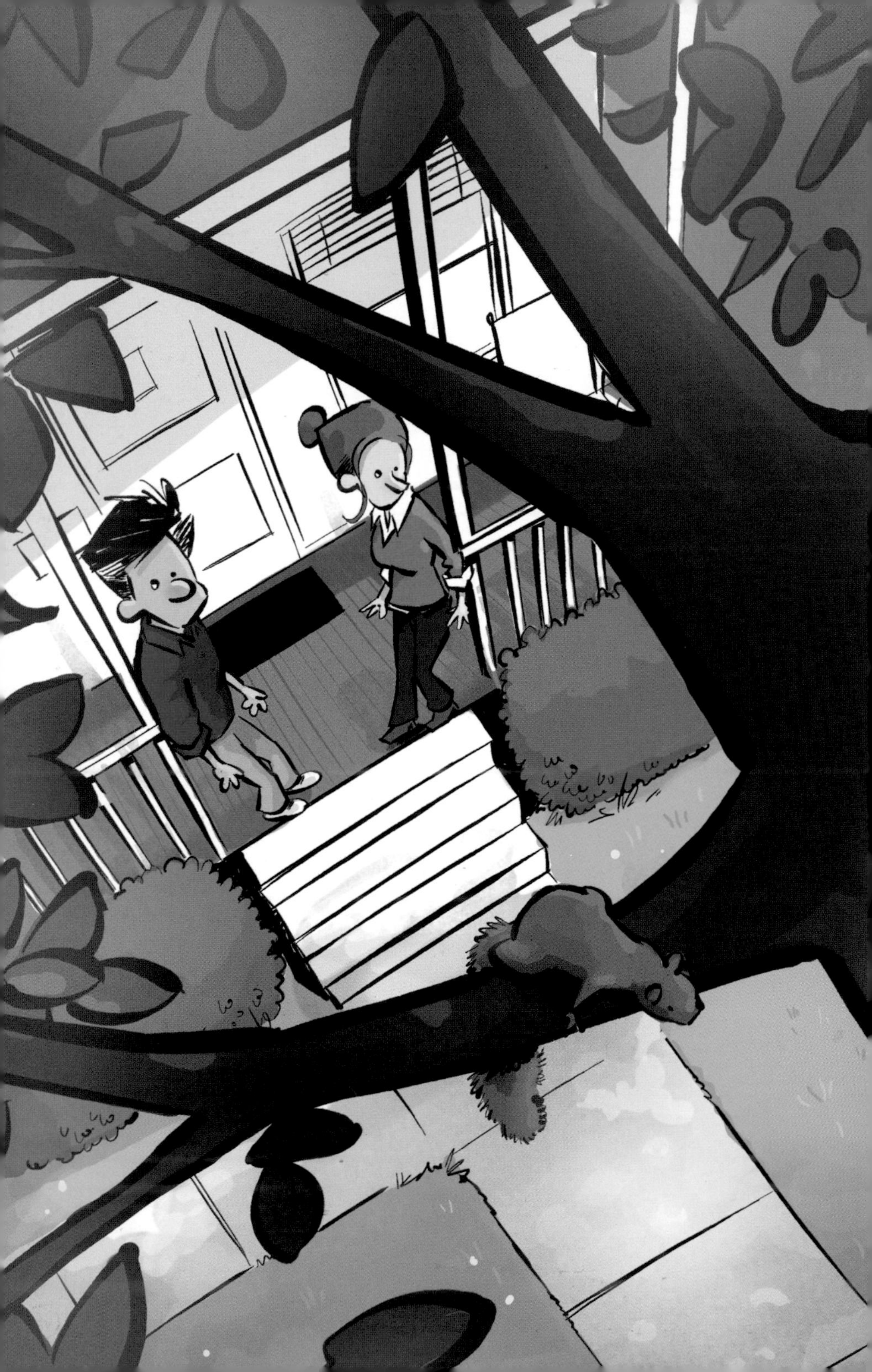

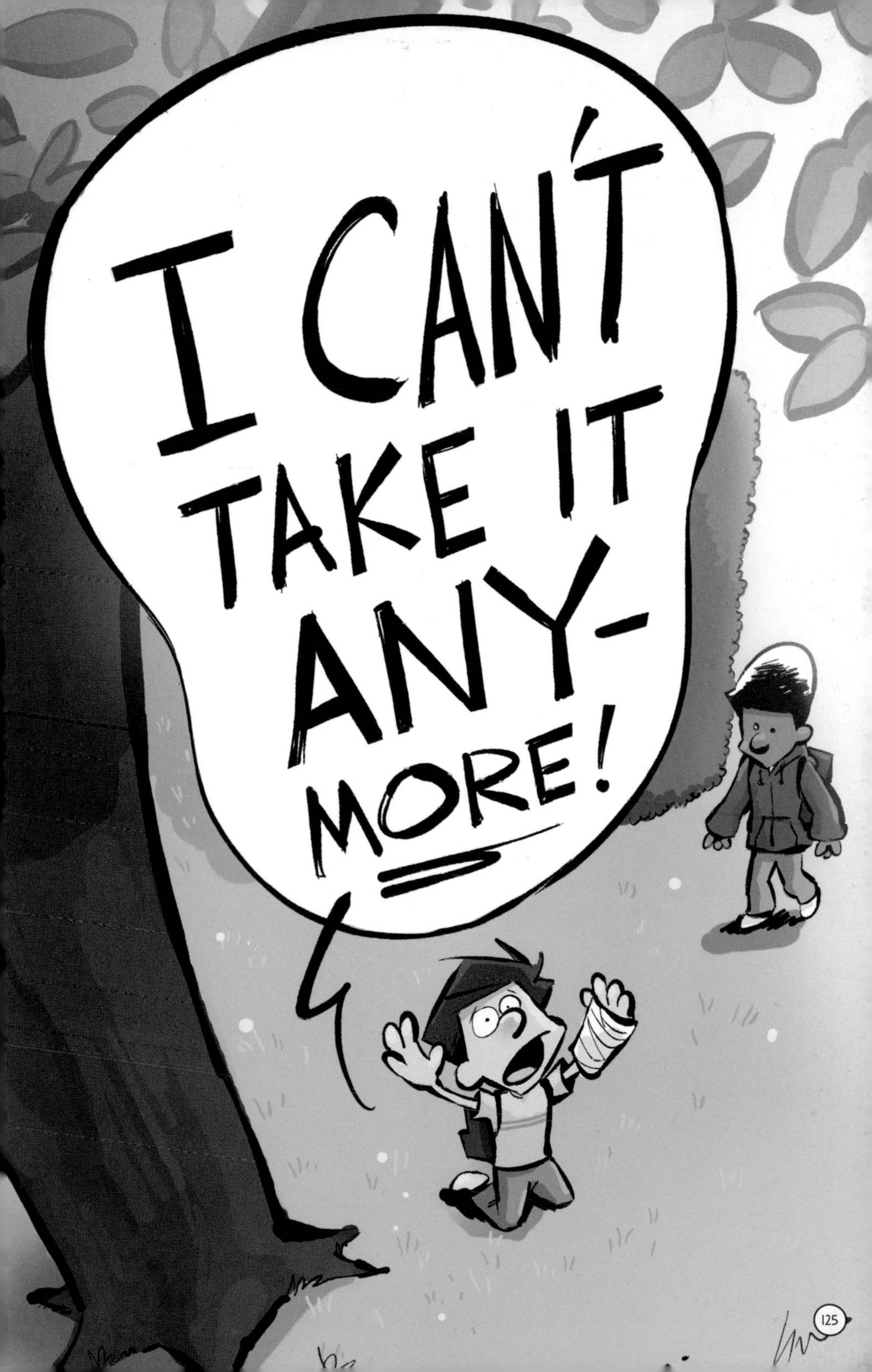
I CAN'T TAKE IT ANY-MORE!

CHAPTER SEVEN
NOTHING IS THE SAME

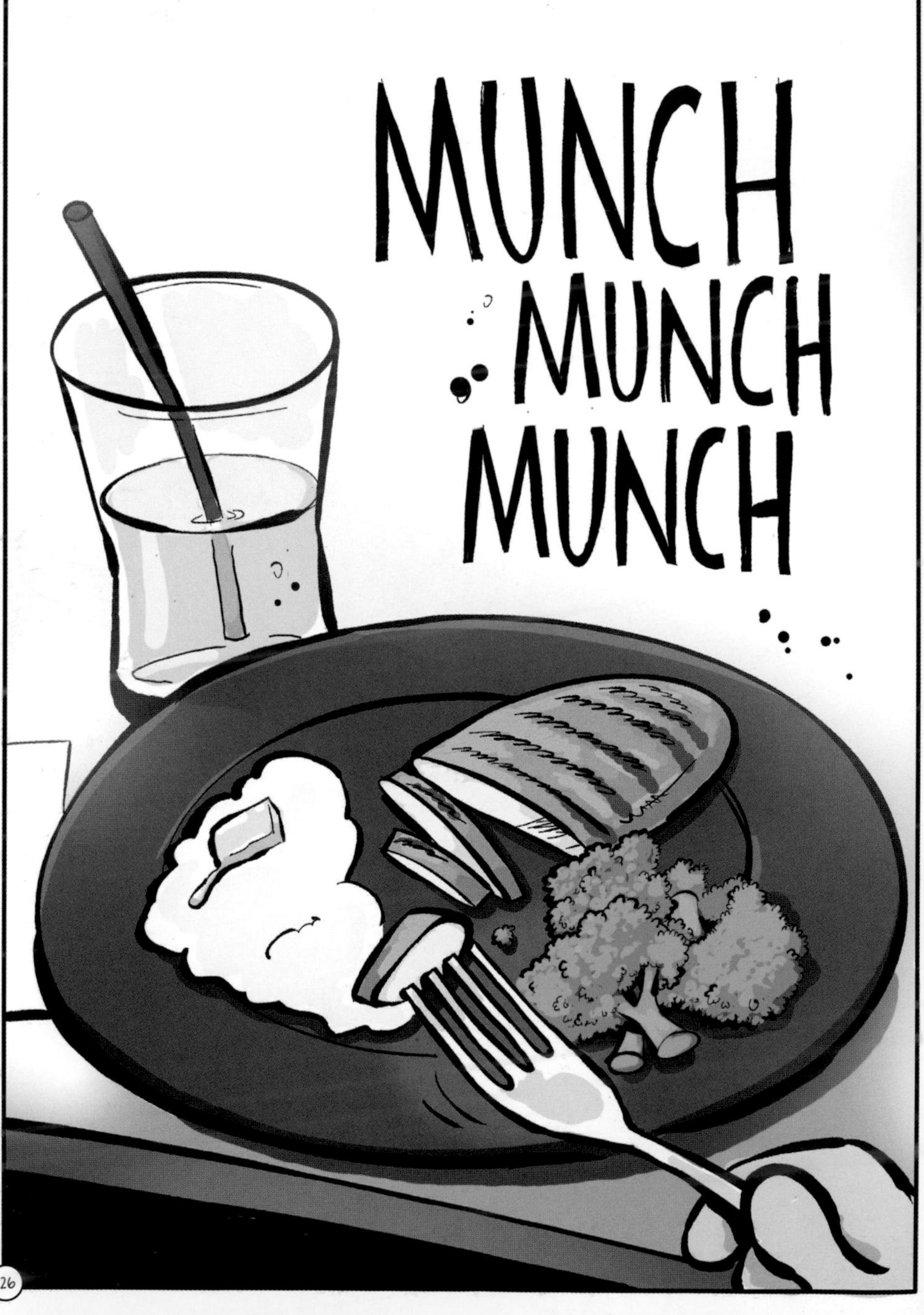
MUNCH
MUNCH
MUNCH

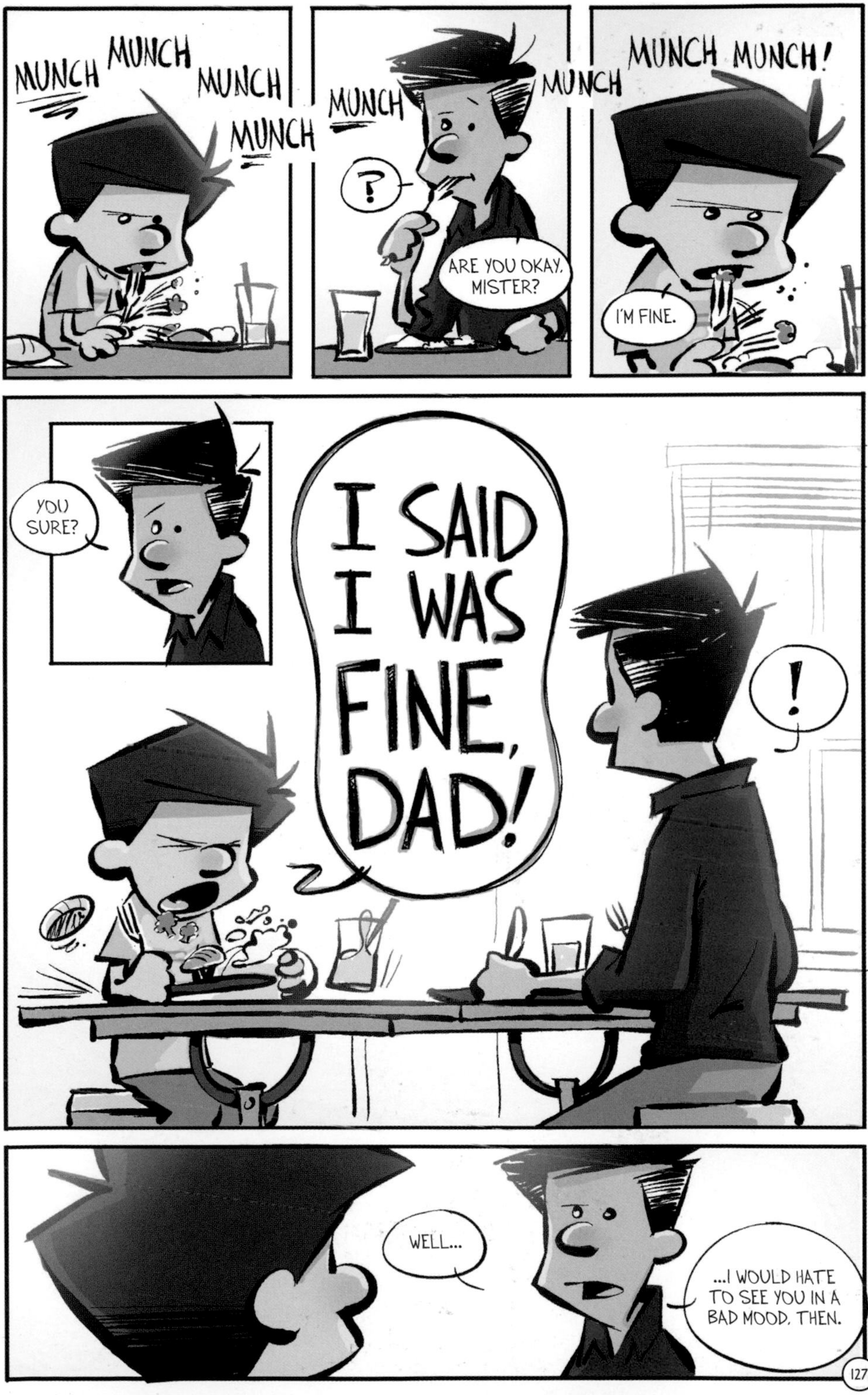
MUNCH MUNCH MUNCH
MUNCH
MUNCH
?
ARE YOU OKAY, MISTER?
MUNCH MUNCH MUNCH!
I'M FINE.
YOU SURE?
I SAID I WAS FINE, DAD!
!
WELL...
...I WOULD HATE TO SEE YOU IN A BAD MOOD, THEN.

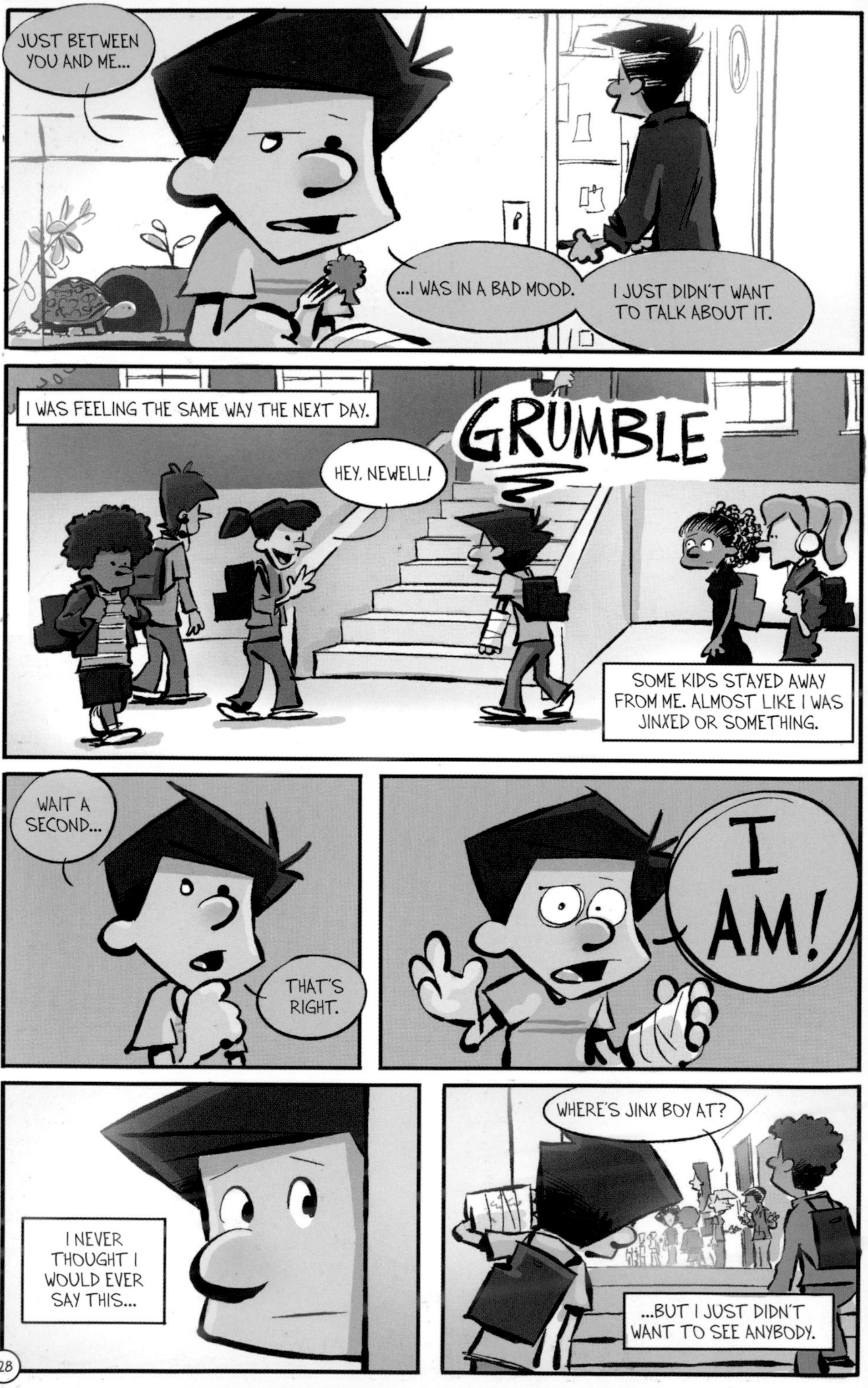
JUST BETWEEN YOU AND ME...
...I WAS IN A BAD MOOD.
I JUST DIDN'T WANT TO TALK ABOUT IT.
I WAS FEELING THE SAME WAY THE NEXT DAY.
GRUMBLE
HEY, NEWELL!
SOME KIDS STAYED AWAY FROM ME. ALMOST LIKE I WAS JINXED OR SOMETHING.
WAIT A SECOND...
THAT'S RIGHT.
I AM!
I NEVER THOUGHT I WOULD EVER SAY THIS...
WHERE'S JINX BOY AT?
...BUT I JUST DIDN'T WANT TO SEE ANYBODY.

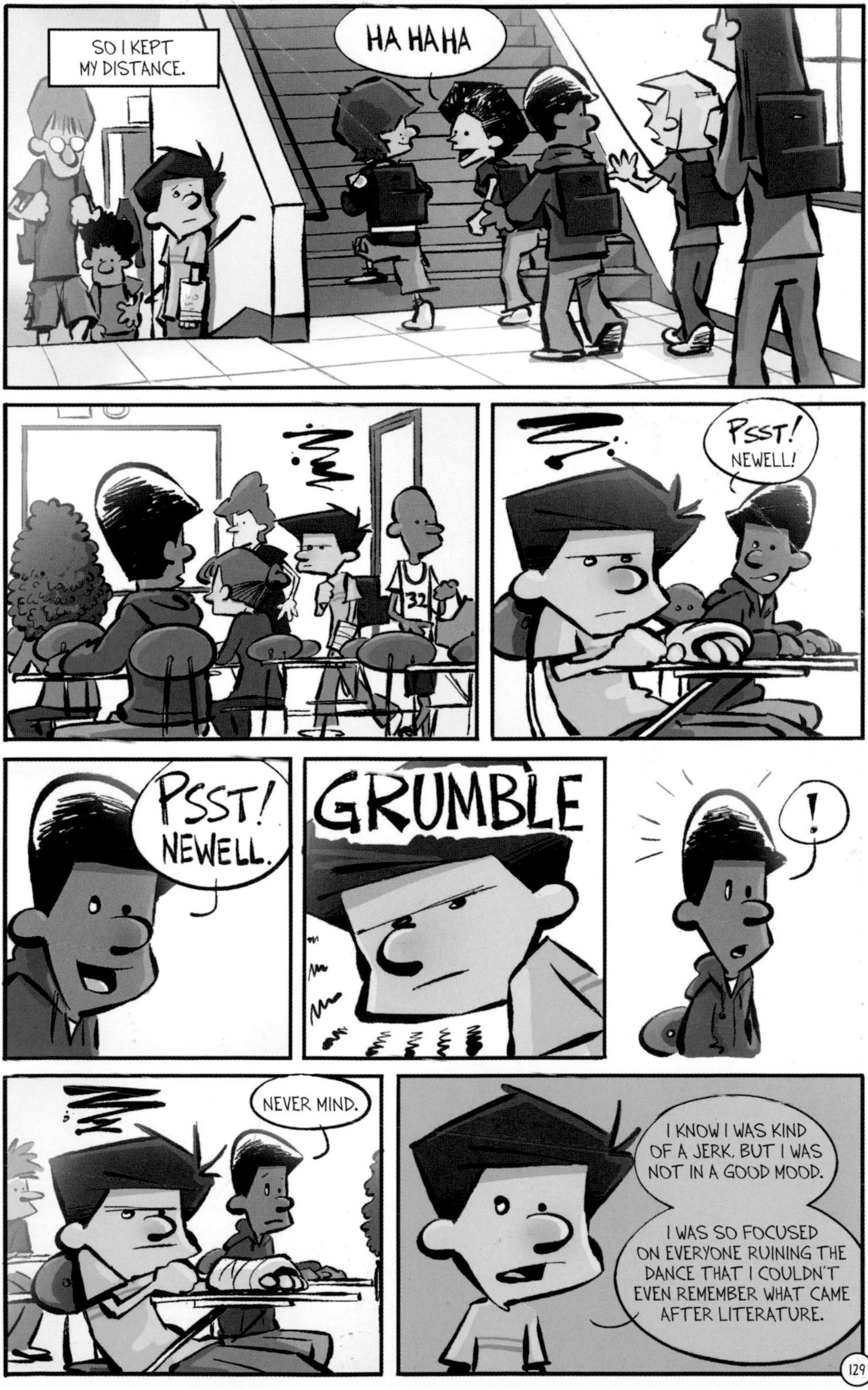
SO I KEPT MY DISTANCE.
HA HA HA
PSST! NEWELL!
PSST! NEWELL.
GRUMBLE
!
NEVER MIND.
I KNOW I WAS KIND OF A JERK. BUT I WAS NOT IN A GOOD MOOD.
I WAS SO FOCUSED ON EVERYONE RUINING THE DANCE THAT I COULDN'T EVEN REMEMBER WHAT CAME AFTER LITERATURE.

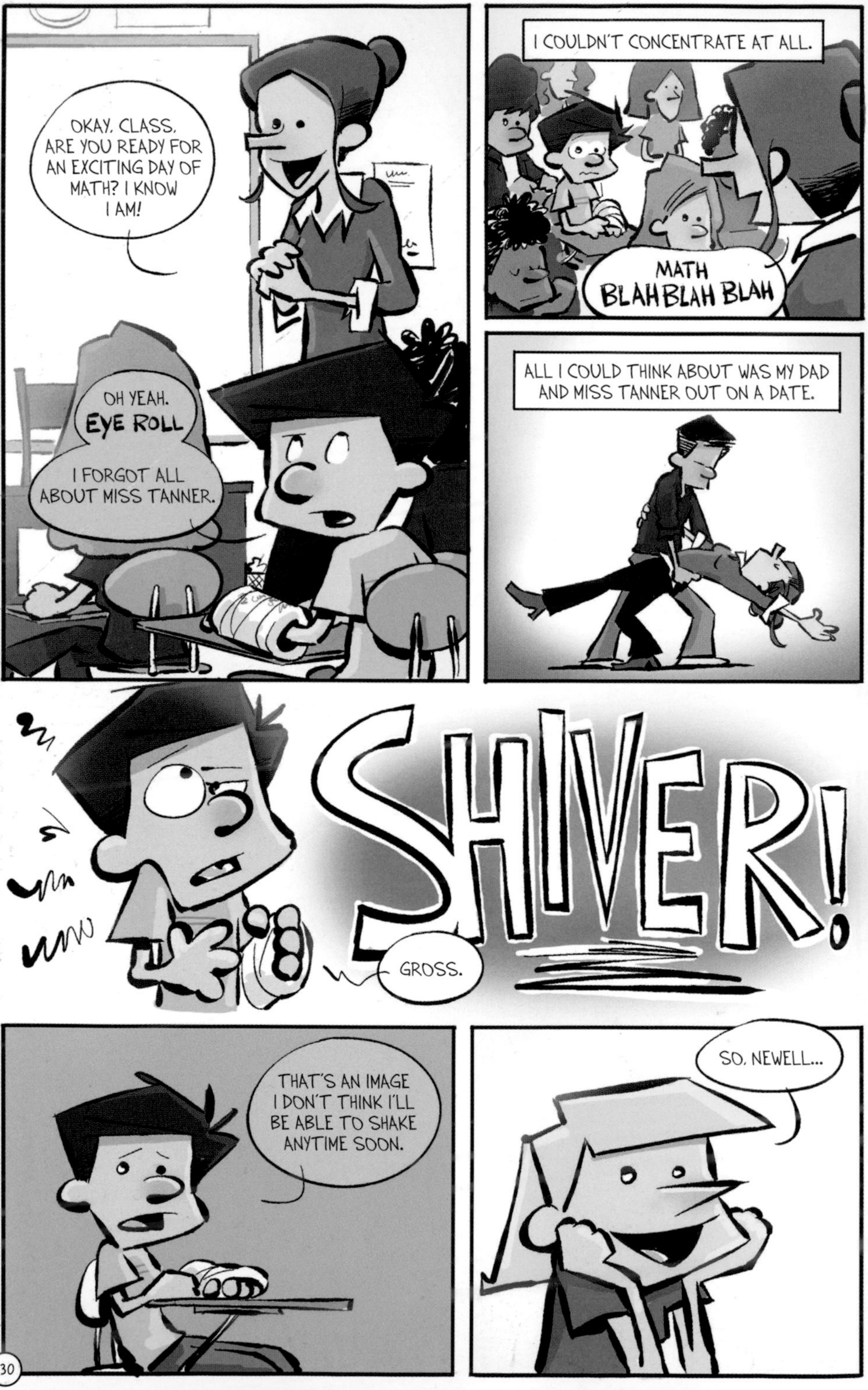
OKAY, CLASS, ARE YOU READY FOR AN EXCITING DAY OF MATH? I KNOW I AM!
OH YEAH. EYE ROLL
I FORGOT ALL ABOUT MISS TANNER.
I COULDN'T CONCENTRATE AT ALL.
MATH BLAH BLAH BLAH
ALL I COULD THINK ABOUT WAS MY DAD AND MISS TANNER OUT ON A DATE.
SHIVER!
GROSS.
THAT'S AN IMAGE I DON'T THINK I'LL BE ABLE TO SHAKE ANYTIME SOON.
SO, NEWELL...

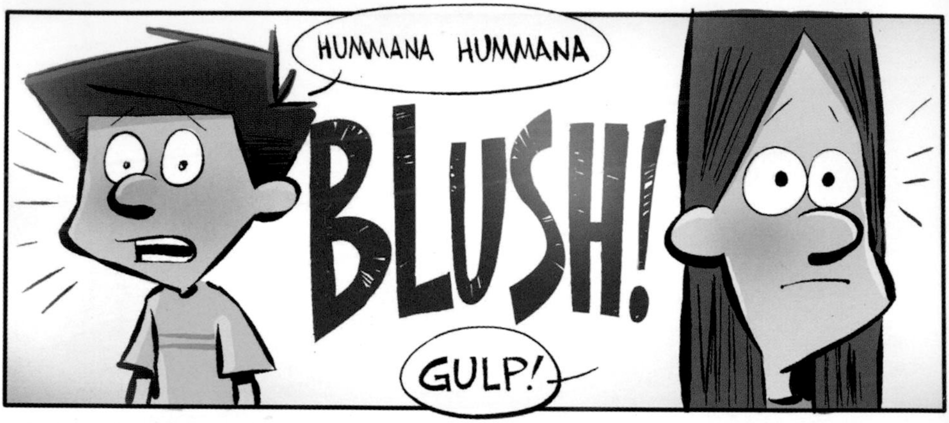
HUMMANA HUMMANA
BLUSH!
GULP!

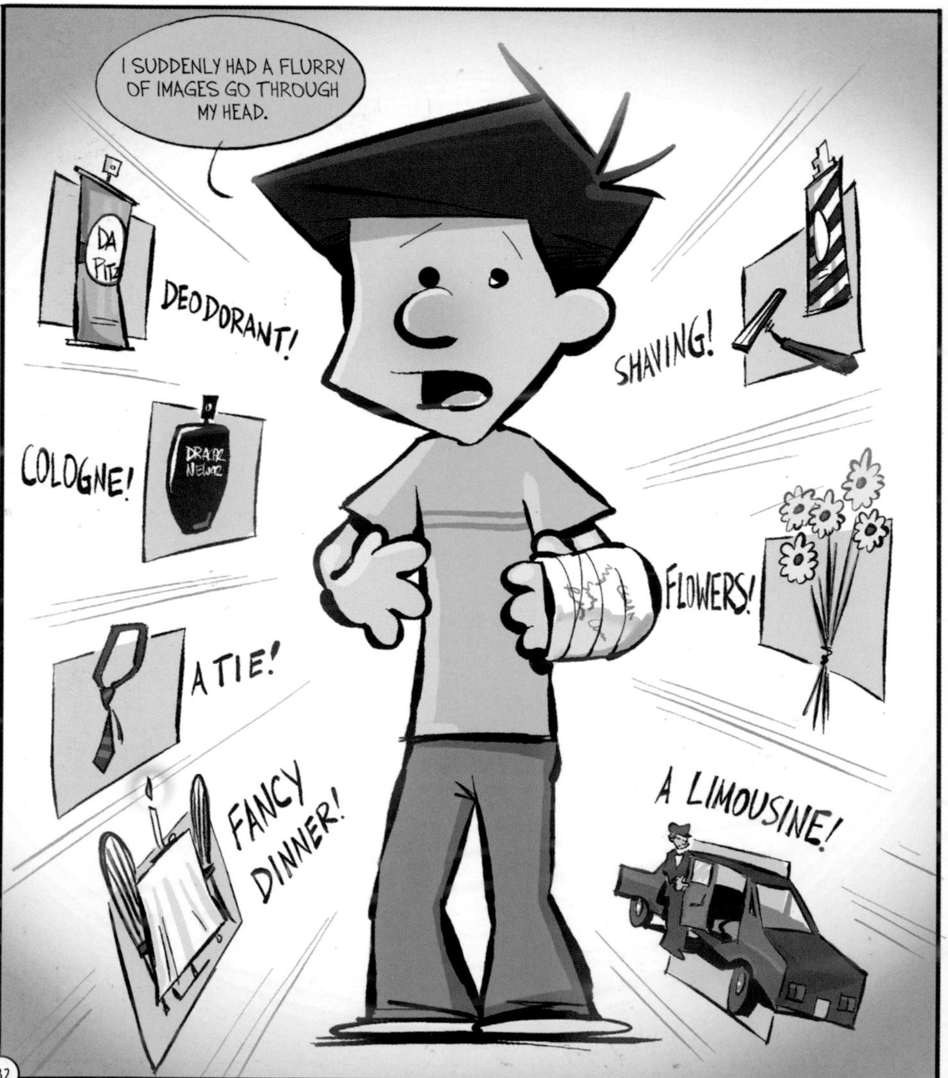
I SUDDENLY HAD A FLURRY OF IMAGES GO THROUGH MY HEAD.
DEODORANT!
SHAVING!
COLOGNE!
FLOWERS!
A TIE!
FANCY DINNER!
A LIMOUSINE!

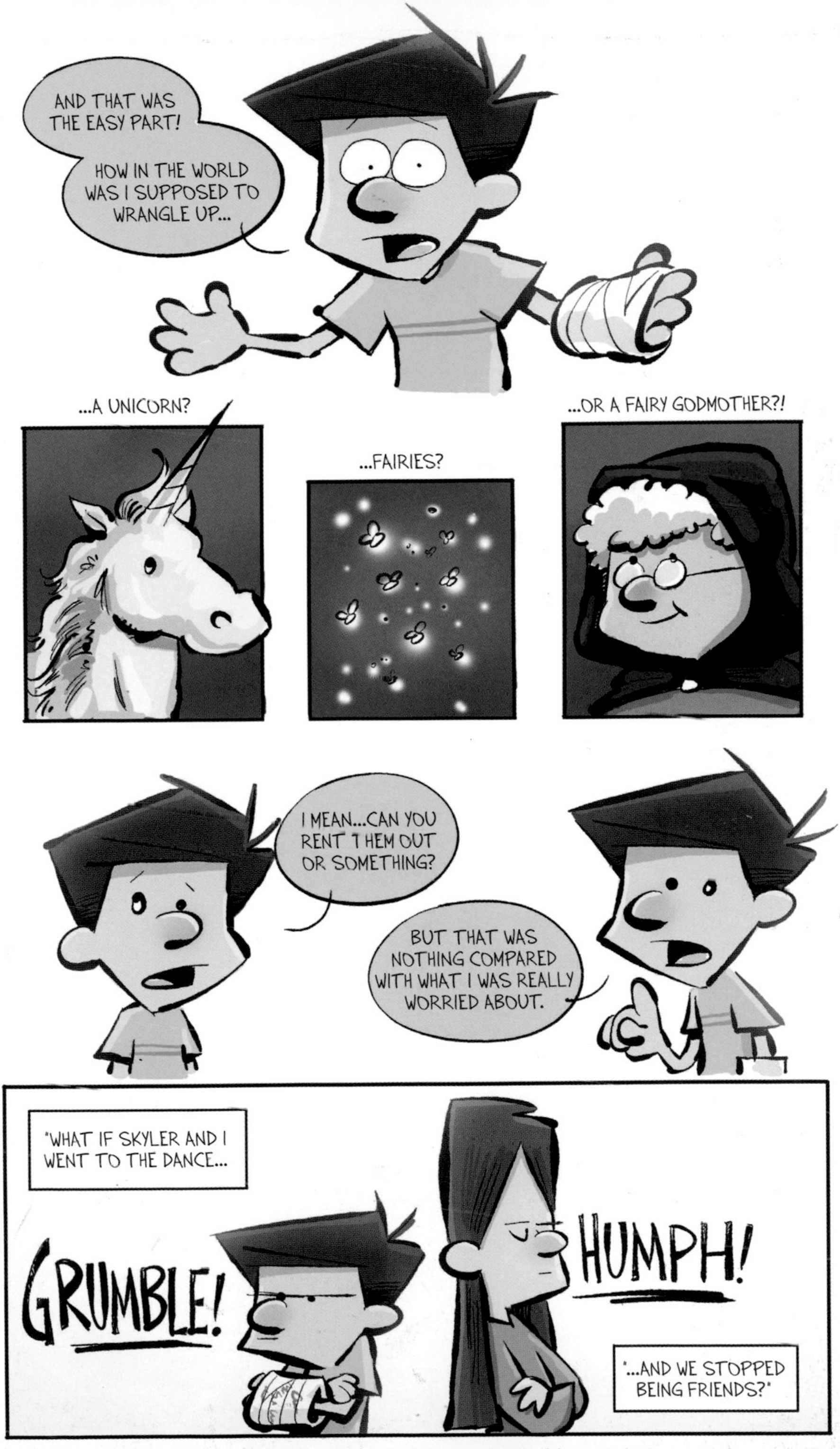
AND THAT WAS THE EASY PART!
HOW IN THE WORLD WAS I SUPPOSED TO WRANGLE UP...
...A UNICORN?
...FAIRIES?
...OR A FAIRY GODMOTHER?!
I MEAN...CAN YOU RENT THEM OUT OR SOMETHING?
BUT THAT WAS NOTHING COMPARED WITH WHAT I WAS REALLY WORRIED ABOUT.
"WHAT IF SKYLER AND I WENT TO THE DANCE...
GRUMBLE!
HUMPH!
"...AND WE STOPPED BEING FRIENDS?"

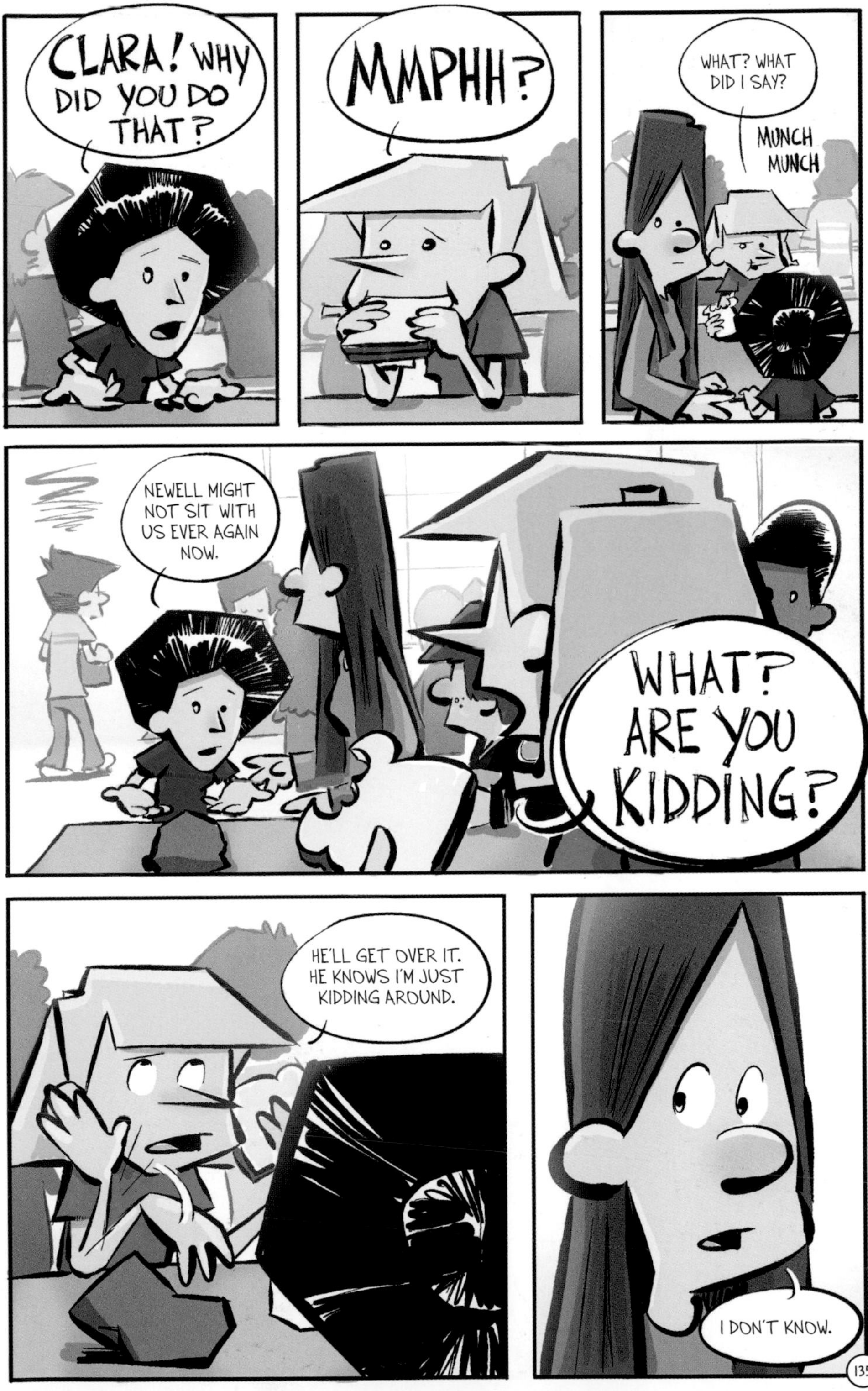
CLARA! WHY DID YOU DO THAT?
MMPHH?
WHAT? WHAT DID I SAY?
MUNCH MUNCH
NEWELL MIGHT NOT SIT WITH US EVER AGAIN NOW.
WHAT? ARE YOU KIDDING?
HE'LL GET OVER IT. HE KNOWS I'M JUST KIDDING AROUND.
I DON'T KNOW.

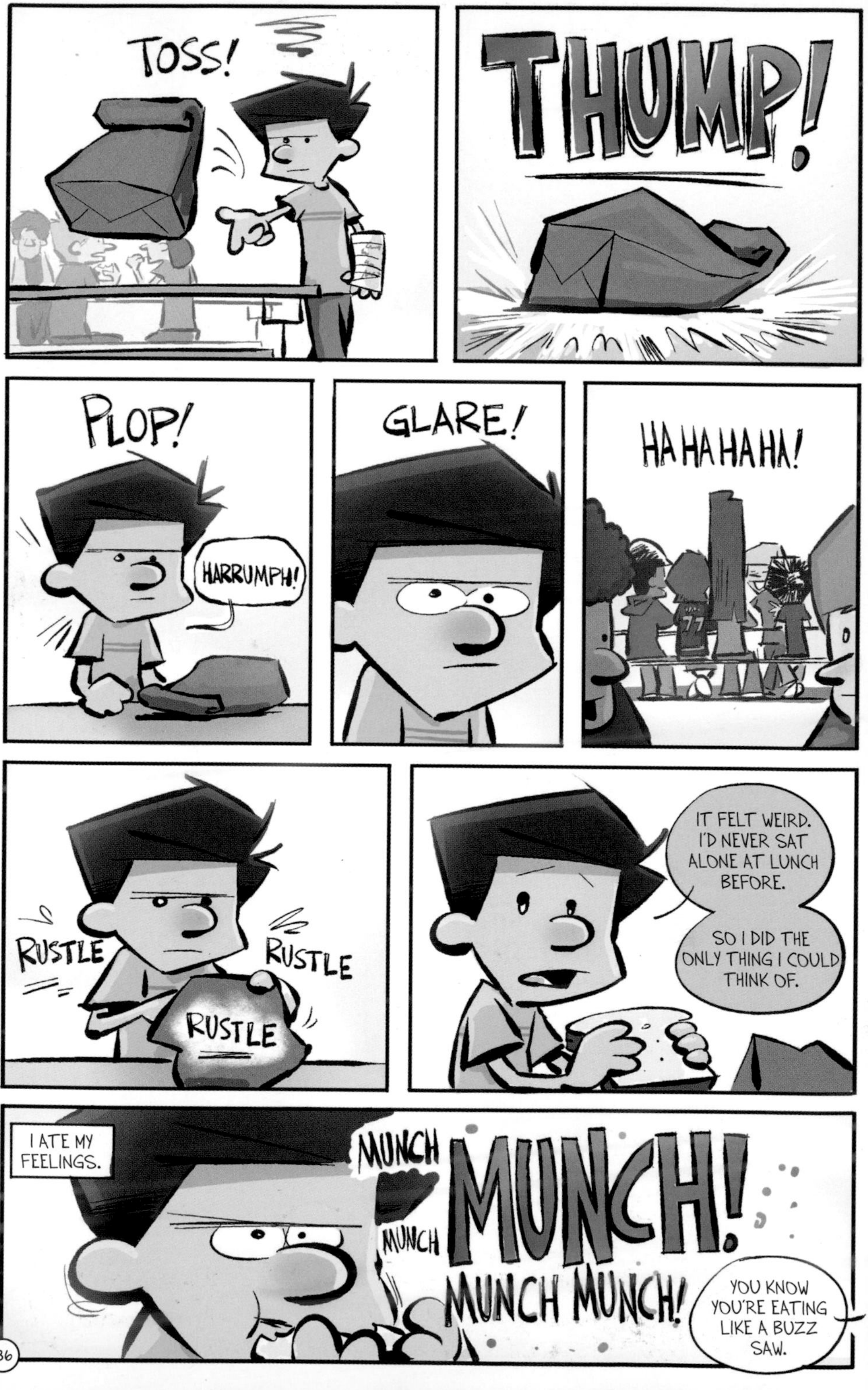
TOSS!
THUMP!
PLOP!
HARRUMPH!
GLARE!
HA HA HA HA!
RUSTLE
RUSTLE
RUSTLE
IT FELT WEIRD. I'D NEVER SAT ALONE AT LUNCH BEFORE.
SO I DID THE ONLY THING I COULD THINK OF.
I ATE MY FEELINGS.
MUNCH
MUNCH
MUNCH!
MUNCH MUNCH!
YOU KNOW YOU'RE EATING LIKE A BUZZ SAW.

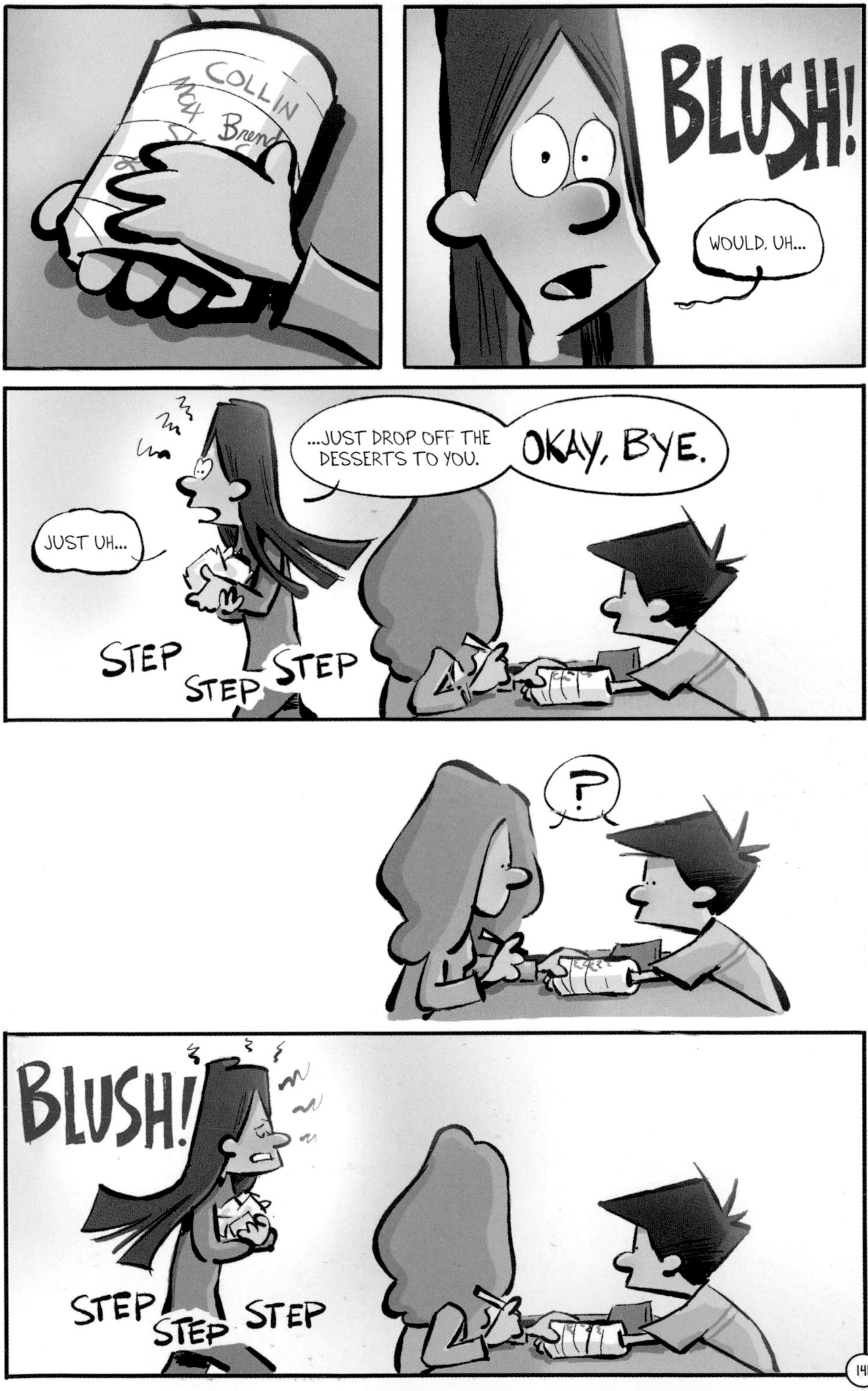
COLLIN
BLUSH!
WOULD, UH...
JUST UH...
...JUST DROP OFF THE DESSERTS TO YOU.
OKAY, BYE.
STEP STEP STEP
?
BLUSH!
STEP STEP STEP

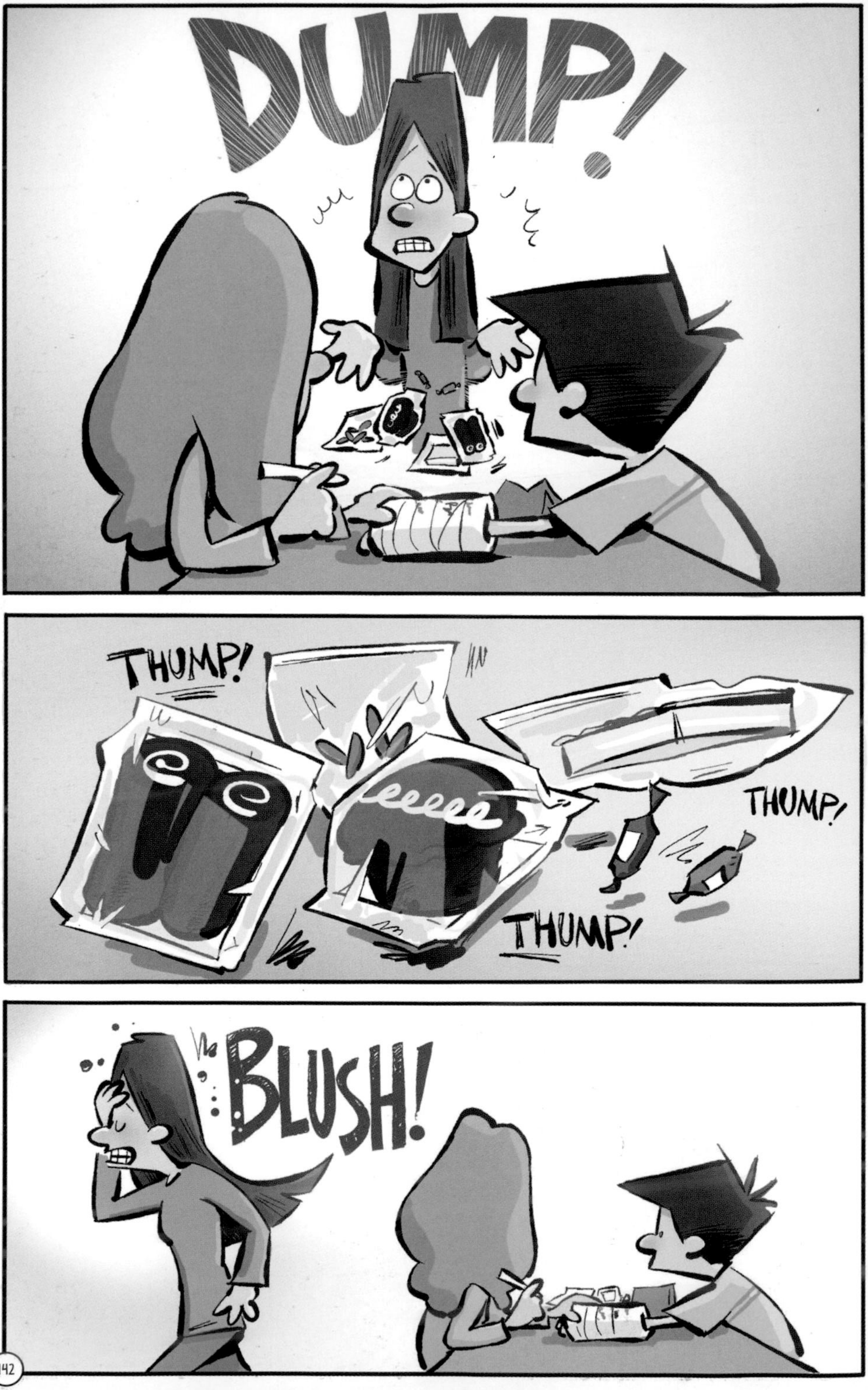
DUMP!
THUMP!
THUMP!
THUMP!
BLUSH!

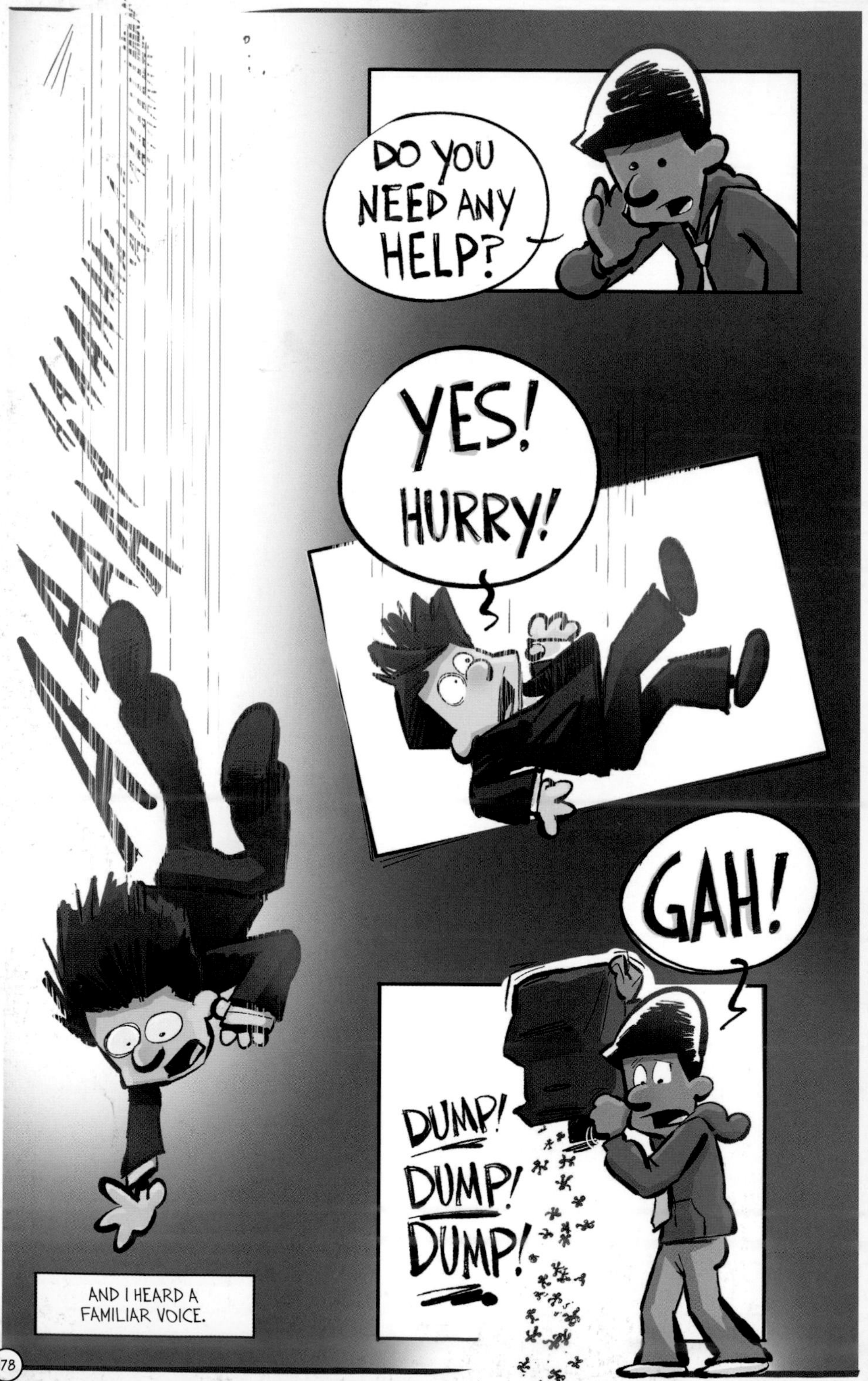
DO YOU NEED ANY HELP?
YES! HURRY!
AND I HEARD A FAMILIAR VOICE.
GAH!
DUMP! DUMP! DUMP!

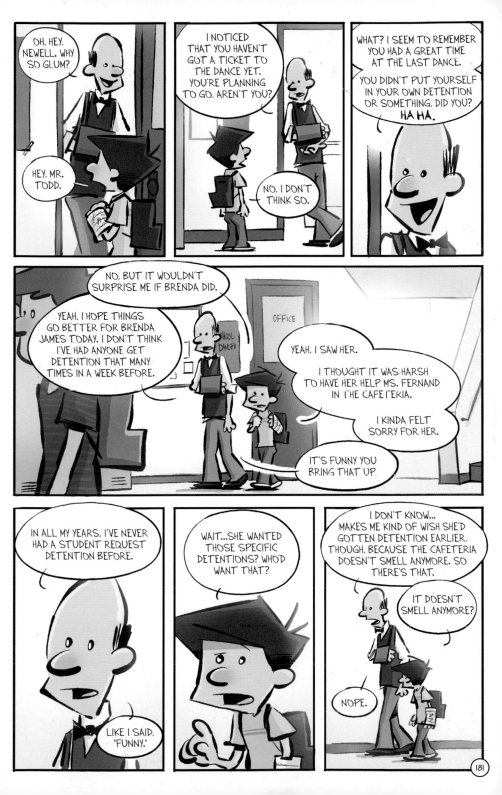

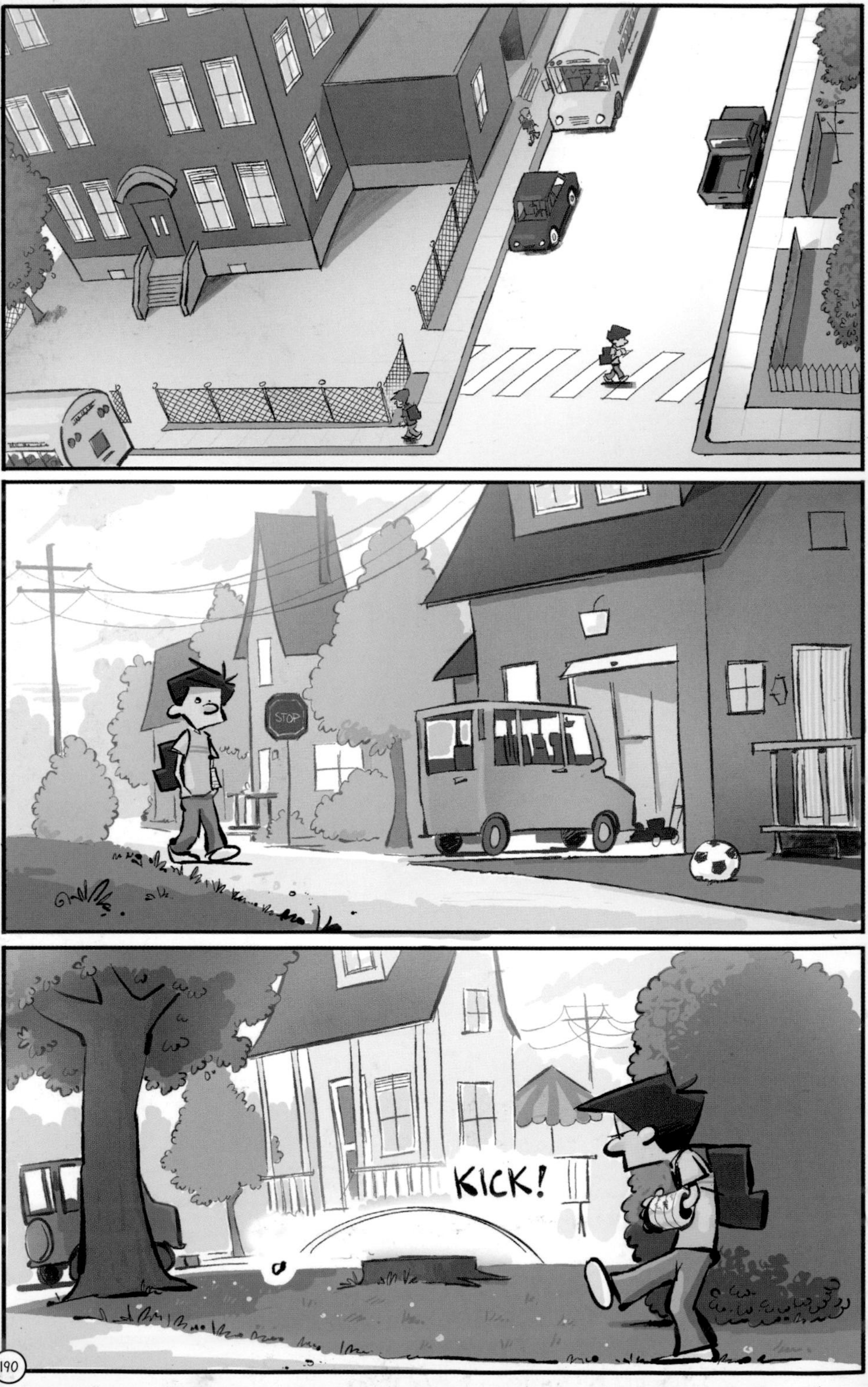
STOP
KICK!

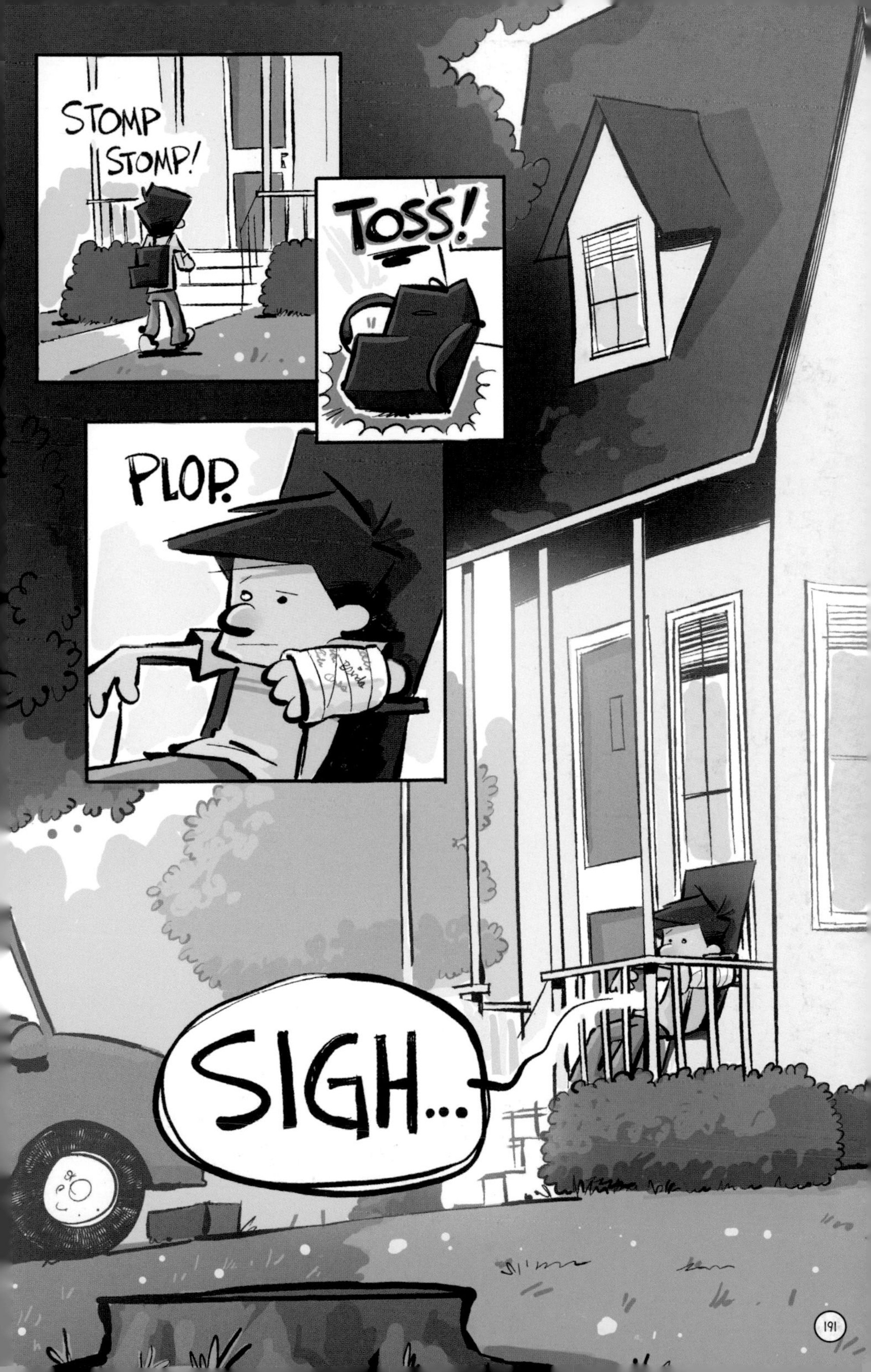
STOMP
STOMP!
TOSS!
PLOP.
SIGH...

CHAPTER TEN
A MESSY REALIZATION

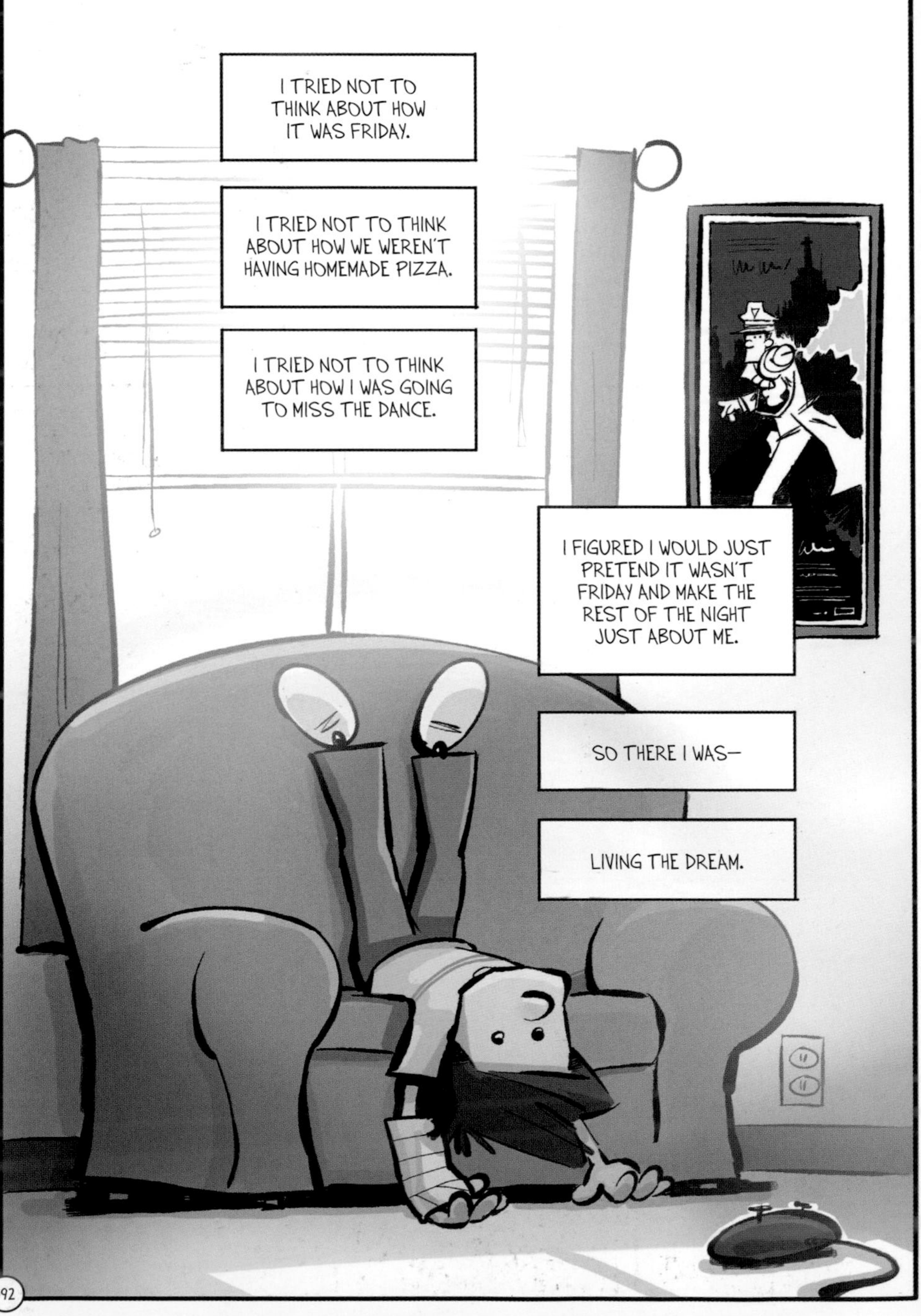
I TRIED NOT TO THINK ABOUT HOW IT WAS FRIDAY.
I TRIED NOT TO THINK ABOUT HOW WE WEREN'T HAVING HOMEMADE PIZZA.
I TRIED NOT TO THINK ABOUT HOW I WAS GOING TO MISS THE DANCE.
I FIGURED I WOULD JUST PRETEND IT WASN'T FRIDAY AND MAKE THE REST OF THE NIGHT JUST ABOUT ME.
SO THERE I WAS—
LIVING THE DREAM.

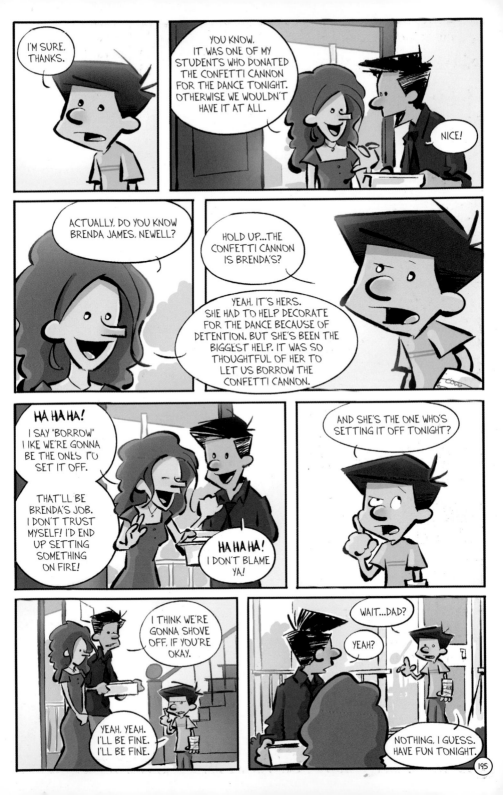

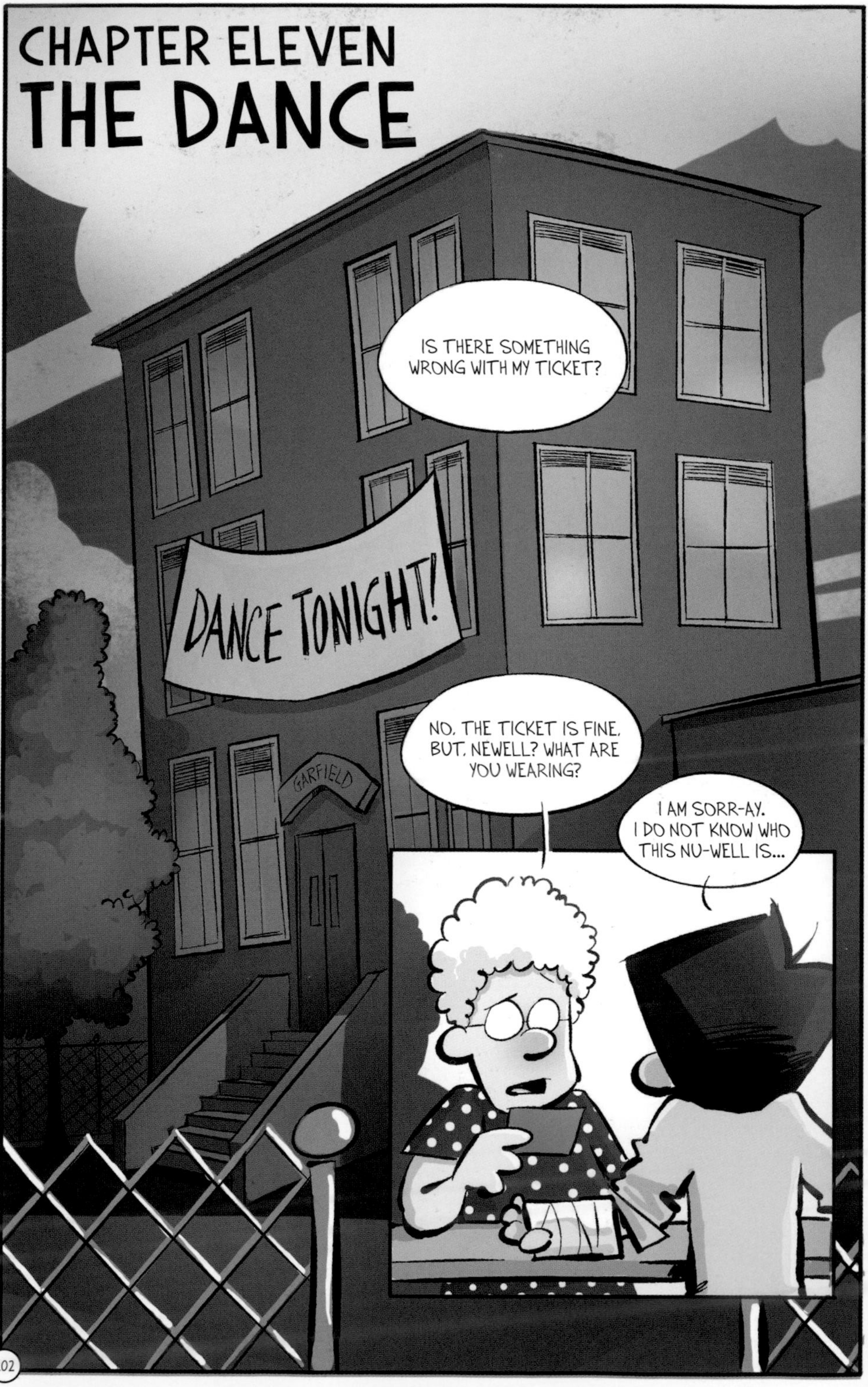
CHAPTER ELEVEN
THE DANCE
DANCE TONIGHT!
GARFIELD
IS THERE SOMETHING WRONG WITH MY TICKET?
NO. THE TICKET IS FINE. BUT, NEWELL? WHAT ARE YOU WEARING?
I AM SORR-AY. I DO NOT KNOW WHO THIS NU-WELL IS...

215

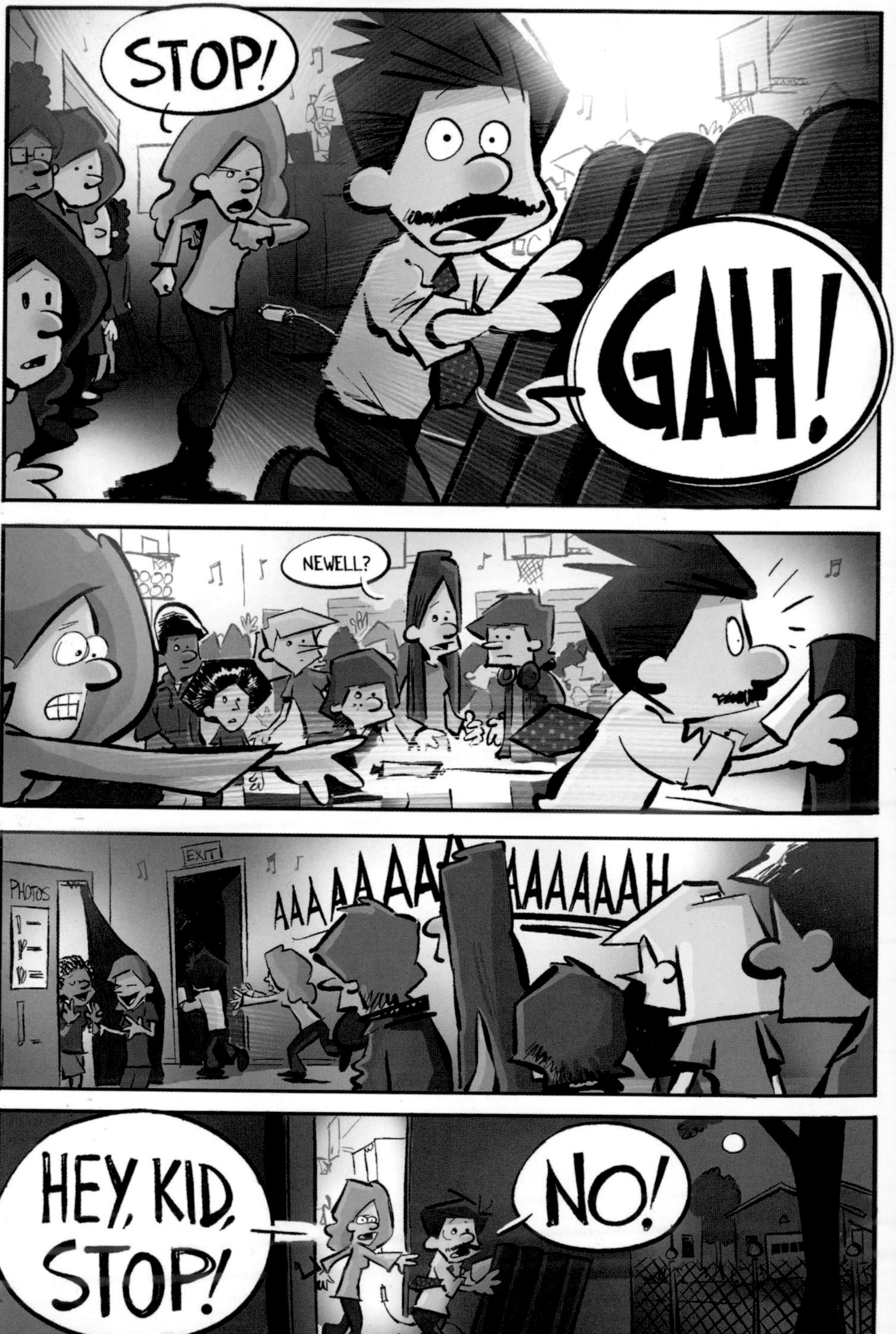
STOP!
GAH!
NEWELL?
AAAAAAAAAAAAAAAH
PHOTOS
EXIT
HEY, KID, STOP!
NO!

217

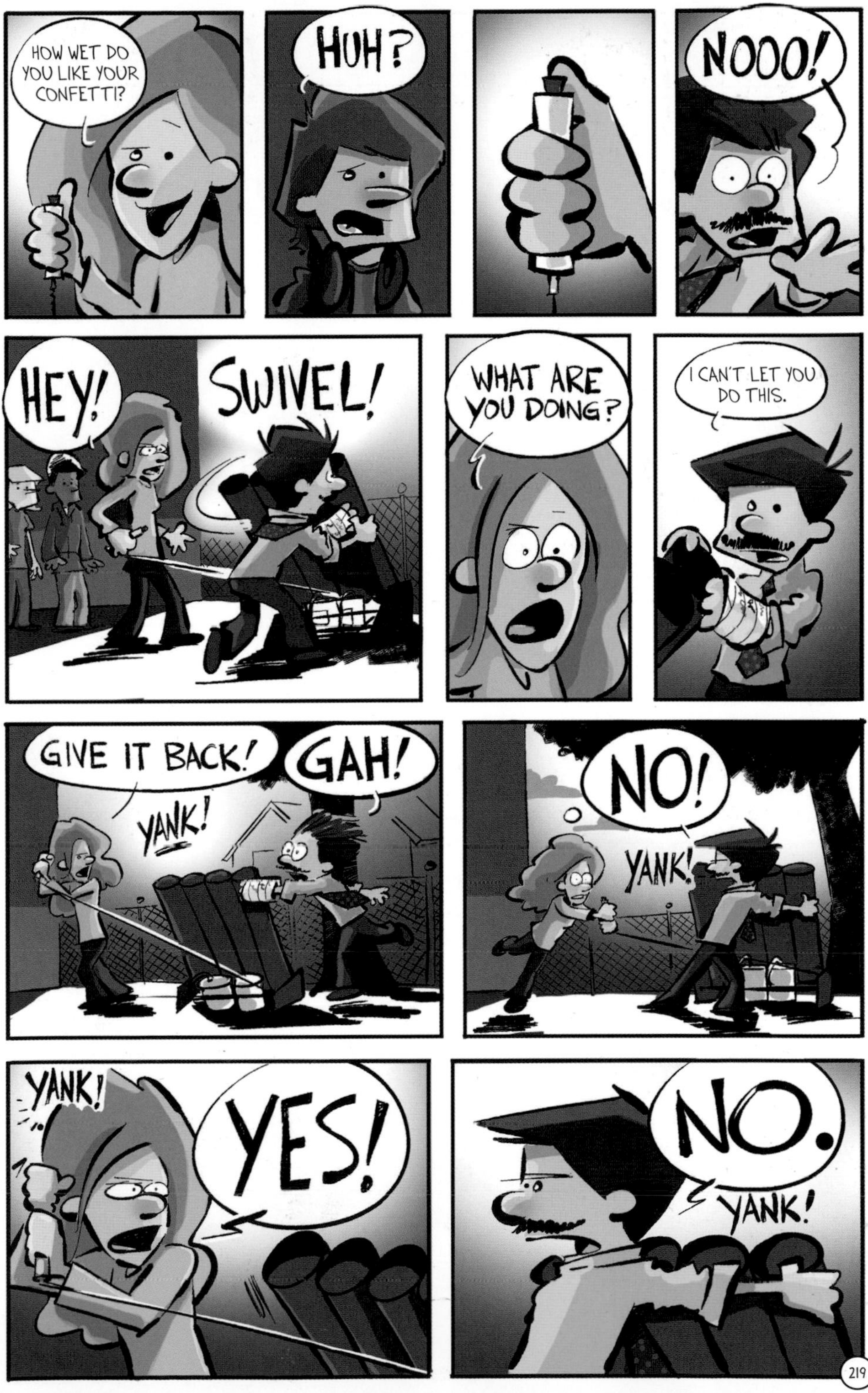
HOW WET DO YOU LIKE YOUR CONFETTI?
HUH?
NOOO!
HEY!
SWIVEL!
WHAT ARE YOU DOING?
I CAN'T LET YOU DO THIS.
GIVE IT BACK!
YANK!
GAH!
NO!
YANK!
YANK!
YES!
NO.
YANK!

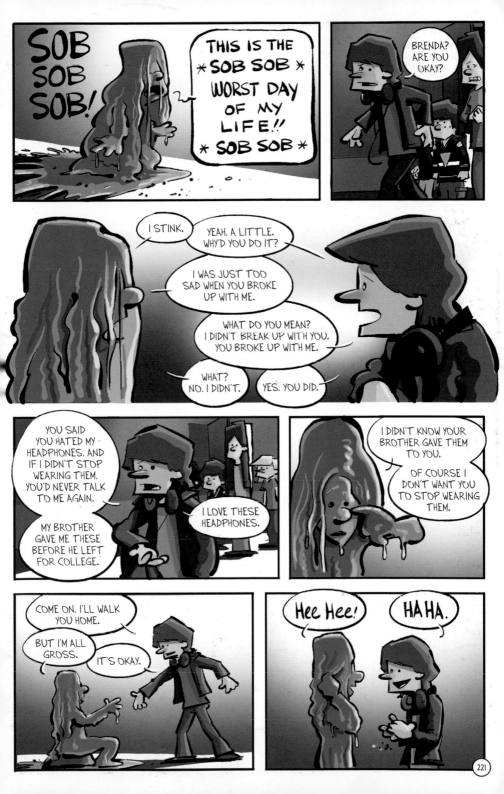

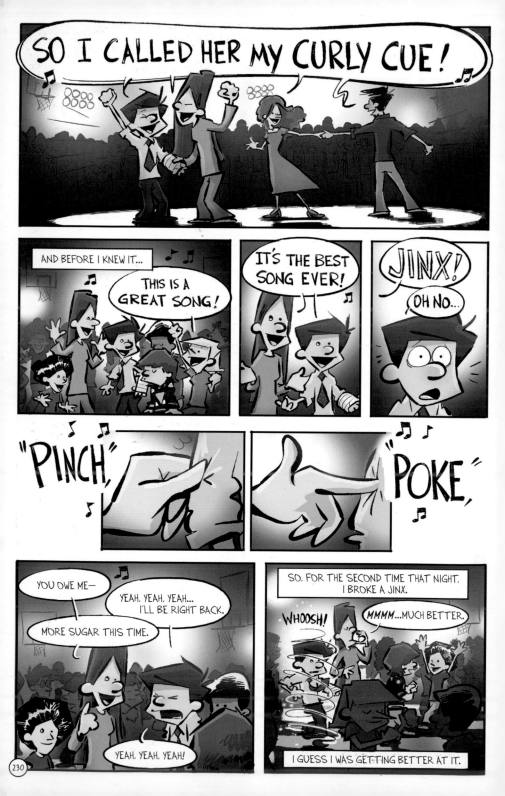

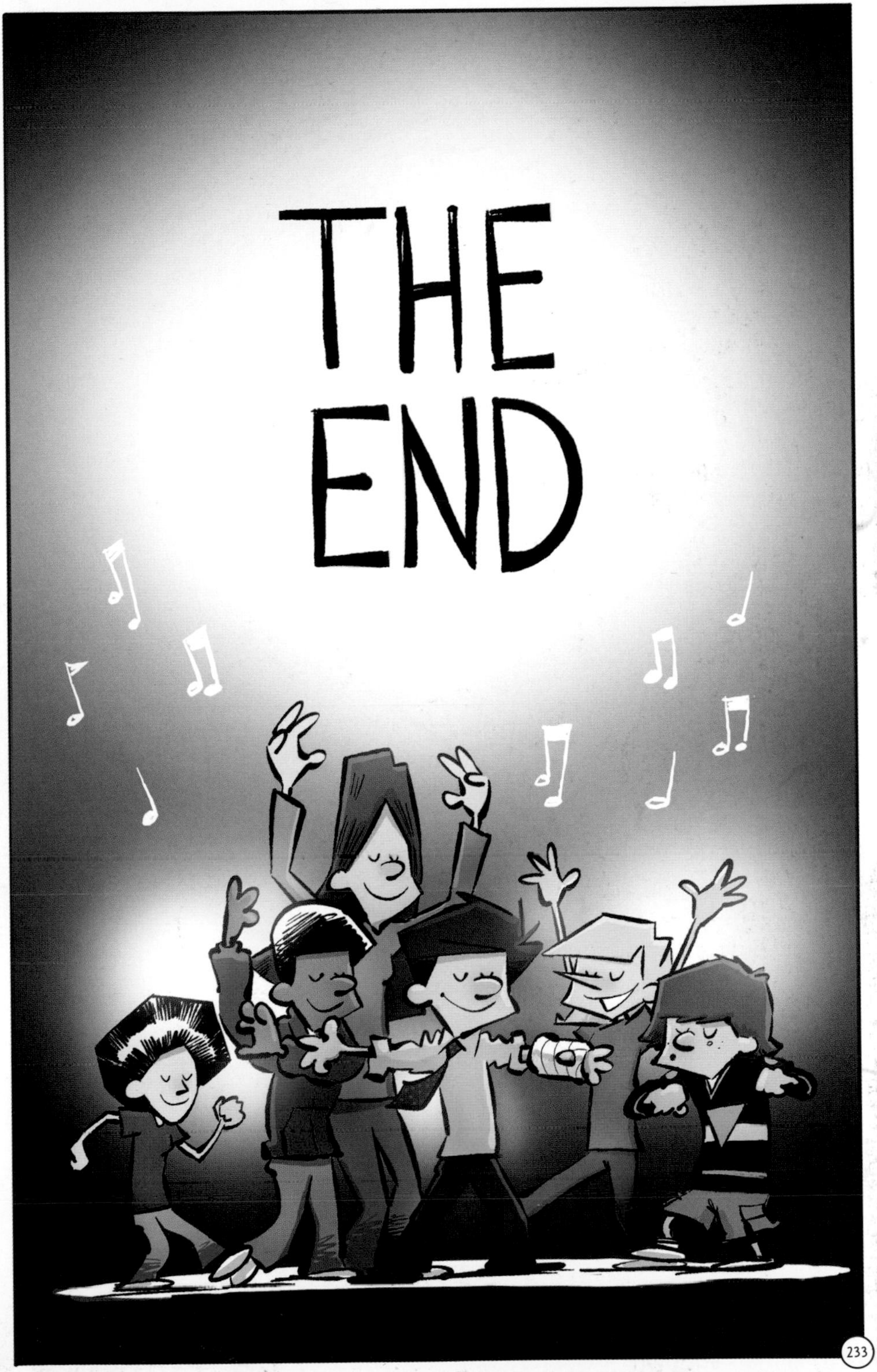
THE END

ACKNOWLEDGMENTS

* * *

MY NAME MAY BE THE ONLY ONE YOU SEE ON THE FRONT COVER, BUT BELIEVE ME, THERE ARE SO MANY PEOPLE WHO HAVE HELPED MAKE THIS MISADVENTURE HAPPEN.

FIRST AND FOREMOST, THIS SERIES WOULDN'T BE WHERE IT IS TODAY WITHOUT THE LOVE AND SUPPORT OF MY FAMILY: MY BEAUTIFUL WIFE, ERIN; MY SON, WYETH; AND MY MOTHER, KATHRYN. THANK YOU. THEY HAVE BEEN THERE FOR EVERY MOMENT OF THIS BOOK, FROM THE PENCILING AND WRITING, TO THE INKING, ALL THE WAY DOWN TO THE COLORS. WHEN YOU SURROUND YOURSELF WITH PEOPLE WHO BELIEVE IN YOU, HALF THE WORK IS ALREADY DONE. I'M A LUCKY GUY.

BIG THANKS TO MY AGENT, TIM TRAVAGLINI, WHO WAS ALWAYS THERE WHEN I NEEDED HIM AND KEPT A FIRE GOING ON THIS PROJECT.

TO EVERYONE AT LITTLE, BROWN BOOKS FOR YOUNG READERS WHO HAS HELPED SHAPE THIS BOOK. BUT MOST IMPORTANTLY TO MY EDITOR EXTRAORDINAIRE, RACHEL POLOSKI, WHOSE LAUGHTER AND INSIGHT KEPT ME ON TRACK; MY DESIGNER, MEGAN McLAUGHLIN, AND HER INCREDIBLE PATIENCE; AND MY EDITOR ESTHER CAJAHUARINGA, WHO HELPED ME ON THE FINAL STRETCH. THANK YOU.

A BIG THANK YOU TO MY SON, WYETH PLATT, FOR PERMITTING ME TO USE THE FICTIONAL PIZZERIA, MOZZIE & HAM, FROM HIS NOVELLA **THE WILL TO DELIVER: A PIZZA MEMOIR.**

EVEN THOUGH NEWELL'S MISADVENTURES THROUGH MIDDLE SCHOOL ARE FICTITIOUS, I COULDN'T HELP REFLECTING ON MY OWN JUNIOR HIGH AND HIGH SCHOOL MOMENTS WHILE WRITING THESE STORIES. SO THANK YOU TO ALL MY FRIENDS WHO HELPED GET ME THROUGH THE DAYS AT CHEWNING JUNIOR HIGH AND NORTHERN HIGH SCHOOL IN DURHAM, NORTH CAROLINA. WHO WOULD HAVE EVER THOUGHT THAT I WOULD BE MENTALLY REVISITING THOSE DAYS ALL THESE YEARS LATER?

AND FINALLY, TO ALL THE KIDS WHO'VE LAUGHED ALONGSIDE NEWELL AND HIS FRIENDS: THANK YOU. YOU'RE THE BEST.